SATAN'S FIRE

Also by P. C. Doherty

Hugh Corbett medieval mysteries

The Song of a Dark Angel
Satan in St Mary's
Crown in the Darkness
Spy in Chancery
The Angel of Death
The Prince of Darkness
Murder Wears a Cowl
The Assassin in the Greenwood

Satan's Fire

P. C. Doherty

St. Martin's Press ✖ New York

Library of Congress Cataloging-in-Publication Data

Doherty, P. C.
    Satan's fire / by P.C. Doherty.
        p. cm.
    ISBN 0-312-14728-7
1. Great Britain—History—Edward I, 1272–1307—
        Fiction.   I. Title.
    PR6054.037S28   1996
823'.914—dc20   96-25615   CIP

First published in Great Britain by
Headline Book Publishing

First U.S. Edition: November 1996

10 9 8 7 6 5 4 3 2 1

To my baby son, Little Paul [Mr. T. T.].

Prologue

On the shores of the Dead Sea, where the djinns and devils rested from their constant war against man, stood the rocky, yellow-stoned eyrie of Am Massafia; the stronghold lair of the Sheikh Al-Jebal, the Old Man of the Mountain. The trackways to the Old Man's lair were narrow, winding and secret, the shadow of vultures' wings a constant presence. The final path, a perilous journey along a roped bridge above a yawning gorge, was guarded by Sudanese swordsmen with broad, razor-edged scimitars clasped to their waists. Once across this bridge of hell, however, and through the iron-studded gates, a visitor would enter a palace with mosaic floors. Cool courtyards, with fountains spouting ice-cold water, offered shade against the setting sun. Peacocks strutted and gaily coloured parrots shrieked amongst the rose gardens or rustled the leaves of the dark mulberry trees. Around the courtyard, wooden lattices, built against the wall, were covered with rare and exotic flowers which turned the dry air heavy with perfume, whilst thuribles, in corners or on shelves, poured amber smoke to the ever-blue sky.

Beneath the fortress, however, lay a different place: dark, hot passageways; galleries without light or air; only the occasional torch flickering against the blood-red rock. The dungeons of the Old Man of the Mountain housed many prisoners. Some had long died, the flesh falling off their bones which now turned yellow in the heat. Others had gone insane and crouched like animals in their narrow chained dungeons, crawling around like dogs, their eyes mad, their tongues constantly baying against the darkness. But, in one cell, the Unknown, the infidel knight with corn-coloured hair and light-blue eyes, squirmed on rotting straw and dreamed of vengeance. For only this, burning brightly within him, held back the Stygian blackness and the demons ever ready to carry away his soul. Hatred, anger and a burning desire for vengeance kept his wits together and body and soul as one. He refused to dwell on the silent horrors around him but lived constantly in the past, on that dreadful night when the great city of Acre had fallen to the Turks. Again and again he would recall the constant beat of the kettledrums as the Muslim hordes poured through the breach in the wall of the city. The armoured regiments of Mamelukes streaming across the ruined moat, over the bodies and broken engines, pressing back the wounded knights, forcing their way into the streets. The prisoner blinked and, lifting his arm, stared closely at the white scabs forming on his arms and legs. He closed his eyes and called on God for life: not a cure for his leprosy but length of days and the opportunity to wreak his revenge.

In the opulent, breeze-filled chambers far above the dungeon, the Sheikh Al-Jebal, the Old Man of the Mountain, sat overlooking a walled garden with marble fountains which tossed sparkling wine into the perfumed air. The Old Man, his eyes heavy with opium, stared down at the silk-carpeted pavilions and beautifully tiled porticoes, where his young men lay sprawled with their Circassian girls and dreamed hashish-filled fantasies of Paradise. So it was, every day, a time of Paradise until the Old Man issued his orders. Once the die had been cast, these young men, dressed in their white robes, red girdles about their waists, scarlet, gold-tipped slippers on their feet, would leave the fortress and go down into the valleys to wreak their master's will. No one could ever oppose him. No one ever escaped his death sentence. Two daggers pressed into the pillows of their intended victim's bed and, on the table beside it, a flat seedcake, a warning from the Old Man of the

Mountain that his Assassins were about to do his will.

The Old Man turned, shifting his body on the purple silk divan between the naked, golden bodies of his concubines. They murmured in their drug-filled sleep whilst he stared up at the ceiling of the chamber, hard cedarwood, inlaid with gold and fresh diamonds. He felt restless and sat up, gazing round the room at the inanimate birds fashioned out of gold and silver with enamel feathers and brilliant ruby eyes. The sheikh's hand went out to the table next to the bed where gold dishes and amber cups stood, filled with the sweetest wines or ripest fruit. He let his hand fall. He had drunk and eaten enough. He was bored and the affairs of men required his attention.

'What does it profit a man,' Sheikh Al-Jebal murmured, quoting the Christians, 'if he gains the whole world but suffers the loss of his immortal soul?'

Yesterday messengers had arrived bringing news of the outside world; whispers from the busy markets of Alexandria, Tripoli, and even further west, from the land of the infidels. From Rome, Avignon, Paris and London. The sheikh got off the divan. He stretched and a slave, standing in the corner, hurried across, a white gauze cloak in his hands, he carefully wrapped this round his master's shoulders. The Old Man ignored him as if the slave didn't even exist. He walked across to a small alcove, pulling back the double-edged curtain of gold-embossed leather and stared down at the ivory chessmen.

'It is the will of Allah!' He murmured. 'It is the will of Allah that I intervene in the game.'

He picked up the figure of the king and, cradling it against his cheek, went and sat on his throne-like chair. He thought of the infidel kings of the west: Edward of England, Philip of France, as well as his inveterate enemies, those monk-soldiers, the Templars, with their red crosses, great castles and immense power. He played with the figure of the king and smiled lazily.

'It is time to go down,' he murmured, 'among the sons of men.'

3

England and France were on the verge of signing a great peace; the Templar order, ever ready, might exploit this peace and turn the eyes of the Western kings and princes to the regaining of Jerusalem and its Holy Places. Once again the fleets of Venice, Genoa and Pisa would be seen off the Palestine coast. The Templars would reprovision their castles and the great iron-mailed knights of the West would pour ashore to plant their standards above Acre, Damascus, Tripoli and Sidon, turning the whole coastline into a sea of blood. And there were other whispers. Strange stories, things the Old Man of the Mountain could hardly believe but hoped to act upon. He closed his eyes and whispered the three sacred messages of the Assassins, always dispatched to every one of their victims.

KNOWEST THOU, THAT WE GO FORTH AND RETURN AS BEFORE AND BY NO MEANS CAN YOU HINDER US.
KNOWEST THOU, THAT WHAT THOU POSSESSES SHALL ESCAPE THEE IN THE END AND RETURN TO US.
KNOWEST THOU, THAT WE HOLD YOU AND WILL KEEP THEE UNTIL THE ACCOUNT BE CLOSED.

He opened his eyes. Few men escaped such a message. Only one, Edward of England, whilst crusading in Palestine in the months before he became king: a poisoned knife plunged into his shoulder but, through God's grace as well as the attentions of his wife, Edward had recovered from the poison. The Old Man of the Mountain played with the rings on his fingers. He must act on the secrets he'd learnt. But how, he wondered, could assassins be sent to Edward's cold, misty isle? He toyed with the rings, watching the light dance on the precious stones, then lifted his head: there were more ways to sting a man than use a scorpion.

'Bring up the prisoner!' he whispered into the scent-filled

air. 'Release the Infidel, the knight we call the Unknown. He will do my bidding!'

Some three months later, Dames Cecilia and Marcia of the Order of St Benedict were journeying along the old Roman road leading to the gate known as Botham Bar at York. The daylight had died. Darkness was beginning to shroud the damp forests on either side of the road. The two good sisters, swathed in their brown, woollen robes, each riding one of their convent's best palfreys, gossiped to hide their own concern. They were not truly frightened. Their guide, Thurston of Guiseborough, striding ahead in front of them, was a burly, thickset peasant. He carried a short, small buckler on his back, sword and dagger were clasped to his belt, and his burly fist held a club which would have dimmed the brains of an ox. Nevertheless, the two good sisters liked to frighten each other. Now and again, they would glance hurriedly sideways at the damp trees and recall the tales about how the Romans had built this road. How, in the cold, wet forest beyond, the ghosts of these ancient people clustered in the vine-covered ruins where the owl, fox and badger made their nests.

The good sisters' fears became more real as daylight disappeared and the undergrowth on either side of the road became alive with night creatures. A boar crashed across the road, his wicked tusks scything the air. Vixens yipped at the rising moon and, from some hamlet hidden in the trees, a dog bayed dolefully against the night. The two good sisters edged their palfreys closer. Secretly they comforted themselves. Who would harm two women consecrated to God? In actual fact they put their faith in Thurston's thick club as well as the king's impending arrival in York. Because of that, the highways and forest tracks had been cleared of outlaws and vagabonds. Moreover, the presence of so many sergeants of the great Templar Order also kept the villains, rascals and wolves heads well away from the city of York. It was the Templars about whom the two good sisters chattered: those iron-clad men with their sunburnt faces, their chainmail covered by great white cloaks of wool bearing a six-sided blood-red cross. The sisters had just passed the great Templar manor of Framlingham and its shadow-shrouded buildings had prompted their conversation about these strange men. The Templars were soldier-monks, virgins dedicated to war, but also the holders of great wealth as well as mysterious secrets. The two good sisters had learnt all this whilst staying at their mother house in Beverley. In the refectory there the sisters had gossiped about how the great Templar lords had swept into the convent courtyard demanding provisions for themselves and their horses. How they had guarded so securely a covered wagon bearing a six-locked coffer which, so Mother Perpetua informed them, must carry some great relic of tremendous force.

'Why else?' Mother Perpetua had concluded, 'had the wagon been closely guarded by knights, foot-soldiers and crossbowmen all wearing the insignia of the Order?'

Dames Cecilia and Marcia had spent their long journey speculating on the many rumours about the Templars. Now, as the owls began to hoot, they wondered if these same Templars had brought a curse upon the land.

'We are definitely living in dreadful times,' Dame Marcia declared. 'Look you, Sister; where else have we had rain at seed times to smother the young crops and rot the wheat in the ear of corn?'

'Aye,' Dame Cecilia replied. 'There's talk of famine and hunger. How the poor are mixing chalk with their flour.'

'And other stories.' Dame Marcia chattered on. 'Outside Hull, a vicar saw three witches come riding towards him, a yard and a half above the ground.'

'And at Ripon,' Dame Cecilia interrupted, eager to show her knowledge, 'the noon-day devil was glimpsed under the outstretched branch of the yew tree, glaring, with horrid eyes, at the priory gates.'

The two sisters heard a sound on the road ahead of them. Dame Cecilia gave a small scream and reined in. Thurston strode on, cursing under his breath at these chattering women. He stopped and peered down the road.

'It's nothing,' he murmured in his broad Yorkshire burr, 'though . . .' He hid his grin and scratched his tousled beard.

'What?' Dame Cecilia snapped.

'Well,' Thurston replied slowly, thoroughly enjoying himself, 'there have been rumours . . .'

'Rumours about what?'

'Well, ever since those Templars came back to York,' Thurston continued, staring into the darkness, 'there've been stories of devils, in the form of weasels, riding huge, amber-coloured cats along these roads.'

The two good nuns drew in their breath sharply.

'Or there again,' Thurston continued, his voice dropping to a whisper, 'outside Walmer Bar, the Lord Satan himself has been glimpsed. He was clad in a purple gown with a black cap upon his head.' He walked back and stared up at Dame Cecilia's wrinkled face. 'His face was terrible,' Thurston continued hoarsely. 'He had the nose of a great eagle, burning eyes, his hands and legs were hairy and he had feet like a griffin.'

'Now that's enough,' Dame Marcia interrupted. 'Thurston, you are frightening us. We should be in York.'

Aye, Thurston thought, and we'd have been there an hour ago if it hadn't been for your constant gabble and chatter about imps, Templars, demons and magic. He looked up at the starlit sky.

'Don't worry, good sisters,' he called back over his shoulder. 'Two more miles and we'll be at Botham Bar; even sooner if you can make those palfreys trot a little faster.'

The two nuns needed no further urging. They dug their heels in, shouting at Thurston not to walk too far in front of them. Their guide strode on, quite pleased at teasing these plump,

7

well-fed gossips who, ever since they had left Beverley, had spent more time talking about Satan than their devotions. Thurston stopped abruptly. A country man, a born poacher, Thurston knew the forest and could distinguish between what sounds and smells spelt danger and what to ignore. Now something was wrong. He lifted his hand, even as his neck went cold and his heart began to beat faster. A strange smell in the night air of smoke, fire and something else, smouldering human flesh. Thurston recognised that smell. He'd never forgotten the time they'd burnt the old witch in the market place at Guiseborough. The village had stunk for days afterwards, as if the old crone had cursed the air at the very moment of dying.

'What's wrong?' Dame Cecilia shrilled, fighting hard to control her usually meek palfrey which had now become restless, as it too caught the smell.

'I don't know,' Thurston replied. 'Listen!'

The two nuns obeyed. Then they heard it: the mad galloping of a horse coming along the trackway ahead. Thurston moved them quickly to the side of the road just as the horse appeared, pounding along, neck out, ears flat against its head. Thurston wildly wondered whether he could stop the charging animal. The horse saw them and, skittering on the trackway, turned sideways then up, back on its hind legs, before charging on. As it did, Thurston's blood ran cold: the severed legs of the horse's former rider were still clasped firmly in its stirrups.

'What is it?' Dame Cecilia whispered.

Thurston crouched on the edge of the road, his hands across his stomach.

'Thurston!' Dame Marcia yelled. 'What is wrong?'

The guide turned and vomited on the grass. He then grabbed the wine skin slung over the horn of Dame Cecilia's saddle. He ignored their protests, undid the clasps, almost throwing the wine into his mouth.

'We'd best move on.' He put the stopper back, thrust it at Dame Cecilia and, without a backward glance, continued along the trackway. They rounded the bend and fearfully approached the fire burning so fiercely on the edge of the forest. Dame Marcia gagged at the terrible stench, her palfrey, unwillingly, drew close to the flames. Dame Marcia took one look at the fire greedily consuming the upper, severed part of a man's corpse; she screamed and fell like a sack from her saddle, swooning in terror at the hideous sight.

Chapter 1

York. Lady's Day, 1303

'The Lord knows I need it!' Edward of England ran a hand through his iron-grey hair then brought his fists down on the refectory table in the priory of St Leonard outside York. The crash echoed round the long whitewashed room. 'I need money!' the king yelled.

The commanders of the Temple, the principal officers of Christendom's monastic fighting order, however, were not frightened by the English king's play-acting. Indeed, all four looked to the other end of the table where Jacques de Molay, Grand Master of their Order, recently arrived from France, sat in his high-backed chair, hands linked together as if in prayer.

'Well?' Edward barked.

De Molay spread his hands; his sunburnt face was impassive, his clear grey eyes betrayed no fear at the English king's terrible rage.

'Well?' Edward snapped. 'Are you going to answer or bless me?'

'My lord King, we are not your subjects!'

'By God's teeth, some of you are!' Edward roared back. He straightened in his chair, jabbing his fingers down on the table. 'On my way here, I passed your manor of Framlingham with its elegant gatehouse, fields, pastures, stewponds and orchards. Those lands are mine. The cattle and sheep which graze there are mine. The sparrows which nest in the trees and the pigeons in your dovecotes are all mine. My father gave

11

you that manor. I can take it back!'

'All we have,' de Molay answered quietly, 'comes from God. They were given to us by noble princes like your father, so we can continue our fight against the Infidel and win back the Holy Places in Outremer.'

Edward of England was tempted to reply that, so far, the Templars had made a poor job of it, but then he glanced across the room: the dark-haired clerk who sat in a window embrasure caught the king's gaze and shook his head slowly. Edward breathed out noisily through his nose. He stared up at the polished hammer-beam roof.

'I need money,' Edward continued. 'My war in Scotland is nearly finished. If I can only catch that bastard, that will-o'-the-wisp Wallace . . .!'

'You have no war with France,' de Molay interrupted. 'You and His august Majesty, Philip IV, are about to sign a treaty of eternal peace.'

Edward caught the sardonic note and hid his own smile.

'Your son,' de Molay continued, 'your heir apparent, the Prince of Wales, is set to marry Philip IV's daughter Princess Isabella. She will bring a grand dowry.'

John de Warrenne, Earl of Surrey, seated to the left of the king, belched noisily. His watery blue eyes never left de Molay's face. Edward pressed his boot on de Warrenne's toes.

'The good earl,' Edward intervened, 'may not be elegant in his response but, Seigneur de Molay, you taunt us. Isabella is only nine years old. It will be three years before she can marry. I have to fill my coffers in the next few months. I need a new army in Scotland by mid-summer.'

Edward looked despairingly at each of the four Templar commanders. Surely, he thought, they will help? They are English. They know the problems which beset me. Bartholomew Baddlesmere, his head bald as a pigeon's egg, his grizzled, weather-beaten face showed no compassion. Next to him William Symmes, his face a patchwork of scars: one black patch covered his left eye, his blond hair hung in lank tendrils to frame a narrow, mean face. No hope there, Edward thought: both of them are Templars born and bred. All they care for is their bloody Order. Edward tried to catch the eye of Ralph Legrave who, twenty years ago, had been one of the king's household knights. Now he wore the white surcoat of the Templars emblazoned with their red-pointed cross. Legrave's open, boyish face, however, skin smooth as a maiden, showed no concern for his former lord. Across the table from Legrave sat Richard Branquier, tall and stooped, the Templar's grand chamberlain in England. He just wiped his dripping nose on the back of his hands. His short-sighted gaze refused to meet the king's; instead he glanced down at the accounts book before him, a doleful look on his face.

Just like some bloody merchant, Edward thought, he regards me as a poor prospect. Edward stared down at his hands clenched in his lap. I'd like to break their heads, he thought. Beside him de Warrenne shuffled his feet, moving his head slowly from side to side. Edward caught the earl's wrist and gripped it. De Warrenne was not the brightest of his earls and Edward recognised the signs: if this meeting went on too long and the Templars grew more obdurate, de Warrenne wouldn't think twice about name-calling or even resorting to physical violence. Edward glared across at the man sitting in the window-seat, staring down at the courtyard below. Moody bastard! Edward thought. Sir Hugh Corbett, Keeper of the King's Secret Seal, should be over here sitting at his right hand, instead of staring out of the window, mooning over his flaxen-haired wife. The silence in the priory refectory became oppressive. The Templars sat like carved statues.

'Do you want me to beg?' the king snapped.

Edward scratched at a stain on his purple surcoat. Out of the corner of his eye he watched Branquier lean over and whisper in de Molay's ear. The grand master nodded slowly.

'The King's Exchequer is in York?' de Molay asked.

13

'Yes, my Treasury's here but there's sweet bugger-all in it!' Edward retorted.

Branquier brought his hand from beneath the ledger book and sent a gold coin ringing down the table. Edward deftly caught it. He stared down at the coin, his heart skipping a beat. He grimaced at de Warrenne.

'Another one!' he whispered, passing it to his companion.

The earl looked at it curiously. As large as a shilling, the gold coin seemed freshly minted, with a crude cross stamped on either side. He weighed it carefully in his hand.

'Well?' Edward taunted. 'Is this all you are going to give me?'

'You say you have no treasure.' Branquier leaned on the table. He pointed one bony finger at the coin de Warrenne was now tossing from one hand to the other. 'Yet, Your Grace, those coins are appearing all over York. Freshly cut and neatly minted. Are they not issued by your own Treasury?'

'No, they are not,' Edward replied. 'Since my arrival outside York, scores of such coins have appeared, but they are not from our Mints.'

'But who would have such bullion?' Branquier asked. 'And how can they circulate such precious coinage?'

'I don't know,' Edward retorted. 'But, if I did, I'd seize the gold and hang the bastard who made it!' He took a wafer-thin shilling out of his own purse and tossed it down the table. 'That's what my own Mints are producing, Sir Richard: so-called silver coins. They have as much silver in them as I have in my . . . er . . . hand!' the king added quickly.

'But who would counterfeit such coins?' de Molay insisted. 'Who has the bullion as well as the means to fashion such precious metal?'

'I don't know,' Edward shouted. 'And, with all due respect, Seigneur, that is my business. The counterfeiting of coins in this realm is treason. I can't see what this has got to do with the business in hand.'

14

'Which is what?'

'A loan of fifty thousand pounds sterling,' Edward retorted. The Templars stirred, shaking their heads.

'Could you not,' Baddlesmere declared, staring across at Branquier, 'ask Philip of France for a loan? To be put against the dowry settlement on his daughter? After all, Philip's envoy Sir Amaury de Craon is now feeding his face in the priory buttery.'

Edward glanced across at Corbett. The clerk, at the mention of his inveterate enemy and political opponent, was now listening intently to what was being said.

'What do you think of that, Sir Hugh?' Edward called out. 'Shall I send you to France and ask my brother in Christ to empty his Treasury?'

'You might as well send me to the moon, Sire: Philip is even more bankrupt than yourself.'

'What is it you really want?' de Molay intervened. 'A loan or a gift?'

Edward beamed from ear to ear. He winked at Corbett: the Templars were about to negotiate.

'If you offer me a gift, de Molay,' Edward teased back, 'then I'll take it.'

'Let me explain,' the grand master continued. 'If you confirm all Templar possessions in England and Gascony . . .'

Edward was already nodding vigorously.

'. . . Free passage for our merchants; confirmation of our Templar church in London. Confirmation,' de Molay continued, 'of all our possessions, both movable and immovable.'

The king was now beside himself with pleasure. 'Yes, yes,' he murmured.

'And a quarter of this gold,' de Molay concluded.

Edward sat up in his chair. 'What gold?'

'You mentioned a counterfeiter,' de Molay continued. 'Whoever it is must have a mass of gold. We want a quarter of it.'

15

'Agreed!' Edward snapped.

'And finally,' de Molay leaned forward, clasping his hands together; 'twelve years ago, Acre, the last fortress in Outremer; our door to the Holy Places, fell into Infidel hands.'

'God knows,' Edward murmured piously. 'But the city of Acre still weighs heavily on my soul.' He pressed the toe of his boot on de Warrenne's foot, just in case the Earl began to snigger.

'Yes, yes, I am sure it does,' de Molay observed sarcastically.

'I fought in the Holy Land,' Edward retorted. 'Thirty-three years ago I went there with my beloved wife, Eleanor. You may recall how the Old Man of the Mountain sent an assassin to kill me.'

'And you were cured by a Templar physician,' de Molay interrupted.

'My lord King, you were cured for a purpose. We want you to take the cross.' He watched the smile fade from Edward's face. 'We want you to swear an oath that you will go on Crusade and join the Temple in liberating Acre with one great, holy war against the forces of Islam. Do that and our Treasury in London, through its Italian bankers, will deliver to your Exchequer, by the feast of St Peter and St Paul, fifty thousand pounds sterling.'

'Agreed!' The king shouted.

'We want your oath now.'

'Impossible!' Edward replied. 'I am still fighting the Scots!'

'When that war is over, will you take the oath?' William Symmes called, touching the patch over his eye. 'The war in Scotland will soon be over. We have agreed to your gift. You must agree to our request.'

The Templar's one eye gleamed fanatically. Edward regretted his impetuosity. You are all in this together, he thought. You had this planned before we ever met. He glanced across at Corbett and saw the I-told-you-so look in his clerk's eyes.

'Tomorrow morning,' de Molay continued. 'You will enter

York to hear Mass at the abbey church of St Mary's. We would like you to take your oath after receiving the Eucharist. Swear, your hand on the sacrament, that when the war in Scotland is finished, you will support our Crusade.'

'And I get the money?'

'Will you swear?'

'Yes, yes, I intend to enter York tomorrow by Micklegate and go through Trinity to Mass in the abbey. I'll take the oath but will the money be paid?'

'As I have promised,' de Molay replied. He leaned back in his chair. 'When this meeting was arranged, my lord King, you said there were other matters.'

Sir Hugh Corbett continued to watch the juggler amusing the royal troops in the courtyard below. The man was throwing skittles in the air and deftly catching them, whilst a scraggy-haired bear, with a monkey on its shoulder, danced a shuffling gait to the reedy tune of a piper. He heard de Molay's remark about 'other matters' and sighed. He got to his feet and walked back to sit on the chair to the right of his royal master.

'For God's sake, stop dreaming!' the king hissed. 'You could have been of more help!'

The Templar commanders, pretending to chatter amongst themselves, glanced slyly up the table.

'More like a monk,' Branquier whispered, staring at Corbett's cropped, black hair with flecks of grey at the temples, the smooth, olive-skinned face and deep set eyes. The king's dramatic whisper had been heard and the Templars now waited to see what this most enigmatic of clerks would reply. Corbett leaned his elbows on the table; pushing his face only a few inches away from Edward's.

'My lord,' he whispered. 'You don't need my help. As usual, you have a skill even the devil would admire, though for what . . .?'

The king stared back in mock, hurt innocence.

'You got your money,' Corbett continued. 'The clerks of the

17

Exchequer will draw up the agreement and you will swear whatever you like.'

'You are not going home,' Edward hissed spitefully. 'I want you here, Hugh. Now, tell our guests just what our problems are.'

'Seigneur de Molay,' Corbett began. 'Commanders of the Temple.' He rose to his feet. 'What I say to you is a matter of secrecy. The king mentioned his enemy, the Old Man of the Mountain. You know, as men who have lived and fought in Outremer, how the Old Man heads a sect of dangerous assassins.'

His words were greeted by murmurs of agreement.

'This sect,' Corbett continued, 'prides itself that no man is beyond its reach. Seas, mountains, deserts pose no obstacles to them. They follow the same ritual: two daggers, each wrapped in red silk with a piece of seedcake, are always left in some prominent place as a warning to their intended victims.' He paused, his fingers drumming the table-top. 'Our lord the king has received such a warning. Ten days ago,' Corbett explained, 'two daggers, a seedcake nailed in between, were found thrust into the doors of St Paul's Cathedral in London.' Corbett plucked a piece of parchment from his wallet. 'Each dagger had a red sash tied to it. To one of the daggers was pinned the following notice:

KNOWEST THOU, THAT WE GO FORTH AND RETURN AS BEFORE AND BY NO MEANS CAN YOU HINDER US.
KNOWEST THOU, THAT WHAT THOU POSSESSES SHALL ESCAPE THEE IN THE END AND RETURN TO US.
'KNOWEST THOU, THAT WE HOLD YOU AND WILL KEEP THEE UNTIL THE ACCOUNT BE CLOSED.'

Corbett paused; his words had caused consternation amongst

the Templars. Chairs were scraped back; no longer the calm, impassive warriors, the very mention of their inveterate enemies – as well as the sheer impudence of the message – had the Templars clutching daggers and muttering threats.

Grand Master de Molay, however, still sat as if carved out of stone.

'How could this be done?' Legrave shouted. 'The Assassins live in the deserts of Syria: they have no house in Cheapside.'

His words created a ripple of laughter.

'In London,' Baddlesmere shouted out, 'such an assassin would stand out like a hawk amongst pigeons!'

Corbett shook his head. 'You mentioned Sir Amaury de Craon? True he is here, being attendant upon the king over the marriage negotiations for Philip's daughter.' Corbett paused to choose his words carefully. 'But yesterday de Craon also brought messages from France. A similar message was pinned to the doors of Saint Denis. A short while later, whilst Philip was hunting in the Bois de Boulogne, a mysterious archer tried to kill him.'

The refectory had now fallen silent, all eyes on Corbett.

'Sir Hugh, you have still not answered our question,' de Molay said quietly. 'How could an assassin walk through the cities of Paris and London yet not be seen?'

'Seigneur, aren't there links between your Order and the Assassins?'

De Molay silenced the protests of his companions.

'We have had dealings with them, as your king has with different caliphs and sultans, not to mention the Mongol lords. Say what you are going to.'

'Monsieur de Craon,' Corbett continued, 'believes the assassin is an apostate, a turncoat, a member of your Order!'

Now the Templar commanders jumped to their feet, chairs and stools were knocked over. Baddlesmere drew his dagger. Symmes pointed at Corbett, his face mottled with fury.

'How dare you?' He spluttered. 'How dare you accuse us of

19

treason? We are Christ's monks. We spend out lives and our blood defending God's holy creed.'

'Sit down!' de Molay shouted. 'All of you!' His sunburnt face had now turned an ashy grey and a murderous fury blazed in the grand master's eyes.

'You'd best sit down!' de Warrenne ordered. 'To draw sword or dagger in the king's presence is treason.'

'I have heard rumours about what happened in Paris,' de Molay declared. 'And I reject them as scurrilous scandal until the full facts are known. What proof does de Craon have for his assertions?'

'Quite considerable,' Edward intervened. 'On the day the assault was launched on Philip, a soldier, wearing the Templar livery, was seen fleeing from the Bois de Boulogne. Secondly, Templars are in London and in Paris. Thirdly, the Templars know the rites of the Assassins: the dagger, the red silk, the sesame seedcake and the three-fold message. Fourthly,' Edward straightened in his chair and pointed a finger at de Molay. 'You know, Monseigneur, how there are many in your Order, perhaps even seated round this table, who believe that the Temple was driven out of the Holy Land due, or so they claim, to a lack of support from the kingdoms in the West. Finally,' Edward looked up at the ceiling. 'Yes, finally, and I will say this. Thirty years ago the Assassins tried to kill me. They failed and I brained the man responsible with a stool. Very few people know about that attack. Most of the lords who were with me at the time are now dead, but the Templars knew.'

'And are there other matters?' de Molay asked wearily.

Corbett, ignoring the rancour his words had caused, continued in a matter-of-fact tone.

'Since the reign of the king's father, the Templars have owned the manor of Framlingham on the Botham Bar road, outside York. Usually it is left in the care of bailiffs and stewards. However, over the last two weeks, since the arrival of your good selves in York, petitions have come in about strange happenings: fires are seen glowing at night in the woods. Certain rooms and passageways are strictly forbidden . . .'

'This is nonsense!' Branquier interrupted. 'We are a religious Order. We have our own rituals. Sir Hugh, the Templars are an enclosed community: we would not let any jack-in-the-puddle know what we are doing, no more than the king or yourself allow the common sort to wander through the Chancery rooms at Westminster or the Treasury chamber of the Tower.'

'There are other matters,' Corbett continued. 'Sir Richard Branquier, you showed us a gold coin, certainly not from the Royal Mints. Now, with all due respect, these gold coins appeared during the last month: the very time you and your companions took up residence at Framlingham Manor.'

The Templar commanders objected vociferously, beating their fists on the table, shouting denials at what Corbett had said. De Molay remained impassive, gently clapping his hands, exercising that iron discipline for which the Temple was so famous.

'You'd best finish, Sir Hugh,' he declared resignedly. 'What else are we held responsible for? Surely not the strange death on Botham Bar road?'

Corbett smiled thinly. 'Now you mention it, Monseigneur; two good sisters, Cecilia and Marcia, accompanied by their guide Thurston, came before the mayor and aldermen of this city and swore that, as they approached York, a horse, bearing the lower half of a man's body, charged wildly by them. Further along the trackway, they discovered a corpse being eerily burnt to death by a fire for which they could see no source.'

'Yes, we heard that,' Baddlesmere declared. 'The story is all over York. The man's body was burnt beyond recognition.'

'Not exactly,' Sir Hugh interrupted. 'Only the top half of the man's corpse was burning, the bottom part of his torso and legs . . .' He shrugged. 'Well, you have heard the story.

21

What is strange is no one knows who he was, why he was attacked, the identity of the killer, or where the strange fire came from.'

'I object.' Branquier spoke up, turning to de Molay. 'Monseigneur, we have been brought here and our generosity has been exploited. We have always served the Crown of England well and have just agreed to the bestowal of a most generous gift. Now the king's senior clerk, his Keeper of the Secret Seal, stands in our presence and whispers the most scandalous allegations.'

De Molay placed his elbows on the table, steepling his fingers. 'No, no.' De Molay shook his head. 'You are not saying that, are you, Sir Hugh? You do not really believe the Templars are guilty of such horrid acts?'

'No, Monseigneur, we do not.' Corbett stared bleakly at Branquier. 'But remember, sirs; first, we have not gossiped behind your backs but bluntly informed you about what others have whispered to us. Secondly, there is a remarkable coincidence between your arrival here and those strange happenings. Thirdly, and most importantly, the Templars are a kingdom in themselves. You have houses which stretch from the borders of Scotland to the toe of Italy. From Rouen in the West to the borders of the Slavs. Now gold coins, burning corpses . . .' Corbett shrugged. 'These matters can be dealt with, but treason against our lord the king is another matter. You can use your knowledge and power to acquire information. You listen to the rumours of courts.'

'In other words,' de Molay intervened, 'you would like us to search out why the Assassins have decided now to reawaken old grievances against your king?'

'Exactly,' Corbett replied. 'We do not intend to threaten you.' He turned and bowed to Edward. 'The king has already agreed to the confirmation of your rights and privileges. We simply seek your help in this matter. We would be grateful for what you discover.'

'And it does not affect what we have agreed?' the king asked.

'No,' de Molay replied. 'It does not.'

The king heaved a sigh. 'Then in the abbey church tomorrow, I will take the oath.'

After that the meeting broke up. De Molay and his commanders bowed and took their leave. Edward, de Warrenne and Corbett sat in the refectory, listening to the mailed footsteps of the Templars fade in the distance. The king grinned slyly at Corbett.

'I got what I wanted, did I not?'

'And so did the Templars, my lord. Your oath will be a public statement of support for them.'

'It was a pity,' Edward pushed back his chair, 'that you had to lay such allegations before them.'

Corbett smiled as he began to clear his writing tray from the desk.

'My lord, you have been threatened. These are matters which could be laid at the Templars' door. By raising them, you are warning the Templars that, perhaps, their Order does not enjoy the support it once did.'

'Do you think there is any truth in the Assassins' threat?' De Warrenne asked.

'The knives were found,' Corbett exclaimed. 'Thirty years ago His Grace was attacked by the same sect. We also have the warnings brought by Monsieur de Craon.' He shrugged. 'But it's all too vague.'

'In other words,' Edward declared, getting to his feet and stretching till his muscles cracked, 'not serious enough to hold you here at York, eh, Hugh? So you can scuttle off, back to your manor at Leighton, to the lovely Lady Maeve and Baby Eleanor.'

'It has been three months, Sire. You did promise I would be released from your service at Candlemas, some seven weeks ago.'

Edward glanced down at him. 'Affairs of state, Sir Hugh.' The king held up his long, scar-studded fingers. 'We have a council in York and the French envoy is here. We have the marriage negotiations for my son. There's the business of the counterfeit coins and the matter of the Templars.' He gripped Corbett's shoulder. 'I need you here, Hugh.'

'And my lady wife needs me at home.' Corbett retorted. 'You gave your word, Sire. You, Edward of England, whose motto is, "My word is my troth".'

The king shrugged. 'Well, sometimes it is . . .' He picked up his cloak from the back of the chair and swung it round his shoulders. '. . . and sometimes it isn't.'

'We'd all like to go home to our wives and families,' de Warenne exclaimed, glaring like an angry boar at Corbett. Deep in his heart the earl could never understand why the king tolerated this clerk's bluntness. Corbett bit his tongue. He felt like reminding the earl that if he was married to Lady de Warenne, he'd spend as much time as he could as far away as possible from her. He looked at the king.

'So, when can I leave, Sire?'

Edward pursed his lips. 'By mid-April. I promise you, by the feast of Alphage, you will be released. But, meanwhile,' Edward strode to the door, snapping his fingers for de Warenne to follow, 'I want that counterfeiter unmasked. I want you to keep an eye on the Templars. There are also over a hundred petitions from our good burgesses at York. You and that green-eyed rapscallion clerk of yours, Ranulf, can deal with them.' The king paused, one hand on the latch. 'Oh, and to show there's no ill-feeling between myself and the grand master; go to the vintner, the master taverner Hubert Seagrave. He owns the largest tavern in York, just off Coppergate. Ask him for a tun of his best Gascony. Tomorrow, after I have sworn the oath, take it out to Framlingham. A gift from me to him.'

Corbett turned in his chair. 'And will you go on Crusade, Sire?'

Edward looked innocently back. 'Of course, Hugh. I have given my word. Once all the affairs in England are settled, then you and I, de Warrenne and all the rest, will go on Crusade to Jerusalem.'

And, chuckling softly to himself, the king swept out of the chamber, de Warrenne plodding behind him. Corbett sighed and got to his feet. He stared round the refectory, the huge, black cross hanging on the far wall and the brightly coloured triptych above the fireplace. He went back to the window and stared down into the courtyard. The king's soldiers had persuaded two blind beggars to have a duel with wooden swords. The two hairy, ragged men lurched and struck at each other, staggering about, their wooden swords beating the air. Now and again the circle of soldiers pushed them back into the ring with roars of laughter.

'Didn't you have enough?' Corbett whispered to himself. 'Didn't you see enough humiliation and bloodshed on the Scottish march?'

He sat in the window-seat. Since the end of January the king had been in his northern shires, launching raids across the Scottish border, trying to bring to battle or capture the elusive Scottish leader William Wallace. Corbett had become sickened by the hamlets and villages left as a black, smouldering mess, the corpses strewn about in pools of scarlet across the damp, broken heather. The columns of grey smoke, the stench of death and putrefaction, the gibbets full of corpses naked as worms. Cattle and sheep slaughtered, their bloated bodies fouling streams and wells, all consumed by the sea of fire which Edward, in retreat, had lit to burn everything behind him.

Corbett didn't just want to go back to Maeve and Eleanor because he was missing them; he was also sickened by Edward's ruthless drive to bring the Scots to heel; and by the intricacies and subtleties of court intrigues; by nobles like de Warrenne who believed they were lords of the soil and every other man

25

and woman had been born to serve them. The two beggar-men were now crying. Corbett was tempted to ignore them but, rising, he thrust open the window.

'Stop it!' He yelled.

One of the soldiers was about to make an obscene gesture back, but his companion immediately recognised Corbett and whispered in the soldier's ear. Corbett called over to a serjeant.

'Take the beggars to the almoner!' He shouted. 'Give them bread and wine and send them on their way!'

The grizzled veteran nodded. 'The lads are just amusing themselves, sir.'

'There has been amusement enough!' Corbett snapped. 'Make sure your lads pay for their enjoyment. Organise a collection for the beggars!'

Corbett waited for the serjeant to carry out his orders then closed the window. He heard a rap on the door.

'Come in.'

Ranulf, his manservant, now a fully fledged clerk in the Chancery of the Green Seal, swaggered in, his red hair tied in a knot behind his head. Proud of his clerkly tunic of light blue edged with squirrel fur, Ranulf stuck his thumbs in the broad swordbelt fastened round his waist. His cat-like eyes twinkled in a smile.

'Are we going home, Master?'

'No!' Corbett snapped, 'we are not.' And he went back to the table.

Ranulf quickly made a face at the blond-haired, bland-faced Maltote, Corbett's messenger.

'Good,' he whispered.

Corbett whirled round. 'What holds you at York, Ranulf?'

'Oh, nothing, Master.'

Corbett studied him carefully. 'Do you ever tell the truth, Ranulf?'

'Every time I open my mouth, Master.'

26

'And you have no lady-love here? No burgess's buxom wife?'

'Of course not, Master.'

Corbett turned back to his writing tray. Ranulf pulled a face behind him and quietly thanked God that Corbett hadn't questioned him about the burgess's buxom daughters.

'So, we are staying?'

'Yes,' Corbett wearily replied. 'We'll take lodgings in St Mary's Abbey. Meanwhile, we have work to do. You have the petitions?'

Maltote hurried across, carrying a thick roll of vellum. 'This is what the clerks have received.'

Corbett gestured at his servants to sit on either side of the table.

'We'll work for two more hours,' he declared.

As Corbett reopened his writing case, Ranulf looked across at Maltote and raised his eyes heavenwards. 'Master Long Face', as Ranulf had secretly nicknamed Corbett, was not in the best of humours. Nevertheless, both men helped as Corbett began to work through the roll of vellum containing all the petitions the council had received, once the good burgesses of York knew the king was visiting their city. Every town had the right to petition the Crown, and Edward took such matters most seriously. The Chancery clerks would collect individual petitions, write them out again in a fair hand on sheets of parchment which were then sewn together. One of Corbett's functions, whenever he was at Court, was to deal with such requests. This collection of petitions covered a multitude of affairs: Francesca Ingoldsby complained against Elizabeth Raddle for assaulting and beating her with a broomstick on a pavement in the presence of their neighbours. Matthew Belle complained against Thomas Cooke for assault and striking him in the face with a poker at the Green Mantle tavern. Thomasina Wheel sought a licence to go beyond the seas to St James's Shrine at Compostella. Mary Verdell alleged she'd lost a cloak and believed Elizabeth Fryer was the culprit. John de Bartonon and Beatrice his wife complained against the vicar of their church who constantly trespassed upon their property. On and on the petitions went. Corbett ordered some of them to be sent to the city council, others to the sheriff, or the mayor; a few he kept for the king's consideration. One, in particular, he did scrutinise: it was from Hubert Seagrave, 'king's vintner in his own city of York', seeking permission to buy two messuages of land adjoining his tavern.

Corbett smiled across at Ranulf. 'We can deal with this one ourselves,' he muttered. 'I am to collect a tun of wine from Seagrave and take it to the Templars at Framlingham.'

Ranulf, busily writing down his master's decisions, just mumbled a reply. Corbett returned to the roll, noticing how a growing number of petitions from individual citizens, as well as some from the commonality of York, complained about the strange and mysterious events happening at the Templar manor at Framlingham. One man, John de Huyten, complained of lights burning late in the manor house, with hymns being sung at the dead of night. A batch of further petitions complained about how, since the Templar commanders had arrived at Framlingham, the gardens and estates of the manor were very closely guarded, and ancient rights of way across the Templar estates were now closed. A petitioner, Leofric Goodman, carpenter, declared how he had been ejected from Framlingham. He had been hired to work in the manor: he had gone upstairs to repair a shutter on a window but a Templar soldier had accosted him and driven him away with threatening and violent language.

Corbett put his pen down and went out to stand by the window. Daylight was fading: already lamps and torches had been lit, and even Ranulf was muttering that the light was too poor to read by. Corbett tried to marshal his thoughts. He wished to return to Maeve but there was a deep feeling of unease, a sense of growing menace: the warnings against the king in London, the daggers left pinned in the doors of St Paul's; that strange, macabre murder on the road outside York. Who had been that unfortunate rider? Who had cut his body in two then mysteriously burnt the top half? Why was Jacques de Molay in England? And what did the Templars have to hide? Outside in the priory grounds, an owl hooted, proclaiming its coming hunt through the night. Corbett recalled an old soldier he had known in his fighting days along the Welsh march.

'When the owl hoots before dusk,' the man had warned, 'the devil is about to walk!'

Chapter 2

At the manor of Framlingham, Guido Reverchien, Keeper of the Templar Estates in Yorkshire, was making his daily, lonely pilgrimage along the pebbledashed path of the great maze. Guido made this pilgrimage, as usual, on his hands and knees, chanting the Divine Office of the Church in atonement for his sins. Guido, now in his sixtieth year, his hair and beard white, his skin almost burnt black by the sun, still believed he carried a great burden of sin. He had been a Templar knight, a warrior of Christ: one of those who had defended the walls of Acre in 1291 until the Mameluke hordes had swept across its walls and turned that Templar city into a sea of blood. Guido had escaped: shoulder to shoulder with his comrades, he had fought his way down from the quayside to one of the few remaining boats waiting to take him and other refugees out to the Christian fleet. Oh, Guido had fought! At times the narrow, dusty streets of Acre became ankle-deep in blood: yet, still, the city had fallen and he, Guido Reverchien, had been saved. Ever since that terrible night, Guido had suffered nightmares. Every minute of his sleep seemed to be trapped in the destruction of Acre.

As the years passed, Guido had reached the conclusion that he should have died in Acre. He should have fought on until the enemies of Christ had killed him and so given others the opportunity to escape.

'Instead,' Guido had whispered to his father-confessor, 'I came back to England. I was given a comfortable benefice supervising the granaries, granges, fields and meadows of the

Templar Order. Father, I am a traitor to Christ, I failed God. I must go back and be saved.' Time and again his father-confessor had advised him that this was out of the question.

'You are needed in England,' he whispered back from behind the lattice screen. 'You have your duties here.'

But Guido would not be comforted until his father-confessor had mentioned the maze. This lay to the side of the Templar manor: a great sea of high, cruel, privet hedge with narrow paths leading to its centre, where a huge wooden cross stood bearing the image of the crucified Christ.

'You cannot go to Jerusalem,' Father-confessor had confided. 'But, Sir Guido, if you must atone for your sin; if you seek to do reparation; every day, just before dawn, go on your knees through the maze chanting the psalms.'

Now Guido did that. The pebbles dug deep into his knees but Guido saw this as his path to heaven as he shuffled along, the battered, wooden rosary beads slipping through his gnarled fingers. He knew the maze like the back of his hand. Every secret corner, each blind path. Sometimes Guido would deliberately take the wrong turnings intensifying his pain, feeling a release from his self-inflicted tortures. At last he reached the centre. His knees were now bloodied, the pain in his shoulders and arms intense. The sweat ran like water down his face.

'I am in Jerusalem,' he whispered, staring up at the cross. 'I have kept faith!' He crawled on his hands and knees to the stone base of the crucifix and looked up at the stricken face of his Saviour. 'Domine,' he murmured, striking his breast. 'I have sinned before heaven and before Thee!'

Guido took a tinder from his pouch and lit the three squat yellow candles which stood in their iron spigots on the steps before the cross. He moved his knees away from the pools which had formed amongst the pebbles and watched the flames of the candle flicker in the dawn breeze. He stared up at the crucifix.

'Just like Acre,' he whispered. 'A grey dawn, flames flickering.'

Guido narrowed his eyes; even the smell of that damned burning city seemed to haunt him. The candle flame grew stronger, suddenly there was fire all around him. Guido opened his mouth to scream just as a sheet of flame engulfed his body.

Edward of England was entering York with banners and pennants flying. Heralds walked in front of the long procession which wound its way under Micklegate Bar. Behind the king trundled a long train of carts and pack animals, lines of pike men and archers marching on either side. The city had been busy as an upturned beehive, because only at the last minute had the royal heralds proclaimed through which gate the king would come. Now all of York had turned out to greet him: the burgesses in their fur robes and ermine-lined cowls; their wives and daughters, clothed in the most costly sarcanet and samite dresses, their brows plucked, their lustrous hair covered by the most ornate head-dresses and veils. Parish priests in colourful chasubles had brought their parishioners as well as stoups of holy water and asperges rods to bless the king as he passed. The city council had done its best. The streets and sewers had been cleaned, the sore-ridden beggars driven away, the stocks emptied and the gibbets and their iron cages taken down. The Guilds of Corpus Christi and Trinity were well represented under their great many-coloured banners.

The mayor and his aldermen had met the king outside Micklegate Bar and handed him the keys of the city on a purple cushion. They'd widened the king's smile even more with purses full of gold and silver coins. Edward had expressed his thanks, accepting their protestations of loyalty and thrust the purses into de Warrenne's hand.

'Keep your eye on them,' he whispered. 'I don't want a penny to go amiss.'

Just within Micklegate Bar, they stopped and listened as a

choir of boys in white surplices sung a three-voiced hymn welcoming the king, praising his rule and extolling his victories. Then the royal progress had continued into the city itself, along the narrow streets, past the great houses with their beams painted a polished black, the plaster between gleaming a brilliant white in the morning sun. Despite the city ordinances, all the colourful underworld of York was also present. The whores and prostitutes in their low-cut gowns and orange and red wigs eyed the soldiers and tried to catch the eye of the mounted knights and sergeants-at-arms. The masterless and penniless alley folk were also there, sheltering in the shadows away from the sunlight, ready to flee at the approach of any city bailiff. The cripples, the song-chanters, the cut-throats, the foists and pickpockets had gathered around looking for easy prey. The stalls had been put away and the merchants and their apprentices, each in the colour of their guild, stood gawping, eager to catch a glimpse of their great king.

Edward did look the image of the Conquering Prince: a gold circlet round his iron-grey hair, his coat of chainmail, which Corbett had insisted he wear, covered by a golden samite surcoat. Edward rode his great destrier, Black Bayard, and its saddle and harness were of dark purple leather edged with silver. The king rode easily, one hand holding the reins, the other bearing a magnificent snowy-white hawk from Paris. Beside him, John de Warrenne, Earl of Surrey, dressed in half-armour, carried the king's personal banner, a golden lion rampant on a field of blood. Corbett rode just behind the king, restless and worried: his eyes constantly surveyed the crowds and the open windows on either side of the procession. Now and again he would feel the hilt of his dagger and glance anxiously sideways at Ranulf. His manservant, however, was more interested in smiling and blowing kisses at the wives and daughters of the burgesses. Every so often the procession would pause and the gloriously garbed heralds blew a silver fanfare before advancing further into the city, behind the fluttering banners bearing the arms of England, Scotland, Wales, France and Castille.

At the corner of Trinity, the king paused to watch a pageant. A scene from the Last Judgement; a massive tapestry from the Corpus Christi Guild, had been hung between two long poles on a frame mounted across three great carts. In garish colours the tapestry depicted the fate of sinners: legislators who had made bad laws were dressed in burning cloaks of sulphur, whilst corrupt lawyers were impaled and broken on the wheel. Edward chuckled at another scene depicting a group of monks, their pates shaven, being led by a monkey-faced demon to a boiling hot pit filled with venomous serpents. In front of this makeshift stage were groups of young women, all dressed in white, with green chaplets on their heads, singing a sweet carol welcoming the king. Edward listened attentively whilst stroking the hawk on his wrist. He then threw silver coins in front of the cart, kissed one of the young girls, and ordered the procession to continue. Corbett glared as Ranulf tried to imitate the king's example, reaching out to seize one of the young maids by the arm.

They had just turned into Trinity when Corbett heard the whistle of the crossbow bolt flying by his head, between him and the King. One of the men-at-arms, walking alongside, dropped his spear and collapsed screaming and gurgling on the blood spurting out of his mouth. Corbett raised himself in the stirrups and yelled at the men-of-arms who ran forward: under Corbett's and de Warrenne's instructions, these circled the king, raising their shields to form a wall of iron around him. Corbett glanced quickly at the houses on either side.

'There!' Ranulf yelled.

Corbett followed his direction to the top-storey window of a tavern on the corner of an alleyway. He saw the casement and wooden shutter being pushed open again, a cowled figure lurking there and the thick snout of a crossbow. Again there was a whirr like a hawk falling to the kill, but this time the bolt

35

smashed against one of the upraised shields.

'Follow me!' Corbett urged.

He dismounted, drew his sword and, with Ranulf and Maltote following behind, forced his way through the crowd, ignoring the chaos breaking out around them. They reached the shadows of the houses. Corbett looked up and cursed. He had lost his way. Then he saw the corner of the alleyway: a hooded beggar squatted there, hands extended. Corbett knocked him aside as he ran towards the entrance under a garish tavern sign swinging from its jutting pole. Yelling at Ranulf to go down the alleyway and guard the back entrance, Corbett entered the narrow, dark hallway. The people gathered there had no idea what was going on. Most of them were tapsters, scullions and maids. Corbett ordered them out of the way and ran up the narrow, shaky, wooden stairs. By now he was covered in sweat and had to grip the sword more tightly: he desperately wondered what he would do if he met the assailant. He tried to recall the window.

'It's at the top,' he muttered to himself, and gingerly climbed the next flight of stairs. He was half-way up when he saw the smoke seeping out from under a doorway in a recess at the top of the stairs. He turned round.

'Maltote!' he ordered, 'go back! Tell the taverner his house is on fire!'

Corbett, pinching his nostrils, tried the garret door. It was locked. He stepped back and kicked it open. Smoke curled and twisted, though most of this was pouring out of the open window. There was a chair just under the sill on which an arbalest lay, a collection of bolts beside it. On the floor next to this sprawled the corpse of a man blackened and burning. For a while Corbett could only stare, horrified by the eerie blue and yellow flames which danced over the blackening corpse.

'God save us!' Maltote muttered, coming up behind him. 'Master, what kind of fire is that?'

Coughing and spluttering, Corbett broke from his reverie. He wrenched off a heavy curtain, tattered and holed, which hung on the back of the door and, urging Maltote to help, threw it over the burning corpse, dousing the flames. Others came up: the landlord and his helpers carrying pails of water. They threw these over the blanket and around the rest of the room. Corbett, however, noticed that, apart from some scorching, the fire had not caught either the walls or floorboards. At last the fire was doused. Nothing to show except the stench, scorch-marks, and a horrid sizzling as the water seeped through the curtain covering the corpse.

'Clear the room!' Corbett urged. 'Maltote, get them all out!'

The landlord, a pot-bellied, balding fellow, began to protest as Ranulf burst into the room.

'I saw no one!' He gasped. 'No one at all! What happened here?'

'Clear the room!' Corbett shouted. 'You, sir –' he pointed at the taverner – 'wait for me below!'

Maltote and Ranulf shoved them from the room. Corbett pulled back the heavy curtain then gagged at the terrible stench. Maltote turned away to vomit on a pile of straw in the corner; Ranulf coolly squatted down beside the remains.

'How did this happen?' he asked, pointing to the crossbow and bolts on the stool.

'I don't know,' Corbett replied. 'Here we have a man full of life and malice. He takes a crossbow, shoots two bolts in an attempt to kill the king and then, a few minutes later, is a burning cadaver. He is consumed by a strange fire which does not spread to the walls or floorboards.'

'It would have done,' Ranulf retorted. 'Eventually, the wood would have smouldered and then burst into flames. Our arrival here stopped it. The question is, who is he; and how did he die?'

Corbett forced himself to examine the corpse. The face and upper torso were all burnt. The eyes had turned to water. Any hair on scalp and face was now flakes of ash. Corbett swallowed hard.

'Look.' He pulled the blanket further down. 'The top half of

37

the body has been terribly burnt.' He pointed to the hose and boots the man wore. 'Yet these are only scorched.'

Corbett eased himself up and went across to the bed. A battered leather saddlebag lay pushed just under the dirt-stained bolster. Corbett pulled this out, cut the straps and emptied the contents on to the woollen coverlet: a Welsh stabbing dagger; a purse full of silver coins, and the soiled white surcoat of the Templar Order with its red cross on either side.

'A wealthy man, at least for a soldier,' Corbett observed.

He opened the neck of the purse and shook the coins into his hands. He put the silver on the bed and unrolled the scraps of parchment he'd also found. One was a very crude diagram which Corbett immediately recognised as a rough map of the road leading from Micklegate Bar up through Trinity. The other was a list of provisions bought by one Walter Murston, serjeant of the Templar manor at Framlingham. Corbett sat down on the bed.

'Ranulf, put everything back into the saddlebag. For God's sake,' he waved at the blackened remains, 'cover that. Here we have,' he continued, 'Walter Murston, a member of the Templar Order, who tried to commit treason and regicide. He fired two bolts at our king but then, in a matter of minutes, is consumed by a mysterious fire.'

'God's punishment,' Maltote intoned.

'If that was the case,' Ranulf jibed, 'most of York would burst into flames.'

Corbett got up and stared out of the window. The royal cavalcade was now on its way. The crowd was staring up at the tavern. A curtain of men-at-arms, shields locked together, lances out, now ringed the tavern. On the stairs outside there was a heavy footfall and a deep voice cursing every taverner as 'fatherless, misbegotten spawns of Satan'. Corbett grinned.

'My lord of Surrey is about to arrive,' he murmured.

The chamber door crashed back on its leather hinges.

'Poxy knaves! Ingrate bastards!' de Warrenne shouted, his red face covered in sweat. He lumbered into the room like an old bear. 'Well, Corbett, you bloody clerk! What do we have here?' The earl pulled back the ragged coverlet and stared down at the corpse. 'Fairies' tits! Who's he?'

'Apparently a serjeant, probably an arbalester of the Temple Order,' Corbett replied. 'He came into this chamber with his crossbow and tried to slay our king.'

'And who killed him?'

'We were just debating that, my lord. Maltote thinks it was God, but Ranulf believes that if every sinner in York was to be so punished, the whole city would be a sea of fire.'

De Warrenne hawked and, going back to the door, bawled down the stairs. A group of royal archers came up.

'Take that out!' de Warrenne ordered. 'I want it dragged to the Pavement in York and hung from the highest gibbet!'

The archers neatly stripped the bed and wrapped the corpse in soiled sheets. De Warrenne looked out of the corner of his eye at Corbett. 'Oh, and get some bloody lazy clerk to write out a notice: SO DIE ALL TRAITORS. Fix it around the bastard's neck!'

De Warrenne hustled the archers and their grisly burden out of the room, slamming the door behind them. 'And the bastard's name?'

'Walter Murston.'

'The king will want an answer to all this.' De Warrenne snapped. 'I don't trust those bloody fighting monks!' He came over and kicked the ash away with his boot, spurs jingling on the wooden floor. He stared through the window. 'I am frightened, Corbett.' He whispered. 'I am terrified. I was with the king thirty years ago when the Assassins tried to kill him. A man pretending to be a messenger.' The old earl narrowed his eyes, breathing heavily through flared nostrils. 'He got so close, so quickly. The king was quick. He brained him with a stool. Now they are hunting him again.' He gripped Corbett's arm; the clerk stared unflinchingly back. 'For God's sake, Hugh, don't let them do it!' De Warrenne glanced away. 'We are all dying,' he murmured. 'All the king's old friends.'

'Tell His Grace,' Corbett replied, 'that he will be safe. Say that I will join him at the abbey of St Mary's.'

De Warrenne stomped across the room.

'Oh, my lord Earl?'

'Yes, Corbett.'

'Tell the king I will not return to Leighton Manor.' He forced a smile. 'At least, not until this present business is finished.'

He paused and listened as de Warrenne stamped down the stairs, hurling abuse at everyone in the tavern below. Ranulf and Maltote were standing in the corner watching open-mouthed.

'What's the matter, Ranulf?' Corbett asked. 'If you don't close your mouth, you'll catch a fly.'

'I've never heard de Warrenne call you Hugh,' Ranulf replied. 'He must be very frightened . . .'

'He is. The Assassins' boast is never hollow.' Corbett closed the window. 'But let's leave. This place stinks. Ranulf, bring that saddlebag.'

'Who are the Assassins?' Maltote asked.

'I'll tell you later. What I want to know is why a member of the Templar Order is carrying out their instructions!'

They walked back down the stairs and into the taproom, a low, dank chamber, its ceiling timbers blackened by a thousand fires. At the far end, near the scullery door, sat the landlord surrounded by his slatterns; he was gulping wine as if his life depended on it. He took one look at Corbett's face and slumped to his knees, clasping his hands before him.

'Oh, Lord have mercy on me!' He wailed, staring piteously, though Corbett's grim face did nothing to ease his panic. He almost grovelled at the clerk's feet. 'Master, believe me, we had nothing to do with it!'

Ranulf drew his sword and brought the flat of its blade down on the man's shoulder. 'If you had,' Corbett's red-haired servant taunted, 'within a week you'll hang, then you'll be quartered and your pickled limbs dangled above Micklegate Bar.'

The landlord grasped Corbett's cloak. 'Master,' he groaned, 'mercy!'

Corbett knocked away Ranulf's sword and pushed the man back on to his stool.

'Get your master a cup of the best wine. The same for me and my companions,' he ordered one of the slatterns. 'Now, listen sir,' Corbett pulled a stool up and sat close, his knees touching the landlord's. 'You have nothing to fear,' he continued, 'if you tell the truth.'

The landlord could hardly stop shaking. Ranulf's sword was one thing, but this soft-spoken clerk was absolutely terrifying. For a while he could only splutter.

'You are in no danger,' Corbett reassured him. 'You can't be held responsible for everyone in your tavern.' He took the wine a servitor had brought and thrust it into the man's hand. Corbett sipped from his own then put it down: the wine was good but the sight of a fat fly floating near the rim turned his stomach. 'Now, who was the man?'

'I don't know. He came here last night. A traveller. He gave his name as Walter Murston. He paid well for the garret: two silver coins. He ate his supper and that's the last I saw of him.'

'Didn't he come down to break his fast?'

'No, we were busy preparing for the king's entry to York.' The landlord groaned and put his face in his hands. 'We were going to have a holiday. One minute we are by the doorway cheering the banners and listening to the trumpets, the next . . .' The man's hands flailed helplessly.

'And no one else was with him?' Corbett insisted. 'No one came to visit him?'

'No, Master, but there again the tavern has two entrances:

41

front and back. People come and go, especially on a day like this.' The man's voice trailed away.

Corbett closed his eyes and sat, recalling how he had struggled through the crowds. He had knocked that beggar aside as Ranulf had gone down the alleyway. Corbett opened his eyes.

'Wait there,' he ordered, and went out of the tavern.

'What are you looking for?' Ranulf hurried up behind him.

Corbett walked to the mouth of the alleyway and stared down. It was a narrow, evil-smelling tunnel between the houses, full of refuse and wandering cats. Two children were trying to ride an old sow which was lumbering amongst the litter, but there was no sign of the beggar.

'Master?' Ranulf asked.

Corbett walked back into the taproom.

'Master taverner, in London, and I suppose York is the same, beggars have their favourite haunts: certain corners or the porch of some church. Does a beggar-man stand on the corner of the alleyway, on the other side of your tavern?'

The landlord shook his head. 'No, Master, no beggar would stand there. It's well away from the stalls, and the alleyway really goes nowhere.' He smiled in a display of red, sore gums. 'After all, my customers are not the sort to part with a penny.'

'In which case, Master taverner, go back to your beer barrels. You have nothing to fear.'

Corbett beckoned at Ranulf and Maltote to follow and they walked back into Trinity Lane.

'Sir.' A serjeant of the royal household came up, one hand on the hilt of his sword, the other cradling his helmet. 'The Earl of Surrey told us to stay here until you were finished.'

'Take your men, Captain,' Corbett ordered. 'Rejoin the king at the abbey. Tell my lord of Surrey I will be with him soon. Our horses?'

The soldier raised his hand and an archer came forward, leading their three mounts.

'You'll have to walk them,' the soldier observed. 'The streets are now packed.'

Once they had left Trinity, Corbett was forced to agree. Now the royal procession had swept on, Micklegate was thronged. The stalls had been brought out and it was business as usual: traders, hawkers and journeymen trying to earn a penny in the holiday atmosphere of the city. Corbett walked his horse, Ranulf and Maltote trailing behind: they made slow progress. Outside St Martin's church, a troupe of players had erected a makeshift stage on two carts and were depicting, to the crowd's delight, a play about Cain and Abel. As Corbett passed, God, a figure dressed in a white sheet with a gold halo strapped to the back of his head, was busily marking Cain with a red cross. If only it was so easy, Corbett reflected: if the mark of Cain appeared on the forehead of every assassin or would-be murderer.

'Do you think that Templar acted by himself?' Ranulf asked, coming up beside him.

'No,' Corbett replied. 'How long, Ranulf, did it take us to leave the king's side and reach that garret room?'

Ranulf paused as a group of children ran by, chasing a wooden hoop; a mongrel followed, the corpse of a scrawny chicken in its mouth, hotly pursued by an irate housewife, screaming at the top of her voice.

'They talk strangely here,' Ranulf declared. 'Faster, more clipped than in London.'

'But the girls are just as pretty,' Corbett replied. 'I asked you a question, Ranulf; how long do you think it took us?'

'About the space of ten Aves.'

Corbett remembered pushing through the crowds, losing his way, then entering the tavern and going up the stairs.

'You think there were two, don't you?' Ranulf asked.

'Yes, I do. The door to the room was locked, probably by the crossbowman's accomplice as he left. I noticed the key was missing.'

43

'So it was the beggar you went looking for?'

'Perhaps, though that doesn't explain it,' Corbett continued. 'Murston must have fired those two bolts. Yet how could a professional soldier be killed in such a short time, offering no resistance? And then his body be consumed so quickly by that terrible fire?'

'The other person could have killed him,' Ranulf replied, 'then ran downstairs and pretended to be the beggar you knocked aside.'

'That's only conjecture,' Corbett replied.

He gripped his horse's reins more tightly as they entered the approaches to the bridge across the Ouse. The bridge was broad; stalls had been set up alongside the high wooden rails where traders could offer fish 'Freshly plucked', so they shouted, 'from the river below.' Corbett stopped, told Ranulf to hold the horses, and went to look through a gap between the palings. To his right, he could see the great donjon of York Castle then, turning to his left, he glimpsed the towering spires of York Minster and St Mary's Abbey.

'What shall I tell the king?' he murmured to himself, ignoring the curious looks of passers-by. He looked down at the river swirling past the starlings of the bridge, and the fragile craft of the fishermen bobbing there. These rowed against the tide, struggling to hold their nets, whilst avoiding the mounds of refuse which swirled about, trapped by the great pillars of the bridge. Corbett couldn't make sense of the Templar's death: a fighting man, so expertly reduced to burning ash! He walked back towards Ranulf and, as he did so, a little beggar boy ran up, a penny in one hand, a piece of parchment in the other. He chattered to Corbett. The clerk smiled and squatted down.

'What is it, boy?'

The smile on the urchin's thin face widened. He thrust the dirty piece of parchment into Corbett's hand. The clerk unfurled it and the boy ran away. As he read it, despite the bustling crowds and the warm sunlight, Corbett's blood ran cold.

KNOWEST THOU, THAT WHAT THOU POSSESSES SHALL ESCAPE THEE IN THE END AND RETURN TO US, the message read. KNOWEST THOU, THAT WE GO FORTH AND RETURN AS BEFORE AND BY NO MEANS CAN YOU HINDER US.

KNOWEST THOU, THAT WE HOLD YOU AND WILL KEEP THEE UNTIL THE ACCOUNT BE CLOSED.

Corbett studied the scrawl on the parchment: the sequence of the verses was slightly changed but the threat was just as real. He glanced up: the boy was gone, impossible to follow. Somewhere in the crowds the Assassin had been watching them, tracking their every footstep. The dead Templar had not been alone, he had merely been a pawn – and the game was only just beginning.

Chapter 3

Edward of England sprawled in the great wooden bath in the private chamber of the archbishop's palace. The tub's surroundings had been covered by a purple buckram cloth, filled by a troop of servants carrying buckets of scalding water, then sweetened by rose-hips and other herbs. The king sat with his arms out on either side, allowing his body to float in the sweet-smelling, soapy water. He glared over the rim at Corbett who was sitting next to de Warrenne. The clerk was trying to keep his face straight: not that Edward lost any of his royal dignity in taking a bath, the clerk was more amused by the pretensions of the archbishop, the owner of this tub, whose coat of arms, not to mention a few crosses, were painted on the bath.

'Do you think it's amusing?' Edward snarled. 'I have just been promised a loan of fifty thousand pounds sterling by the Templars. I have taken their bloody oath to go on Crusade: now you say the bastards are trying to kill me!'

'It wasn't a loan,' Corbett retorted, 'it was a gift. If you go on Crusade, Your Grace, then with all due respect, that tub will sing the Te Deum.'

Edward rose to his feet, shaking himself like a dog. He stepped out of the bath; de Warrenne placed a woollen cloth round his shoulders.

'I enjoyed that,' Edward declared. 'I wish I didn't have to wait until mid-summer for the next.' He padded over to Corbett, shaking the water from his hair. 'You bathe once a week, don't you?'

'An Arab physician, a student of Salerno, said it would do me no harm.'

'It makes you soft!' Edward grumbled.

The king went across to a small table, filled three gold-encrusted goblets with wine and brought them back, thrusting one each into de Warrenne's and Corbett's hands.

'So, this Templar loosed two arrows at me then burst into flames?'

'Apparently, my lord, though there must have been someone else there,' Corbett replied. 'The same person followed me through York and delivered that warning message.'

'But why should the Templars want me dead?' Edward asked. And does this attack have anything in common with that poor bastard those two nuns found burning on the road outside York?' He breathed in deeply. 'You still look fresh, Corbett. I want you to go out to Framlingham.' He slipped a ring from his finger and dropped it into Corbett's hand. 'Show that to de Molay. He'll recognise it.'

Corbett looked at the amethyst sparkling on the gold ring.

'The Templars gave it to my father,' Edward explained. 'I want it back, till then it's your authority to act. You are to investigate, Corbett! Use that long nose and sharp brain, ferret out the assassin and, when you do, I'll kill him!'

'Is that all, my Lord?'

'What more do you want?' Edward sneered. 'The archbishop's tub to sing the "Te Deum" for you? Oh,' he called out as Corbett rose, bowed and made his way to the door, 'I want you to stay at Framlingham until this business is finished. However, to show my friendship to the grand master, take that tun of wine I promised.'

There was a rap on the door and it was abruptly pushed open, almost knocking Corbett over. Amaury de Craon, Philip IV's envoy to the English council, stalked into the room all afluster. He scarcely seemed aware of de Warrenne, but immediately sank to one knee before the king.

'Your Grace,' he murmured. 'I heard about the attack on you.' He raised his red-bearded, foxy face. 'On behalf of my own master I give thanks to God for your safe deliverance. I pray that your enemy will soon be brought to destruction.'

'As he will be. As he will be.'

Edward stretched his hand out for the French envoy to kiss. De Craon did so, then rose to his feet.

'Our dear and well-beloved clerk, Sir Hugh Corbett, Keeper of our Secret Seal,' the king continued, 'will search out the truth.'

'As I have done on other occasions,' Corbett added, closing the door and leaning against it.

De Craon turned. 'Sir Hugh, God save you!' And, going over, he grasped the English clerk by the arms and kissed him, Judas-like, on his cheek. 'You look well, Sir Hugh!'

Corbett stared at his inveterate enemy: Philip's spy-master and the source of all his intrigues. He admired the Frenchman's ostentatious dress: the damask tunic, edged at the neck and cuffs with gold; the hem over shiny red leather boots, studded with miniature gems.

'And you, Sir Amaury, have not changed.'

De Craon smiled, though, keeping his back to the king, his eyes betrayed a deep antipathy for this English clerk he'd love to kill.

'Congratulate me, Sir Hugh. I am married and my wife is already with child.'

'Then you are twice blessed, Sir Amaury.'

'But I did not come to share pleasantries.' De Craon turned. 'Nor even to rejoice in His Grace's narrow escape.'

'Then what?' Corbett snapped.

'Warnings from my master,' de Craon continued. 'You heard of a similar attack on him whilst hunting in the Bois de Boulogne?'

'Continue,' Edward said softly.

'The culprit was found,' de Craon explained. 'A Templar, a

49

high-ranking serjeant from their fortress in Paris. My master's agents arrested him. He made a full confession after a short sojourn in the dungeon of the Louvre.'

'And?' Corbett asked.

'Apparently there are high-ranking Templars who view their expulsion from the Holy Land as the fault of the Western kings, the Holy Roman Emperor, even the Pope himself; more especially, Philip of France and Edward of England.'

Corbett walked across. 'And so you bring warnings?'

'Yes, Sir Hugh, I bring warnings. England and France are about to sign a great treaty of peace. It will be cemented by a royal marriage between the two houses. Both our countries have had their differences. However, this is a common danger which threatens us both and could shatter that peace.'

'And what else did this serjeant confess?' Edward asked.

De Craon plucked a parchment from his sleeve and thrust it at Corbett. 'See for yourself!'

Corbett unrolled the parchment and read it; as he did so, he realised that his suspicions about de Craon were, on this occasion, apparently unfounded.

'What does it say?' the king asked, sitting down on a bench.

Corbett studied the manuscript, taking it over to a window for better light. 'It's a confession,' Corbett explained. 'By a serjeant based in the Temple at Paris. He admits to trying to kill Philip in the Bois de Boulogne. Apparently, the serjeant was carrying out the orders of a high ranking officer known only to him as "Sagittarius" or "The Archer".'

'And Philip's torturers wrung this out of him?' Edward asked.

'No,' Corbett looked up, 'not the royal torturers.' He saw de Craon's smile of satisfaction. 'No less a person than the grand inquisitor.'

'And you know,' de Craon intervened, 'the Holy Inquisition is a law unto itself.'

'Apparently,' Corbett continued, studying the manuscript

carefully, 'certain artefacts were found in the Templar's possession: a pentangle, a picture of an inverted cross, and other tools of the black magician.' He glanced up. 'Which is why the Inquisition took the matter over. The serjeant maintained that he and other Templars were part of a warlock's coven, participating in Satanic practices, the worship of demons and a disembodied head.'

Corbett glanced at the bottom of the paper. He studied the blood-red seal of the Holy Inquisition as well as the personal signature of the master grand inquisitor and his two witnesses.

'So,' Edward leaned forward, 'this is a serious threat.'

De Craon nodded tersely. 'My master has already written to Pope Boniface the Eighth demanding the order be investigated.' He rose and sank to one knee before the king. 'But I shall inform my master about your safe deliverance. And,' he added slyly, glancing out of the corner of his eye at Corbett, 'your sacred vow to go on Crusade.'

'In which,' Corbett intervened, 'my master will call on other Western princes to join him.'

De Craon got to his feet and bowed at Corbett. 'You shall not find Philip of France lacking. He is ready to spill his blood, as his grandfather did, to win back God's fief.' And, making further obeisances, de Craon left the room as swiftly as he had arrived.

'It must have been hard,' Corbett declared, going over to make sure the door was closed. 'For de Craon, once in his life, to tell the truth.'

'Go to Framlingham,' Edward declared. 'Take up residence there. Tell their grand master that if any Templar is found outside the grounds of that manor, he will be arrested on suspicion of high treason!'

Ranulf and Maltote complained bitterly at being pulled away from their game of dice with the royal archers. Their wails grew even louder as Corbett told them where they were going.

51

'Stop moaning,' their master ordered. 'First, it's only a matter of time before the archers realise you cheat. Secondly, Ranulf, a period of abstinence from chasing the ladies will do your soul the world of good.'

As they later rode through the streets of York, Corbett did not bother to look, though he knew Ranulf was scowling behind him and muttering under his breath about 'Master Long Face' and his killjoy actions. Maltote was more resigned. As long as he was with horses and able to know what the great lords of the soil were planting, he was content. So, he let Ranulf mutter on whilst trying to manage a vicious sumpter pony who deeply resented being plucked from a comfortable stable and taken through the noisy, dusty streets of York.

Ranulf, who had got to know the city well, eventually pushed his horse alongside Corbett's.

'Master, surely we should be going in the other direction? Framlingham lies beyond Botham Bar to the north of the city.'

Corbett paused just before they entered the Shambles, York's great meat-market.

'We have business, Ranulf, with Master Hubert Seagrave, King's vintner and proud owner of the Greenmantle tavern in Coppergate. We are to take the grand master a present.'

Corbett stared down the narrow streets ahead of him. He saw the blood and offal which coated the cobbles in a bloody mess; from the stalls on either side of the street hung the gutted carcases of sheep, lambs and pigs. He pulled his horse's head round.

'Let's find another way.'

As he turned, an arrow bolt whirred by his face, smashing into the plaster wall of the house alongside. Corbett stared open-mouthed: Ranulf seized the reins of his horse, pulling it into a gallop down a narrow alleyway leading into Coppergate. Tradesmen, apprentices, beggars, children, scavenging dogs and cats fled before the pounding hooves. The more quick-witted picked up fistfuls of refuse and threw it at these three riders, for Maltote had quickly followed suit. Once in Coppergate, Corbett reined in.

'Who fired that?' he demanded.

Ranulf wiped the sweat from his face. 'God knows, but I don't intend to go back and find out.'

Corbett hurriedly dismounted, ordering Ranulf and Maltote to do the same.

'Keep the horses on the outside!' he urged.

They walked down Coppergate. A trader ran up, protesting at their feckless ride. Ranulf drew his sword, shouting that they were on the king's business, so the fellow backed away.

'What was it, a warning?' Ranulf asked.

'I don't think so,' Corbett replied. 'If I had not turned, that arrow would have found its mark.'

'Shall we go back?' Maltote asked. 'Perhaps—'

'Don't be stupid!' Ranulf snarled. He gestured at the houses on either side. 'Windows, doors, alleyways, nooks and crannies; you could hide an army in York.'

Corbett walked on. He just wished his stomach would stop heaving. The narrowness of his escape made him feel light-headed, and the sweat coating his body was turning cold. He tried to distract himself by looking at the crowds on either side, the different colours, the shouts and cries, but he was afraid. He felt like drawing his sword and dashing into the crowd. He also found he could not stop thinking about Maeve and his baby daughter Eleanor. They will be cleaning the rooms, he thought, now spring was here; Maeve will turn the house inside out. Oh God! he thought. Would she be doing that when the messenger came riding up the manor path? Would she run down to meet him? How would she take the message sent by the king that his trusted and well-beloved clerk, her husband, was dead, killed by some assassin in York? He heard, as if from far off, his name being called.

'Master? Sir Hugh?'

Corbett stopped and glanced at Ranulf.

'What is it?' Corbett rasped. His throat and lips were bone dry.

'Do you know where we are going?' Ranulf asked quietly, alarmed by Corbett's pallid face.

'I made a mistake, Ranulf,' Corbett confessed. 'I am sorry. We should have left York.'

'Nonsense.' Ranulf leaned over and gripped his master's hand, ice-cold to the touch. 'We are going to the Greenmantle tavern,' Ranulf said quietly. 'We'll collect the tun of wine, Master, and go on to Framlingham. We'll tell those Templar bastards they cannot leave the place: then you'll ask your questions. You'll sit and you'll brood like you always do. And, before Ascension Day has arrived, you'll have dispatched another felon to his well-deserved fate. Now, come on,' Ranulf urged. 'Cheer up. After all, I am leaving Lucia.'

'Lucia?' Corbett asked.

'Master, she's the most beautiful girl in York.' Ranulf walked on. 'She has hair as black as midnight, skin like white silk and eyes,' he pointed to the sky between the overhanging houses, 'bluer than that.' He looked over his shoulder at Maltote. 'And she has a sister. Indeed,' Ranulf chattered on, 'the two of them remind me of a story I heard about the bishop of Lincoln who had to take refuge in farmhouse at the dead of night . . .'

Soothed by Ranulf's chatter, Corbett found himself relaxing. They paused at the corner of Hosier Lane where Ranulf hired a young lad who led them down into the courtyard of Master Seagrave's tavern.

The Greenmantle was a spacious, four-storeyed mansion with wings built on either side, standing in its own grounds off Newgate. The courtyard at the front was bounded by a curtain wall: the tavern was really a small village in itself, with outhouses, smithies, stables, a small tannery, and workshops for coopers and carpenters. Its owner, Hubert Seagrave, came out to greet them. He was dressed like a merchant rather than a landlord, in pure woollen robes. A straw hat was perched on his balding head against the heat of the day. He swaggered across the courtyard, swinging his cane.

'Just like a bishop in his palace,' Ranulf whispered.

Seagrave was apparently used to meeting royal officials, but his harsh face and gimlet eyes became more servile when Corbett introduced himself.

'I am sorry, sir, I did not realise,' he stammered. 'Usually servants from the royal household come . . .'

'The king wants a tun of your best wine, Master Seagrave,' Corbett remarked casually. 'And I mean your best. It's his gift to the Templar grand master.'

Seagrave's face became worried.

'What's the matter?' Corbett asked. 'Are you out of wine?'

Seagrave plucked Corbett's sleeve, pulling him closer as if they were fellow conspirators.

'No, no,' the vintner whispered. 'But the rumours have swept the city, of strange doings at Framlingham as well as the attack on the king this morning.'

Corbett gently detached his arm. 'Aye, tell a taverner,' he said. 'And you have told the world. But you shouldn't listen to every bit of tittle-tattle.'

Seagrave agreed. 'I have a cask,' he declared, 'from the best year in Gascony. Ten years it has been in my cellar. I hoped to give it to the king. My servants will pull it out but, come, you wish some refreshment?'

'In a while, Master Seagrave, there is another matter: the two messuages of land you wish to purchase.'

Seagrave became even more servile, rubbing his hands together as if he sensed a profit. He insisted on taking Corbett, a cynical Ranulf and an awe-struck Maltote, on a tour of his domain: the stores and smithies in the courtyard, the deep cellars where Seagrave pointed out the tun of wine he had selected. He then took them up through sweet-smelling rooms where the scent of fresh rushes mingled with the cooking smells

55

from the kitchen, and out into the pleasant garden beyond. This was bounded on all four sides by a high bricked wall covered by creepers and lichen. The garden itself was divided into small patches where, Seagrave explained, the tavern grew its own herbs and vegetables for the kitchen.

Ranulf impatiently asked about the two messuages, so Seagrave led them over to a small postern gate. Corbett paused just before this and stared at the sheet which covered a great yawning hole near the wall.

'You are building again, Master Seagrave?'

'Aye. We intend to build arbours, small drinking places screened against the wind, where select customers can sit and eat during the pleasant days of summer.'

Corbett nodded and stared round. The garden was beautiful; a small dovecote stood at the far end with beehives on either side. He closed his eyes, smelt the fragrance of the flowers, and listened to the gentle hum of the hunting bees.

'A pleasant place, eh, Sir Hugh?'

'Aye, it makes me homesick.' Corbett opened his eyes: Ranulf was still looking at him curiously. 'But come, Master Seagrave, let me see the land you wish to buy.'

The taverner opened the gate and led him through. The area beyond was nothing more than a common where wild grass and brambles grew, a broad triangle of land stretching between the tavern and the back of houses on either side.

'Who owns this?' Corbett asked.

'Well, at first I thought the city but, on examination of the deeds, I discovered it was granted to the Order of the Templars. They own many such plots throughout the city.'

'Ah!' Corbett sighed. 'And, of course, such sales can only be made with the permission of the king.'

Seagrave drew his bushy brows together. 'Of course, Sir Hugh. No land granted to a religious Order can be resold without royal permission.'

They returned to the tavern. Corbett gathered from Ranulf's

hungry look that they should accept Seagrave's offer of refreshments, so they stayed for a while sharing a dish of lampreys and succulent chicken slices. Seagrave himself served them a white wine specially chilled in his cellars. After they had eaten, the taverner's ostlers fastened the small tun of wine on to the sumpter pony and they made their farewells. They went up Colney Gate through Lock Lane, up Petergate and under the yawning, cavernous mouth of Botham Bar. Corbett rode ahead. Ranulf and Maltote felt better after eating what they described as the best meal they'd been served since arriving at York.

The afternoon was now drawing on, and Corbett wondered how he would manage his meeting with the Templars.

'Do you think they'll know?' he called out over his shoulder.

'What, Master?'

'Do you think the Templars have heard about the attack on the king?'

'God knows, Master.'

Ranulf pulled a face at Maltote. Despite all the banter on their journey to Framlingham, Ranulf was anxious. Corbett was determined to leave the royal service and go back to Leighton Manor. The recent attack would only strengthen his resolve. But what, Ranulf wondered, would happen to him? Leighton could be beautiful, particularly in summer. However, as he had often told Maltote, one sheep tends to look like another, whilst trees and hedgerows do not contain the same excitement as the crooked alleyways of London. He now began to discuss this with Maltote, as the houses and small cottages gave way to green open fields and they entered the open countryside which Ranulf disliked so much. He watched Corbett tense in the saddle and Ranulf himself grew uneasy as the trackway narrowed. Thick hedgerows rose high on either side, and the trees leaned so close that their branches entwined to form a canopy over their heads. Now and again a wood-pigeon's liquid cooing would be offset by the raucous cawing of hunting rooks. Ranulf tried to ignore these, listening for any sound, any movement which could presage danger. He relaxed as the hedgerows gave way and the road became broader. Corbett, however, would stop now and again, muttering to himself. He would look down at the trackway and then ride on.

'For the love of God, Master!' Ranulf shouted. 'What's so exciting about stones and mud?'

Corbett reined in. 'The severed, burning corpse,' he remarked, 'was found near here.' He dismounted, ignoring Ranulf's protests. 'That's right.' He pointed to the trackway. 'There, just before the corner near the small copse of trees: that's where the good sisters found the remains.'

'Are you sure?' Ranulf asked.

'Yes, their guide said they were approaching a bend in the road. The horse came pounding round and passed them. When they turned the corner, they found the corpse, or part of it, burning like a torch.' He remounted and grinned at Ranulf. 'Let's see if my memory fails me. The good sisters did say that, within half an hour of leaving the spot, they reached Botham Bar. We have travelled the same distance.'

In the end Corbett was proved right. They rode on into the small copse of trees. Corbett stared into the darkness, then down at the pebble-covered soil, and pointed to the great scorch-mark.

'Why are you so interested in this murder?' Ranulf asked.

Corbett dismounted, crouched down, and ran the scorched earth through his fingers.

'Here we have a traveller to York. We don't know who he was, where he was going or what he was doing on this lonely road. But, apparently, he was attacked by a master swordsman.'

'How do you know that?' Ranulf asked.

'Only a professional soldier, someone capable of using a great two-handed sword could slice a man through his waist: the horse careered off, leaving the decapitated upper part of the torso to be consumed by a mysterious fire. And where did that come from, eh?'

'The Templars?' Ranulf interrupted. 'They carry two-handed swords.'

Corbett smiled. 'Now you understand my interest. So, stay where you are.' Corbett drew his sword. 'Right, Ranulf, you are the victim and I am your assailant.' He grasped his sword hilt with two hands, ran forward and gently smacked the flat of the blade against Ranulf's stomach.

'Is that how it was done, Master?'

Corbett resheathed his sword. 'Possibly. But why should the victim ride on to the sword? Why didn't he turn his horse and flee?'

'It was night,' Ranulf remarked.

Corbett shook his head. 'It doesn't make sense. Why cut a man in half then burn the upper part of his body? And, if you are the victim, some innocent traveller, why not flee?'

'How do we know he was innocent?' Ranulf asked.

'Well, no other weapon was found.' Corbett stared back along the trackway. 'So there was little resistance.'

'Was the victim going to or from York?' Ranulf asked.

Corbett shook his head. 'According to what I have seen, not one petition has come in asking about the whereabouts of any citizen, nor has anyone been reported missing.'

'What makes you think,' Maltote asked, 'that the assailant was a Templar knight?'

Corbett patted his horse's neck. 'That's what I like, Maltote. Good, searching questions. I think it was a knight,' he continued. 'As I've said, for a man to cut through another man's body requires terrible force as well as skill. You must think, Maltote, of this murderer running towards his victim, sword in hand, then he brings it back, like a farmer's scythe, and cuts straight through the middle just above the crotch. Now only a trained knight, an experienced warrior, could swing a sword with such position and force. I have seen it done in Scotland and Wales. Such skill only comes after years of experience in war.'

'But why a Templar?' Maltote insisted.

'Because of their skill and their proximity to Framlingham. Also, as far as I know, the only other knights capable of such a blow were with the king.'

'So, the murder on this lonely trackway, and the death of the assassin in the city are linked?' Ranulf asked.

'Yes, both men were killed and their bodies burnt. But why, and by whom, is a mystery.'

'What happens if the victim was a Templar?' Maltote asked, now preening himself at Corbett's praise.

'Possible,' Corbett replied. 'And that could explain why no one has come forward to claim the remains, as well as why the whereabouts of the horse and the rest of the poor victim's body remain a mystery. But,' he added slowly, 'somehow I think he wasn't a Templar.' He shrugged. 'But there again I have no proof.' Corbett stared down at the scorch-mark then into the green darkness of the trees. 'We will see,' he murmured and, mounting his horse, they continued on their journey.

For a while they jogged along in silence, Corbett assessing in his mind the sea of troubles mounting against him. Who was the victim on the lonely trackway? Why was he killed, then his body set alight? Why didn't anyone recognise the corpse? Why had that Templar serjeant tried to kill the king and, in turn, been consumed by a mysterious fire? Was the Templar Order so rotten with intrigue and greed? Was there some dark coven plotting the destruction of princes through murder and black magic? Who was Sagittarius? Corbett closed his eyes, letting his horse find its head. Then there was this business of the coins: who had the means to issue good gold coins? Where had the precious metal come from? How was it distributed? Was that, too, linked to the Templars? Had they discovered the secret of alchemy, of transmuting base metals into gold? Corbett opened his eyes. And what could he do at Framlingham? He carried the king's ring in his pouch and the royal authority in his wallet, but how would the Templars react? They could scarcely reject him but, there again, there was no guarantee that they would cooperate. Corbett found his mind whirling round and round like a little dog turning a kitchen spit. So engrossed was he in the problem, he was startled to find himself on the trackway leading down to the gates of Framlingham Manor. As soon as he and his companions approached the heavy, iron-studded gates, Corbett knew there was something wrong. The small watch-tower above the gates were manned and a troop of crossbowmen stood on guard, resplendent in their white livery and great red crosses.

'Stay where you are!' a voice rang out.

Corbett reined in, lifting his hand in a gesture of peace. A Templar soldier walked forward, his face almost hidden by the chainmail coif and heavy helmet with broad noseguard. Questions were asked. Only when Corbett produced the king's ring and warrants were the gates opened and he was allowed on his way. Two of the soldiers went before him, up the shady path which wound between the trees. Now and again Corbett could hear the bracken on either side of him crackle, and the barking of a dog nearby. Ranulf pushed his horse alongside.

'What's happening?' he whispered. 'The gates are fortified. Templar soldiers with war dogs are in the trees.'

'Is anything wrong?' Corbett called out.

One of the soldiers stopped and came back. 'Haven't you heard?' the Templar asked. 'Sir Guido, the keeper of the manor, was killed early this morning. He died at the centre of the maze, consumed by fire.'

'Fire?' Corbett asked.

'Aye. Whether from heaven or hell we don't know. The grand master and all the commanders are now in council.'

He led Corbett on, they turned a corner and entered the great, grassy area which stretched in front of Framlingham Manor. This was a large, four-storeyed building, as huge as any merchant's, greatly extended, with two wings coming out on either side. It was shaped in the form of a horseshoe: a rich, palatial residence. The bottom storey was built of stone, the upper storeys consisted of black beams, the plaster between painted a dull gold. The roof was tiled with red slate. The windows were filled with glass gleaming in the afternoon sunlight. Nevertheless, the silence and sense of oppression made itself felt. The serjeant took them round the manor into the stableyard: the grooms and ostlers looked frightened. They scurried forward as if desperate for something to do to break the tension. Corbett told Ranulf and Maltote to guard the sumpter pony and followed the serjeant in through a back door along wainscoted passages.

The knight whom Sheikh Al-Jebal had called the 'Unknown' slipped from the saddle of his horse outside the Lazar hospital near the church of St Peter-Le-Willows just inside Walmer Gate Bar. For a while the Unknown rested against his horse, one hand on the high saddle-horn, the other on the hilt of his great two-handed sword which hung from it.

'I am dying,' the Unknown whispered.

The terrible sickness raging within him had manifested itself in more great open sores. He had tried to hide these behind the cowled cloak which shrouded him from head to toe, the gauntlets on his hand and the black band of cloth which covered the lower half of his face. The old war horse which he'd bought at Southampton snickered and whinnied, its head drooping in exhaustion.

'We are both finished,' the Unknown murmured. 'God be my witness, I can go no further.'

He had spent days journeying around York, then out through Botham bar towards Framlingham Manor. He had seen the Templar commanders and their seigneur, Jacques de Molay, as he'd sat hidden in the shadow of the trees. The sight of their surcoats, flapping banners and pennants had tugged at his heart and brought tears to his fading eyes. Since his release, the Unknown had found his thirst for vengeance had faded. Before he died, he wanted to make peace with his brothers and with

God. Death was very close. For years, in the dungeons of the Old Man of the Mountain, the Unknown had evaded death, but now, out in God's sunlight, back in a country where church bells tolled across lush green meadows, what was the use of vengeance? God had already intervened . . .

'Can I help?'

The Unknown turned, his hand dropping to the dagger thrust in his belt. The kindly face of the aged friar didn't flinch as the Unknown dragged down the black, silk mask over his face.

'You are a leper,' the brother whispered. 'You want help?'

The Unknown nodded and stared into those gentle, rheumy eyes. He opened his scarred mouth to speak, his horse jerked and the Unknown grew dizzy; the friar was hazy, the walls of the lazar hospital behind him seemed to recede. He closed his eyes, sighed, then crumpled into a heap at the friar's feet.

Chapter 4

At Framlingham, the Templar serjeant led Corbett up the dark mahogany staircase and along a bare, hollow-sounding gallery. Crosses and shields bearing the escutcheons of different knights hung on the walls, interspersed by the stuffed heads of wolves and stags which stared glassily down at him. Only a window at the far end lit the gallery and gave it an eerie atmosphere, where light and darkness mixed so mysteriously. On corners and in doorways, men-at-arms stood on guard, silent as statues. They went up another short flight of stairs and into the council chamber. Oval-shaped, the walls were bare apart from two great banners bearing the Templar insignia. There was no fireplace, just an open stone hearth with a flue high in the roof; it was a bleak, awesome room, bereft of furniture and carpets, the windows mere arrow-slits. It smelt strangely of sizzled fat, which curdled Corbett's stomach and brought back memories of the burning villages in Scotland. The Templar commanders, sitting in heavy carved choir-stalls formed in the shape of a horseshoe, fell silent as he entered. De Molay, in the centre, waved Corbett forward to a stall on his immediate right. The clerk made his way past a table which bore a corpse covered by a sarcenet, gold-edged pall and ringed by purple wax candles. A ghastly sight, the source of the sour smell, made rather pathetic by the dirty boots peeping out from beneath the cloth.

'We thought you'd come, Sir Hugh.' De Molay gestured at the table. 'We are holding a coroner's court according to the rule of our Order. The keeper of the manor here, Sir Guido

Reverchien, was mysteriously killed this morning, burnt alive in the centre of the maze.'

Corbett glanced round at the Templar commanders; they looked alike with their stony, sunburn faces. Not one of them made a gesture of welcome.

'Every morning, just before dawn,' de Molay continued, 'whatever the weather, Sir Guido did his own private pilgrimage to the centre of the maze. Over the years he'd come to know it so well, he could find his way in the dark, chanting psalms and carrying his beads.'

Corbett looked down at the burial pall. He'd heard about the construction of such mazes, so those who were unable to perform their vow to go on pilgrimages or Crusade, could make reparation by following the tortuous path of a carefully contrived maze to a cross or statue of Christ in the centre.

'How could a man meet such a death in the centre of a maze?' Corbett asked.

'That is why we are assembled,' Legrave explained. 'Apparently Sir Guido reached the centre. He had lit the candles at the foot of the cross when this mysterious fire engulfed him.'

'And no one else was present?' Corbett asked.

'Nobody,' Legrave replied. 'Very few people knew the mysteries of that maze. His old friend Odo Cressingham, our archivist, used to stand on guard at the entrance. No one had gone into the maze before Sir Guido, and no one followed him. Odo was sitting on a turf seat, as he did every morning: Sir Guido's knees and legs would be sore by the time he left the maze and he always required help to go back to the refectory. Odo said it was a beautiful morning; the sky was lighting up when he heard Sir Guido's terrible screams. Standing on the turf seat, Odo could see a heavy pall of smoke rising from the centre. He raised the alarm. By the time he and some serjeants reached the centre, this was what they found.' Legrave got up and lifted back the pall.

Corbett took one look and turned away. Reverchien's body had been reduced to a cinder. From the frizzled scalp to those pathetic boots, the fire had burnt away all features and reduced flesh, fat and muscle to a cindery ash. If it hadn't been for the shape of the head and the holes where the eyes, nose and mouth had been, Corbett would have thought the corpse was a blackened log.

'Cover it!' de Molay ordered. 'Our brother Guido has gone. His soul is in Christ's hands. We must decide how he died.'

'Shouldn't the corpse be handed over to the city coroner?' Corbett asked.

'We have our rights,' Branquier snapped. 'Approved by the Crown.'

Corbett wiped his lips on the back of his hands.

'And why are you here?' the treasurer continued harshly.

'Let's be courteous to our guest,' William Symmes intervened.

Sitting next to Corbett, he smiled across the choir-stall, but then the clerk started as a small, furry bundle leapt from Symmes's lap into his. Corbett's consternation eased the tension. Symmes sprang to his feet apologising, and deftly plucked the little weasel from Corbett's lap.

'It's my pet,' Symmes explained.

Corbett peered over the stall at the weasel's small, russet body, its white pointed features, twitching nose and the unblinking stare of those little black eyes. Symmes cradled it as if it was a baby, stroking it gently.

'He's always like this,' Symmes explained. 'Curious but friendly.'

De Molay rapped his fingers on the side of the stall and all eyes turned to him.

'You are here, aren't you, Sir Hugh, because of recent happenings in the city? The attack on the king!'

'Aye, by a serjeant of your Order, Walter Murston.' Corbett ignored the indrawn hiss of breath. 'According to the evidence,

Murston fired two crossbow bolts at the king as the royal procession was moving up Trinity.'

'And?'

'By the time I reached the tavern garret where Murston was lurking, he, too, had been killed by a mysterious fire which consumed the top half of his body.'

'How do you know it was Murston?' Legrave asked.

'We found his saddlebag, Templar's surcoat and a list of provisions in his name. I am sure,' Corbett added, 'that if you search, you will find the serjeant gone and your armoury lacking an arbalest.' The clerk stared across at Branquier. 'And you will not be sitting in judgement on his corpse. Sir John de Warrenne, Earl Marshall of England, has ordered it to be gibbeted on the Pavement in York.'

De Molay leaned back in his choir-stall. Corbett saw how his saintly, ascetic face had now turned an ashen grey. Dark rings under the grand master's eyes showed he had slept very little, and betrayed the anxieties seething within him. You know, don't you, Corbett thought; you know there's something rotten here. Something festering within your Order.

De Molay drew his breath in. 'Murston was one of my men,' he explained. 'A member of my retinue. He was of Gascon birth and belonged to the French chapter of our Order.'

'Why should he try to kill our king?' Corbett asked.

De Molay tapped the side of his head. 'Murston served in Outremer: the heat there can boil a man's brain. He was a good serjeant but his wits were slightly addled.'

'The same could be said of many in York, but they do not try to commit treason and regicide.'

'There are those in our Order,' Legrave spoke up, 'who claim the Western princes' lack of support cost Christendom the city of Acre. The Templar Order lost many good knights at Acre, not to mention treasure, as well as their foothold in the Holy Land. If Acre had been relieved . . .' Legrave wrinkled his brow. 'If Edward of England had done more,' he continued, 'perhaps that tragedy would never have occurred.'

'But that was twelve years ago!' Corbett exclaimed.

'Some wounds fester,' Baddlesmere snapped. 'Others heal quickly. Murston was one of those who felt betrayed.'

'In which case,' Corbett continued, 'there are others, aren't there? Somebody else was with him.'

'What proof do you have of that?' Symmes shouted.

'I simply don't believe that fire consumes every would-be murderer, even if their intended victim is a crowned king.'

'But you have no proof,' Legrave said.

'No, I don't. But I do possess proof that, as I came through York earlier today, I received the Assassins' warning as well. A message thrust into my hand. Someone scrawled it out then paid a beggar to give it to me. A short while later,' Corbett continued, 'a crossbow bolt narrowly missed my head. This was not imagination, I have all the proof I need.' Corbett held up his hand bearing the king's ring.

'I see it,' de Molay remarked softly. 'You act for the king in this matter?'

'So, let's not sit here engaging in tittle-tattle,' Corbett said. 'Some days ago, a grisly murder occurred on the road outside York near Botham Bar. A man's body was cut into two, the top half consumed by fire. Only a trained knight, with a two-handed sword, could have performed such a terrible feat.' He glanced at de Molay. 'You have recently all come from France, Grand Master.'

De Molay nodded, running his fingers through his beard.

'We attended a grand chapter there,' Branquier explained.

'Aye, and shortly afterwards,' Corbett replied, 'a Templar serjeant tried to kill Philip of France.'

'Rumour,' Branquier scoffed. 'More of your tittle-tattle, Master Clerk.'

'You will hear the truth soon enough,' Corbett replied. 'We have news from France. This Templar serjeant has been captured and handed over to the Inquisition. He confessed that there's a coven within your Order of high-ranking knights who dabble in black magic and wage a secret war against God's anointed princes.'

Corbett's words created an uproar. Legrave and Symmes sprang to their feet. The latter still stroked his pet weasel, so lovingly that Corbett idly wondered if it could be his familiar, but he dismissed the thought as both unfair and superstitious.

Richard Branquier put his face in his hands: he glared through his fingers at Corbett with such intense hatred that the clerk wished he had brought Ranulf and Maltote with him. Old Baddlesmere just sat shaking his head. Only when de Molay brought his high-heeled boots crashing down to the floor and shouted for silence, did the knights resume their seats.

'We heard about this attack,' he announced. 'Sooner or later the Temple in Paris will send us the truth of these matters, though Edward of England's own emissary would never lie. What else do you know, Sir Hugh?'

'The French Templar confessed that members of this coven are led by a high-ranking officer who calls himself Sagittarius, or the Bowman.' Corbett turned and jabbed a finger at de Molay. 'You, Sire, know there is something wrong. It's written on your face: that's why your soldiers now patrol the grounds and heavily armed men stand guard in the galleries outside. What do you fear?'

'Nothing but superstition,' de Molay snapped back, 'of course.' He shrugged. 'There are Templars who are bitter at what happened at Acre and elsewhere, just as there are English barons who do not want peace with France.'

'Is that why you acceded so quickly to the king's demand for money?' Corbett asked. 'Are you trying to buy his protection?'

This time Corbett knew he had hit his mark. There were no dramatic outbursts or cries of disapproval.

De Molay smiled faintly. 'Sir Hugh,' he replied. 'Templars are fighting monks. All of us here are warrior-priests. We came into this order for one purpose, and one purpose only: to defend

Jerusalem and the Holy Places. To protect Christ's fief from the infidel. Now look at us . . . Merchants, bankers, farmers. Of course, we hear the rising tide of protest. They call us idle, time-wasters! But what can we do? Men like Guido Reverchien, Murston, myself; all the knights in this room who would love to give our lives on the walls of Jerusalem and spill our blood so the likes of you can kneel and kiss the ground in the Holy Sepulchre. It is politic,' he added slowly, 'for us to seek out friends in high places, whether it be Philip of France or Edward of England.'

'We are the king's loyal subjects.' Legrave's boyish face looked even more youthful.

'Then you can prove it,' Corbett replied. 'Where were you all, today, between the hours of ten o'clock and two o'clock, the time of the attacks on both the king and myself?'

'Why single us out?' Baddlesmere snapped. 'We are not the only Templars.'

'You were in France and Philip was attacked. Murston was from Framlingham Manor. He carried a purse of silver, far too much for a common serjeant. Above all, the murderous attack outside Botham Bar was, I believe, carried out by a knight. More importantly, the only people who knew which street the king would use in going to the archbishop's palace were me, John de Warrenne and yourselves.'

'Nonsense!' Baddlesmere exclaimed.

Corbett shook his head. 'No, sir, the only time that route was mentioned was when you were present in the priory yesterday afternoon. I deliberately arranged it so that the king could take four, even five routes through the city. The decision to go up Trinity was reached just before the king met you. It was announced publicly only very shortly before the king entered York, yet Murston was in that tavern from the night before.'

The Templars now looked frightened. Baddlesmere shuffled his feet, Branquier fingered his lips, Legrave stared in outrage at Jacques de Molay, whilst Symmes sat, head bowed, stroking

71

and muttering under his breath to his pet weasel.

'If what you say is true,' de Molay remarked, 'the traitor must be in this room.'

'You are forgetting one thing, Master Clerk,' Branquier pointed down to the corpse covered by the pall. 'Guido Reverchien was killed this morning just before dawn. Concedo, there is a link between the death of the stranger outside Botham Bar, that of Murston, and the mysterious death of Guido Reverchien. However, you cannot prove any person here was present on the road outside Botham Bar or with Murston. On the other hand, we can prove, every man in this room, that when Sir Guido Reverchien died we were lodged at St Leonard's Priory.' He saw the surprise on Corbett's face. 'Didn't you know that, Clerk? We stayed there overnight. We arrived back here, shortly before you did, to discover the tragedy.'

'And, before you ask,' de Molay intervened, 'this morning we were in the city. We had business there with our bankers.'

'Together?' Corbett asked, trying to conceal his confusion.

De Molay shrugged. 'Of course not. Legrave came with me, my colleagues went hither and thither. There was business to be done.'

'So, any one of you,' Corbett asked, 'could have been with Murston? Or written that message or loosed a crossbow bolt at me?'

'Sir Hugh,' de Molay almost shouted, raising his voice over the cries of protest, 'you have no proof of these matters!'

'I returned here just after noon,' Branquier protested, 'to speak to Brother Odo our archivist.'

'And the rest?' Corbett asked.

Different replies were given; clearly all the Templars had been back at Framlingham shortly before Corbett's arrival.

'We heard about Guido's death,' Branquier explained. 'We deemed it mysterious. The gates were locked, the guards doubled and this court held.'

'You may well be innocent,' Corbett replied, 'but I act on

orders from my king: no Templar may leave the grounds of Framlingham Manor until this matter is resolved. None of you is to enter the city of York.'

'Agreed,' de Molay answered quickly. 'And I suppose you and your companions are to be our guests?'

'Until these matters are resolved,' Corbett replied. 'Yes, we are.'

'In which case Ralph,' de Molay gestured at Legrave, 'will show you to our guesthouse.'

Corbett pointed to the corpse. 'And your companion's death?'

De Molay pulled a face and got to his feet. 'Either an act of God or . . .'

'Murder,' Corbett added.

'Yes, Sir Hugh, murder. In which case we can use your skills. After Legrave has shown you your chambers, you are free to go into the maze. A rope has been laid, as a guide, from the centre to the entrance. Use that and you'll not get lost!'

Corbett followed Legrave to the door.

'Sir Hugh!' De Molay came forward. 'Tomorrow morning, the brothers will sing a Requiem Mass for Sir Guido. You are most welcome to attend. As for the rest, you are an honoured guest. However, we ask you to observe the courtesies. We are a monastic Order; certain parts of this building are our enclosure: outsiders are not permitted to enter.'

Corbett nodded and followed Legrave out into the corridor and back to the hallway where Ranulf and Maltote were sitting in a small recess just inside the front door. Legrave took them all out across the gravel path to the bottom floor of the east wing.

'They are just cells,' Legrave explained. He opened one door. 'Sir Hugh, your servants can share this.'

He then pushed open another chamber door and ushered Corbett into a large, cavernous cell with a single arrow-slit window. The walls were lime-washed. A large crucifix hung above the trestle bed; at the foot of this stood a large, leather chest with an iron-bound coffer on the table beside it. Beneath the window was a writing table and a throne-like chair, its back and arms intricately carved.

'You may join us in the refectory for meals,' Legrave told him. He looked over his shoulder at Maltote and Ranulf who were still standing in the corridor. He closed the door and leaned against it, his eyes crinkled into a smile.

'Sir Hugh, do not take offence at the reception given. Our Order is in turmoil. We are like a ship without a rudder, blown this way and that by different winds. The Holy Land is lost. The Infidels squat in our sacred places and what are we supposed to do now? Many of our companions left family, home and hearth to become Templars. This is their family, yet all they can see is their beloved Order being plundered by princes.'

'There is still no excuse for murder or treason,' Corbett retorted.

'No, no, there isn't, but that, Sir Hugh, is still to be proved. Anyway, you'll hear the bells ring for supper.' And with that Legrave slipped quietly out of the room.

Ranulf and Maltote entered, carrying Corbett's saddlebags.

'The horses are stabled,' Maltote said. 'Including that vicious brute of a sumpter pony: it gave the stable boys all the devil's bother.'

'What do you think, Master?' Ranulf asked, placing Corbett's saddlebags into the great trunk and pulling across a stool.

'Mysterious,' Corbett replied. 'The Templars are a closed book: hard-bitten, fighting men. They don't like us. They resent our interference, yet, beneath it all, there is something wrong.'

'You mean the death of the keeper? We heard all about it,' Ranulf declared. 'Oh, not from the Templars, they're all tight-lipped and soft-footed, but from the ordinary servants.'

'And did you learn anything?'

'No, they are just terrified. The usual mumblings about

strange lights at night, comings and goings. Apparently, all was peace and quiet until de Molay and the commanders arrived. Usually, the manor is left empty under its keeper and a few servants. Now everything has been turned topsy-turvy. They believe the keeper was murdered by black magic, consumed by flames sent up from hell. They are already deserting, refusing to work here.'

Corbett stared out of the window. The sky was scarred with the red-gold flashes of a setting sun. He wanted to lie down and compose his thoughts but he kept remembering that grisly burden lying on the table in the council chamber.

'Look, Ranulf, Maltote, unpack our belongings. Lock the door after me. I am going down to the maze. Meanwhile you two can try blundering about, acting the innocent.' Corbett winked at Maltote. 'For you, that won't be hard. Try and see where you can go. Ranulf, if you are turned away, don't argue. We'll meet back here within the hour.'

Corbett left the guesthouse and walked round the manor. He sauntered by the stables, smithies, outhouses and, going through a huge gate, entered a large garden, a place of silent peace, beautifully laid out. It contained a tunnelled arbour along one side, covered by white roses, lily of the valley and honeysuckle. Corbett sat down on a turf seat and stared round in admiration.

'Oh,' he whispered. 'If only Maeve could see this!'

His wife had a passion for gardens, yet this was better than any Corbett had seen even in Edward's palaces. There were chequerboard beds in one corner, and the sweet fragrance from the herbs growing there hung heavily in the evening air. After a while Corbett rose, walked across and stared down at the periwinkle, polypody, fennel, cowslip and white orris. Next to these were nerbers, small raised flower beds containing yarrow, daisy and Lady's bedstraw. Corbett walked on, into a small orchard with apple, pear and black mulberry trees, all providing cool shade against the brightness of the setting sun. He looked back towards the manor, its arrow-slit windows and small bays full of glass, and wondered if he was being watched.

He left the garden through a small postern gate built into the wall. This led to a meadow, which sloped down to a small copse at the edge of a broad, shimmering lake. From the nearby byres, Corbett heard the cattle lowing as they were brought in for the night. A man was singing and, on the breeze, he heard the crash of a blacksmith's hammer on the anvil. An idyllic scene which brought back bitter-sweet memories of his own manor at Leighton. Nevertheless, Corbett felt uneasy: he was sure someone was studying his every movement. He turned right and walked behind the manor house to a fringe of trees. Behind these stood the maze, a sea of high, green, prickly hedgerows which stretched out to the curtain wall of the manor. He walked along, staring into each entrance, then he found the long line of rope lying on the ground. Corbett made his way, following the rope as it twisted through the hedgerows.

'Lord save us!' Corbett whispered as he stared up at the thick green bushes on either side. 'Guido Reverchien must have been a glutton for punishment.'

He started as a bird flew out of the hedge and soared above him in a whirr or wings. The sound reminded Corbett of a crossbow bolt. He walked on: the maze became silent, as if he was lost in some magical, secret forest. He followed the rope along the path. The ominous silence seemed to intensify; he felt his heart skip a beat and sweat prickle the nape of his neck. Shadows were beginning to fall and, in some places, the high hedgerows blocked the rays of the dying sun. Corbett trudged on. He was regretting not waiting till the following morning when suddenly he heard a crunch on the gravel. Corbett whirled round. Was someone following him? Or did the sound come from some bird or animal on the other side of the hedgerow? He stood listening for any noise then, satisfied, walked on. At last the rope snaked round a corner and into the centre of the maze. A large stone crucifix stood here; in front of it were paved steps on which Reverchien must have knelt. Now the stonework and the heavy iron candelabra were cracked and scorched. Corbett stared up at the carved face of his Saviour.

'What happened?' he asked. 'How can an old soldier saying his prayers be consumed by a mysterious fire?'

Corbett studied the area where the fire had blazed: he could not detect how the inferno had been caused. The candles were gone, mere streaks of wax: these might spark or scorch but not turn a man into a living flame. Corbett sat on a turf seat and tried to visualise the scene: Reverchien would have come out along the same path he had, chanting his psalms, his beads in his hand. Dawn would be breaking, there would be enough light for Reverchien to notice anyone hiding in this small enclosure. Moreover, although Reverchien was old, he had been a soldier: his hearing would be sharp and sensitive. He would know if someone had followed him through the maze. Yet if the killer was a Templar commander, one of the five he had met in the council chamber, he could not have possibly been here when Reverchien had died. Corbett stared at the great scorch-mark.

'But what happens,' he murmured, 'if there was more than one killer? If there was a coven here at Framlingham? If someone entered the maze long before Sir Guido?'

But if that was the case, the killer would have to have got out again, and that would have been impossible without being detected.

Corbett looked up at the sky. As he did so, he heard the crunch of a boot on gravel from behind the wall of privet, then a creak, like a door opening. Corbett immediately threw himself to the right as a long yew arrow smashed into the cross. Corbett moved behind this, drawing his dagger. Again the crunch on the gravel and an arrow whipped by his head into the privet beyond. Corbett did not wait for a third but ran to the entrance where he could see the rope lying. He fled, keeping his eyes on that rope as it wound and snaked through the maze. Behind him Corbett heard the sounds of quiet pursuit. He turned a corner and suddenly the rope was no longer there. Corbett stopped, sobbing for breath. Should he go to the left or the right? He tried to climb the hedge but the branches were stubby, pointed, and cut his hands. He found it impossible to gain a foothold. Corbett crouched, fighting for breath, trying to calm the thudding of his heart. He remembered how far he had run and quickly gauged that he must be somewhere near the entrance. However, if he took the wrong path he could find himself lost, trapped, a clear target for the assassin. For a while Corbett waited, straining his ears, listening for any sound: all he could hear was the cawing of the crows and an occasional rustle as some bird nesting in the hedgerow burst up into the sky.

At last Corbett felt he was calm enough to move. He took off his cloak and began to cut strips of cloth from it, which he tied around twigs.

'At least,' he muttered, 'I will know if I am going round in circles.'

He crept forward, trying to recall how he had entered the maze.

'Turning left,' he whispered. 'I kept turning left.'

He chose the path to his right and began to work his way forward. Now and again he lost his way, coming round to find a strip of cloth hanging from the bush. He cursed and tried again, a mixture of trial and error. Only once did he hear the pursuer. A crunch of gravel and his heart skipped a beat, the assailant was now in front of him. Darkness was beginning to fall. Somewhere a dog howled mournfully as the daylight began to fade. After a while Corbett felt secure, no longer pursued or watched. He realised the rope had been removed, not to trap him, but as a means of delaying him, should he survive and the assailant had to flee. Corbett edged forward, then he heard Ranulf's voice.

'Master?'

'Here!' Corbett shouted and, doffing his cloak, waved it high above his head.

'I saw that!' Ranulf shouted back.

'Keep shouting!' Corbett ordered.

Ranulf happily obliged, bawling out encouragement as Corbett made his way, following the sound of Ranulf's voice. The hedgerows thinned and he was out on the path where Ranulf and Maltote stood, grinning from ear to ear.

'You should be more careful,' his manservant exclaimed.

'I was bloody careful,' Corbett grunted. 'Some bastard removed the rope and tried to kill me.'

Ranulf looked round. 'Then where is he? He must be still in the maze.'

'No, he's gone. Ranulf, did you see anyone?'

'Only a gardener pushing a wheelbarrow.'

'What did he look like?'

'He wore a cowl and cloak, Master. But the manor is full of servants.'

Corbett closed his eyes. He remembered seeing a wheelbarrow near the maze, covered by a dirty sheet.

'Why should they kill me?' he rasped. 'If this secret coven of Templars wants the destruction of the king, how can murdering me bring that about?'

'They don't want you to investigate.'

'But the king will send someone else. Why create more suspicion?' Corbett glanced up at the darkened sky. 'Well, they failed for the second time today. That's the last time I'm wandering round this benighted manor by myself. Well, what did you find?'

A bell began to toll, the sign for evening supper. They walked back to the main entrance, Ranulf explaining how they had wandered the galleries and passageways. He paused, clutching his master's arm.

'Framlingham is a mysterious place. There are chambers, stairways, cellars, even a dungeon. The place is well guarded: armed men everywhere. Never once did they try to stop us, except when we tried to climb to the garret at the top of the manor. The stairway is guarded by soldiers. They were polite and shook their heads. When I asked them why not, they just smiled and told me to mind my own business.'

'Oh, and tell him the other thing,' Maltote interrupted.

'Oh, yes, Master.' Ranulf leaned closer. 'On the second floor of the main building there are eight windows.'

'So?' Corbett asked.

'But, Master, on the gallery inside there are only seven chambers.'

Chapter 5

Corbett and his companions returned to the guesthouse and changed for supper.

'Make no mention about the attack on me,' Corbett warned them as they returned along the passageway to the refectory.

The Templars were already assembled, seated round a table down the centre of the hall, which was a small, comfortable room, brightly caparisoned by banners hanging from the hammer-beam rafters. De Molay quickly said grace, blessing the food on the table, but then, before they sat down, a servant came in bearing a tray with goblets and an equal number of dishes containing bread sprinkled with salt. Each Templar and their three guests were given a cup and a piece of the salted bread.

'Let us remember,' de Molay intoned, 'those of our brothers who have gone before us. Those of our comrades who have gone down into the dust.'

'Amen!' the Templars chorused.

Corbett glanced round the shadow-filled hall and suppressed a shiver, as if the ghosts of those on whom de Molay had called were now thronging all around them. He sipped from his cup and bit into the salted bread. Ranulf began to cough, but Corbett nudged him and Ranulf hurriedly ate the salted morsels.

'Let us remember,' de Molay continued, 'those fair cities and fortresses which have fallen to our foes.'

Again the wine and bread were tasted.

'Let us remember,' de Molay spoke for a third time, 'the

Holy Places where the Lord Jesus ate, drank, suffered, died and rose again.'

After this the cups and plates were cleared. De Molay gestured at them to sit and the supper began. Despite such a sombre toast, the meal proved to be delicious: spiced pheasant, jugged hare, dishes of fresh vegetables, cups of claret, and whilst the sweetmeats were served, iced wine from Alsace. Corbett sipped the wine and remembered the king's gift to de Molay as he listened to the conversation around him. Most of the talk was about matters abroad, as if the Templars wished to forget the recent occurrences. They talked of ships, corsairs in the Middle Sea, the recent Chapter in Paris and the great question of whether they should unite with the Hospitaller Order. Corbett and his two companions were not ignored, but never once were they drawn into the conversation. Only when Odo the librarian, a thin, bald-pated man with a flowing white beard joined them, did the conversation lighten. Odo was a carefree soul with a smiling mouth and laughter-filled eyes. Corbett immediately warmed to him.

'You are boring our guests,' Odo declared from the foot of the table. 'You are not knights and gentlemen but grizzled old soldiers who don't know any better.' He bowed to de Molay. 'Grand Master, I apologise for being late.'

'Nonsense.' De Molay smiled back. 'We know you and your books, Brother Odo, and what you say is right. We should improve our manners.'

A scullion came from the kitchen and laid a fresh trancher in front of the librarian. Odo rested his elbows on the table and Corbett gaped: Odo had no left hand, nothing but a polished, wooden stump. Legrave, sitting opposite, leaned across.

'We put up with Brother Odo,' he whispered loudly, smiling down at the librarian who stared back in mock anger. 'He will not like us telling you this, but Odo is a hero, a veritable paladin.'

'It's true!' Branquier trumpeted. 'Why do you think we put

up with his speeches and bad manners?'

Corbett felt the deep admiration, even love for the old Templar.

'In his time,' Symmes declared, 'Brother Odo was a knight of whom even Arthur or Roland and Oliver would have been proud.'

'Oh, stop it!' The librarian gestured with his good hand, though he openly revelled in this warm-hearted badinage.

'He was at Acre,' Legrave continued, 'as we all were, but he defended the breach when the walls were broken. He was the last to leave. Tell us, Brother, tell our guests what happened.'

Corbett realised this was a ritual time-honoured, only this time with a difference. These men were desperate to show Corbett that, despite the rumours and whispered allegations, once, in a different age, they had been defenders of Christendom: heroes, saints in armour. The other Templars joined in, so Odo took a deep swig of wine and raised the polished stump.

'I lost my hand in Acre,' he began. 'Yes, I was there when the city fell in March 1291.' He stared round at the four Templar commanders. 'You were there too.'

'We broke and ran.' Legrave did not lift his eyes. 'We fled the city, our shields on our backs, our faces towards the sea.'

'No you didn't,' Odo replied gently. 'You had to retreat. I have told you hundreds of times: there's no glory in dying. There's no honour in a bloody corpse. There's no pride in captivity.'

'You didn't flee,' Branquier remarked.

'Brother,' de Molay tapped the hilt of his knife on the tablecloth. 'In truth, you all have the advantage of me, I wasn't even there. I have never known the scorching heat of the deserts of Outremer. I have never heard the blood-curdling cry of the Mamelukes nor felt the savage fury of battle. Acre did not fall because of us. But, because . . .' He caught Corbett's gaze and his voice trailed off. Then the grand master looked up, eyes brimming with tears. 'Tell us once again, Odo,' he whispered. 'Tell us how the city fell.'

'The siege began in March.' Odo's voice was deep and mellow. He leaned back, closing his eyes, painting pictures with his words. 'As you all know, Acre was a doomed city, yet the streets were full of life and the taverns thronged, feasting far into the night. Syrian and Greek girls filled the upper rooms of wine shops. A feverish excitement seized Acre as the Turks began to ring the city.' He opened his eyes. 'Why is it?' he asked, 'that when people are about to die, they dance even faster? Sir Hugh, have you ever been in battle?'

'Ambuscades in Wales and in the wet heather on the Scottish march, but nothing like you, Brother Odo.' Corbett glanced round at the Templars. 'I cannot condemn any man for what he did in battle. I am not too sure how I would behave.'

Odo toasted him silently before continuing. 'The final attack came in May. The thudding of the siege engines, the cracking of boulders against the crumbling walls of the city, the crash and roar of exploding fire – and those drums. Do you remember them, Brothers, the Mameluke drums constantly rattling?'

'Even now,' Branquier declared. 'Sometimes at night, when I lie down to sleep in my cell, I can still hear that drumming.' He stared round sheepishly. 'I get up and stare through the window into the shadows amongst the trees. I wonder if Satan and all his army have come to taunt me.'

Odo nodded. 'I was on the western wall,' he continued. 'A breach was caused and oil poured in, blackening the ground, creating a curtain of smoke. The Mamelukes filled in the ditches by stampeding columns of beasts of burden. These fell into the moat, were slaughtered, and so formed a bridge over which they could pour across. There were not many of us left. I was weary, blinded by smoke, my arms heavy.' He paused. 'Behind the smoke we could hear the songs of the dervishes, the rattle of their drums drawing closer. In the half-light, just before dawn, the first attack came: dark masses, as if hell was spitting out legions of demons. We fought them off but then armoured regiments of Mamelukes followed and the walls were taken. We fell back. We passed a group of monks, Dominicans. They had gathered together to sing the "Salve Regina". We could do nothing to save them. All around us men were dying, burning in their towers, in the entrances to houses, or on the barricades across the alleyways.'

'But you stopped them,' Branquier intervened. 'For a while, Brother Odo, you stopped them.'

'Aye. There was a street leading down to the docks; everyone was fleeing there. All command had collapsed and the ships were filling up as fast as they could. I and about two dozen other Templars – chosen men – manned the last barricade.' Odo straightened up. His face became youthful, his eyes bright with excitement. 'We fought all afternoon,' he declared. 'And, as we did, we sang the *"Paschale Laudes"*, the Easter hymn, until even the Infidels pulled back and promised us our lives. We laughed at them. They closed again. Balls of fire rained down on the barricades; then there was blackness.' His shoulders slumped. 'When I woke up I was in one of the transports fleeing out to the open sea. My left hand was gone; Acre had fallen. I later learnt one man had survived; he'd dragged me down to the quayside steps. He found a boat.' Odo's voice trembled. 'Sometimes, I wish to God I had died there with my brothers.'

'Nonsense.' William Symmes, his scarred face now softer, rose and went to kneel beside the old librarian. 'If you had died,' he said softly, 'we would never have heard the story and Framlingham would not have its favourite librarian.'

'So,' Corbett asked, 'apart from the grand master, you were all in Acre?'

'We came back with the rest,' Legrave replied. 'Each of us is now a principal commander. I at Beverley, Baddlesmere in London, Symmes at Templecombe in Dorset, Branquier in Chester.'

'And at your Grand Chapter,' Corbett insisted, hoping to

85

lighten the atmosphere, 'were fresh plans laid? Will the Order attempt to regain what it has lost?'

'In time,' de Molay replied. 'But where are your questions leading, Sir Hugh?' He flicked his fingers and a servant came out of the shadows to fill their wine goblets.

'Perhaps this is not the time nor occasion.' Corbett glanced quickly at Ranulf and Maltote who, having filled their stomachs, were now staring, round-eyed, at these strange men who had witnessed scenes they could never imagine.

'Nonsense,' de Molay replied. 'What is it you want to know, Corbett?'

'You all went to France for the Grand Chapter? Grand Master, why did you come back to England? And why did you all stay together instead of returning to your different posts?'

'It is my duty to visit every province,' de Molay replied. 'And when I do, I am to be attended by the senior commanders.'

'When did you return?'

'Seven days before the warning was pinned to the doors of St Paul's Cathedral,' de Molay replied sardonically, 'and a few days after the attack on Philip of France in the Bois de Boulogne.'

'Do continue.' Legrave put his elbows on the table, licking his fingers.

'And you came to Framlingham?' Corbett asked.

'Yes,' Legrave replied, taunting him. 'We were here at Framlingham when that terrible murder occurred outside Botham Bar.'

'And we were in York,' Branquier spoke up. 'When your king was attacked and you were so nearly assassinated.'

'But all this,' Baddlesmere declared, 'is coincidence, not proof of any treason.'

'And remember,' Brother Odo intervened, 'none of my comrades was here when Sir Guido died at the centre of that maze. They had all left Framlingham the previous evening for their meeting with the king at St Leonard's Priory.'

'Sir Guido was your friend?' Corbett asked.

'Yes and, before you ask, the reason why I am not grieving is that I am glad Sir Guido is dead. He was a man who constantly tortured himself. Now he's at peace in the arms of Christ. No more pain, no more doubt.' The old librarian's eyes blinked quickly. 'Tomorrow we bury him and he'll be at rest.'

'You were there,' Corbett said. 'You went to the mouth of the maze with him?'

'Yes, I did, just before dawn. It was a beautiful morning. The sky was turning a deep blue. Sir Guido said it reminded him of Outremer. He knelt down, his rosary in his hand, and began his pilgrimage. I just sat there, as I always did, revelling in the sweet smells of the morning breeze and wishing Sir Guido would not torture himself. I was dozing when I heard his terrible screams. I stood up and saw a black pall of smoke rising above the maze. The rest you know.'

'And you are sure no one else was there?' Corbett asked.

'God be my witness, Sir Hugh, there was no one.'

Corbett now looked at the Templars. 'And then you all came back, late in the afternoon?'

'As we have said,' de Molay replied. 'We were in the city. We had business to do. Brother Odo could see no point in sending a message to us. Sir Guido was dead, no hustle or bustle would bring him back.'

'Except Branquier,' Odo declared. 'He came back early. He had asked to meet me at one o'clock.' He smiled and picked at his food. 'I was asleep, Branquier had to wake me.' He grinned. 'Sometimes I feel my age,' he added. 'But what hour was it?'

'The hour candle had scarcely reached the thirteenth ring,' Branquier replied. 'You saw that yourself.' He glanced across at Corbett. 'I wanted Brother Odo to find me a book. However, when I arrived at Framlingham, a servant told me about Sir Guido, so I went to my cell, left my belongings, then visited Brother Odo.'

'And this is the information I need,' Corbett declared. 'Grand

Master, I apologise, but I must interrogate all of you about your precise movements.' He lifted his hand in a gesture of peace. 'I am sure these questions will clarify matters. Neither I, nor His Grace the King intend insult. Indeed, Grand Master, I have brought a tun of wine from the Greenmantle tavern, the best wine Gascony has ever produced, as a gift from His Grace.'

'Ah.' De Molay smiled his thanks. 'From the king's own vintner, Hubert Seagrave. He has applied to purchase certain lands from us. A waste area . . .'

He broke off at the terrible screaming from the kitchen. Ranulf was the first to react: throwing back his chair, he hastened into the kitchen. Corbett and the rest followed into a large, cavernous room, its walls lined with hooks from which skillets, pots and pans hung. Now it was transformed into a scene from hell: near the oven one of the cooks stood screaming, watched by his horror-struck companions, as flames roared about him. The fire had run along the man's apron, which was fully alight, whilst tongues of flame caught his hose and the cloth around his neck. He staggered forward then crumpled to his knees. Ranulf poured a large bucket of water over him and, helped by Maltote, seized a piece of heavy sacking lying near a bread basket and threw it over the tortured man to damp down the flames. Corbett quickly glanced at the Templars. De Molay had turned away, his face to the wall. Brother Odo and the four commanders just stared, a look of horror on their faces as the cook's screams faded to a whimper then died completely. At last, the writhing figure lay still. Ranulf, his hands and face black with smoke, pulled back the sacking. The cook lay dead, his entire body terribly burnt. A horrid sight. Maltote retched and headed straight for the door leading to the yard.

The other servants, spit boys, scullions and cooks, edged away from the Templars. One knocked a pewter pot, which fell with a resounding crash.

'He was laughing,' one of the cooks whispered. 'He was just

laughing, then he was on fire. You saw it? Flames all over him.'
The man's eyes rolled in panic. 'We were just having a joke. He
was laughing.' The fellow's hand flew to his nose as he became
aware of the terrible stench.

'Who was he?' Corbett asked quietly.

'Peterkin. He lived with his mother in Coppergate. Had
grand ambitions, he did, to open his own cookshop.'

'Take him away.' De Molay turned to the Templar serjeants
now thronging in at the door of the refectory. 'Cover him with
a sheet and take him to the Infirmary.'

The servants continued to edge to the door. The principal
cook, with massive shoulders and balding head, stepped forward.
He took off his leather apron and threw it on the floor.

'That's it!' he snorted. 'We are leaving. Try and stop us, but
in the morning we'll be gone.' He pushed his hand towards the
Templars. 'We want payment and then we'll be gone.'

Corbett saw the red, angry abscess on the palm of the man's
hand, and his stomach churned a little at what he had eaten. The
cook's demands were echoed by the rest. The mood in the
kitchen perceptibly changed. One of the scullions picked up a
fleshing knife, another a cleaver still red with the blood of the
meat it had cut. Behind him Corbett heard the Templar serjeants
drawing their swords.

'This is ridiculous,' Corbett exclaimed. 'I am the king's
commissioner here. Grand Master, pay these men, and, once
they've answered certain questions, let them go. But not here.
God save the poor wretch but the place stinks with his burning.'

De Molay turned to his commanders. 'Make sure the manor's
secure.' He declared, 'Our supper is ended. Sir Hugh and I will
question these good people,' adding diplomatically, 'and don't
worry.' De Molay smiled faintly. 'I am sure Master Ranulf
here will protect us all.'

At first all four commanders seemed about to refuse. Hands
on dagger hilts, they glared at the cooks and then at Corbett.

'Go on,' de Molay urged quietly.

The group broke up. Corbett led the cooks back into the refectory towards the dais. He stood on this, the cooks thronging together. Out of their kitchen they became more anxious, frightened, shifting their feet, eager to be away.

'What happened?' Corbett asked.

'It's as they say,' the principal cook spoke up. 'The meal was finished. We were clearing up the kitchen. Peterkin was pastry cook. He was raking the coals out of the oven, laughing and talking. The next minute I heard him scream. I turned round and there was fire all along his front.'

He turned and snapped his fingers. One of the scullions took off a thin, leather apron and handed it to Corbett.

'He was wearing one of these.'

Corbett examined it curiously. The leather was very thin, a loop at the neck so it could go over the head and a cord to fasten it around the middle. It would protect a man against stains and the occasional spark but not the angry fire Corbett had seen.

'What was he wearing on his hands?'

'Thick woollen mittens,' the cook replied. 'They covered his arms up to the elbow.'

'Show me what he was doing,' Corbett urged. 'Come, just you and me.'

The cook was about to protest, but Corbett stepped off the dais and held a silver coin in front of the cook's face.

'I'll be with you all the time,' Corbett assured him.

The silver coin disappeared and the two went into the kitchen. The cook led Corbett to the great fire-grate: on either side of this was a large oven built into the wall.

'He was here,' the cook explained, pulling open the iron door.

Corbett gingerly peered in, only to flinch at the blast of heat from the burning charcoal piled high beneath a steel wire netting. The cook picked up a pole with a wooden board at the end. He pointed into the oven.

'You see, Master, Peterkin would put the pies on to the netting, shut the door and allow them to bake. He knew exactly how long to leave them.' The man's greasy face broke into a sad smile. 'He was a good cook. The crusts of his pies were always golden and light, the meat fresh and savoury. He leaves a mother,' he continued. 'And she is a widow.'

Corbett put a silver piece into the man's blackened hand. 'Then give her that,' he said. 'Now the king is in York,' he added, 'tell her to petition him for mercy.'

'Much good that will do,' the fellow grunted.

'No, it won't,' Corbett replied. 'The petition will come to me. Now, what was Peterkin doing?'

The cook pointed to an iron tray full of dust which lay on the floor.

'Once the baking's done, the ovens have to be doused. Peterkin always insisted on doing it himself in preparation for the next day. He knew exactly how clean the oven must be, how to spread the charcoal. Well, he was raking it all out into the tray when I heard him scream.'

'What do you think happened?' Corbett asked, walking away from the oven.

The cook followed. 'I don't know, sir. Oh, I have seen men burnt in kitchens, especially when they mix oil with fire – bad burns to hands and faces. Now and again we scald our legs or feet.' The man took a rag from beneath his leather apron and wiped the sweat from his face. 'But, Master,' he edged so close that Corbett could smell his stale odour. 'But, Master,' he repeated, 'I have seen nothing like that. A good man turned into a sheet of flame within seconds.'

Corbett walked to the back door of the kitchen which had been flung open. The acrid smell of burning flesh still hung heavily in the air. From the hall he could hear the faint murmur of voices, as well as the clink of mailed men outside in the darkness. He stood, just within the kitchen, watching the moonlight reflected in the puddles in the cobbled yard.

'What did you see?' Corbett asked. 'I mean, the first time you saw Peterkin burn?'

'The flames.' The man brushed his apron. 'Along his front, chest, stomach and his hands. Yes, even the woollen mittens were ablaze.'

'And did you notice anything untoward during the evening?'

'No, sir!'

'Nothing?' Corbett asked.

'We were busy, sir.'

'And no one came in? Either before the meal or during the day?'

'Not that I saw, sir!'

'Then what have you seen?'

The cook pulled a face. 'There's the horseman . . .'

'What horseman?'

'Masked and cowled, a great two-handed sword hanging from his saddlebag.' The man shifted uncomfortably. 'I've only seen him once. I was, er, hunting for rabbits in the woods nearby. He was sitting like the shadow of death amongst the trees, staring at the manor. He never moved – I just fled.'

Corbett's heart skipped a beat. Was there, he wondered, a secret assassin lurking in the woods between Framlingham and York?

'Do you think this masked horseman was from Framlingham?' he asked.

'I don't know, but this place is accursed,' the cook continued in a rush. 'Some of us live here. Others, like Peterkin, live in the city. We heard about the strange murder outside Botham Bar. This was a quiet manor, sir, before those commanders arrived with their soldiers. Now they are singing strange hymns at night, up all hours. You can't go here and you can't go there! Then there's the death of Sir Guido. He was a good man. A little forbidding, but kind – that's what Peterkin was laughing about.'

Corbett turned abruptly. 'What do you mean?'

'He said the fire which killed Guido came from hell: Satan's fire.'

'Why should it?' Corbett asked.

The man glanced back at the door to the refectory, then at another silver coin held between Corbett's fingers.

'Well,' he said, 'there are rumours.'

'Rumours about what?' Corbett insisted. 'Come on, man, you have nothing to fear.'

'Well, a scullion saw one of the Templars.' The cook paused.

'You mean one of the commanders?'

'Yes. I don't know which one but, well, he saw him kissing a man. You know, sir, like you would a woman. And before you ask, he couldn't make out who it was.'

'You are sure?' Corbett asked.

'Certain. He was coming down a passageway. He glimpsed the commander who had his back to him. He knew it was one of the visitors from the cloak he wore. I think the other was one of the Templar serjeants, a youngish man. You've seen how dark this place is, sir. They were in the shadows. The scullion was frightened so he turned and fled. Anyway, Peterkin was laughing about that. He made a joke of everything. He said the place smelt of Satan's sulphur and then it happened.' The man plucked the coin from Corbett's fingers. 'And now I am going, sir.'

He strode out of the kitchen in the hall. Corbett heard raised voices and, by the time he returned, the cook was marching the rest down towards the door.

'I couldn't stop them,' de Molay murmured. 'They can visit the almoner, collect their wages and go. What do you think, Sir Hugh?' The grand master stepped into the pool of light from the candles on the table and wearily sat down, face in hands. Ranulf and Maltote also took their seats. Both had drunk deeply and were now feeling its effect.

'I have seen similar accidents,' Ranulf declared. 'Men

93

getting burnt, in cookshops in London.'

'Not like that,' Corbett replied, sitting down opposite de Molay.

The grand master looked up. He seemed to have aged years; his iron-grey hair was tousled, dark shadows ringed his eyes. His face had lost that serene, rather imperious look. 'Satan attacks us on every side,' he murmured.

'Why do you say that?' Corbett asked. 'What happened in the kitchen could have been an accident.'

De Molay leaned back in his chair. 'That was no accident, Corbett. The murder outside Botham Bar, the attack on the king, the death of Sir Guido. Now this!'

'So why should Satan attack you?'

'I don't know,' the grand master snarled, rising to his feet, 'but when you meet him, Corbett, ask him the same question!' De Molay strode out of the refectory, slamming the door behind him.

Corbett, too, rose, beckoning Ranulf and Maltote to follow.

'Listen! From now on, we sleep in the same chamber. Each does a watch. Be careful what you eat and drink. No one travels round the manor by themselves.' Corbett sighed. 'As far as I am concerned, we're back on the Scottish march. The only difference being that there we knew our enemy, here we don't!'

They walked back towards the guesthouse: Corbett stopped, heart in his throat, as a figure came rushing out of the darkness but it was only a servant, belongings packed into a fardel, scurrying towards the gates.

'By morning they'll all be gone,' Ranulf muttered. 'If I had my way, Master, we'd follow!'

'Where to?' Corbett asked. 'Edward in York or Leighton Manor?'

Ranulf refused to answer. Once they were back in the guesthouse, a sleepy-eyed Maltote stood guard outside whilst Corbett told Ranulf to join him. The servant sat down on a stool. Corbett studied him curiously: Ranulf's usual cheeky face was now pallid, his attitude no longer devil-may-care.

'What's wrong?' Corbett asked.

'Oh, nothing.' Ranulf kicked at the rushes. 'I am so happy I am thinking of becoming a Templar.' He glared at Corbett. 'I hate this bloody place. I don't like the Templars. I can't make them out, monks or soldiers. The librarian may be a grand old man but the rest make my skin crawl.'

'You are frightened, aren't you?' Corbett sat down on the edge of the bed.

Ranulf scratched his head. 'No, Master, I'm not frightened. I am terrified. All Maltote thinks about is horses, that's all he talks about. What's happening here hasn't yet sunk into his thick skull.' Ranulf plucked at the dagger in his belt. 'I can deal with enemies, Master: the footpad in the alleyway, the assassin in the darkened chamber. But this? Men mysteriously bursting into flames, Reverchien at the centre of a maze, that poor bastard in the kitchen . . .'

'For every natural phenomenon,' Corbett replied, 'Aristotle said there must be a natural cause.'

'Bugger that!' Ranulf snarled. 'Bloody Aristotle's not here. If he was, the silly bastard would soon change his mind!'

Corbett began to laugh.

'Oh, you're amused, Master,' Ranulf snapped. 'We have only been here a few hours and we've been threatened, shot at and hunted in a maze.'

Corbett grasped Ranulf's hand. 'Yes, I am frightened, Ranulf.'

He got to his feet, stretched and stared at the black carved crucifix on the wall. 'In all my years of pursuing murderers I have never seen the like. Yes, I was hunted in the maze.' He turned, his face set hard. 'I don't like being hunted, Ranulf. I don't like being threatened. I don't like nightmares about a royal messenger telling Maeve and Baby Eleanor that I am gone but my corpse will soon arrive for burial.' He sat down. 'I am a clerk. I deal with wax and parchment. I resolve problems.

I protect the king and hunt down his enemies. Sometimes I am frightened; so terrified that I wake up sweating from head to toe.' Corbett paused. 'This morning I was frightened. If it hadn't been for you, I would have fled. But that's what the assassin wants, everything to be in chaos. But we *will* impose order and, once we do, we wait!'

'If we live long enough.'

'We'll live. I'll make my mistakes, but in the end I'm going to see the cruel bastard behind all this arrested and pay the price. So, let's impose order. We have the Templars. They have houses in England and throughout Western Europe. They have been driven from the Holy Land. They have lost their purpose and have provoked the hostility and, because of their wealth, the envy of men. They, too, are frightened: that's why they have offered our king the princely sum of fifty thousand pounds. That cunning old fox knew he could get it. So come on Ranulf, Clerk of the Green Wax, what has happened so far?'

'It began with the Grand Chapter in Paris.'

'De Molay presided over that meeting,' Corbett continued. 'The four English Commanders were present. They left for England just after the attack on Philip IV was launched. Whilst they are in London, the Assassins' warning is pinned to the doors of St Paul's Cathedral. They come to York; there is unease about their stay here at Framlingham. The manor house is heavily defended, certain places carefully guarded. Then we have the deaths: the strange murder outside Botham Bar, the attack on the king and on me. The slaying of Reverchien and now the death of Peterkin the pastry cook. Well, Ranulf, what logic is there to all this?'

Ranulf scratched his head. 'Only one: where de Molay and his four commanders are, trouble occurs. There is neither rhyme nor reason for what happens. Most assassins have a motive. True, there could be divisions in the Templar Order, a secret coven dabbling in black magic. One or all of the Commanders, even de Molay, could be intent on wrecking vengeance against the kings of France and England.'

'But that does not explain,' Corbett added, 'the strange deaths outside Botham Bar and the slaying of Peterkin. Why should a poor pastry cook be consumed by fire? And, more importantly, how do these strange fires occur?'

Ranulf got up and paced restlessly up and down the chamber. 'Master, you said that for every natural phenomenon there's a natural cause. But what happens if this is not natural? People don't just break into flames?'

Corbett shook his head. 'I hear what you say, Ranulf. Yet, I suspect, that's what we are supposed to think.'

'But how can it happen?' Ranulf persisted. 'True, the Templars were in the city when the attack was launched on the king. But they weren't here when Reverchien was killed. We know that for a fact.'

'Brother Odo was,' Corbett replied. 'He was here. He may be old but, by his own confession, he is a fighting man. He could have killed Sir Guido, left the manor, joined Murston, then prowled the streets of York waiting for us. After that he could have hastened back to Framlingham before the others arrived. Legrave did say he found him asleep.'

'He's missing one hand.'

'So? I have heard of men with greater handicaps committing murder. How do we know he didn't follow Reverchien into the maze and kill him? Or somehow arrange for Peterkin's death?'

'And outside Botham Bar?' Ranulf asked. 'Swinging a two-handed sword?'

Corbett spread his hands. 'Concedo, that would be difficult – but not impossible. There again, the cook told me of a masked horseman lurking in the woods near the manor.'

'An assassin?' Ranulf asked.

'Possibly, though the cook could be lying. Finally one other matter remains. The counterfeit coins. Or perhaps they are not counterfeit . . .' Corbett continued, 'Anyway, these appeared in York just after the Templars arrived.'

97

'Then we are back to alchemy or magic,' Ranulf snapped. 'Master, when I ran wild in the streets of London, I knew some counterfeiters. What they do is take a good coin and make two bad ones out of it. I have never heard of anyone producing solid gold coins.'

Corbett sat down on the bed and rubbed his face with his hands. '"If you analyse everything,"' he quoted, '"And you can only reach one conclusion, then that conclusion must be the truth."' he glanced over at Ranulf. 'Perhaps it is magic.' He added slowly, 'Perhaps Satan's fire is burning amongst us.'

Chapter 6

The two knights took up position at either end of the tilt-yard. Down the dusty yard which separated them ran the tilt barrier, a long wooden fence covered with a leather sheet. The knights were fully armoured, great jousting helmets on their heads. Squires passed up shields and then the long wooden tourney lances. Corbett watched as each rider, guiding his horse with his legs, balanced his lance expertly. A trumpet shrilled. The knights began to move slowly. Another trumpet call and the horses burst into a gallop, their iron-shod hooves kicking up the dust, heads straining as each knight, keeping to the tilt barrier on his left, headed straight for his opponent. Shields came up, lances lowered. They met with a resounding crash in the centre. Lances shattered. Both knights swayed in the saddle but both kept their seats and passed to the other end of the tilt-yard.

'Well done!' Brother Odo cried, leaning against the wall and banging his stick on the ground. 'Good lance, Legrave. Symmes!' the old librarian bawled, 'bring your lance down sooner or you'll land on your arse!'

This sally provoked laughter from the watching knights and serjeants. Corbett and his two companions kept to the shadows of the wall. The sun was strong and the dust from the tilt-yard caught at their eyes and throats. Again the knights prepared. Fresh lances, shields in position and, with another trumpet call, the great destriers, caparisoned in gaily coloured harnesses, lunged forward, breaking into a gallop as each rider bore down on his opponent. The two jousters met, but this time Symmes was too slow: his lance missed Legrave whilst at the same time his shield slipped, making him vulnerable to his opponent's lance. There was a terrible crash. Symmes's horse went down on its hind legs and Symmes toppled from the saddle.

'Oh, well done!' de Molay cried, sitting on his throne-like chair under a silken canopy. He beckoned Corbett forward.

'Did you see Legrave? He changed his lance, held it in his left! Such expertise! Come, Sir Hugh, have you seen that amongst the king's knights?'

'No, Grand Master, I have not.'

Corbett spoke the truth. Ever since they had broken their fast after the morning Requiem Mass, the Templars had jousted. Corbett, though tired and suffering rather badly from the heat and dust, had been quick to admire the consummate skill of the Knights Templar. He looked across the tilt-yard where squires were now helping Symmes to his feet, taking off his helmet, offering him ladles of water to slake the dust from his throat and the sweat from his face. Legrave also dismounted and took off his helmet. He walked over to his fallen opponent. Symmes was a little dazed and shaken, but he met his former adversary: they embraced, exchanging the kiss of peace on each other's cheeks.

'If only all such differences were settled so peacefully,' de Molay murmured. He passed a cup of chilled white wine to Corbett, indicating to a servitor that the same be given to Ranulf and Maltote. 'Sir Hugh, I would like to thank you.' De Molay leaned forward so only Corbett could hear. 'It was chivalrous of you to let us bury our dead and salute his memory in a passage of arms.' He sighed. 'Now it's all finished. You wish to speak to us?'

'Yes, Grand Master.'

De Molay shrugged. 'I have instructed my comrades. You can question us in the refectory.'

Corbett drained his cup and handed it back to the servitor, motioning to Ranulf and Maltote to follow him. They walked across the tilt-yard, which lay at the opposite side of the manor to their quarters, and returned to the guesthouse.

'Thank God,' Ranulf groaned, easing himself down on a stool, 'I am not a Templar. They attack with such vehemence.'

'They are superb horsemen,' Maltote declared. 'Did you see how they guide their war-horses with the inside of their knees?'

'We are wasting time,' Ranulf replied crossly. 'I thought that Requiem Mass would never end!'

Corbett, standing at the window to catch the cool breeze, thought differently but kept his own counsel. The Requiem had been beautiful. Reverchien's body, in a wooden casket draped with the flags and banners of the Order, had been placed in front of the high altar of the beautifully decorated Templar chapel. The small church had been packed and the deep voiced singing of the Templars intoning the 'Requiem Dona Ei' had possessed its own solemn majesty. Corbett had sat in one of the side aisles, moved by de Molay's elegant panegyric on Sir Guido Reverchien. True, now and again, the clerk had carefully studied the congregation. The four Templar commanders had sat with their grand master in the sanctuary, whilst the serjeants, squires and other retainers had stood in the nave of the church just beyond the wooden rood-screen.

Corbett had tried to concentrate on the Mass but the cook's story was still fresh in his mind, and he wondered which of the Templar commanders and other members of this congregation were enjoying a homosexual relationship. Time and again the clerk had tried to dismiss this as a distraction for himself and a terrible danger to those concerned: in the eyes of the Church, homosexuality was a great sin. If the culprits were found they would face the cruellest of deaths. Yet his curiosity got the better of him. At the 'osculum pacis', the kiss of peace just before communion, he'd watched Baddlesmere and a young Templar serjeant meet at the entrance to the rood-screen. Now the kiss of peace was exchanged by all, but Corbett glimpsed something different between the grizzled Templar knight and

101

the youthful, fair-haired serjeant. Ranulf, of course, found it very difficult to keep his eyes open in church but, alerted by his master's tenseness, followed his gaze. He leaned forward.

'God forgive me, but, are you thinking what I am?'

Corbett had grabbed Ranulf by the shoulders and kissed him lightly on his cheek.

'*Pax frater,*' he whispered. 'Peace brother.'

'*Et cum spirituo tuo,*' Ranulf whispered back.

'Keep your thoughts to yourself,' Corbett had hissed, and returned to concentrate on the Mass.

After Reverchien's body had been buried in the vaults below the chapel, Corbett and Ranulf had attended a light collation in the refectory, followed by the tournament held in memory of the dead knight.

'Do you think they'll come?' Ranulf broke into his reverie.

Corbett turned away from the window. 'If de Molay has ordered them to, they will.'

'Do they like women?' Ranulf abruptly blurted out.

Corbett shrugged. 'They are supposed to. The only difference between them and us, Ranulf, is they take vows of celibacy and chastity. Their bride is Christ's Church.'

Ranulf whistled under his breath. 'But they must have feelings,' he added teasingly.

Corbett sat down at the small table and undid the saddle panniers containing his writing equipment. 'Why not be more blunt, Ranulf? Every member of the Templar Order is dedicated to a life of celibacy and chastity. It's part of their sacrifice. However, like all such male communities, there are men attracted to each other.'

'But that's a sin,' Maltote declared. 'And if they are caught?'

'God help them: the Templar Order has been known to put such men into a cell, brick the doors and windows up and leave them to starve.'

'Will you question de Molay about the secret chamber?' Ranulf asked. 'On the second floor where there's one window extra. I checked it again this morning after Mass. Between two of the chambers there's fresh wooden panelling. I think a door was once there.'

'The grand master has many questions to answer,' Corbett answered. 'I'm eager to learn what they keep hidden here.'

'Could that be the cause of the fire? Some secret weapon or even powerful relic!' Maltote exclaimed. 'I met a man in London who claimed to have travelled deep into Egypt, beyond Alexandria, to a tribe who possessed the Ark of the Covenant. They say that, if you touched it, strange fire burst out and consumed you. It's true!' Maltote's voice rose as Ranulf began to laugh behind his hand. 'I paid him tuppence for a piece of the wood!'

'I'll wager, the fellow never got further than Southampton,' Ranulf chortled. 'Have you seen Maltote's collection of relics, Master? It includes a rusty sword which Herod's soldiers are supposed to have used when killing the Holy Innocents . . .'

A sudden rap on the door ended the banter. Corbett answered it, expecting to find a messenger from the grand master. Instead the young Templar serjeant he had glimpsed during Mass stood there. Beside him was a squat, thickset man with the features of a fighting mastiff. He had a jutting jaw, firmly clenched mouth, eyes which never blinked, and ridiculously cropped black hair shaved high on all sides, leaving the rest to stand up like some unruly bush.

'Well?' Corbett asked.

'A visitor for you, Sir Hugh.'

'Didn't you expect me?' the stranger barked and, without further ado, walked into the chamber. He almost knocked Corbett aside, slamming the door behind him in the young Templar's face. He stood, his squat legs apart, his fingers jammed into his swordbelt. He took off his dark-maroon cloak and slung it over a chair.

'Devil's tits!' He smacked his lips. 'I'm as dry as a whore's armpit!'

'You'll be drier still if you don't explain yourself!'

Ranulf got to his feet. 'Who in God's name are you?'

'Roger Claverley, Under-sheriff of York.' Their visitor unbuckled his pouch, took out a warrant and thrust a piece of parchment at Corbett. 'This is my warrant from the mayor and sheriff. I'm here to help you.'

Corbett chewed his lip to stop himself smiling: the more he watched Claverley's confrontation with Ranulf, the more his visitor reminded him of the small fighting mastiff that Uncle Morgan, Maeve's kinsman, always had trotting behind him. The mastiff didn't like Ranulf and the feeling was warmly reciprocated.

'Get our visitor some wine, Ranulf,' Corbett said, studying the letter closely. 'He's a very important official and, if this letter is correct, he can provide us with valuable information about the gold coins as well as other matters.' Corbett put the parchment down on the table and came forward, extending a hand.

Claverley clasped it in a bone-crushing grip.

'You are very welcome, Roger,' Corbett said, trying to hide his wince.

The under-sheriff relaxed, his ugly face breaking into a warm smile.

'I am really the city thief-taker,' he declared grandly. 'I know all the villains of the city and they know me. A bit like the good shepherd, only in reverse: where they go, I follow.'

Corbett waved him to a seat, warning Ranulf with his eyes to stand off. Claverley looked first at Maltote who, as usual, was staring open-mouthed, and then at Ranulf.

'I'll wager a month's provisions you have seen the inside of a gaol, my lad. Even across a crowded room, I know a felon when I see one.'

'Yes, I have been inside Newgate.' Ranulf replied tartly. 'I ran wild with the rufflers, the foists, the palliards, the upright men. But tell me, Claverley, were you just born this

104

discourteous? Or does it come with the office you hold?'

Claverley suddenly leaned forward, hands extended, that charming smile back on his face. Ranulf clasped his hand.

'I didn't mean to give offence. I have been there as well,' Claverley remarked. 'After all, the best gamekeepers were once poachers. Now, Sir Hugh, I have been told to assist you, so that's what I'll do. I'll be honest: if I help, would you mention my name to the king?'

Corbett grinned at this ambitious little man's blunt honesty.

'Master Claverley, I will not forget you.'

'Good,' the under-sheriff replied. 'First, we've found the remains, the decomposing bottom half of that man's corpse. Do you remember, the good sisters' guide, Thurston, glimpsed it as the horse careered by them. Some of our young merchants went hunting and their dogs unearthed it.'

'And the horse?'

'Neither hide nor hair has been seen.'

'Anything else?' Corbett asked.

'Well, the Templar crossbowman: I was responsible for having him gibbeted on the pavement. Hung him up in a nice metal cage I did. With a placard, proclaiming this to be the fate of traitors and regicides, tied to it.'

'And?'

'Well, this morning the placard was removed. This was attached by a piece of wire to the gibbet cage.' Claverley handed over a piece of parchment.

'Oh Lord!' Corbett groaned as he read it.

'KNOWEST THOU, THAT WHAT THOU POSSESSES SHALL ESCAPE THEE IN THE END AND RETURN TO US.

'KNOWEST THOU, THAT WE GO FORTH AND RETURN AS BEFORE AND BY NO MEANS CAN YOU HINDER US.

'KNOWEST THOU, THAT WE HOLD YOU AND

WILL KEEP THEE UNTIL THE ACCOUNT BE CLOSED.'

Corbett held the parchment up. 'The verses are slightly changed but it is the Assassins' warning.'

'But the Templars could not have done that,' Ranulf exclaimed. 'They are confined here at Framlingham on the king's orders.'

'They can climb a wall as easily as anyone,' Maltote declared.

'I doubt it,' Claverley intervened. 'We have our orders in the city. No Templar is allowed in.'

'He might have gone disguised,' Maltote added.

Claverley shrugged. 'The guards at the gates have been doubled. Strangers have been stopped and searched but, I suppose, it's possible.'

'There might be an assassin in York,' Corbett replied, and described the masked horseman the cook had seen.

Claverley scratched his chin. 'An assassin hiding along the Botham Bar road?' He pulled a face. 'I've heard nothing about that. Anyway,' Claverley indicated with his head, 'what's happening here? There are no servants, just Templar soldiers and squires.'

'They have all fled,' Corbett retorted. 'There was a death here last night.'

He paused at a knock on the door and Legrave came in. 'Sir Hugh, we are ready in the refectory. The grand master . . .' He paused and glared at Claverley. 'Your visitor from the king?'

'Yes,' Corbett replied. 'Ranulf, you stay here and tell our guest what we know. Sir Ralph, I'll join you now.'

Corbett followed the Templar out of the guesthouse and across into the refectory. De Molay was seated at the head of the table, his companions on either side. De Molay indicated for Corbett to sit at the far end facing him. He noticed the leather bag of writing implements which Corbett laid out on the table, together with parchment, pen and ink-horn.

'Sir Hugh, this is a formal occasion.'

Corbett agreed.

'You will interrogate us on behalf of the king. So you will not object if we, too, keep a fair record of what is said. Sir Richard Branquier will be our clerk.'

'Grand Master, do what you wish, but time is short, so I'll be blunt. If I give offence then I apologise. And you'll forgive me if I repeat what I have asked before?'

De Molay nodded.

'Grand Master, are there divisions in your Order?'

'Yes.'

'Are there those, amongst your principal commanders, who are bitter at the lack of support from the Western Princes?'

'Of course, but that does not mean we are traitors!'

'Have you ever heard,' Corbett continued remorselessly, 'of a high-ranking officer in the Templars who carries the nickname of Sagittarius, the Archer?' He watched the rest but they remained inscrutable.

'Never!' de Molay snapped. 'Though some of the knights, indeed all, are accomplished archers, with the arbalest, the Welsh longbow and even with Saracen weapons.'

'Have you heard any news about the Templar interrogated by the Inquisition?'

'No, but we expect news daily. We do not even know his name.'

'But you knew Murston?'

Corbett watched as Branquier, holding his pen in his left hand, conscientiously scribbled what was being said.

'Murston was my retainer. A weak man, not liked by his colleagues. He drank a lot. He had become bitter.'

'But not a traitor?'

'No, Sir Hugh, I think not.'

'Wasn't he missed from his quarters? After all, he hired the garret in that tavern the night before the attack on the king?'

'You must remember, Sir Hugh, all of us had met the king at

St Leonard's Priory the previous day. My companions and I then went into York. It could have been some days before Murston was missed.'

Corbett paused to write down what he had learnt. His quill skimmed across the soft parchment, writing in a cipher known only to himself.

'And on the day the king entered York?' he asked, placing the quill down.

'We left the priory of St Leonard,' de Molay replied, 'and entered York. Legrave and I visited our bankers, goldsmiths in Stonegate.'

'What are their names?'

'Coningsby,' Legrave replied. 'William Coningsby and Peter Lamode.'

'And you stayed there all the morning?'

'There is no need for this,' Branquier broke in. 'We are knights of the Cross, not felons seized by the Crown!'

'Hush!' De Molay raised his hand. 'All we are telling, Brother, is the truth. Legrave and myself were in Stonegate well into the afternoon. I inspected our accounts, then journeyed up Petergate and through Botham Bar. The king's procession was in the grounds of York Minster. I would have liked to have visited the place.' The grand master smiled thinly. 'But I let it wait for another day.'

'And you, Sir William?' Corbett asked.

Not a muscle moved in Symmes's scarred face, though his good eye looked threateningly at Corbett.

'For a while I was with the grand master, but then I visited merchants in Goodramgate and journeyed to see a friend, a priest who serves the church of St Mary. I arranged to meet the grand master just outside the parchmenters' house within sight of Botham bar. I journeyed back with him.'

'And Sir Bartholomew?' Corbett made a few notes on the parchment.

'I went to Jubbergate where the armourers and fletchers

keep their shops. I was to buy arms.'

'And you were alone?' Corbett asked innocently.

'No, I was with a serjeant.'

'And his name?' Corbett asked.

The Templar swallowed hard. 'John Scoudas. He's here in the manor.'

'You needn't ask me!' Branquier almost shouted down the table. 'I left St Leonard's Priory after the rest. When I reached York, its streets were thronged because of the royal procession. I lingered for a while but the city grew hot and packed. I came back here, as Brother Odo will tell you.'

Corbett quickly studied what he'd written: de Molay and Legrave, he reasoned swiftly, could vouch for each other, Brother Odo for Branquier. But Baddlesmere? Corbett suspected he was lying. And the same went for Symmes, who sat stroking his pet weasel which he kept under the rim of the table. Corbett stared at the parchment. He was aware that the Templars were becoming impatient: chairs were scraped back with loud sighs of exasperation.

'Where do you think we were?' Legrave abruptly asked. 'Helping Murston to try and kill the king? Or sending you messages on Ouse Bridge?'

'Or setting an ambush for you?' Baddlesmere scoffed.

'Grand Master.' Branquier threw his quill down, splashing the table with ink. 'This is the last time I will answer such questions. Just because an idiot of a serjeant, with addled wits, attempts to kill the king, and silly pretentious warnings are sent hither and thither, does that make us all guilty?'

His words provoked a murmur of assent. De Molay looked distinctly uncomfortable, his dark, aristocratic face betrayed an unease. Corbett glanced to the left and right. Baddlesmere sat scratching his grizzled, weather-beaten face. Was he the murderer, Corbett wondered, with his secret sin? Or Legrave, with his neatly combed brown hair and olive-skinned, boyish face? A consummate soldier. Or one-eyed Symmes? Or

Branquier, tall and stooping over the table? Yet Corbett was certain that one of these men, or perhaps all, were assassins, and that other murders could soon occur.

'We have sent Peterkin's body into the city,' de Molay spoke up, 'suitably coffined.' He raised a hand. 'Don't worry. No Templars accompanied it, only one of our stewards with a letter of commiseration and a purse of silver for the man's mother. Sir Hugh, why should anyone kill a poor cook? What profit lay in his death?'

'Or even poor Reverchien?' Baddlesmere snapped.

'I don't know,' Corbett replied. 'But, Grand Master, why have you come to York?'

'I have told you: it is the duty of every grand master to visit each province.'

'And, before you came,' Corbett continued easily, 'Framlingham Manor was supervised by Sir Guido Reverchien, its bailiff and steward?'

'Yes.'

'So why are certain stairwells now guarded? What other secrets does this manor hold?'

'Such as?'

'A masked horseman has been seen hiding in the woods near Framlingham.'

De Molay looked at his companions then shook his head. 'We know nothing of that. What else?'

'A sealed room on the second floor of the manor?'

'Silence!' de Molay ordered as his companions began to accuse Corbett of snooping. 'Have you finished your questioning, Sir Hugh?'

'Yes.'

'Then let me show you our secret room.'

De Molay rose. Corbett put away his writing implements as quickly as possible and followed him out of the room.

'Sir Richard Branquier,' de Molay called over his shoulder. 'You may follow us.'

The grand master, fighting hard to control his temper, led Corbett up the stairs and along the second gallery, a wooden-floored passageway with carved panelling on the walls on either side. De Molay walked half-way down and stopped.

'Branquier, open this room for Sir Hugh!'

The Templar shouldered by Corbett roughly, almost knocking him aside. He pulled open a panelling and pressed a lever. There was a click and part of the wooden wainscoting came away to reveal a door. De Molay took a key from his pouch, inserted this into the lock and a door opened. Inside was a small, narrow cell, the floor bare, the walls whitewashed. A small casement window provided light.

Corbett, slightly embarrassed, stared round at the trunks and coffers stored there.

'It's our treasure house,' Branquier explained. 'Many of our houses and manors have such a room. Doesn't the king have the same?' Branquier pushed his face near Corbett's. 'Perhaps even you, Keeper of His Secret Seal. Are all your rooms and chambers, Sir Hugh, open to the curious and inquisitive?'

'I simply asked,' Corbett replied.

'And you have your answer.'

Corbett stared at a tapestry on the wall: a beautifully embroidered piece of cloth held in place by a thin wooden frame. The tapestry depicted the taking of Christ down from the cross by Nicodemus and St John. Mary knelt, arms outstretched, waiting to receive him. The artist had executed a brilliant scene: the gold, blue, red, green and purple colours seemed more like a picture than a tapestry.

'It's very costly,' de Molay explained. 'Done by an Italian artist. The goldwork alone is worth the profits of this manor. But come, Sir Hugh, we have more to show you.'

Corbett left the chamber. De Molay made the door secure and Branquier closed the wooden partition before leading him along the gallery and up some steps. In the stairwell at the top, two soldiers guarded a flight of stairs to what must be the garret. De Molay told them to stand aside. He unlocked the door, ushering Corbett inside. The room was long, rather musty, a small oval window at the far end just above a makeshift dais on which stood a wooden altar with candlesticks at either end.

'Look around,' Branquier taunted Corbett.

'There's no need to,' Corbett retorted. 'It's as bare as a hay-loft.'

He glanced up at the slanted ceiling and, through chinks in the tiles, glimpsed the sky beyond. He walked towards the altar, noticing the two cushions on the floor before it. He picked at the wax on top of the table.

'There's nothing here!' Branquier snapped, but he looked uneasy, as if frightened to be here.

'So why is it guarded so securely?' Corbett asked.

Branquier, startled, opened his mouth to reply. De Molay, however, was quicker.

'Sir Hugh, you are so suspicious. We are the Templar Order. We have our own rites and rituals.'

'You have a fair enough chapel downstairs.'

'True. True,' the grand master replied. 'But go to any religious house in York: Cistercians, Carthusians, the Crutched Friars, Friars of the Sack. They all have their own private chanceries and chapels well away from the public gaze. This is what happens here.'

'For everyone?' Corbett asked.

'No, no,' de Molay replied. 'Only Sir Richard and myself. We have reached that stage of development in our Order.'

De Molay kept in the shadows, his face turned away. Corbett intuitively knew he was hiding something, but what else could he say? He'd asked his questions and de Molay had replied.

'Grand Master.' He walked to the door. 'I thank you for your courtesy. This morning my servant left the king's gift of wine in your kitchens.' He smiled over his shoulder. 'A poor token compared to the trouble I have caused.'

Chapter 7

Corbett left the garret but turned half-way down the stairs.

'Oh, by the way, Grand Master, did anyone leave Framlingham Manor last night?'

'Apart from the servants who fled, no. The rest of our community are under strict orders: they are not to leave Framlingham.'

Corbett thanked him and returned to his quarters. Ranulf and Maltote were deep in conversation with Claverley over the intricacies of spoilt dice and how easy it was to cheat at shuffle penny.

'We are leaving,' Corbett announced briskly. 'Maltote, get our horses ready. Ranulf, collect my cloak and swordbelt, I'll meet you down at the stables.'

'And you, Master?'

'I want to see Brother Odo. Oh, by the way, Claverley,' Corbett called out as he left. 'Whatever you do, don't play dice with Ranulf or buy any of his potions!'

A Templar serjeant showed him to the library: a long, high-vaulted room at the back of the manor house overlooking the garden. It was pleasant and cool. Books filled the shelves along all the walls: some were chained and padlocked, others stood open on lecterns. At the far end were the study carrels each built into a small portico containing a table, chair, a tray of writing implements and a large, metal-capped beeswax candle. At first Corbett thought the library was deserted. He walked slowly down, his footsteps echoing through the cavernous room.

'Who's there?'

Corbett's heart skipped a beat. Brother Odo emerged from the shadows where he had been poring over a manuscript: his one good hand was covered in ink.

'Sir Hugh, I did not know you were a bibliophile.'

'I wish I was, Brother.'

Corbett shook his hand and the librarian led him into one of the study carrels.

'All these books and manuscripts belong to the Templars,' Odo explained. 'Well, at least to its province north of the Trent.' He fingered his ink-stained lips and looked round wistfully. 'We lost so many libraries in the East. We even had an original of Jerome's commentary . . . but you haven't come to ask me about that, have you?'

He jabbed a finger at a stool next to his chair. Corbett sat down self-consciously and stared at the manuscripts littered across the desk.

'I am writing a chronicle,' Odo announced proudly. 'A history of the siege of Acre and its fall.'

He pulled across a piece of vellum and Corbett stared at the drawing: Templar knights, distinctive by the crosses on their cloaks, were defending a tower; they were throwing spears and boulders down at evil-looking Turks. The drawing was not accurate, it lacked proportion – yet it possessed a vigour and vibrancy all of its own. Underneath, written in a cramped hand, was a Latin commentary.

'I have done seventy-three pieces,' Odo announced. 'But I hope that the chronicle will include two hundred; a lasting testament to the valour of our Order.'

A piece of parchment fell off the table. Corbett picked it up. There was writing on this but it was strange and twisted. Corbett, fluent in Latin and the Norman French of the Royal Chancery, thought it might be Greek.

'What language is that, Corbett?' Odo teased.

'Greek?'

Odo grinned and seized the parchment.

'No. They are runes, Anglo-Saxon runes. My mother's name was Tharlestone. She claimed descent from Leofric, Harold's brother, who died at the Battle of Hastings. She owned lands in Norfolk. Have you ever been there, Corbett?'

The clerk recalled his recent, and most dangerous, stay outside Mortlake Manor the previous November.

'Yes,' he replied. 'But perhaps it was not the happiest of visits.'

'Well, I was raised there. My mother died young.' The old librarian's eyes misted over. 'Gentle as a fawn she was. No other woman like her: that's probably the reason I entered the Order. Ah well,' he continued briskly, 'my grandfather raised me. He would take me fishing on the marshes. I still do that now, you know: I have a little boat down near the lake. I call it *The Ghost of the Tower*. Anyway, whilst Grandfather and I were waiting for the fish to bite, he'd scratch out the runes on a piece of bark and make me learn them. See that letter there like our "P"? That's "W". The arrow is a "T" and the sign like a gate is "V". I make my own notes.' He plucked the parchment from Corbett's hand. 'So no one really knows what I am doing.' He smiled. 'Ah well, how can I help you?'

'On the day Reverchien died,' Corbett asked, 'did you notice anything amiss, anything wrong?'

'No. Both Sir Guido and I were pleased when the grand master and his commanders left. Framlingham went back to its usual serene ways. We went round checking stores, I spent most of the time here in the library. We met in church to sing the Divine Office. He had a good voice, Reverchien, slightly higher than mine. We thundered out the verses then supped in the refectory. The next morning, just after Matins, Sir Guido went on what he called his little Crusade.' He shrugged. 'The rest you know.'

'And then what?'

'Well, when I smelt the smoke and heard the screams, some

of the servants and I went into the maze. It looks difficult to thread so you must keep moving in a certain direction.' The old man's face became sad. 'But, by the time we reached the centre . . .' His voice faltered. 'Oh, don't misunderstand me. I have seen men burning alive at Acre but, in the centre of an English maze on a warm spring morning, to see a comrade's body smouldering, blackened ash from head to toe. The flames must have been intense. The ground and the great iron candelabra were all burnt black. We sheeted the corpse and took it to the death-house. I went into the buttery. Perhaps I drank more than I should have. I felt sleepy so I went back to my cell. I was snoring my head off when Branquier woke me.'

'What do you think caused the fire?' Corbett asked.

'I don't know. The whispers say the fire of hell.' The old librarian leaned closer. 'But Sir Guido was a good man, kind and generous: a little addled in his wits but he loved God, Holy Mother Church and his Order. Why should such a good man be burnt, whilst the wicked swagger around boasting of their evil?' The librarian blinked; he ran his good hand across the parchment, stroking it gently like a mother would a child.

'I don't believe it was the fire of hell,' Corbett remarked. 'Sir Guido was a good man. He was murdered. But how, and why, God only knows.'

'The flames had died but it smelt so bad.' Odo murmured. 'I could smell the sulphur and brimstone in the air. Just like . . .'

'Like what?' Corbett asked.

The old librarian scratched his unshaven cheek. 'I can't remember,' he whispered. 'God forgive me, Corbett, but I can't.' He looked at the clerk. 'Is there anything else?'

Corbett shook his head and got to his feet. He gently pressed Odo's thin shoulder.

'They'll talk of you in years to come,' Corbett declared kindly. 'They'll talk of Odo Tharlestone, soldier and scholar. Your chronicle will be copied in monasteries, libraries and abbeys throughout the land. The halls of Oxford and Cambridge will bid for it.'

Odo looked up, his eyes sparkling. 'Do you really think so?'

'Oh, yes, the king has a great library at Westminster. He'll want a copy as well but, Brother,' Corbett added, 'reflect on what you saw the morning Sir Guido died.'

And with the librarian's assurance that he would do so ringing in his ears, Corbett went to the stables to join his companions.

A few minutes later, accompanied by Claverley and Ranulf, who were arguing noisily about which was the fairest, York or London, Corbett left Framlingham. They rode down the lonely pathway, past the guards and through the gate, turning left on to the Botham Bar road. The day was drawing on but the sun was still strong. The hedgerows on either side were alive with the rustling of birds and the buzzing of bees searching for honey amongst the wild flowers.

'I have beehives,' Claverley announced. 'At least a dozen steppes in my garden. The best honey in York, Sir Hugh.'

Corbett smiled absentmindedly. His mind was back in that library. Odo had remembered something. Corbett just hoped the old man's long memory would produce a key to unlock all these mysteries. They rode on under the shadow of the towering trees. At last Claverley reined in.

'We have to leave the road here.' The under-sheriff pointed to a small, beaten trackway on the edge of the forest. 'The remains were found deeper in.'

'What happened to them?' Ranulf asked.

'They had been unearthed by some animal. They were rotting, rather mangled, then tossed about by the hunting dogs. They were put into a leather sack; a verderer took them into the city for burial in a pauper's grave. Look, I'll show you.'

They left the trackway and entered the forest. The sunlight began to fade as the path wound along between holm, oak, elm, larch, black poplar, sycamore, beech and copper beech. The sky became shut off, the sunlight blocked out by the thick canopy of leaves and entwining branches. Their horses became uneasy at the rustling amongst the bracken and the sudden, startling song of some bird. Now and again there would be a break in the trees, and they'd cross a clearing where the grass grew long and lush and wild flowers filled the air with their heady scent. Then back into the green darkness, as if entering some strange cathedral where the walls were wooded, the roof green and the distant bird-song the chanting of some choir. Ranulf, frightened of nothing, stopped his banter with Claverley and peered nervously about. Corbett rode ahead, guiding his horse carefully, ears straining for the snap of the twig or a footfall which could mean danger. Now and again his horse would toss its head, snorting angrily. Corbett tightened his reins, stroking his horse's neck, talking to it gently.

'Of course, I've already been here,' Claverley declared in a voice which seemed to boom amongst the trees. 'It's not far now.'

He pushed his horse forward and they entered a small glade. Claverley pointed to an outcrop of rock in the centre where the soil had been dug up and piled on either side of a hole. Corbett nudged his horse forward and carefully examined where the grisly remains of that mysterious victim had been buried. He stared at the rough cross carved on the rock.

'Is there any settlement round here? A village or hamlet?'

Claverley shrugged and scratched his cropped hair. 'Not that I know of.'

'Well, there's nothing behind us.' Corbett remarked. 'And there's no trace of any settlement to the left or right, so let's keep to the path we are following.'

They rode deeper into the forest. Corbett closed his eyes and prayed that the assassin from Framlingham had not followed them; he reined in, his horse whinnying at the acrid tang of the woodsmoke.

'There's something ahead,' he called back.

'Possibly a verderer,' Claverley replied. 'Or a woodcutter.'

At last the trees thinned and they rode into a clearing. At the far end, just in front of the line of trees, was a large, thatched cottage, its roof heavy and sloping. On either side of it were wooden sheds or byres and stacks of logs, around which scrawny-necked chickens pecked at the earth. A gaggle of geese, alarmed at their approach, turned from their feeding and fled screeching towards the house. The door opened and a mongrel dog came yapping at them, followed by two children dressed in ragged tunics, their hands and faces covered in soot, their thick hair greasy and matted. They showed no fear but stared up at these unexpected visitors, chattering in a dialect Corbett couldn't understand.

'What do you want?'

A man stood in the doorway. He was dressed in a dark-brown tunic, a piece of rope around his protuberant belly, leggings of the same colour pushed into black, battered boots. Over his shoulder a woman peered nervously at Corbett and his companions. The clerk raised his hand in peace. The man put down the axe he carried, called off the dog and walked towards them.

'Are you lost?' he asked.

'No. We are from the city.' Claverley edged his horse forward. 'We are investigating the remains found in the clearing.'

The man glanced away. 'Aye, I heard about the excitement,' he muttered. He shuffled his feet nervously and turned to shout something at the children.

'Can we come in?' Corbett asked. He pointed across at the well. 'Perhaps a stoup of water and something to eat? We are hungry.'

'Master,' Maltote spoke up, 'we have just—' He shut up as Ranulf glared at him.

Corbett dismounted and held his hand out. 'I am Sir Hugh Corbett, King's Clerk – and you?'

The woodcutter lifted his windburnt face, though he refused

119

to meet Corbett's gaze. 'Osbert,' he muttered. 'Verderer and woodcutter.' He glanced back at his wife. 'You'd best come in!' he declared grudgingly.

Corbett told Maltote to guard the horses and they followed the woodcutter and his family into their long, shed-like house. A fire burnt on the stone hearth in the centre, the smoke escaping through a hole in the room. At the far end was a loft reached by a ladder where the family slept: there were a few sticks of furniture and shelves with some cooking pots on them.

'You'd best sit where you can.' The woodcutter pointed to the beaten earth floor.

Corbett, Ranulf and Claverley sat near the hearth. Corbett chatted to Osbert's wife, putting her at her ease whilst her husband filled pewter cups with water. The woman smiled, pushing back her hair, and leaned over to stir the pot which hung above the hearth.

'It smells delicious,' Corbett remarked, though the odour was less than savoury.

'What do you want?' Osbert asked. He served the water and sat down opposite them. 'You are a king's clerk. You are used to eating better than this. Your servants carry water-bottles so you don't need a drink.'

'No, I don't,' Corbett replied. 'And you, Master Osbert, have very sharp eyes. As do I. You buried those remains, didn't you?'

The woodcutter's wife scuttled away to look after the children who sat near the wall, thumbs in mouths, watching their visitors.

'You found the remains,' Corbett continued. 'And, because you are an upright man, you buried them. You dug a hole beneath the boulder, hoping that would keep wild animals out and, with your axe, scratched a faint cross on it.'

'Tell him,' Osbert's wife pointed at Corbett. 'He knows!' she shouted. 'Or we'll all hang!'

'Nonsense,' Corbett exclaimed. 'Just tell me, Osbert.'

'It was just before dawn,' the woodcutter replied. 'I was out hunting a fox, one of the chickens had been taken. I heard a whinny and found the horse just off the road: its leg was damaged. The horse limped towards me. I thought I'd died and gone to hell: the mangled legs of its rider were still in the stirrups. Blood and gore drenched the saddle. The horse was blown: I took the remains and buried them beneath the rock. I said a prayer, then I brought the horse home. I threw the saddle down a pit. I couldn't sell it, it was too soaked in blood.'

'And the horse itself?'

Osbert swallowed hard and pointed to the pot. 'We are eating it.'

Ranulf coughed and spluttered.

'We are hungry,' Osbert continued. 'Hungry for meat. All the deer have gone. They've got more sense than to stay near the city.' He spread his dirty hands. 'What could I do, Master? If I took the horse to market, I'd hang for a thief. If I'd kept it, the same might happen. The animal was sick, its leg was damaged and I know little physic. I killed it: gutted its belly, salted and pickled the rest and hid it away in a little hut deep in the forest, hung over some charcoal to smoke it and stop the putrefaction.'

'And what else did you find?' Corbett asked. He took two silver coins out of his purse. 'Tell me the truth and these will be yours; there'll be no recriminations over what you did.'

Osbert wetted his lips and pondered but his wife acted for him. She went to the far end of the hut, climbed the ladder to the bed-loft and returned carrying a set of battered saddle panniers over her arm. She slung these at Corbett's feet.

'There was a little money,' Osbert grumbled. 'Now it's all gone. I bought the geese with it. What's left is there.'

Corbett emptied the contents out: a jerkin, two pairs of hose neatly darned, a belt, a collection of small metal pilgrim badges and statues of saints, cheap geegaws to be bought outside any

121

church. Finally a few scraps of parchment. Corbett studied the faded ink on these.

'Wulfstan of Beverley,' he announced. 'A seller of religious objects and petty relics.' He glanced at Claverley and Ranulf. 'Why on earth would someone kill poor Wulfstan? Cut his body in two, send his horse galloping madly into the darkness and burn the top half?' Corbett threw the saddlebag at Claverley. He got to his feet and pressed the two coins into Osbert's hands. 'Next time you go to Mass,' Corbett added, 'pray for the soul of poor Wulfstan.'

'I did what I could,' Osbert muttered. 'God assoil him. Is there anything else, Master?'

Corbett asked, 'In the forest, have you ever glimpsed a rider, masked and cowled?'

'Once,' Osbert replied. 'Only once, Master, just after I found the horse. I was out cutting firewood on the edge of Botham Bar road. I heard a sound so I hid in the bracken. A rider passed, dressed like a monk. His horse was a nag and the cloak was tattered but I glimpsed a great two-handed sword hanging from the saddlehorn. I thought he was an outlaw so I stayed hidden until he passed.' The woodcutter pulled a face. 'That's all I've seen.'

Corbett thanked him. They left the woodcutter's, collected their horses and rode back on to the Botham Bar road. Ranulf and Claverley immediately became involved in a fierce argument over the eating of horseflesh. Maltote, pale-faced, could only feebly protest.

'To eat a horse!' he kept exclaiming. 'To eat a horse!'

'You would,' Claverley called back. 'My father told me how, in the great famine outside Carlisle, they caught rats and sold them as a delicacy.'

Corbett urged his horse on, only stopping when he came to the place where Wulfstan's burnt remains had been found.

'What are you looking for?' Claverley called out as Corbett dismounted and walked into the line of trees.

'I'll tell you when I find it,' Corbett replied.

He walked further in and crouched down to examine the great scorch-marks on the earth. He then drew his sword and began cutting the brambles and long grass. As he did so, Corbett glimpsed more, though much smaller, scorch-marks. And on the trees which fringed the undergrowth, Corbett noticed scratch-marks, as if some great cat had clawed the back, gouging and scarring it.

'What on earth caused this?' Claverley exclaimed, coming up behind him.

Corbett looked back towards the road where Maltote sat on his horse staring soulfully at them.

'This is what I think happened,' Corbett explained. 'Someone came here to practise with the fire which burnt Wulfstan and the others.'

'It looks as if the devil himself has swept up from hell,' Claverley intervened. 'His tail scorched the earth and his claws gouged the trees.'

'Yes, you could sell such a story in York marketplace,' Corbett replied. 'But I am sure the Lord Satan has better things to do than journey up from hell to burn grass and brambles on the Botham Bar road. No. Somebody was practising with that fire, whilst the marks on the trees are made by arrows.'

'So, the killer was firing arrows?'

'Possibly,' Corbett explained. 'He created small fires, for God knows what reason, and practised shooting arrows using the trees as targets. Now I think he was so busy, so confident under the cover of dusk, that he failed to notice Wulfstan. Our poor relic-seller came trotting along the Botham Bar road, journeying to some village or market town to sell his geegaws. Now anyone else would have gone hastily by or even turned back. Wulfstan, however, was a pedlar, a man who loved to travel and collect stories as he did. He stopped where Maltote now is, probably calling out through the dusk. The assassin turns. He has been recognised. His horse stands nearby. He

123

hurries up, draws his great two-handed sword hanging from the saddlehorn and rushes towards Wulfstan. The relic-seller would sit startled, frightened, immobile as a rabbit. He'd raise his hands to his face as the assassin swings that terrible sword, slicing his body in two with one savage cut.'

'And the horse bolts?' Ranulf asked.

'Yes, the violent stench of blood sends the poor nag stampeding down the road. Our killer then sets the top half of the corpse alight. In doing so, he not only prevents any identification but finds out, for his own devilish curiosity, the effect of this strange fire on human flesh.'

'And, of course,' Claverley intervened, 'Wulfstan being a pedlar, a stranger to these parts, no one came forward to declare he is missing.'

'Master.' Ranulf pointed to the scorch-marks on the ground. 'How can a man control fire? We have a tinder which can be clumsy to strike, especially in the open air. Or you can kindle a fire and take a burning stick or piece of charcoal, but this killer seems to be able to summon it out of the air.' Ranulf stared into the green darkness of the trees. 'Isn't that magic? The use of the black arts?'

'No,' Corbett retorted. 'I could call up Satan from hell but, whether he comes or not is another matter. This killer wants us to believe he has magical powers, the key to all sorcery.'

'And this mysterious rider,' Claverley asked. 'He might be the killer; he did carry a great two-handed sword.'

Corbett kicked at the scorched path. 'Perhaps. But, Master Under-sheriff, we must go: other matters, just as pressing, await us.'

They remounted their horses and rode down Botham Bar road. As they approached York, the road became busier: traders and pedlars making their way out of the city, packs and fardels on their backs: a dusty-gowned Franciscan of the Order of the Sack leading an even more tired mule. A beggar pushed a wheelbarrow in which an old man sprawled, his legs shorn from the knees down: both looked happy enough after a day's begging and, drunk as sots, raucously bawled out filthy songs as the barrow staggered along the road. Peasants huddled in their carts, their produce sold, and a woman and two children walked wearily, leading a cow. A royal messenger galloped by, his white wand of office tucked into his belt; the soldier riding behind him wore the resplendent livery of the king's chamber. Everyone drew aside to let them pass and, shortly afterwards, had to do the same again as a Templar soldier urged his foam-flecked horse along the road.

'I thought all Templars were confined to Framlingham?' Claverley asked.

'Probably a messenger,' Corbett replied. 'I wonder what's so urgent?'

They pressed on. Botham Bar came into sight, the great iron portcullis raised like jagged teeth over the people passing through. On top of the gatehouse were poles bearing the severed heads of malefactors and, on either side of the gateway, makeshift gallows had been set up. Each bore its own grisly corpse twirling in the late afternoon breeze, placards slung round the necks proclaiming their crimes.

'The king's justices have been busy,' Claverley declared. 'There's been sessions of gaol delivery all of yesterday.'

'Where are you taking us?' Corbett asked.

'To see the Limner.'

'The what?'

'The Greyhound: my nickname for the best counterfeiter in York.'

They continued under Botham Bar, along Petersgate, past the foul-smelling public latrines built next to St Michael the Belfry Church, and into the busiest part of the city. The market stalls were still open. The narrow streets thronged. The taverns were doing a roaring trade. One man lay in the middle of the street in a drunken stupor whilst a friend lying alongside tried to beat off marauding hogs, much to the delight of passers-by.

125

The stocks were also full. Some malefactors were fastened by the neck, others by the arms and legs. One apprentice had his thumbs only clasped into a finger press for helping himself to his master's food. Two whores stood in the pillory, heads shaven, shouting abuse at the crowd whilst a drunken bagpipe player tried to drown their cries as a bailiff birched their bare bottoms. On the corner of a street Corbett and his party had to stay for a while: a group of officials from the alderman's court had raided a tavern to search out old wine, long past its freshness. They'd seized three barrels and were trying to stave these in whilst, from the windows above, the landlord, his wife and family pelted the bailiffs and everyone else with the smelly contents of their chamberpots.

At last the bailiffs restored order and Claverley led them on along Patrick Pool and into the Shambles. The smells and dust caught at their noses and mouths: the butchers' and fletchers' narrow street, which ran between the overhanging houses, was covered in offal and black blood. Flies massed there, dogs and cats fought over scraps. The crowd, eager to buy fresh meat, thronged around the stalls from which gutted pigs, decapitated geese, chickens and other fowl hung. At last Claverley lost his temper. He drew his sword and, shouting, '*Le roi, le roi!*' forced a passage out on to the Pavement, the great open area fronting All Saints Church.

Here the crowds thronged before the grim city prison. Outside its main door stood a line of scaffolds, each three-branched, on which executions were being carried out. The condemned felons were led out from the prison, taken on to a platform, pushed up a ladder, where a noose was fixed round their neck. The ladder was then turned and the felon would dance and kick as the hempen cord tightened round his throat, choking his life out. Corbett had seen such sights before in many of the king's great cities. The royal justices would arrive, the gaols would be emptied, courts held and swift sentence passed. Most of the felons didn't even have time to protest. Dominicans, dressed in their black and white robes, moved from one scaffold to another whispering the final absolution. The crowd thronging there sometimes greeted the appearance of a prisoner with curses and yells. Now and again a friend or relative would shout their farewells and lift a tankard in salute. Claverley waited until the prison door opened, then pushed his way through into the sombre gatehouse. The doorkeeper recognised him.

'We are nearly finished, Claverley!' he shouted. 'And by dusk York will be a safer place.'

'I've come for the Limner!' Claverley snapped, leaning down from his horse. 'Where is he?'

The porter's beer-sodden face stared up. 'What do you want him for?'

'I need to talk to him.'

'Well, only if you know the path to hell.'

Claverley groaned and beat his saddlehorn.

'The bugger's dead,' the porter laughed. 'Hanged not an hour since.'

Claverley, conscious of his companions, their horses growing restless in the enclosed space, cursed colourfully.

'What now?' Corbett asked.

Claverley turned, spat in the direction of the porter, then tapped the side of his nose.

'There's nothing for it,' he whispered. 'Let me introduce you to one of my great secrets!'

On the other side of York, another man was dying. The Unknown lay on a pallet bed in a small, stark chamber of the Lazar hospital, his sweat-soaked hair fanned out against the white bolster.

'It's all over,' he whispered. 'I shall not leave here alive.'

The Franciscan, crouching by the bed, grasped his hand and did not disagree.

'I can feel no life in my legs,' the Unknown muttered. He

127

forced a smile. 'In my youth, Father, I was a superb horseman. I could ride like the wind.' He moved his head slightly. 'What happens after death, Father?'

'Only God knows,' the Franciscan replied. 'But I think it's like a journey, like being born all over again. A baby struggles against leaving the womb, we struggle against leaving life but, as we do after we're born, we forget and journey on. What is important,' the Franciscan added, 'is how prepared we are for that journey.'

'I have sinned,' the Unknown whispered. 'I have sinned against Heaven and earth. I, a knight of the Temple, a defender of the city of Acre, have committed dreadful sins of hate and a desire for vengeance.'

'Tell me,' the Franciscan replied. 'Make your confession now. Receive absolution.'

The Unknown needed no further prompting but, staring up at the ceiling, began to recite his life: his youth on a farm in Barnsleydale; his admission to the Temple; those final, bloody days at Acre followed by the long years of pent-up bitterness in the dungeons of the Old Man of the Mountain. The Franciscan listened quietly; only now and again did he interrupt and softly ask a question. The knight always answered. At the end the Franciscan lifted his hand, carefully enunciating the words of absolution. He promised that, the following morning, he'd bring the Viaticum after Mass. The Unknown grasped the friar's hand.

'Father, in all truth, I must tell what I know to someone else.'

'A Templar?' the Franciscan asked. 'The commanders are gathered at Framlingham.'

The Unknown closed his eyes and sighed. 'No, the traitor may be there.' He opened his cracked lips, gasping for air. 'The King's Council is in York, yes?'

The Franciscan nodded. The Unknown squeezed his hand tightly.

'For the love of God, Father, I must speak to one of the King's Council. A man I can trust. Please, Father.' The eyes in that thin, disfigured face burned with life. 'Please, before I die!'

Chapter 8

Claverley led Corbett and his companions from the Pavement up towards the Minster, and into a more refined, serene quarter of the city. The streets were broad and clean, the houses on either side had their plaster painted pink and white, the upright beams a polished or a dark mahogany, sometimes gilt-edged around windows and doors. Each stood, four or five storeys high, in its own little garden. The windows on the bottom floors were filled with glass and on the top storey with horn or oiled linen. Claverley stopped in front of one which stood on a corner of an alleyway, across from the Jackanapes tavern. He brought up the iron clanger carved in the shape of a monk's face, and rapped loudly. At first there was no sound, though Corbett could see the glow of candlelight through the windows.

'Don't worry.' Claverley grinned over his shoulder. 'She'll be at home.'

At last the door swung open. A maid poked her head out. Claverley whispered to her and the door closed. Corbett heard chains being removed, then it swung open and a small, grey-haired lady, dressed in a white, gold-edged veil and a gown of dark burgundy, came out. She smiled and kissed Claverley on his cheek; bright button eyes in a swarthy face studied Corbett and his companions.

'Well, you'd best come in,' she said huskily. 'You can leave your horses in the stable at the Jackanapes.'

Whilst Maltote led their mounts off, the woman took them

into what she called 'her downstairs parlour', a long, comfortable chamber which must have stretched the length of the house. Through the open window at the far end, Corbett glimpsed flowerbeds and a small orchard of apple trees. The room was luxurious. There had been rushes in the passageway outside, but in here carpets lay on the floor and broad strips of bright cloth hung against the wall. A tapestry was fixed above the hearth, and on a long beam which spanned the ceiling stood row upon row of flickering candles.

'Sir Hugh Corbett,' Claverley made the introductions. 'May I introduce Jocasta Kitcher, gentlewoman, merchant, the maker of fine cloth, owner of the Jackanapes tavern and, in her time, a much travelled lady.'

'Once a flatterer always a flatterer,' Jocasta retorted.

She ushered her visitors towards the hearth as a maid, hurrying from the kitchens, pulled up chairs around the weak fire. At first there was confusion: Ranulf knocked a stool over and then Dame Jocasta insisted that they 'partake of her hospitality', telling the maid to bring goblets of wine and a tray of marzipan biscuits.

Corbett's stomach was still unsettled after the executions, but the effusive bonhomie of this little lady and the air of mystery around her soon distracted him. He sat on his chair and sipped the wine, surprised at its sweet coolness.

Dame Jocasta leaned forward. 'My cellars are always flooded,' she declared. 'Oh, not with sewer muck. York has underground rivers and the water is icy cold, it keeps the white wine chilled.'

'Are there many such rivers?' Corbett asked.

'Oh, Lord above.' Jocasta twirled her cup, inlaid with mother-of-pearl, between her hands. 'York is two cities, Sir Hugh. There's what you see in the streets, but – ' her voice dropped to a deep whisper – 'underneath the lanes there's another city built by the Romans: it has sewers and paths, long forgotten.' She grinned. 'I know, my husband and I used those sewers a great deal. Oh, don't look so puzzled,' she rattled on. 'Hasn't Claverley told you?'

'That's the reason I brought him here!' Claverley declared. 'I haven't yet told him our secrets, Dame Jocasta, but I thought you could help. There's a counterfeiter in York,' he continued hurriedly.

'Then trap and hang him!'

'This is different,' Corbett replied. He took a gold coin and handed it over.

Jocasta's hand was warm and soft, her fingers covered with expensive rings. She grasped the coin and examined it with a sigh of admiration, letting it drop from hand to hand, weighing it carefully, studying the rim and the cross carved on either side.

'This is pure gold.'

'Whatever they are,' Corbett intervened, 'they are not from the king's Mint and are issued without royal licence. Now, I agree, Dame Jocasta, counterfeiters usually take one good coin and make two bad, adulterating the silver with base alloys and metals. However, I've never heard of anyone using the finest gold to counterfeit coins.'

Dame Jocasta lifted her head. 'Sir Hugh, you need not tell me about counterfeiting. Forty years ago – aye I look younger than I am,' she added merrily, her small eyes bright with laughter. '. . . forty years ago I ran wild in this city. My parents could not control me. On a hot midsummer's day I went to a fair outside Micklegate Bar. I met the merriest rogue on God's own earth, my husband, Robard. Now he was a clerk, fallen on hard times. He couldn't abide the stuffy Chanceries and the long, miserable-faced clerks.'

She paused as Ranulf choked on the biscuit he was eating. Corbett's glare soon made him clear his throat. Ranulf hid his face, staring into the wine cup as if something very precious lay there.

'Robard was a knave born and bred,' Jocasta continued.

'He could sing like a robin and dance the maypole into the ground. He was attracted to mischief like a cat to cream. I loved him immediately. I still do, even though he's ten years dead.'

Claverley stretched over and touched her hand. 'Finish your story,' he murmured.

'Well, well, well.' Jocasta held up the gold piece, she turned it so it caught the candlelight. 'Robard would have loved this. He wanted to be rich, amass silver and go to foreign parts to be a great merchant or warrior. I became part of his knavery. I'd steal out of my house at night and join him in the moonlight. We'd lie on the tombstones of St Peter's Church and he would tell me tales of what we could do. We became handfast, betrothed, then Robard's desire to become rich led him into counterfeiting. He became known amongst the cunning and upright men of the city, the cranks, the palliards, the foists, pickpockets, all the scum of the earth.' She shrugged. 'We hired a small forge just off Coney Street and began to counterfeit coins. This was in the old king's time, when the governance of the city was not what it should be . . . Then we were caught. At the assizes Robard was given two choices: either hang from the gallows on the Pavement or join Prince Edward's Crusade. Of course, he chose the latter. The levies massed outside in the meadows in Bishop's Fields just across the river. Robard, however, was a pressed man: he was kept in chains until he boarded the king's ships. I went with him.'

'You went to Outremer!' Corbett exclaimed.

'Oh, yes. Three years in all. But we came back rich. We bought the tavern across the alleyway: Robard became a landlord, an ale-master and a taverner. My parents were dead. I became his wife, but old habits die hard, Sir Hugh. Once the rogues of the city knew he was home, we were never left alone. Robard would receive visitors at the dead of night but he always kept within the law.' She laughed self-consciously. 'Or nearly so. Once again we were drawn into counterfeiting but, this time, I swear to God, I was not party to it. Now pride always goes before a fall. The king's justices returned to York, a grand jury was convened, and allegations were laid against my husband.'

Claverley interrupted. 'Twice convicted, Robard would have hanged. Moreover, his first crimes were still remembered. Dame Jocasta came before the sheriffs and a secret pact was made. Robard would receive a pardon but Jocasta swore a great oath that in future she would let the sheriffs and thief-takers know of crimes and felonies being planned in the city.'

'I turned king's evidence,' Dame Jocasta quietly added. 'And my husband never knew. Oh, I was selective. I still am. The little foists, the petty criminals, I ignore, but not those who kill and maim, the rapists and violators of churches. As any tavern-keeper does, I hear the whispers and I pass them on . . .'

'But your husband never knew?'

'Never,' Jocasta declared. 'And nor does anyone else except Claverley.' Her face became hard. 'I don't dress in widow's weeds.' She tapped her chest. 'Robard's still here. I close my eyes and I can hear him singing. At night, if I turn on the bolster, I see his face smiling at me. He wasn't a bad man, Sir Hugh, but oh, Lord save us, he loved mischief.'

'And yet you tell us now?' Corbett asked.

'Before I left York to meet you, Sir Hugh,' Claverley interrupted, 'I came here. If Limner refused to help you, Dame Jocasta promised she would.' He shrugged and turned to the woman. 'But Limner's hanged,' he announced flatly.

'God grant him safe passage.'

'Dame Jocasta and I have known each other for years,' Claverley explained. 'True,' he wagged a finger, 'the art of counterfeiting may well be a subtle one but, in this city, Dame Jocasta knows everything about it.'

Corbett stared through the window at the far end of the room and watched the sunshine die. A wild thought occurred to him: what if Jocasta was the master counterfeiter?

'I couldn't do it,' she declared, as if reading his thoughts. 'I don't have a forge or the precious metal. More importantly, I know all the secret whispers. Yet, I've heard nothing.' She held the coin up. 'And, believe me, tongues would certainly clack about this.'

Corbett cleared his throat and glanced away in embarrassment.

'So, how is it done?' Ranulf asked. 'Who's responsible?'

Jocasta put her cup down. 'Sir Hugh, I have never seen a coin like this before. Most counterfeiters debase the king's coin, yes?'

Corbett agreed.

'So, why should someone produce gold coins except . . .' She paused.

'Except what?'

'Well, let us say, Sir Hugh, you found a pot of gold. No, not at the end of a rainbow, but a treasure trove: cups, mazers, ewers, crosses. What would you do?'

'I'd take it to the sheriffs or the royal justices.'

Dame Jocasta laughed: Claverley and Ranulf joined in. The old woman shook her head.

'I am not mocking you, Sir Hugh; you are an honest man.' Her face became serious. 'But what would happen then?'

Now Corbett smiled. 'Well, the royal clerks would seize the gold. They'd examine it then come back and interrogate me.'

'And how long would that last?'

'A year, maybe even two: until I'd proved both my innocence and that the gold was truly treasure trove.'

'So!' Jocasta exclaimed. 'You found some treasure. You are honest but the king's clerks take it and all you get is a sea of troubles.'

'Aye,' Corbett added. 'And at the end of it all, half of what I found, though, knowing the Exchequer officials as I do, I'd be lucky if I got a quarter.'

'So,' Ranulf spoke up. 'Dame Jocasta, this gold.' He paused.

'By the way, Master, Maltote has not returned.'

'Oh, he's probably in the tavern,' Corbett replied. 'You know Maltote: he'll be talking horses with the stable boy and grooms and downing tankards as if his life depended on it. What were you going to say?'

'Someone in York,' Ranulf continued, 'has found a treasure trove, melted it down and made coins. He has then used those coins to buy comforts and luxuries for himself.'

'Precisely,' Dame Jocasta agreed. 'It's the only way. If you take gold and silver objects to a goldsmith, you immediately become suspect, either as a felon or someone who's found treasure trove and is flouting the king's rights in the matter. Now, such treasure is easy to trace. No goldsmith would be party to that.' She played with the coin in her hand. 'Whoever made this has a very good forge and the means to buy all the coining tools.'

'But wouldn't anyone become suspicious?' Claverley asked. 'If gold vessels can be traced back to their original owner, so can gold coins.'

'Not if fifty or sixty appeared at the same time,' Jocasta replied. 'And that's what Robard used to do with his counterfeit coins. The more you distribute, the safer you are. The man who counterfeited these coins did the same. He must have the means to move round York and bring these coins into circulation without raising suspicion.' She rubbed the coin between her fingers. 'And that's the whole beauty of it. All a goldsmith and a banker will do is weigh coins on a scale. After all, its not their fault if these coins end up in their possession. They have become party to the crime but can act the innocent. They have sold foodstuffs or cloths, wines or whatever. They have a right to be paid: the coins are accepted and people become forgetful.'

Corbett leaned back in the chair. 'Brilliant,' he whispered. 'You find gold. You melt it down into coins, you distribute them and, by doing so, bring everyone else into your game. At

the same time you evade the law and become very, very rich.'
He looked at Dame Jocasta. 'And you have no idea . . .?'

'Don't stare at me like that, Clerk,' she teased back. 'This
counterfeiter is no ruffian or miscreant clipping coins or melting
them down over a charcoal fire. This cunning man is very
wealthy: he has the means and the wherewithal.'

'But couldn't the coins be traced?' Ranulf asked insistently.
'Someone, somewhere, would remember?'

Dame Jocasta pointed to Corbett's purse. 'Master Clerk,
you have good silver there? Can you remember exactly which
coin was given to you by what person?'

'But I'd remember a gold coin,' Ranulf replied.

'Would you?' Jocasta retorted. 'If you thought it might be
seized and taken away from you? However,' she handed the
coin back to Corbett, 'you have a point. This counterfeiter
probably doesn't use coins to buy anything from city merchants.
After all, anyone paying gold here and there would eventually
be recognised.'

'So?' Corbett asked.

Dame Jocasta looked into the flames of the fire. She watched
the small, sweet-smelling pine logs crackle and snap on their
charcoal bed.

'I wish Robard was here,' she whispered. 'He'd know.' She
glanced up quickly. 'You are staying at Framlingham, the
Templar manor?'

Corbett nodded.

'Why not start there?' Jocasta murmured. 'The Templars
have the means: woods and copses to hide a secret forge. They
import foodstuffs and goods from abroad. They have connections
with bankers and goldsmiths. And, unless I am mistaken, this
gold appeared at the time the Templars arrived in York.'

'Yes, it did,' Corbett replied. 'The king and Court moved
down from the Scottish march and stayed outside York. Shortly
after the Templar commanders arrived, these coins began to
appear.'

138

'But where would they get the gold from?' Claverley asked.

Corbett toyed with his Chancery ring which bore the insignia of the Secret Seal.

'They did grant the king a huge gift,' Ranulf remarked. 'And they have treasures not known to anyone.'

Corbett recalled the secret room at Framlingham. Was there a connection between this gold and the murders?

'Sir Hugh?'

Corbett shook himself from his reverie. 'I am sorry, Dame Jocasta.' He rose to his feet, took her hand and pressed it with his lips. 'I thank you for your help.'

'You are not just hunting a counterfeiter, are you?' she asked shrewdly. 'Not the king's principal clerk!'

Corbett stroked her cheek gently with his finger. 'No, Domina, I am not. As usual,' he added bitterly, 'I am hunting demons: men who kill for the-devil-knows-what reason.'

'Then you should be careful, Clerk,' she replied softly. 'For those who hunt demons either become hunted, or demons themselves.'

Ranulf, standing in the shadows of the doorway, saw his master start, as if Jocasta's words had struck home, but then the old lady smiled and the tension eased. Corbett and Claverley made their farewells and followed Ranulf out and across into the yard of the Jackanapes tavern: here, a guilty-faced Maltote, brimming tankard to his lips, was declaiming to the round-eyed ostlers and slatterns what an important man he was. Ranulf, ever with an eye for mischief, joined the group and began to tease Maltote, whilst Corbett and Claverley went into the taproom. They took a table overlooking the small garden. For a while Corbett stared out, watching the sun set in a glorious explosion of colours. Claverley ordered some ale. Corbett sipped his, thinking of Dame Jocasta's warning as he fought the waves of homesickness. The flowers and the garden reminded him of home and, in his heart, Corbett knew that he would not stay here much longer. He wanted Maeve and Eleanor. He'd even sit for hours and listen to Uncle Morgan's fabulous boasting about the great Welsh heroes. He wanted to sleep in a bed with no dagger by his side and walk without a warbelt strapped round his waist.

'Was that helpful?' Claverley interrupted.

'Oh, yes, it was.' Corbett smiled an apology. 'We at least know the counterfeiter is powerful, wealthy, has access to gold and knows how to distribute these coins.'

'Could it be the Templars?' Claverley asked. 'At the Guildhall we've heard rumours . . .'

'I don't know,' Corbett replied. He leaned across the table and clapped the man on his shoulder. 'I am not the best of companions: Roger, are you a family man?'

'Twice married,' the under-sheriff replied with a grin. 'My first wife died but my second has given me lovely children.'

'Do you ever tire of hunting demons?' Corbett asked.

Claverley shook his head. 'I heard what Dame Jocasta said, Sir Hugh.' He sipped from his tankard and continued. 'We all bear the mark of Cain. Like you, Sir Hugh, I've seen the breakdown of law and order, when the demons come out of the shadows. So no, I don't ever tire of fighting them. If we don't hunt them, as God is my witness, they'll eventually come hunting us.'

Across the rim of his tankard, Corbett stared at Claverley. A good man, Corbett thought, just and upright. He promised himself to mention Claverley's name to the king. Ranulf and Maltote joined him: they would have continued their banter but one look at Corbett's face made Ranulf change his mind.

'Where now, Master?'

Corbett leaned back against the wall. 'We are not going back to Framlingham,' he declared. 'Not tonight. The Botham Bar road is dark and dangerous. Master Claverley, one favour, or rather four.'

'My orders are to give you every assistance.'

'First, I'd like rooms here.'

'That can be arranged.'

'Secondly,' Corbett said, 'our counterfeiter must have a forge. Now the city has tax rolls, forges are always part of an assessment.'

'Unless it's a secret one,' Claverley added.

'I also want a list,' Corbett persisted, 'of all those who have a licence to import goods into the city. Finally, if this gold is treasure trove, it must have been found during some building work. No burgess can do that without a licence from the aldermen.'

'Agreed,' Claverley said. 'So, you want a list of blacksmiths or anyone owning a forge: those with a licence to import and any citizen who has received a writ permitting him to build?'

'Yes, as soon as possible!'

'The Templars,' Claverley continued, 'will be on all three lists.'

'That's an extra favour,' Corbett replied. 'On the morning of the attack on the king, the grand master, Jacques de Molay, and four of his principal commanders, Legrave, Branquier, Baddlesmere and Symmes, came into the city. Now Branquier left early, or so he said. Baddlesmere and Symmes were by themselves for a long period of time whilst Legrave accompanied the grand master to a goldsmith's in Stonegate. Now York is a great city, but people know each other. The Templars would stand out. I want you to find just exactly what they did that morning.'

Claverley whistled under his breath. 'And where do I start?'

Corbett grinned and gestured around him. 'Ask the tavern-masters and landlords. Whatever you find, I'll be grateful.'

Claverley finished his drink and made his farewells. He promised that, if he discovered any information, he would personally travel out to Framlingham. Then he went across to talk to the landlord, standing behind a counter made out of wine barrels. Corbett saw the fellow nod. Claverley lifted his hand, shouted that all would be well and went out into the street.

'I am tired,' Corbett declared. 'Ranulf, Maltote, you can do what you want, provided you are back in our chamber within the hour.'

And, leaving his companions to grumble about 'Master Long Face', Corbett followed the landlord up to the second floor to what was grandly described as the tavern's principal guest-chamber. The room had only two beds but the landlord promised to provide a third. Whilst servants brought up straw-filled mattresses, new bolsters, fresh jugs of water and a tray containing bread and wine, Corbett went and lay down on a bed. This time he did not think of Leighton Manor and Maeve but tried to marshal his thoughts. He heard a noise in the passage outside, then Ranulf and Maltote burst into the room.

'For the love of God!' Corbett groaned, swinging his legs off the bed.

Ranulf, his face a picture of innocence, pulled across a stool and sat opposite Corbett.

'That old woman frightened you, didn't she?' he demanded.

'No, she did not frighten me, Ranulf,' Corbett replied. 'I am already frightened.' He pointed to his writing implements laid out on the table. 'Think of the murderers we have hunted, Ranulf. There's always been a motive: greed, lechery, treason. There's always a pattern to the killings, as the assassin removes those who block his way or may have guessed his identity. Yet this is different: here we have a man killing without purpose.'

'But you said the Templars were divided? They want revenge on the king.'

'In which case,' Corbett retorted, 'why kill Reverchien? Why attack me? And what threat in God's name did poor Peterkin pose? Moreover, there's no connection between the three.' Corbett continued. 'Oh, yes, if the king was injured or killed: if his principal clerk suffered some dreadful mishap, I suppose there's a logic to that. But why Reverchien and Peterkin?'

'Perhaps they knew something,' Ranulf retorted.

'Perhaps,' Corbett replied. 'But then we come to the second problem. How? Murston may have shot an arrow at the king but how did he die so quickly? How was that fire caused? Reverchien died in the centre of a maze early on a spring morning, Peterkin burst into flames in the middle of a busy kitchen.'

Corbett paused, chewing the corner of his lip. 'And what progress have we made? We know the Templar Order is demoralised, possibly splitting into factions: I'm sure that is why de Molay has come to England. These factions may be manifesting themselves through the attacks against Philip of France as well as our own king. We also have these warnings, sent by that strange sect "the Assassins". We know there's some mystery in the Order, hence those secret rooms at Framlingham. We've learnt Murston was eaten up with revenge and bitterness, yet he must have been managed by someone else.'

Corbett paused. 'The killer,' he continued after a while, 'is using some form of secret fire. He was practising with it amongst the trees along the Botham Bar road: that poor pedlar paid for his curiosity with his life. We think it's a Templar commander but, if all the Templars are confined to Framlingham and the city gates are so closely guarded, who attached that notice to Murston's gibbeted corpse? And who could have sent a similar warning to me? Whatever the Templars did in York, we have established that by the time these arrows were fired at me, they were on the road back to Framlingham Manor.'

'That masked rider, maybe he's the assassin?' Maltote asked hopefully. 'Or one of the commanders in disguise?'

'The counterfeit coins,' Ranulf interjected, 'may also be Templar villainy.'

'Possibly,' Corbett said. 'But whatever, Ranulf . . .' He lay back on his bed. 'If there's no method in this madness, if the assassin is killing for the sake of it, then he'll strike again and again.'

143

'And what will we do?' Ranulf asked.

'In the end,' Corbett replied, 'we will go back to the king and report what we have found: a divided, demoralised Order, bereft of its original purpose.' He half sat up, leaning on one arm. 'And if I report that,' he concluded, 'it will only be a matter of time before the Exchequer officials begin to ask why such a wealthy Order should exist when it lacks purpose and, moreover, is riddled with treason, sorcery, murder and other scandals?'

The serjeant patrolling the great meadow at Framlingham Manor stared down at the boat bobbing on the lake. 'It's time the old man came in,' he grumbled.

Hitching his swordbelt higher, he began the long walk down to the lakeside. Nevertheless, the sunset was glorious, and a cool evening breeze soothed the serjeant's sweat-soaked brow.

'Oh, let the old one fish,' he muttered to himself.

He sat down on the grass, took off his helmet and pulled back the mail coif beneath. He studied Odo: the old librarian had taken his boat *The Ghost of the Tower*, and had been fishing for some time.

'More bloody use than what I've been doing,' the serjeant grumbled as he grabbed a clump of grass to cool his sweaty cheeks.

The garrison at Framlingham had relaxed after that snooping royal clerk and his companions had left: that is, until the messenger had arrived and de Molay and the other great ones had gathered in the hall for a secret council. Orders had gone out, reinforcing the grand master's edict that no one was to leave Framlingham, whilst any stranger found wandering on the estate was to be arrested immediately. The Templar serjeant chewed on a piece of grass, narrowing his eyes against the setting sun as he watched Brother Odo's black cloak flap and curl in the evening breeze. The old librarian was apparently fighting to hold the long rod and line he was wielding. The

144

Templar serjeant envied the serenity of the scene after the turbulence of the last few days. The news of the attack upon the king, the killing of Reverchien and Peterkin the cook were known to all. Very few mentioned Murston's death, though many felt guilty at what he had done. Nevertheless, Murston had always been a hothead: just because he had served in Outremer, he'd set himself up as an authority on what was right and what was wrong.

The Templar lay back in the grass and stared up at the fleecy clouds.

'I wish I was away from here,' he whispered. 'But where?'

The fall of Acre had put a stop to service abroad. No more dark-skinned girls, no more wandering around the bazaars. There was now little excitement about battle or talk of guarding the holy sepulchre. The best one could expect was lonely garrison duty in a God-forsaken manor house or, if you were lucky, some expedition into the Middle Sea to fight the corsairs. The serjeant rubbed his eyes; it wasn't his duty to wonder or to speculate. Murston's fate had put an end to all that. And who was he to question the masters of his Order? They knew best. They had the secret knowledge which they discussed behind closed doors. The serjeant remembered that lonely garret at the top of Framlingham Manor. What *did* go on there, he wondered? Why were only de Molay and Branquier allowed to go in? Why the purple wax candles and the chanting? He'd once been on guard outside, when his superiors had come out, he'd noticed how both were covered in dust from head to toe. What was so special in that room, the serjeant wondered, that such important men should lie face down in the dust? He heard a sound and struggled to his feet. Odo was moving as if straining at the rod, but then the Templar serjeant glimpsed the fire burning in the prow of the boat. He dropped his helmet and began to run.

'Brother Odo! Brother Odo!' He shouted, but still that black cowled figure sat as if impervious to the leaping flames. The serjeant undid his swordbelt, running until his lungs were fit to burst. He watched as the boat and Brother Odo suddenly erupted into a sheet of fire. The Templar fell to his knees, shaking with fright. He watched the fire consuming the boat and its occupant from prow to stern; even the water of the lake seemed to provide no protection.

'Oh, Lord save us,' he gasped, 'from Satan's fire!'

Chapter 9

Corbett and his companions arrived back at Framlingham to find the manor in complete uproar. As soon as they dismounted in the stable yard, Baddlesmere, whiskers bristling, hurried out to greet them.

'Sir Hugh!' He swallowed hard. 'You'd best come to see the grand master!'

Despite the warm sun and blue skies, Corbett felt his feeling of oppression return. He glanced round the stables: Templar soldiers, now doing the tasks of the ostlers and grooms, stared blankly at him.

'There's been another death, hasn't there?' Corbett asked.

Baddlesmere nodded, indicating with his hand for Corbett to follow him.

The clerk told Maltote to take care of the horses and, with Ranulf striding beside him, walked into the manor. Baddlesmere took them across a small cloister-garth and into the grand master's chamber: a stark, unfurnished cell, much bigger than Corbett's but just as austere with its whitewashed walls, black crucifix, and its stone floor covered with rushes. De Molay sat behind a small table, a metal crucifix in the centre. The other Templar commanders were already assembled, their agitation apparent from their grave faces and red-rimmed eyes.

De Molay rose as Corbett came in, snapping at Baddlesmere to bring in extra chairs. Once they were seated, the grand master tapped the top of the table.

'Sir Hugh, whilst you were gone yesterday, Brother Odo

died. Or rather, he was killed. Late in the afternoon he went fishing, as he often did, in his small boat, *The Ghost of the Tower*. He stayed on the lake some time: this was not out of the ordinary. A Templar serjeant watched him and was about to go down to tell him it was time for Vespers and the evening meal, when he saw flames in the prow. He was too late: Brother Odo and the boat were consumed in a sheet of fire.'

Corbett put his face into his hands and said softly, 'I spoke to him just before I left for York, I visited him in the library. He showed me his chronicle; I could see how proud he was of it.' Corbett gazed at the others. 'Why?' he asked. 'How could it happen?'

'We don't know,' Branquier retorted. 'We don't bloody know, Corbett: that's why we're waiting for you. You are the king's clerk.' He jabbed a finger at him. 'You were sent here to find out. So, find out!'

'It's not as easy as that.' Legrave leaned forward. 'How can Sir Hugh deal with this? Brother Odo went fishing, everything was calm and serene. For the love of God, the boat was in the centre of the lake! Nobody swam out. Nobody else was with him. Yet both he and the craft were consumed by a fire which not even the water of the lake could extinguish.'

'What remains have been found?' Ranulf asked abruptly.

The Templars looked at him with disdain.

Corbett spoke up. 'My friend's question is an important one.'

'Very little,' De Molay replied. 'Brother Odo's corpse was charred beyond recognition. A few burnt planks of the boat but that's all.'

'Nothing else?' Corbett asked.

'Nothing,' de Molay replied. 'Just floating, charred remains. It was difficult to tell one thing from the other.'

'And who pulled these out?' Corbett asked.

'Well,' Branquier replied, 'the Templar serjeant could do

nothing. He raised the alarm and we all hurried down to the lakeside. Another boat, moored some distance away, was used: by then the flames were beginning to die down. Brother Odo's remains have already been sheeted and coffined, he'll be buried tonight. What we want to know, Sir Hugh, is why this happened? And how can it be stopped?'

Corbett gazed across the room: the tun of wine he'd brought as a gift from the king stood broached on a side-table, the red wax seal of the vintner now hanging down like a huge blob of blood. He sighed and pushed back his chair.

'I don't know,' he replied. 'Though I tell you this: forget the tittle-tattle and gossip about fires from hell.'

Corbett then told them what he had found on the Botham Bar road. De Molay sat up, his eyes bright with excitement.

'So you know the name of the victim and how he died?'

'Yes. I also believe someone was in that wood, using a strange form of fire. Now, when I listened to Brother Odo's account of the fall of Acre the evening before last, he talked of the Turks throwing fire into the city.'

'But that was nothing,' Branquier intervened. 'Just bundles of wood faggots, soaked in tar, lit, then thrown as a fire ball by a catapult or mangonel.'

'Are you saying the same thing is happening here?' Symmes asked.

Corbett saw movement beneath the knight's gown and realised the Templar still had his pet weasel with him.

'But that's impossible,' Baddlesmere scoffed before Corbett could reply. 'Such fires are clumsy. Nothing more than heaps of burning material. How can that explain the death of Reverchien at the centre of a maze? Nobody else was there. Or Peterkin in the kitchen? And, as for Brother Odo . . .'

'What about a fire arrow?' Corbett interrupted. 'Covered in tar and pitch.' He shrugged. 'I know, before you answer, if a fire arrow had been loosed into Brother Odo's craft, he would have tried to put it out and, if that failed, just jumped into the

149

water and swam for shore.' He paused. 'Grand Master, may I ask one favour?'

De Molay spread his hands.

'Permission,' Corbett continued, 'to go round this manor, to question whom I like, to poke my long nose – as others put it – into your affairs.'

'Granted,' de Molay replied. 'On one condition, Sir Hugh. The chambers I showed you yesterday? You must stay well away from those. As for the rest, we are in your hands.'

Corbett thanked him and left.

'Did you really believe that?' Ranulf hissed as they walked back to the guesthouse.

'Corbett stopped. 'Believe what, Ranulf?'

'Fire arrows!'

'What else could I say? Here we have a man fishing in the centre of a lake. Within minutes, nay, seconds even, both he and the boat are consumed by fire. What else could have caused it?' Corbett shrugged. 'It's a wild guess but the best I can do.' He plucked Ranulf by the sleeve and drew him into a window embrasure. 'Whatever we discover,' he whispered, 'we keep silent about it. I believe the assassin was in that room.'

'What about the masked rider in the woods?' Ranulf asked.

'I don't know, but he wasn't in that kitchen when Peterkin died. Now the assassin, this Sagittarius, could be de Molay, or one of the other four, or any combination of them working together. I don't know why the assassin strikes and I don't know how but, whoever it is, he now realises, thanks to our discovery on the Botham Bar road, that we have glimpsed some of the truth.'

'In which case he may try to shut our mouths.'

'He's tried that already,' Corbett retorted, 'but yes, he may try it again. In doing so, though, he might make a mistake.'

Corbett poked his head out and looked down the empty passageway. 'I said that we would stay together, but now we'll have to work separately. You and Maltote are to scour this manor. Examine the smithy, go out into the fields and copses. Look for any trace of fire or scorch-marks and, if possible, some secret forge.'

'And you, Master?'

'I am going to the library. Brother Odo may have died not because he lived in this manor but also because he discovered something. The assassin must have seen me visit him. I believe the truth, or some of it, lies amongst Brother Odo's papers.'

Ranulf went back to the guesthouse to collect Maltote whilst Corbett, taking directions from one of the guards, traced his steps back to the library. The door was open. He went inside and stared round the long, shadow-filled room.

'God rest you, Brother Odo,' he whispered. 'And God forgive me if I was responsible for your death.'

He walked down the library to Brother Odo's carrel; the table was littered with scraps of paper and the great roll of vellum containing Odo's chronicle. Corbett laid this out flat: he turned over the squares of vellum, following the dramatic history of the fall of Acre. Corbett searched this carefully, wondering if the manuscript contained some reference to the secret fire. However, although Odo's drawings contained mangonels throwing flaming bundles of tar, there was nothing significant. Corbett closed it with a sigh and picked up the scraps of parchment. Some were old scribblings but one caught Corbett's eye. Apparently done on the day he died, Odo had drawn the picture of a long-nosed clerk and beside it a rough drawing of a crow. Corbett smiled at the pun on his own name, '*le Corbeil*', the French word for 'crow'. The rest of the jottings, however, were in some form of shorthand. Corbett remembered Brother Odo's description of Anglo-Saxon runes. There were the same markings, done time and time again, all with question marks beside them. A few he could decipher, though he found it impossible to make sense of them all. He went back along the library, searching amongst the shelves until he found what he was looking for: a thick, yellow-leaved *'Codex Grammaticus'*, bound in calf-skin and kept together by a huge clasp. Corbett pulled this from the shelf and took it back to the carrel. He opened it and began to leaf through: the codex contained references to Greek and Hebrew and, in a well-thumbed appendix at the end, all the letters of the alphabet with the Anglo-Saxon runes beside them. Corbett seized a quill, took Odo's scrap of paper and tried to decipher the dead librarian's scrawls. At first he could make no sense, the runes formed words which did not exist, then Corbett remembered that Odo had used Latin in his chronicle. He tried again and the words were deciphered: *'Ignis Diaboli'*, 'Devil Fire'; *'Liber Ignium'*, 'The Book of Fires', and, finally a phrase repeated time and again, 'Bacon's Mystery'.

'Sweet God in heaven!' Corbett whispered. 'What on earth can that refer to?'

The Devil's fire, he thought: that's how Odo described the flames which consumed poor Peterkin and his colleague Reverchien. The 'Book of Fires'? Was that some sort of grimoire? A book of spells? And 'Bacon's Mystery'? What had that got to do with the terrible fires? Corbett, mystified, got to his feet: for a while he searched for an index to what the library contained but, when he found it, he could discover no reference to a 'Book of Fires', or anything which would clarify the phrase 'Bacon's Mystery'. He was just clearing the desk, rolling up the notes he had made, when he heard a sound at the back of the library, the creak of a door followed by the bolts being driven home. Corbett rose. Drawing the dagger from his belt, he stared down the library, but all he could see were the dustmotes dancing in the sunbeams above the highly polished floor.

'Who's there?' he called. Corbett moved to one side. 'Who's there?' he repeated.

'Knowest thou that we go forth and return.' The voice was low and unrecognisable, though the words rang hollow round the library, like the sombre tolling of a death knell.

Corbett heard another sound, a metallic click. He threw himself sideways even as the crossbow bolt whipped by his head and smacked into the wall behind him.

'Knowest thou,' the voice grew louder, 'that what thou possesses shall escape thee in the end and return to us.'

Again the click. Corbett, now hiding behind the shelves, heard the thud as another barbed quarrel sank into the woodwork above his head. Corbett fought hard to control his breathing. He stared wildly around: the windows were too small, no escape there.

'Knowest thou,' the voice again intoned, 'that we hold you and will keep thee until the account be closed!'

Corbett, lying flat, peered round the shelves. His heart skipped a beat. At the far end of the library stood a figure, a tilting helm on his head, a jet black robe covering him from head to toe, an arbalest in his hand. Corbett watched the winch being pulled back, he heard the catch click and a third bolt speed to where his head had been. Another sound, a footfall, the assassin was slowly drawing closer. If Corbett rose and ran towards him, he'd never be fast enough: a crossbow bolt would take him before he reached his mysterious assailant. Corbett's mouth went dry. He fought hard to curb his fear. For some strange reason he kept thinking of a royal messenger riding up the pathway to Leighton Manor, Maeve hurrying down to greet him . . .

Corbett wiped the sweat from his face and gripped his Welsh dagger even more firmly. He looked across the library and glimpsed a small postern door behind one of the carrels. 'Oh, Christ Jesus,' he prayed, 'let it be unlocked.'

He pushed his head out but drew back quickly as another crossbow bolt whirred like a hawk through the air. Then he was up before the mysterious archer could fit another bolt. Swearing and cursing, Corbett pulled the carrel aside and raised the latch, but the door wouldn't move. Corbett blindly crashed against it even as the footfalls behind him drew closer. Then he glimpsed the bolts on the top. He drew these back, the door opened, creaking on its leather hinges. Corbett was through it, slamming it shut even as the crossbow bolt thudded into the other side. The door led into a passageway and Corbett ran blindly round a corner, so quickly he knocked a Templar serjeant flying. Ignoring his shouts, Corbett continued running until he was through an open door which led into a small disused garden behind the tilt-yard.

For a while Corbett crouched to catch his breath then, resheathing his dagger, he made his way back to the guesthouse. He slammed and locked the door behind him, checked the chamber carefully and sprawled on the bed. Eventually relief gave way to anger, a terrible fury at how he had been so nearly trapped. It was tempting to sweep through the manor demanding to see de Molay and seek an investigation, but what would that prove? Nothing except his own fear. The assassin would have slipped out of the library and be impossible to trace. Corbett got up and splashed water over his face. He dried himself slowly, recalling the cloaked figure, the arbalest and the bolts whistling through the air all around him.

'At least,' Corbett whispered, 'I know you are not from Hell.'

He paused: the attack in the library had been a desperate move. Was that why Odo had been killed? To prevent him discovering the cause of that dreadful fire? The assassin would have checked the carrel but, unaware of the runes, he would have overlooked the piece of parchment Corbett now kept in his wallet. There was a knock on the door.

'Master!'

Corbett went and unlocked it. Ranulf and Maltote swept excitedly into the room.

'They are here!' Maltote exclaimed.

'Shut up!' Ranulf shouted. 'I found them, Master, scorch-marks, the same as we found on the Botham Bar road. You remember the trees which ring the curtain wall around the manor? Well, Maltote and I discovered them there.' He peered at his master's face. 'Don't you want to come? Master, what has happened?'

Corbett told them.

'In the library!' Ranulf exclaimed. 'Why there, Master?'

'First, because the assassin knew I was there. Secondly, he wanted to stop me from finding anything.' Corbett withdrew the scrap of parchment from his wallet. 'Forget the scorch-marks. Maltote, I want you to go back into York.' Corbett crossed to the table and, seizing a quill, wrote a short note listing the phrases he had found in Odo's carrel. 'Go to the king, he's staying in the archbishop's palace at York Minster!' He handed over the message. 'Give this to him. If he interrogates you about what has happened here, tell him—' Corbett pulled a face – 'well, tell him the truth. But I need an answer to that as soon as possible.'

'Can I go with him?' Ranulf asked expectantly.

'No, you can't. A few more days away from the fleshpots of York will do your soul, not to mention your body, the world of good.'

Maltote hurriedly went to fill the saddlebag. He came back to make his farewells and almost ran down the passageway.

'Well, there goes a happy man,' Ranulf remarked. 'But what do we do?'

'Let's go for a walk, Ranulf. The sunshine and fresh air will do us good.'

They sauntered out into the grounds. Corbett did his best to relax. They first went back to the library. The door was now open but when Corbett returned to the carrel, he found the crossbow bolts had been pulled from the woodwork. Apart from a few scratches on the carrel and postern door, there was little sign of any disturbance. They walked back to the stables. After making a few inquiries, Corbett found the serjeant who had seen Odo and his boat burst into flames.

'Come,' Corbett said, 'let's walk to the edge of the lake. Tell us what you saw.'

The serjeant shrugged, threw down the belt he had been mending and walked with them, describing what he'd seen.

'How long had Brother Odo been fishing?' Corbett interrupted.

'Oh, it must have been some time, two or three hours.'

'And you were on guard?'

'Yes, I was patrolling the meadow, bored out of my mind. Every so often I would look down at the lake. I was hot, I grew tired.' He paused as they entered the cool shade of the trees which fringed the edge of the lake. 'When I looked up, I saw the flame; it was as if the fire had sprung from the lake itself.'

Corbett pointed to the wooden causeway which stretched out into the lake.

'Odo's boat, *The Ghost of the Tower*, was moored here?'

'Oh yes. Odo would climb in, row himself out, then sit for hours with his rod and line.'

Corbett walked on to the causeway. It felt strange to have the lake moving and shimmering on either side. At the end of the platform, he peered down at fire-blackened fragments being washed to and fro.

'And you came down here?'

'Well, by the time I reached where you stand there was nothing left, just fire.'

Corbett looked over his shoulder. 'What do you mean?'

'Well, the fire burnt out the bottom of the boat but the lake seemed to make little difference to it.' The Templar looked worried. 'That's what made me think it was Devil's fire.'

'And when the flames did die?' Corbett asked.

'It took some time. Afterwards all that remained was wood, a few scraps of cloth and Brother Odo's mangled remains.'

'Is the lake well stocked with fish?' Ranulf asked.

'Of course,' the serjeant replied. 'Especially with trout. The

156

kitchen often serve it, nice and fresh, covered in a cream sauce.'

'But you saw no fish?' Ranulf asked. 'I mean, if Brother Odo had been fishing for hours and the lake's well stocked, he must have made a considerable catch.'

'I didn't see any fish but they may have burnt.'

Corbett thanked him and the serjeant walked back into the line of trees.

'You think Odo was already dead when the fire broke out, don't you?' Corbett asked.

'Yes, Master, I do.' Ranulf walked carefully backwards along the wooden causeway. 'Have you noticed, Master, how the trees on either side of the lake grow out and conceal this platform from view? Odo wouldn't be seen until he was in the centre of the lake. I think he was killed before he ever got into that boat. His body was lashed upright. He wore his cloak and cowl so nobody from the shore would notice. And why should an old Templar wear a cloak and cowl on a warm spring day? Moreover, if he was fishing, where is his catch, burnt or not?'

Corbett nodded. 'Very good, Ranulf, but the question still remains: how did the fire start?'

'Well, that's why I think he was dead,' Ranulf continued. 'Remember, Master, the serjeant said he saw flames licking the boat but Odo never moved to douse them, nor did he spring up in alarm or attempt to escape.' He blew his breath out. 'But that's all I can say. How the fire was started is a mystery.'

They walked back up the meadow. Half-way up, Corbett sat down, stretching his legs in the long grass. He leaned back on his hands, stared up at the blue sky, then closed his eyes. He savoured the warmth, the sweet smell of crushed grass and wild flowers, the chattering of birds in the trees and the melodious bee hum.

'If I keep my eyes closed,' he murmured, 'I'd say this was paradise.'

Ranulf moaned. 'If I was in a tavern in Cheapside with a

blackjack of ale in my right hand and the other on the knee of a pretty doxy, I'd agree, Master.' He tore at the grass. 'Master, these warnings from the sect of Assassins. Why has the killer chosen them?'

Corbett opened his eyes. 'The Assassins are an Islamic sect,' he replied. 'Garbed in white, with blood-red girdles and slippers. They live under the command of their leader, the Old Man of the Mountain, in their castle, the Eagle's Nest near the Dead Sea. I have heard the king speak of them. Their fortress stands on the summit of an unclimbable mountain. Inside it are walled gardens filled with exotic trees, marble fountains, beautiful flowerbeds and silk-carpeted pavilions. The members of this sect, the 'Devoted Ones', are fed saffron cakes and wine drugged with opiates. They dream of Paradise: every so often the Old Man sends them out to kill those he has marked down for death.

'Now the Assassins did terrible work amongst the Crusaders.' Corbett sat up and stared down at the lake. 'They are a nightmare, phantoms from hell, who stir up black terrors, particularly in our king's soul. Edward still dreams about the attack on him some thirty years ago.'

'Could there be Assassins in the Templar Order?' Ranulf asked, 'apostates who have renounced their vows? Or better still,' he hurried on, 'what if the Assassins are using this Templar coven to weaken the Western Kingdoms?'

Corbett got to his feet, brushing the grass from his hose.

'I can't answer, Ranulf, but I do think it's time we spoke to the grand master.'

They returned to the manor house and, after a while, secured an audience with de Molay. The grand master sat at his desk littered with manuscripts. He gestured for them to sit.

'Sir Hugh.' De Molay rubbed his face. 'This cannot go on for ever. I have to travel back to France. The king's ban must be lifted.'

'Why?' Corbett asked, recalling the messenger he had seen

pounding along the Botham Bar road. 'Is there a fresh crisis in Paris?'

De Molay sifted amongst the documents. 'Yes, of course there is. The attack on Philip of France was carried out by a Templar. The serjeant in question was one of those hotheads. He was handed over to the Inquisition and, yes, he did confess.'

'But I told you that.'

'What you don't know,' de Molay replied, 'is that a few days ago Philip of France was crossing the Grand Ponte, returning to the Louvre Palace after visiting the tombs at St Denis. Apparently,' de Molay threw the piece of parchment back on the desk, 'another attempt was made on his life. Paris is swept by rumours and scandals, the Chapter demands my return.'

'And is there any truth in the rumours?'

De Molay refused to meet his gaze.

'Grand Master,' Corbett insisted, 'I am not your enemy. I admire your Order. Men like Brother Odo and Sir Guido were true knights of the Cross but, for God's sake, open your eyes, there's something rotten here. Did you know,' Corbett continued, 'about the rumours and allegations of sodomy amongst your company?'

De Molay glanced up angrily. 'Don't preach to me, Corbett! I can list bishops and their mistresses, priests who visit whores, noble lords with a penchant for page-boys. Of course there are brethren here who are subject to the frailties of the flesh, as you or I!' he snapped.

'And these murders?' Corbett asked. 'Grand Master, can you explain them? Or why a Templar should send the same warnings as those of the Old Man of the Mountain? Could one of your Order, or more, be apostates, Assassins? What is your relationship with that sect?'

De Molay leaned back in his chair, playing with a thin-bladed parchment knife. 'For centuries,' he replied, 'the Templar Order guarded the Holy Places. We built our castles. We put down roots. We made peace with those around us. Just because a man worships Allah and meets you in battle does not mean that in peace you can't sit down at the same table to exchange ideas, gifts and presents.'

'But the Assassins?' Corbett asked.

'Aye, even with the Assassins. They control some trade routes: certain territories are under their jurisdiction. They are as amenable to bribes as any other.'

'So, your Order did business with them?'

'Yes and, before you ask, Sir Bartholomew Baddlesmere and William Symmes once served an embassy to the Eagle's Nest. They were entertained by the Old Man of the Mountain.'

'Why didn't you tell us this before?'

'I didn't think it was relevant,' de Molay snapped. 'Baddlesmere and Symmes have seen the beautiful gardens, drunk the iced sherbert, listened to the Old Man's speeches. Yes, they've been his guests, but that does not make them apostates. The Assassins are not our enemies.'

'Then who are?' Corbett asked.

'The Western princes,' de Molay replied. 'They see our manors, our granges, our barns, our well-stocked herds and fertile fields. The treasures of the Temple in Paris, London, Cologne, Rome and Avignon make their fingers itch. What do the Templars do, they ask? Why do they need such power and wealth? Should it not be better used for other purposes?'

'So you have no idea who the assassin could be?' Corbett insisted.

'No more than you do, Sir Hugh!' De Molay pushed the parchment aside and picked up a letter. 'I am sending a messenger to the king.'

Corbett nodded.

'I am going to beg him,' de Molay continued, 'for licence to return to France.' He leaned on the table and glared across at Corbett. 'Now there's a thought, Sir Hugh: here am I, Grand Master of Christendom's premier fighting Order, yet I have to beg to travel home, offer money as a surety for my good conduct.' De Molay's face became suffused with rage. 'Now, God forgive me Sir Hugh for saying so, but such humiliation would make a saint plot revenge!'

A few hours later, in the woods overlooking the lake, Sagittarius sat on the trunk of a fallen tree. He picked at the lichen and moss and stared at the cross-hilt of his sword buried in the ground before him. He looked at the cross engraved on the hilt and his face became hard. He rocked himself backwards and forwards. His master, or at least his new one, was right, the Order was finished. And what good would it do then? He stared out across the lake and thought of Brother Odo.

'I am sorry,' he whispered.

Yes, he was truly sorry the old one had to die but, with his long memory and meddling ways, the librarian could have proved a danger. Sagittarius licked his lips as he remembered the wine tun Corbett had brought. He had seen it broached, noticing the red seal with the vintner's mark stamped on it, round as a coin, boldly displaying the year 1292. The wine had tasted rich and mellow on his tongue. Perhaps one day he would have such riches and be able to call up what he wanted. And who could oppose him? The Templars? Stupid, brawny men, frightened by their own secrets and mysterious rituals, scampering about like chickens without their heads. He grasped the hilt of his sword, pulled it out of the soil and lay it over his lap, cleaning the dirt from its point. Corbett was his only danger. The first time the clerk should have been frightened but, in the library, if it hadn't been for that bloody door, he'd have caught and killed him. What a storm that would have provoked! He dared not creep out of the manor and try to enter York, that would be dangerous. So what next? He recalled the gossip and rumours he had heard, the hints and the sniggers. The assassin sat down on the log and coolly planned other murders.

Chapter 10

The tolling of the bell woke Corbett. Ranulf was already up, searching for his swordbelt. Outside the corridors echoed with the running of feet and shouted orders. Other bells in the Templar manor began to toll. Corbett dressed hurriedly. He wrapped his swordbelt around him and peered through the window: the darkened sky was brightening under the first light of dawn.

'Are we under attack?' Ranulf exclaimed, hopping around, putting his boots on.

'I doubt it,' Corbett gasped.

There was a hammering at the door. Ranulf drew back the bolts. A Templar serjeant, his face blackened, hair awry, his surcoat and hose scorched and filthy, almost fell into the room.

'Sir Hugh!' he gasped. 'The grand master's compliments but you are to come. There's a fire in the main building!'

Once outside the guesthouse, Corbett saw the smoke billowing out of the far wing of the manor. The courtyard was now filling with Templars: half-dressed, coughing and spluttering, they were forming a chain so buckets could be passed along. Corbett pushed his way through the door. Inside the passage was full of smoke and, as it parted in a breeze, Corbett saw the orange glow of fire at the far end. Now and again a Templar would dash in, a slopping pail of water in his hand. Branquier, followed by de Molay, came out of the smoke coughing and spluttering. They pushed by Corbett, staggering into the morning air.

'It's Baddlesmere's cell!' de Molay gasped. 'It's a lighted torch from one end to another.' He squatted on the cobbles and greedily drank from the water stoup a servant brought, then threw the rest over his face. 'The water's having no effect,' he muttered.

Corbett crouched beside him. Branquier stumbled off into the darkness, unable to speak, his eyes streaming because of the acrid smoke. Other Templars were now staggering out of the building, shouting that they could do nothing.

'The cell's burning!' de Molay exclaimed. 'If the flames are not brought under control, it will engulf the entire manor house.'

His frustration soon spread to the rest: the chain of buckets faltered. Legrave, a wet cloak covering his nose and mouth, dashed into the passageway. A few minutes later he re-emerged, the top part of his face a mask of ash. Corbett recalled Murston's smouldering corpse.

'Forget the water!' the clerk exclaimed. He pointed across the cobbles where a huge mound of sand, probably used in some building work, lay heaped against the wall. 'Use that!' he said. 'Sand, dirt, soil. Smother the flames rather than drown them!'

At first everything was confusion but then Symmes arrived, his pet weasel popping his little head out of the top of his tunic. He forced the retainers into one long line. Soldiers were sent in, wet cloths over their nostrils and mouths: each carried buckets of sand whilst another was armed with a heavy blanket. An hour passed, eventually the flames died and the fire was brought under control.

'Thank God!' de Molay murmured. 'Thank God, Sir Hugh, the walls are of stone, as is the floor: the whole manor could have been turned into a blazing pyre.'

'It's bad enough,' Legrave remarked, coming up. 'The cell on the other side is damaged, as are the two rooms above. The beams and floor joists are burnt away.' He stared around. 'Where's Baddlesmere?' he exclaimed. 'I'm sure I saw . . .' His voice faltered.

Branquier hastened away, calling Baddlesmere's name. He came back, shaking his head.

'That was Baddlesmere's chamber?' Corbett asked.

Symmes nodded.

'What happened?' Corbett asked.

Symmes turned away and shouted out names. Two Templars hurried up, stripped to the waist, their bodies covered in soot. They looked like two demons from hell.

'You raised the alarm?' Branquier asked one of them.

'Yes, Domine. I was on patrol. I turned the corridor and saw the smoke coming out beneath the door. I hurried down and banged with all my might.' He extended his bloody, scorched fist. 'The door was boiling hot so I called for help. Waldo and Gibner came. Gibner ran off to ring the bell and raise the alarm, whilst Waldo and I tried to force the door, which was locked and barred. We took a bench from the corridor and smashed it on the left so as to snap the hinges. We were successful,' he gasped, 'but the flames and the smoke seemed to leap out at us. Inside it was terrible, fire and smoke. It was like the heart of hell, an inferno.'

'Did you see Sir Bartholomew?' Legrave snapped. 'Speak the truth!'

'Yes, he was lying on the bed. The flames had already reached it. I only saw him for a few seconds.' He stammered. 'Him and . . .'

'And?' Corbett asked.

'There was another,' the Templar mumbled. 'They were sprawled on the bed: the flames were already taking hold of the tester and counterpane. I shouted once, then we ran. Honestly, Master, we could do nothing.'

'Who was the other?' Branquier cried. 'Oh, for God's sake, man! We have lost two of our Order!'

165

'One was Sir Bartholomew,' the serjeant replied. 'I think the other was Scoudas.'

De Molay cursed under his breath and walked away. Corbett stood aside, watching the dirty and blackened Templars wash themselves in buckets of water from the well. Above him the sun was rising fast and strong whilst, a short distance away, de Molay and his commanders waited for it to be safe before re-entering the building. Eventually a serjeant reported the fire was extinguished. De Molay ordered his companions to stay where they were and, beckoning Corbett and Ranulf, entered the charred, stinking corridor. The walls and woodwork were all scorched; when they reached Baddlesmere's chamber, Corbett was surprised at the intensity of the fire. It had reduced the chamber to nothing but a blackened charnel-house. The floor was ankle-deep in ash. The bedding, furniture and ornaments had been turned to cinder. Above them, the ceiling had been gutted; they stared into the upper chamber where the hungry flames had roared, consuming all in its path.

'Are the beams safe?' Corbett asked.

'We always build well,' de Molay replied. 'Fire is our great enemy. Three, possibly four, chambers will have to be gutted and repaired.'

He walked across and stopped where the bed had been. Very little remained of the two dead Templars: charred skeletons lying next to each other made unrecognisable by the horror which had occurred. Despite the ash and dirt, de Molay, tears streaming down his face, knelt down and crossed himself.

'*Requiem aeternam dona eis Domine,*' he intoned. 'Eternal rest give unto them oh Lord and let perpetual light shine upon them.' He blessed the remains with his hand. 'Turn not your face away from them,' he prayed. 'And, in your infinite mercy, forgive their offence.'

He rose to his feet, stumbled, and would have fallen if Corbett had not grasped his arm. De Molay lifted his face. Corbett was shocked: the grand master had aged, his face grey, mouth slack, eyes like a lost child.

'What is happening, Corbett?' he whispered hoarsely. 'For the love of God, what is happening? The fire is terrible enough but Bartholomew? A good soldier, to die in his bed with another man beside him. How will that be seen by the Judge of us all? What terrible damage to the name of our Order!'

He pulled his hand away and stumbled towards the door. Corbett indicated Ranulf to help him. The grand master hobbled like an old man into the passageway. He leaned against the wall and closed his eyes.

'I have heard the rumours,' he whispered. 'Friendships are formed. Sometimes we, who can have no sons, look for someone we would have liked to have had as one. Perhaps that was the case with Bartholomew. Now God's judgement has caught up with him and the power of the Evil One has made itself felt.'

Corbett wiped the soot and ash away from his face. 'Nonsense!' he snapped. 'Baddlesmere and his companion were murdered. Their deaths were planned.'

'But rumours will go out amongst the wicked.' De Molay looked glassy-eyed at him. 'He cast his lot.'

'Shut up!' Corbett shouted.

The grand master bowed his head. For a while he stood sobbing quietly, then, wiping his eyes on his sleeve, he grasped Corbett's arm like a man who had lost his sight. He stumbled down the passageway towards the door. Outside he ignored his companions but, accompanied by Corbett and Ranulf, walked slowly back to his own chamber. Once there, the grand master relaxed a little, bathing his face in a bowl of water, washing the grime and sweat from his face and hands. He then poured three goblets of wine, serving Ranulf and Corbett. He apologised deeply for the early hour, but quoted St Paul that they should take a little wine for their stomach's sake. Then he sat for a while, staring out of the window, mouth open, now and again sipping from the wine goblet. Ranulf looked at Corbett but he shook his head, bringing his finger to his lips. The door opened.

167

Branquier, Symmes and Legrave crept into the room and sat down. At last de Molay sighed and, turning, looked squarely at Corbett.

'It was no accident, was it?'

'No,' Corbett replied. 'It was murder.'

'But how?' Symmes exclaimed. 'Grand Master, I have just studied what remains of the lock and bolts. The key was welded into the lock on the inside. The bolts at top and bottom were secure.'

'What about the window?' Ranulf asked. 'If that was open, a firebrand could have been tossed through.'

'I have checked that,' Symmes retorted. 'The serjeants on duty outside say that the shutters of Bartholomew's window were firmly closed.'

Everyone concentrated on the fire: no one dared to mention the circumstances in which Baddlesmere had died.

'The flames were so intense,' de Molay exclaimed, 'burning savagely. What on God's earth would cause such a fire?' He waved his hand. 'Oh, accidents happen. Candles fall on to the rushes or an oil-lamp is tipped over, but the speed of that fire!' He shook his head. 'It can't have been anything like that.'

'And if such an accident had occurred?' Corbett remarked. 'Why didn't Baddlesmere and his companion raise the alarm, douse the flames themselves?'

'According to the serjeant,' Legrave said. 'Baddlesmere and Scoudas were either unconscious or dead.'

'They were sodomites.' Symmes's face twisted in revulsion. 'They died in their sin.' His voice had risen.

'That's for God to decide,' Corbett retorted. 'What concerns me is how they died. The windows and doors were barred, so how could someone get into a room and start such an inferno?' He stared round. 'Did anything untoward happen yesterday evening?'

His question was answered by headshakes and murmurs of dissent.

'Was Baddlesmere . . .' Corbett paused to marshal his words more carefully. 'Was his liaison with Scoudas well known?'

'There were rumours,' Symmes replied. 'You know, the sort of gossip which runs like a river through any enclosed community . . .'

He paused at a knock on the door. A serjeant hurried in. He whispered in Branquier's ear, laid a pair of saddlebags at his feet and left. Branquier undid the straps carefully. He shook the contents into his lap whilst the rest watched curiously.

'The bag belongs to Scoudas,' Branquier explained. 'I told the serjeant to collect anything he might find in his quarters.'

He held up a small steel ring by its stem. Corbett recognised a sighting which skilled arbalesters used on their crossbows. The rest were a few paltry objects: a knife, a sheath and small squares of parchment. Branquier undid these, cursed and handed them over to Corbett.

The first was a diagram: Corbett recognised it as a street plan of York: Trinity, the road the king had ridden up, its line of houses, the place where Murston had lurked, was marked with a cross.

'It's in Baddlesmere's hand,' Branquier explained. 'As are the rest.'

Corbett stared down at the cramped writing and the fatal message it bore.

KNOWEST THOU, THAT WE GO FORTH AND RETURN AS BEFORE AND BY NO MEANS CAN YOU HINDER US.
KNOWEST THOU, THAT WHAT THOU POSSESSES SHALL ESCAPE THEE IN THE END AND RETURN TO US.
KNOWEST THOU, THAT WE HOLD YOU AND WILL KEEP THEE UNTIL THE ACCOUNT BE CLOSED.

'It's the Assassin's warning.' Corbett put the parchment on the table in front of the grand master. De Molay studied it.

'Sir Hugh?' he asked. 'Could the assassin have been Baddlesmere? Remember the morning we entered York, Baddlesmere was with Scoudas.'

'But he returned to Framlingham with us,' Symmes intervened. 'He couldn't possibly have been in York when Corbett received his warning or narrowly missed the assailant's arrows.'

'True,' de Molay replied, 'but Scoudas was. He came back much later in the afternoon . . . He was Genoese by birth, a professional crossbowman.'

'And this,' Branquier held up a yellowing stub of parchment he'd taken from the saddlebag, 'is a billa with Murston's mark on it, acknowledging the receipt of certain monies.'

'Are you saying,' Corbett looked at the billa and passed it over to de Molay, 'that Baddlesmere and his lover Scoudas were the assassins?'

'It stands to reason,' Branquier retorted.

'Yes, it does,' de Molay declared. 'Baddlesmere was discontented. He had knowledge of the Assassins and their secrets. He attended the Chapter in Paris after which Philip of France was attacked. He was in London when the Assassins' message was pinned to the door of St Paul's Cathedral. He knew when the king was entering York and what route he would take. Scoudas, his lover, paid Murston, the most harebrained of men, a large amount of money. Copies of the Assassins' message are found in Scoudas's saddlebag together with a map of York. Finally, Scoudas was a professional crossbowman.'

'But why?' Corbett asked. 'Why did the fire break out in Baddlesmere's room? And, when it did, surely he and Scoudas would have tried to escape?'

'I can't answer that,' the grand master replied. 'Perhaps they held some secret which went wrong and they were overcome by the smoke.'

'Did any of you see Baddlesmere last night?' Corbett asked.

'Yes, yes, I did,' Branquier replied. 'We dined together.' He smiled weakly. 'We finished up the excellent wine you brought. Baddlesmere did like his wine. He always took a small jug into his chamber.'

'And Scoudas?' Ranulf asked.

'Sir Hugh,' Legrave exclaimed, 'we are a fighting community, bound by vows and a rule of discipline. Nevertheless, we are free men. Our Order is our family; friendships are formed. We do not poke our fingers into every man's pie. We have enough troubles without checking on every man, where he goes and what he does.'

'May I have those pieces of parchment?' Corbett asked, getting to his feet.

De Molay handed them over. Corbett abruptly made his farewells and returned to the guesthouse.

'Do you believe all that?' Ranulf asked, hurrying beside him.

'It's possible,' Corbett replied. 'It would make sense: Scoudas was in York when I was threatened and later attacked. I believe the grand master; this map of York and the Assassins' warning is written in Baddlesmere's hand. But why was it found in Scoudas's possession? Why wasn't it better hidden?'

'Perhaps Scoudas was his messenger boy?'

'In which case we face three possibilities,' Corbett retorted as they entered his chamber.

'First, Scoudas and Bartholomew were the assassins and, due to some dreadful accident, they were killed: that seems a strong possibility. We have documentary evidence and there is no valid explanation of how the fire could begin.' Corbett went over to the table and laid the scraps of parchment out. 'Secondly, Bartholomew and Scoudas were part of a coven, so others in this manor and elsewhere could be implicated in their treason.'

171

'And thirdly?' Ranulf asked.

'That Baddlesmere and Scoudas were victims and the real assassin, the Sagittarius, still walks free. Now,' Corbett sat down at the table, 'we are still awaiting Claverley and Maltote's return.' He grinned over his shoulder at Ranulf. 'You are free to play dice whenever you wish. I am going to be busy.'

For a while Ranulf stayed, kicking his heels, pacing up and down the chamber, peering through the window, muttering about Maltote's good luck at getting away. At last Corbett told him to shut up and go for a walk. Ranulf needed no second bidding and sped off like a greyhound. Corbett returned to drafting the letter he was writing, then threw his quill down in exasperation. Murder, treason, attempted regicide, sodomy, perhaps black magic! He got up and went to the door and bolted it. Corbett knew how Edward would react. He would rant and rave, but others in the Council would urge more pragmatic steps: the closing of all ports to the Templars as well as the possible seizure of their lands and chattels.

Corbett abandoned the letter and, for the next two hours, began to write down everything that had happened, everything he had heard and seen since this business began: conversations and conclusions. These, however, led nowhere, so he went back to the scraps of parchment he had found in Brother Odo's desk, as well as the ones taken from Scoudas's saddlebags. Corbett scrutinised the Assassins' warning again. The first pinned on the doors of St Paul's; the second given to him in York; the third handed over by Claverley, and the fourth plucked from Scoudas's saddlebag. Corbett rose and stretched. And the fifth? Ah yes, the assassin in the library. Corbett seized his quill and wrote this down. He looked at all five, particularly the last, then, his curiosity aroused, he studied them again. There was a difference: he had noticed it before, but was it significant? Corbett bit his lips in excitement. The one delivered by Claverley and the one given to him in York were different. In the other three the message had stated:

KNOWEST THOU, THAT WE GO FORTH AND
RETURN AS BEFORE AND BY NO MEANS CAN
YOU HINDER US.
KNOWEST THOU, THAT WHAT THOU POSSESSES
SHALL ESCAPE THEE IN THE END AND RETURN
TO US.
KNOWEST THOU, THAT WE HOLD YOU AND WILL
KEEP THEE UNTIL THE ACCOUNT BE CLOSED.

Now the scribbled notice mysteriously attached to Murston's
gibbet and the one given to him in York had read as follows:

KNOWEST THOU, THAT WHAT THOU POSSESSES
SHALL ESCAPE THEE IN THE END AND RETURN
TO US.
KNOWEST THOU, THAT WE GO FORTH AND
RETURN AS BEFORE AND BY NO MEANS CAN
YOU HINDER US.
KNOWEST THOU, THAT WE HOLD YOU AND WILL
KEEP THEE UNTIL THE ACCOUNT BE CLOSED.

Why the difference, Corbett wondered? A simple error? He
went to the window and stared down into the yard, watching the
Templar soldiers hurry backwards and forwards as they began
to clear up the debris from the burnt chambers. Was it a simple
mistake? But, if it wasn't, what was the significance?

'Let us say,' Corbett murmured, 'that there were three
conspirators: Murston, Baddlesmere and Scoudas. Each
delivered warnings at certain times. Would that explain why
the message was written out wrongly?'

Corbett went across to the lavarium and splashed water over
his face. He looked down at the grimy water and realised that
he had been so absorbed that he still bore traces of the smoke
and fire, so he went into the corridor and asked a serjeant to
bring fresh water. The man agreed and, once he'd returned,

Corbett stripped, washed and shaved himself in a small steel mirror, then changed into fresh clothes. Still thinking of the problem, he went down to the kitchen where he begged some bread, cheese and a jug of ale. Everyone else ignored him. The murders, the secret scandals and the hard work in dousing the flames had all wrought their effect on the Templar community. Ranulf joined him, his grimy face now furrowed by streaks of sweat.

'A good game?' Corbett asked.

His manservant grinned.

'You look more like an imp from hell than ever. Be careful, Ranulf,' Corbett added. 'People might want to examine the dice you are using.'

'I always throw honest,' Ranulf replied.

'Aye, and pigs fly,' Corbett replied.

Ranulf left to change and wash, Corbett finished his food and went and sat on a stone bench outside the front door of the manor. He revelled in the sun's warmth, his mind still concentrating on those warnings; he was trying to remember something which was out of place, but he couldn't for his life remember it. He closed his eyes, letting himself relax, and thought of Maeve's last letter.

'You must come home,' she had written. 'Eleanor misses you. Uncle Morgan swears you have some pretty doxy in every city. I lie awake every night hoping that the next morning I'll hear the servants' excited cries and you will be back.'

'Sir Hugh?'

Corbett's eyes flew open. Claverley was standing staring anxiously down at him.

'Roger!'

The under-sheriff's ugly face broke into a smile.

'How long have you been here?' Corbett asked.

'Oh, I left my horse in the stables and went up to your chamber. Ranulf was there.' Claverley's face grew serious. 'He told me the news.' The under-sheriff sat on the bench beside Corbett. 'This place is like a morgue,' he murmured. 'And when the news gets out . . .'

'What has happened?' Corbett asked.

'Well, we have already received our orders. Any Templar seen in the city of York is to be arrested on sight. In the Guildhall there are whispers and rumours that the king has sent messengers ordering the keepers of all the ports and the harbourmasters to seize any Templar coming into the country, as well as all letters and writs bearing their seal. Finally, under pain of forfeiture of life and limb, no Templar is allowed to leave the kingdom.'

Corbett got to his feet. 'I just hope,' he declared, 'that His Grace knows what he is doing. The Templars are under the direct control of the Pope. Any attack on them,' he added drily, 'is seen as an attack upon Christ's Vicar himself.' Corbett linked his arm through Claverley's and they walked back into the manor. 'The king doesn't give a damn about the Templars,' Corbett continued. 'He and his great lords would love to get their fingers on their possessions. Anyway, Claverley, what else do you have for me?'

Claverley handed him a small scroll of parchment.

'Bad news going to worse,' he replied. 'I have had my clerks list all those who have access to forges, all those who have licences to import into York, as well as all those who've applied for licence to build.'

'And?' Corbett asked, ushering Claverley into his chamber. 'See for yourself.'

Corbett unrolled the small parchment. Each of the three lists were very short. Corbett recognised the names of some of the leading aldermen and merchants of York, including Hubert Seagrave, vintner and owner of the Greenmantle tavern. However, the only name which appeared in each of the three small columns was that of the Templars. They owned smithies and forges in York. They had the right to import foodstuffs and other goods into the city. They also owned tenements and dwelling houses under the care of their steward, the now deceased Sir Guido Reverchien; he had apparently sought permission from the mayor and aldermen to build or renovate some of those places. Corbett groaned and tossed the parchment on to the bed.

'There's nothing new here!' he exclaimed.

Claverley handed him a gold coin. 'I went to see Mistress Jocasta. She thanks you for your gift but, in view of her past history, she thought it best to send it back. She asked you to examine the coin carefully, especially the rim.'

Corbett did so and saw the faint red marks.

'What are they?' Corbett asked, scraping at one and noticing how it came away under his nail.

'Mistress Jocasta thinks it's wax. She also said the gold is very old.' Claverley sat down on the stool, undoing his swordbelt. 'Apparently gold is like cloth, of different textures and makes: this is soft, precious and very rarely seen nowadays.'

'But why should the Templars be minting their own coins?' Corbett asked.

'I don't know, Sir Hugh. They may be bankrupt and beginning to melt down their bullion, or they may have simply found treasure trove which they do not wish to hand over to the king. Sir Hugh, I travelled fast, the road was dusty . . .'

Corbett apologised and poured out a goblet of wine. He'd hardly finished when Ranulf burst into the room, loudly protesting at how he had been searching high and low. He forgot his moans when Corbett handed him a cup of wine.

'Thank God you've come, Claverley!' Ranulf exclaimed between sips from his cup. 'As I said, this is a morgue, a death-house.'

'Did you make inquiries about the Templars in York, the morning the king was attacked?' Corbett asked.

'Yes, and I didn't find much. Apparently one of them left the city early.'

'Yes, that would be Branquier.'

176

'And one of the guards near Botham Bar definitely saw the grand master and the others meet and ride off.'

'But what were they doing before?'

Claverley explained. 'Well, the one-eyed one, Symmes, he apparently spent a great deal of his time in the tavern watching the doxies, though he wandered about and was seen in different locations throughout the morning.'

'And the dead one, Baddlesmere?'

'Well, some of the market bailiffs remember him, walking amongst the stalls near the Pavement. They definitely saw him and a young serjeant standing there when Murston's corpse was gibbeted.'

'And the grand master and Legrave?'

'De Molay did visit the goldsmith's but, Legrave spent a great deal of the time in the streets outside. It's the glovers' quarter, and some of the shopkeepers recall him making purchases. They thought he was guarding the entrance whilst de Molay was inside.'

'So any of them could have slipped down to that tavern near Trinity where Murston was lurking?'

'Yes they could have done so,' Claverley replied. 'Oh, and one final thing.' Claverley sipped from the goblet. 'Much later in the afternoon, the guards at Botham Bar remember a Templar serjeant, the same young, blond-haired one glimpsed with Baddlesmere, leaving the city. He was riding fast, shouting at people to get out of his way.'

Corbett sighed. 'That would be Scoudas, who's also died. So we know all the Templars, including Baddlesmere, were in York when the attack was launched on the king. We know they separated, but that they met before Botham Bar and left the city before I received that threatening message on Ouse Bridge. They were certainly gone by the time that hidden archer tried to kill me. The only Templar in York when that happened was Scoudas.'

Corbett sat down on the edge of his bed. Was it possible, he thought, that the men behind these attacks – Baddlesmere and Scoudas – were already dead? Is that why Baddlesmere had left the city with de Molay, to put himself beyond suspicion whilst his friend and lover, Scoudas, carried out the attack? If that was the case, Corbett hid the tingle of excitement in his stomach, there would be no more deaths and he could report as much to the king. He glanced at his two companions.

'Can you leave me alone for a while?' he murmured.

Claverley drained his cup. 'I have another message.'

'Yes?'

'A lazar, an unknown knight, is dying in the Franciscan hospital. He claims he was a Templar and wishes to speak to you.'

'A Templar, a lazar!' Ranulf exclaimed. 'Could he be the mysterious hooded rider glimpsed in the woods near the Botham Bar road?'

Claverley shrugged.

'Look,' Corbett smiled faintly, 'Ranulf will look after you. But don't go far. We may have to leave quickly.'

Once they had gone, Corbett tried to marshal his thoughts. All the evidence pointed to Baddlesmere's guilt, yet there was something amiss. Only he was too absorbed to catch and hold it in his mind. He'd certainly go to York and visit the Lazar hospital. He picked up the list which Claverley had brought and fished the gold coin out of his purse. He stared at the red wax on the rim of the coin, then absentmindedly felt for his wine cup. He paused, recalling the tun of wine he'd brought to Framlingham, and stared at the list again.

'Of course!' he breathed. '*In vino veritas*: in wine there is always truth!'

Chapter 11

Hubert Seagrave, tavern master and vintner to the King, mopped his sweaty face, now turned a dull pasty hue. He stared in terror across his counting-room at Sir Hugh Corbett. Roger Claverley, under-sheriff, sat on the clerk's left, whilst that cat-eyed servant stood just behind him. Seagrave's gaze shifted to the gold coin lying on the table.

'Naturally, naturally,' he stuttered, 'I have seen such coins. They are good gold.' He stared piteously at the door where his ashen-faced wife and young sons stared fearfully at him.

'Close the door, Ranulf,' Corbett murmured. 'Now, Master Seagrave.' The clerk pulled his chair to the edge of the counting table, admiring the black and white squares laid out on top. 'I shall begin again. This coin and others like it are not the work of some petty counterfeiter but a wealthy, powerful man. This person discovered a treasure trove which should rightly belong to the Crown but, instead, he decided to melt that gold down in the furnace of his forge and recast it into coins. He used the same moulds he has for forming the red wax discs with which he seals his goods. Now, no one but a fool would go out into the market place with such coins and start buying goods from foreign merchants. He used those coins to purchase his merchandise, and these foreign merchants would then enter the markets of York with the same gold to buy their own purchases. The subtlety of this trick is apparent: the Crown does not get its treasure trove; the merchant keeps it to amass further wealth, whilst four or five foreign merchants use these gold coins to buy goods to import into their own countries. So, who can trace them back? Indeed, who will ask questions? The traders of York are only too pleased to see good gold pouring into their coffers, their memories would soon grow dim.'

Corbett paused and sipped from the excellent wine Seagrave had served when he mistakenly thought the clerk had just arrived on a courtesy visit.

'Now,' Corbett struck his breast, 'I made a mistake. I thought it might be the Templars. They are always applying for licences to refurbish their tenements in York. They have the licence to import goods from abroad and, of course, they have their own forges and ironsmiths. But why should the Templars incur royal anger?'

Corbett paused. He felt truly sorry for this fat merchant whose greed had got the better of him. 'However, the same applies to you, Master Seagrave. You have at least two forges at the Greenmantle. You have also applied for a licence to build on an adjoining piece of waste land. Before I left Framlingham I scrutinised the steward's accounts. You offer a price well above the market value for the wasteland on the other side of your tavern.'

Seagrave opened his mouth but then put his face in his hands.

'The mistake I made,' Corbett continued remorselessly, 'was assuming that the guilty party must have applied for a licence to import from abroad. But, as the King's own vintner in his royal city of York, you need no such licence. Foreign ships bring the wine down the Ouse, they unload their barrels, and you paid them with these gold coins.'

'You don't want that field for more buildings,' Ranulf intervened, 'but because it might contain more treasure trove.'

'You made one mistake,' Corbett added. 'The die casts you used to make your wax seals, you also used to mint the gold. On a few of the coins some of the red wax is still embedded, very deeply in the rim.'

'There are other merchants,' Seagrave mumbled, not raising his head. He dragged his hands across the table and Corbett saw the sweat-marks left by his fingers.

'Master Seagrave,' Claverley spoke up, 'you are an important burgess. A merchant prince. Your tavern is famous, not only in York but well beyond the city walls. You were born and bred here. You have heard the stories: how once the Romans had a great city here and, in the time before Alfred, the Vikings turned the city into a great fortress where they piled their plunder. Such treasure trove is common – the odd cup, a few coins. But what did you find?'

'We can go away,' Corbett added. 'And come back with the king's soldiers. They will tear this tavern apart, dig up every inch of soil.' He leaned against the table. 'Master Seagrave, look at me.'

The merchant glanced up fearfully. 'It was so easy,' he muttered. 'Different merchants at different times. I knew they'd keep their mouths shut. After all, Sir Hugh, who objects to being paid in gold? But you found wax engrained in the rim?'

Corbett nodded.

'Well, God knows how that got there.' Seagrave got to his feet, pushing his chair back. He smiled sourly as Claverley's hand went to his dagger. 'Don't worry, Under-sheriff, I am not going to flee or do anything stupid. I want to show you what I found.'

The merchant left the counting-house. A few minutes later he came staggering back with a small chest about two feet long and a foot high. He dropped this on the table with a crash and threw back the lid.

'Sweet God and all his angels!' Ranulf exclaimed, staring at the gold coins which lay heaped there.

'There's more,' Seagrave added.

He went out and returned with a leather sack. He undid the cord at the neck and spilled the precious objects on to the table: a gold, jewel-encrusted pyx, a drinking horn inlaid with mother-of-pearl. Two small goblets, the cups thick with silver. An agnus dei of pure jade, a pectoral cross, amethysts gleaming in each of the four stems.

'Riches in abundance,' Seagrave murmured. 'I found it all about three months ago when the builders were digging in the garden. They paused because of the snow and frost. I went out to inspect. My children were playing in the trench: they'd pulled a piece of paving stone away from the side of the hole which had strange markings on it. I got down and investigated.' Seagrave paused. 'I don't know whether it was a sewer or a pipe made of elm. I put my hand inside.' He shook his head. 'I thought I was dreaming. I pulled out one bag after another, all full of coins.' He slumped down. 'For God's sake, Sir Hugh, I couldn't mint coins like that.'

'But they look so new!' Corbett exclaimed. 'The cross on each side, the red wax on the rim.'

'I made my own inquiries amongst the chronicles and histories of the city,' Seagrave replied. 'Once York was called Jorvik; the Viking war gangs set up camp here.' He pointed to the precious objects which lay gleaming on the table. 'Perhaps some chieftain took church gold and melted it down and, being superstitious, carved a cross on either side.'

'Candlesticks,' Claverley explained. 'Sir Hugh, they must have been candlesticks, which explains the red wax.'

Corbett lifted up the gold and let the coins run through his fingers.

'Strange,' he murmured. 'In my cleverness I thought the coins were newly minted.'

'They are,' Seagrave replied. 'Whoever made those coins, Sir Hugh, never used them but hid them away with the rest of the treasure. They must have brought him the same ill luck as they did me. The wooden pipes were scorched, as was the earth around it. I didn't know what to do,' he continued. 'I was tired of poor silver coins and, if I handed them over to the Exchequer, what recompense would I have got? Royal officials questioning me, hinting I may have stolen it, using every legal nicety to keep the treasure to themselves. How much of this, Sir Hugh, would have found its way into the royal treasury? Kings' clerks are no different from Kings' vintners: everyone has sticky fingers.'

'You could have petitioned the king yourself,' Corbett retorted.

'I thought of that,' Seagrave replied, 'the day you came here. I nearly broke down and confessed but . . .' He shrugged. 'I was committed. I'd waited until the king arrived in York. The great lords, the royal household, clerks, liveried retainers, so many strangers in the city, an opportune time to spend that gold. Royal purveyors were out buying the goods, the markets were doing a roaring trade.' Seagrave's face crumpled, tears rolling down his ashen cheeks. 'Now I have lost everything,' he muttered.

Suddenly the door to the counting-house was flung open and Seagrave's wife entered, two small children clinging to her skirts.

'What will happen?' Her pretty face was now drawn, her eyes dark pools of fear.

'Wait outside, Mistress Seagrave,' Corbett replied. 'The king wants his treasure, not a man's life. What your husband has done is understandable.'

Corbett waited until the door closed. Seagrave had now dried his eyes and was looking expectantly at him.

'What you must do, Master Seagrave,' Corbett declared gently, 'is seek an audience with the king. Take the treasure with you. Do not mention me or my visit here . . .' Corbett paused. 'No, tell him I supped here and that you asked would it be possible to see His Grace.'

'And then what?' Seagrave asked anxiously.

'Throw yourself on the royal mercy,' Corbett continued. 'And then open the sacks. Believe me, Master Seagrave, the king will kiss you as a brother, provided you hand over everything!'

'You mean . . .' Seagrave gabbled.

'Oh, for heaven's sake, man!' Corbett exclaimed. 'You found some gold and spent some of it: that will be taken from your share.'

'Then there will be no fine, no imprisonment?' Seagrave exclaimed.

Corbett got to his feet. 'Master Seagrave,' he replied drily, 'if you play your part well, you'll probably be knighted.'

The tavern master tried to make him stay, saying he would like to reward his generosity. Corbett did remain for a while, finishing his wine and reassuring the flustered Seagrave that his family should fear nothing from him.

'Is this right?' Claverley muttered, seizing a moment when they were alone in the room together.

'What else is there, Roger?' Corbett laughed sharply. 'Seagrave only became greedy. If we punished everyone for that, we wouldn't find enough gibbets in the country.' Corbett held his hand up. 'You are to keep your mouth shut.'

'Sir Hugh, you have my word.'

Once they had finished, Seagrave led them out to the stables where they'd left their horses. The merchant plucked anxiously at Corbett's sleeve.

'Sir Hugh, I have one final confession to make.'

'There's more treasure!' Corbett exclaimed.

'No, it was the day you came here. I thought you were following someone.'

'What do you mean?' Corbett asked.

'Well, the day the king entered York, this tavern, like every other in the city, was very busy. Two Templars came here. One was a senior commander. I knew that by the way he talked. He was balding, grizzle-faced, a short, stocky man.'

'Baddlesmere!' Corbett exclaimed.

'Yes, well, he was accompanied by a young serjeant. A youngish, blond-haired man with a foreign accent. I thought they'd come about the adjoining piece of land so I entertained them and talked about my plans.' Seagrave coughed to clear his throat. 'Now, to put it bluntly, they humoured me. They asked for a chamber, claiming they had matters to discuss, well away from the eyes and ears of the curious. So I obliged: that was early in the morning. About noon the old one left, followed by the younger one, shortly before you arrived . . .' Seagrave's voice trailed off. 'I thought I should tell you.'

Corbett thanked and reassured him. Once they were out of the stableyard he dismounted, leading his horse by the reins. Claverley, staring curiously at him and Ranulf, wondering what was the matter, followed Corbett through the busy, narrow alleyways and streets, then into the silent graveyard of a small church. Corbett sat down on a weather-beaten tombstone, watching his horse lazily munch the long, fresh grass.

'If I was half as clever as I thought I was,' he began, 'then I'd be the most subtle of royal clerks.' He sighed. 'The truth is I blunder about like the hooded man in Blind Man's Buff. If I strike something then it's more chance than skill.'

'You still found the counterfeiter,' Ranulf offered hopefully.

'Mere chance. I thought the wax proved Seagrave was a counterfeiter: it didn't.'

'Why didn't you arrest him?' Claverley asked.

'I've told you,' Corbett replied. 'He was greedy but, still, he's a father, a husband, I don't want his blood on my hands. And now we have Baddlesmere and Scoudas,' Corbett continued. 'They visited the Greenmantle tavern for a love tryst, using Seagrave's desire to purchase some land as a possible pretext. Baddlesmere, to avoid any scandal or rumour, left to join the grand master. More importantly, Scoudas couldn't have attacked me, he was in the tavern. So,' Corbett let his horse nuzzle his neck, 'Baddlesmere and Scoudas were no more interested in attacking the king and myself than the queen of the fairies. They came into York to be together. Baddlesmere and Scoudas were in that tavern all the time.'

'But the warning?' Ranulf asked. 'The map found in Scoudas's possessions: they all bore Baddlesmere's hand.'

Corbett got to his feet. 'I wonder,' he replied. 'Did Baddlesmere have his own suspicions? Did he draw that map in order to help his own inquiries?' He gathered the reins in his hands and remounted.

'Sir Hugh?'

Corbett broke from his reverie and stared down at the under-sheriff.

'If you want,' Claverley offered, 'I can ride back with you to Framlingham or accompany you to the Lazar hospital.'

'No,' Corbett smiled. 'As the gospels say: "Sufficient unto the day is the evil thereof".' He extended his hand and grasped Claverley's. 'You did good work, Roger. I shall make sure the king knows of it: I thank you for your courtesy and help.'

'They said you were a hard man,' Claverley told him. He jerked his head back in the direction of the tavern. 'But Seagrave will always remember your compassion.'

Corbett shrugged. 'I have seen more blood and death in the last year, Master Claverley . . .' His voice trailed off. 'Keep well.'

And, urging his horse forward, Corbett left the graveyard. Ranulf stayed to make his own farewells.

'He's homesick,' the manservant whispered, leaning down from his horse. 'Old "Master Long Face" is pining for his wife.'

'And you, Ranulf?' Claverley grinned.

Ranulf pulled his most sanctimonious face. 'Virtue is its own reward, Master Under-sheriff,' he intoned solemnly.

And, with Claverley's laughter ringing in his ears, Ranulf spurred his horse on before 'Old Master Long Face' really did fall into one of his melancholic fits.

Corbett dismounted in the courtyard of the Lazar hospital. A lay brother came out, Corbett whispered to him, and the little man nodded. 'Yes, yes,' he murmured, 'we have been expecting you. Stay here!'

He hurried into the hospital and came back a little later, accompanied by a friar. 'This is Father Anselm, our infirmarian.'

The Franciscan grasped Corbett's hand. 'You'd best come,' he urged, but turned as Ranulf made to join them. 'No,' he apologised. 'I am afraid the knight only asked for Sir Hugh.'

Mystified, Corbett looked at Ranulf, then shrugged and followed the friar in through the door and up the stairs. They went along through the long infirmary where the sick lay on beds on either side. Each bed was cordoned off by dark-blue sheets which hung from steel rods bolted to the wall. The room was clean and fragrant, the sheets and bolsters of each bed a snowy white.

'We do our best,' Brother Anselm muttered. 'Many of these had no dignity in living, at least they'll have some in dying.'

At the end of the room he ushered Corbett into a small chamber, stark and austere. The white washed walls and gaunt crucifix above the bed reminded Corbett of his cell at Framlingham: the 'Unknown' lay propped against the bolsters; his yellow hair, soaked with sweat, fanned out across the pillow. Corbett fought to hide his disgust at the terrible sores and ulcers eating into the man's face. The Unknown opened his eyes and tried to smile.

'Don't worry,' he whispered, the spittle bubbling on his cracked lips. 'I am no beauty, Sir Hugh. Brother, a stool for our visitor.'

Friar Anselm brought one across and, when Corbett sat down, whispered in his ear: 'He has not got much time. I doubt if he'll see the night through.'

Then he left, closing the door quietly behind him.

The Unknown turned his face, closed his eyes, drawing deep breaths, summoning up his last resources of strength.

'You are Sir Hugh Corbett, Keeper of the King's Secret Seal?'

187

'I am.'

'They say you are a man of integrity.'

'People say a lot of things.'

'A good answer. My strength is ebbing, Sir Hugh, so I'll be brief. Death will be here soon. Who I am, or where I came from does not concern you. I was a Templar. I fought at Acre and, when that city fell, I was taken prisoner and handed over to the Assassins who kept me imprisoned for years in their fortress of the Eagle's Nest.'

The Unknown stirred, moving his limbs to find relief. 'The Old Man of the Mountain,' he whispered, 'released me to cause chaos in my Order, to lay allegations of cowardice.'

'Why?' Corbett asked. 'What allegations?'

'I know a great secret,' the Unknown gasped. 'Those commanders at Framlingham, they were all at Acre. When the city fell . . .' The Unknown stopped, fighting for breath. '. . . Some Templars died. I and others were wounded and taken prisoner, many retreated. But,' his fingers scrabbled at the blankets, 'according to the Old Man of the Mountain, one English Templar was an arrant coward. He deserted his post and, because of that, the Mamelukes took a wall, cutting me and my companions off. On the day I was captured they told me about a Templar knight running away, dropping his sword and shield whilst others died.'

'Which one?' Corbett asked.

'I don't know,' the Unknown retorted. 'But, for years, hidden in that dungeon, I dreamed of returning, of asking the survivors where they were and so account for their actions. When I was released, all the Old Man told me was that the Templar concerned was now a senior officer in the English province.' The Unknown paused again. 'I asked him how he knew the Templar's nationality but not his name.'

'And?'

'He replied that at Acre there were only six English Templars: myself, Odo Tharlestone, Legrave, Branquier, Baddlesmere and Symmes. The coward screamed in English, so it must have been one of them. Now each is a lord! Oh, how they have all advanced themselves while I rotted.' The Unknown smiled weakly. 'I went out into the woods near Framlingham and saw them sweep by in their power.'

'Why would the Old Man release you and send you back?' Corbett asked.

'I've thought of that,' the Unknown replied haltingly. 'The divisions in the Order are well known: further scandal would weaken it even more in the eyes of the Western princes.'

'But now you are dying,' Corbett exclaimed. 'When you were in the woods near Framlingham, why didn't you seek an audience with de Molay?'

'Because . . .' The Unknown closed his eyes. 'Because, Sir Hugh, I want to die clean before God. No, no.' He shook his head. 'That's not the full truth. As I journeyed through Europe I heard the stories about my Order: why should I drag it down further?'

'So why me?'

'My desire for vengeance has gone, Sir Hugh, but justice must be done. You will inform de Molay of what I know. Tell him to ask each of his commanders where they were in Acre.'

'Nothing else?' Corbett asked. 'No details about which wall or which part of the city?'

'The Templars will know,' the Unknown replied. 'They will ask questions. They will interrogate.' He grasped Corbett's hands. 'Swear, Sir Hugh, that you will!'

Corbett stared down at the Unknown's face, so cruelly ravaged by disease.

'You are not frightened by a leper's touch?' the dying man teased.

'I have learnt it takes more than a touch for the contagion to spread,' Corbett replied. 'But yes, sir, whoever you may be: at my time and my choosing, I will tell de Molay.' He placed the Unknown's hand back on the blanket. 'Is there anything else?'

189

The Unknown shook his head. 'No, my mind's at peace. Now go!'

Corbett rose and walked to the door.

'Sir Hugh!'

Corbett turned.

'I have heard the stories, the terrible fires: whoever it is, he's the coward, I know it.'

Outside in the passageway, Corbett sat for a while on a bench. What the Unknown had confessed was significant, but how and why? Corbett sighed: he'd not tell de Molay – not anyone, he decided, not even Ranulf – until the other pieces of the puzzle were in place.

Corbett and Ranulf reached Framlingham just before dusk. Their ride was quiet, Corbett refusing to answer Ranulf's questions. They found Maltote lying on Corbett's bed, his arms clasping two heavy calf-skin tomes. He woke up with a start, still holding on to the books as he blinked, owl-eyed, up at them.

'Master, I am sorry,' he apologised, 'but I had to wait a while.' He put the books down on the bed beside him.

'His Grace the king?' Corbett asked.

'Well, he's in a fair old rage; closeted in his chamber with de Warrenne and the rest. He has ordered the sheriffs to seal all ports. The Templars are definitely out of favour.'

'We know all that,' Ranulf retorted. 'Did he send any messages?'

'We are to return soon. He will take matters into his own hands.'

'And have you discovered anything about the phrases I wrote down for you?' Corbett asked. He sat down beside Maltote and picked up one of the books and opened it. 'For God's sake, Maltote!' he exclaimed. 'What have you brought? "Jerome's Commentary on St Matthew"?'

'It's a bit further on,' Maltote gabbled. 'I showed those

words to the archivist at the minster, and he sent me back with these books.'

Corbett leafed through the pages and a title caught his eye. '"*Liber Ignium*", "The Book of Fires",' Corbett whispered. 'Yes, the same phrase I found in Odo's manuscripts.'

He picked up the second volume, a collection of philosophical writings. Again Corbett leafed through, stopped and smiled. He'd found what he was looking for: '*Epistola de Secretis Operibus Artis et Naturae.*'

'The writings of Friar Roger Bacon,' Corbett explained, 'concerning the secrets of nature. Bacon was a Franciscan, he studied at Oxford. An eccentric recluse, he built an observatory on Folly Bridge and spent most of his time studying the stars.'

'Did you know him?' Ranulf asked.

'Vaguely,' Corbett replied. 'He sometimes lectured in the Schools, a short, stocky man with a sunburnt face and a beard shaped like a spade. Poor eyesight but he had a voice like a bell. Some people considered him witless, others a deep thinker.'

'And how can these books help us?' Ranulf asked.

'I don't know. Perhaps they can't.'

'You have to take great care of them,' Maltote interrupted. 'That archivist made me take an oath and sign an indenture. They are to be returned immediately to the minster library.'

'Does anyone here know you have them?'

'No,' Maltote replied. 'The Templars paid little attention to me. One of the soldiers told me what had happened: the mysterious fire, the deaths of Lord Baddlesmere and the other one. They're whispering that they were lovers.' He paused as a bell began to toll. 'They are having the Requiem now. Only a few know I am here.'

Corbett got up and walked to the window. The sun was still shining but the clouds were beginning to mass, dark and sullen overhead.

'We'll have a storm later,' he remarked. 'Be careful,' he

warned over his shoulder. 'Don't wander round the manor by yourselves.'

'Master.' Ranulf came up beside him. 'I have been thinking. Do you remember the joust? De Molay remarked how Legrave held his lance in his left hand.'

'Yes, yes, I do.'

'And Branquier, he writes with his left hand.'

'What has that got to do with it?'

'Well, the assassin in the library. You described him as helmeted and cloaked . . .'

Corbett turned and clapped Ranulf on the shoulder.

'Well done, oh sharpest of clerks!' he cried. 'Maltote, bring those books. Ranulf, you have an arbalest. Come on, let's go back to the library.'

Corbett hurried out of the chamber. Ranulf hung back to inform Maltote in hushed tones what had happened since he had left. He told him about Seagrave and the visit to the Lazar hospital, swearing the young messenger to secrecy.

'Or,' Ranulf muttered darkly, 'Corbett will see you reduced to the lowest scullion in the royal kitchens.' He stopped speaking abruptly as Corbett came back into the room.

'I've been waiting!' he snapped. 'Maltote, bring those books! Ranulf, your crossbow!'

Outside the day was dying. The sky was purple-black and, in the distance, came the first faint rumble of thunder and the faint flash of lightning above the forests to the north of the manor. They made their way past the church where the Templars were still gathered, the faint strains of the Requiem Mass echoing eerily through the stained-glass windows. The library was unlocked but dark. Corbett lit a few candles, making sure their capped hoods were secured, then walked down to where he had been sitting when the assassin struck. He told Maltote and Ranulf to stay by the door, then instructed his manservant to pretend he was attacking him.

'I am right-handed, Master,' Ranulf called. 'As most men

are: I hold the arbalest steady with my right and pull back the winch with my left.'

Corbett studied him.

'If I was left-handed.' Ranulf continued, 'then it would be the other way round, like this.' He moved the arbalest to the other hand, holding it more clumsily as he winched back the lever.

Corbett closed his eyes, trying to recall that fateful afternoon. He shook his head and opened his eyes.

'Do it again, Ranulf. Walk forward slowly.'

Ranulf obeyed. Maltote, still holding the books, stood by the door.

'Well, Master?' Ranulf asked, now only a yard away from him. 'Can you remember?'

'He held it in his right hand,' Corbett declared. 'Yes, definitely his right.'

'So, the assassin could have been Symmes or de Molay? Legrave and Branquier are left-handed. Baddlesmere's a blackened corpse, and the same goes for Scoudas. Moreover, we now know, or think we do,' Ranulf continued, 'that neither Baddlesmere nor Scoudas had a hand in this business.'

Corbett just shook his head and extinguished the candles. They walked out of the library, back across the square. The Templars were now leaving the chapel; de Molay, surrounded by his commanders, beckoned Corbett over.

'Sir Hugh.' The grand master forced a smile. 'We wondered where you were. We even thought you might have forgotten us.'

'King's business in York,' Corbett replied. He glanced quickly over his shoulder and thanked God Maltote had had the sense to hide the books under his cloak.

'We buried our dead,' de Molay continued flatly, staring up at the darkening sky. 'And it seems their passing will not go unnoticed by the weather. Sir Hugh, we have certain decisions to make. You will be our guest at dinner tonight?'

'No funeral obsequies?' Corbett asked.

'Not for Baddlesmere!' Branquier snapped, stepping forward. 'Sir Hugh, this business is finished.'

'And Baddlesmere is the guilty party?' Corbett retorted.

'The evidence points that way,' de Molay replied. 'His lustful relationship with Scoudas; his resentments; the map of York showing where the king was stopping; the Assassins' warning. What further proof do we need? Royal writ or no, we have been prisoners here far too long. In three days' time I intend to go into York to seek audience with the king. My companions here also have business. We cannot wait. These matters are resolved: Baddlesmere was the guilty party.'

'I don't think so,' Corbett replied.

The Templar commanders, openly hostile, now took up a more threatening stance. They moved round him, throwing back the white ceremonial robes of their Order, hands touching the swords and daggers in their belts. Corbett stood his ground.

'Don't threaten me, Grand Master.'

'I am not threatening,' de Molay retorted. 'I am sick and tired of the intrigue and the mystery, the fires and the murder of old companions. Those things are a tragedy, but I am a French subject, Grand Master of the Order of Templars. I object to being a prisoner in one of my own manors.'

'Then go if you wish, Grand Master. But I tell you this, everyone of you will be arrested as a traitor. And don't quote Baddlesmere's name to me. He may have been a sodomite, a man who grumbled, but he was totally innocent of any crime. The day the king was attacked in York he was closeted with his lover in a chamber at the Greenmantle tavern. He'd left before I was warned. Nor could Scoudas have had that warning pushed into my hand, or tried to kill me as I went through York.'

De Molay's gaze faltered. 'But the map?' he questioned. 'The warning? The receipt of monies?'

'Aye, I've reflected on that,' Corbett replied. He glanced sideways at Symmes, his dagger half-drawn from his belt.

'Keep your hand away from your dagger,' he warned. 'And look after your pet weasel.'

Symmes's good eye glared at de Molay, who nodded imperceptibly.

'You were telling us about Baddlesmere,' the grand master said.

'Baddlesmere believed that the assassin was a member of his Order,' Corbett continued. 'He was making his own inquiries. He drew that map for some purpose which, at this moment in time, I don't understand. He also transcribed that warning so as to study it more closely. To put it bluntly, Grand Master, the man I am hunting still lives and breathes. Poor Baddlesmere died as a pretext, nothing more.'

They all turned as a serjeant ran up and, pushing his way through, whispered into de Molay's ear.

'What's the matter?' Corbett asked.

'Something or nothing,' the grand master replied. 'But one of our squires, Joscelyn, is missing, probably deserted.' De Molay looked over Corbett's shoulder at Ranulf. 'Tell your manservant to lower that arbalest.' De Molay raised his hands, snapping his fingers. 'The rest of you follow me. Sir Hugh,' he smiled apologetically, 'you are still our guest. Do join us for supper tonight.'

Corbett stood his ground as the Templars swept away in a flurry of cloaks, their boots crunching on the pebbles. Maltote gave a groan and crouched down.

'Master, these books weigh like a sack of stones.'

Ranulf tucked the crossbow bolt back into his pouch. Corbett turned clumsily. His legs felt heavy as lead. He moved his neck to ease the cramp.

Ranulf asked, 'Do you think Baddlesmere was killed because he knew too much?'

'Possibly,' Corbett replied. 'But I still don't see any pattern to these killings. The grand master is correct: we cannot detain him here for much longer.'

195

'And would the king arrest them?'

'I doubt it. De Molay is a lord in his own right, as well as a subject of Philip of France. The king could huff and puff, detain him at some port and threaten to confiscate Templar goods. But de Molay would eventually leave and appeal to the Pope.'

'And so the killer will walk free?'

'On this occasion, Ranulf, he might well do that. But let's not disappoint our hosts. We have to wash and change.'

They returned to the guesthouse. For a while Corbett sat studying the books Maltote had brought. He read the first chapters of Bacon's work, though he could find little there of interest. He cradled the book in his hands and remembered the Unknown's dying gasps in the Lazar hospital. What, he thought, was the significance of his confession: allegations about cowardice amongst the Templars at Acre so many years ago? Was the coward here at Framlingham? Outside the storm broke: the rain splattered against the window, the thunder crashed over the manor house, whilst the lightning illuminated the trees and grounds in great bursts of white light.

'Is there anything interesting in the books?' Ranulf asked, coming up beside him.

Corbett scratched his head. 'Nothing.' He got to his feet. 'It will wait.' He took off his jerkin. 'I wonder what will happen now?'

Ranulf just stared at him.

'I wonder if the true assassin thought I'd be happy with naming Baddlesmere as the assassin?'

'So, we are still in danger?' Ranulf asked.

'Possibly. But come . . .' He paused at the tolling of the bell, almost hidden under the rumble of thunder. 'Our hosts await us.'

They finished their preparations, putting their cloaks on, and ran through the rain and into the main door of the manor. De Molay and his commanders were waiting in the hall. Corbett had to hide a shiver at the scene. Outside the windows, thunder crashed and lightning flared. In the hall itself, all the torches had been lit, and a row of candles along the table threw long shadows which danced and moved against the wall. Corbett and his companions received a frosty welcome. De Molay indicated with his hand where they should sit: Corbett on his left, Ranulf and Maltote further down the table. The grand master said grace, then servants brought out the dishes from the kitchen. Corbett found it difficult to eat, scrupulously studying his goblet, only sipping from it after the others drank wine poured from the same jug.

'You don't trust us, Sir Hugh,' de Molay murmured, popping a piece of bread into his mouth.

'I have enjoyed more festive banquets,' Corbett replied.

The meal continued. Legrave attempted a conversation, but de Molay was lost in his own thoughts, whilst Symmes and Branquier gazed stonily down at the table, determined to ignore Corbett and his companions. The meal was drawing to an end when there was a loud knocking on the door. Corbett turned in his chair as a serjeant ran in.

'Grand Master!' he gasped. 'Grand Master, there are royal soldiers here!'

De Molay half rose from his chair, his surprise cut short as the door crashed open and a rain-sodden captain of the royal guard strode into the hall. Behind him, two of his men pushed a chained, manacled figure, the prisoner's cloak dripping with water.

'Grand Master,' the captain declared, 'I apologise for the inconvenience caused by our abrupt arrival. We believe this is one of your men.'

Grabbing the prisoner, he thrust him forward, pulling back the cowl. Corbett stared in utter disbelief at the unshaven, rain-soaked face of Sir Bartholomew Baddlesmere.

Chapter 12

Immediate consternation broke out: the commanders leaping up, daggers drawn, chairs falling back. More soldiers rushed into the hall, swords out, arbalests loaded. The captain of the royal guard rapped out orders, his men gathered in a small circle facing outwards round their prisoners, weapons ready. Corbett recovered from his surprise and shouted for silence. Whilst he did so, he gazed quickly at the Templar commanders; all of them, de Molay included, looked as if they had seen a ghost.

'There will be silence!' Corbett roared. He drew from his pouch the Secret Seal he always carried. 'Every man here will put away his weapons. I am the king's commissioner.' He continued at the top of his voice. 'I carry the Royal Writ. It is treason to oppose me.'

His threats eased the tension: swords were sheathed, de Molay rapped out orders. The Templar serjeants withdrew, the royal guard also relaxed. Corbett approached their captain, who now took off his heavy conical helmet. He cradled it in his arms, wiping the sweat and water from his face. His prisoner stood swaying, oblivious to what was going on around him.

'Sir Hugh.' The captain stretched forth his hand. 'Ebulo Montibus, Knight Banneret. I bring greetings from the king.'

Corbett clasped his hand.

'I never thought,' the captain continued, 'that I would receive such a welcome. After all, the man has done no wrong.'

'It's a long story, Captain.'

Symmes came forward: he caught Baddlesmere just before he fell and helped him to a chair.

'If he's done no wrong, why is he chained?' Branquier snapped. He filled a goblet of wine and passed it down to the prisoner.

'It's quite simple,' Montibus snorted. 'The king's proclamation was very clear: no Templar was to leave Framlingham Manor.'

'And where did you find him?' Corbett asked.

'Trying to smuggle his way through Micklegate Bar. He wore no Templar livery but the saddlebags he carried contained enough evidence about who he was. The city bailiffs arrested him. He was detained in the castle and the king ordered him to be brought back here.' The captain smacked his lips and looked at the table. 'It's a witch's night,' he continued. 'My men are cold, hungry.'

'Then be our guest.' De Molay intervened smoothly. 'Legrave, take our guests into the kitchen. The chains can be removed, can't they?'

Montibus agreed. Baddlesmere's leg irons and wrist gyves were unlocked, falling to a heap on the floor. Baddlesmere, however, sat like a man poleaxed. Now and again he would blink or drink greedily from the goblet. His escort disappeared into the kitchen; only Montibus stayed. Corbett took his seat. Maltote stood staring, open-mouthed, like a cow over a hedge.

Ranulf, delighted by the surprising diversion, grinned from ear to ear. He came down and whispered an Corbett's ear, 'Nothing is what it appears to be, eh, Master?'

'Did he commit a crime?' de Molay asked.

'Not that we know of,' Montibus replied. 'Except that he broke the royal prohibition.'

'It's the first time ever,' Ranulf remarked with a laugh, retaking his seat, 'that I have sat at table with a man who is supposed to be dead, buried and his Requiem sung.'

'Shut up!' Branquier snarled, his face white with fury.

Ranulf just smiled back. Baddlesmere slammed the goblet
down on the table. He gave a deep sigh then slouched forward,
shoulders hunched, the tears rolling down his cheeks. Montibus
was ignoring all this, piling the trancher in front of him with
scraps of chicken and pork. He began to eat hungrily then,
struck at last by Ranulf's words, and by the tense silence,
looked up. 'What is this?' His face grew serious as he stared
round at the company. 'What did you mean, a man who's
supposed to be dead and buried?'

'Captain,' Corbett intervened. 'Eat your food and drink
your wine. You and your men can stay the night. I am sure
the grand master's hospitality will extend to that. Sir
Bartholomew, there are questions I must ask, though this is
not the place.'

'No, it is not,' de Molay remarked, rising to his feet.
'Branquier, Sir Hugh, bring Baddlesmere to my chamber.'

Corbett whispered to Ranulf to look after the royal guard,
then followed a shuffling Baddlesmere, held by Branquier, out
of the hall and along the corridors into the grand master's
chamber. For a while Baddlesmere just sat muttering to himself,
rubbing his mouth and staring vacuously around.

'He's lost his wits,' Branquier commented.

'Sir Bartholomew,' de Molay thundered. 'You must tell us
what happened! Your chamber was burnt. The corpses of two
men were found on the bed, blackened and burnt beyond
recognition. We thought one of them was you.'

Baddlesmere lifted his head. 'I am a worm and no man,' he
intoned. 'My sins, my sins are always before me!'

'What sins?' Corbett asked quietly, moving the stool so he
sat directly opposite the Templar. 'What sins, Bartholomew?'

Baddlesmere lifted his head. 'The sin of sodomy,' he rasped.
'Which cries out to God for vengeance.'

'And yet,' Corbett replied, quoting from the Bible, '"though
your sins be as scarlet, they shall be as white as snow." You
loved Scoudas, didn't you?'

201

Baddlesmere plucked at a loose thread in his rain-sodden hose.

'I became a Templar,' he began slowly, 'as a young man. I wanted to be a knight in shining armour, dying for the Cross. No, even before that, as a child: I used to sleep in my mother's room. She would bring men home. I'd hear her groaning and scrabbling in the bed. I was only a stripling. By the time I was fourteen, I knew I could never take a woman. I wanted to be pure, cold as ice and white as snow: clean and God-fearing before the Lord.' Baddlesmere pulled a face. 'And so I was. I became a Templar, a warrior, a monk, a priest. I had temptations of the flesh but I could control them, until I met Scoudas. At first I loved him like the son I never had but always wanted. His skin was smooth, white as satin . . .'

'And on the morning you went to York,' Corbett interrupted, 'you saw Murston being gibbeted and then went to the tavern, the Greenmantle?'

Baddlesmere nodded.

'And Scoudas went with you?'

'Yes, we shared the same chamber. However, Scoudas had changed. He began to threaten me, insinuate that he would complain.' Baddlesmere paused. 'He shouldn't have done that: he mocked me as an old man, telling me that he had met someone else, Joscelyn, a member of Branquier's retinue. I left in a temper, rejoined de Molay and journeyed back to Framlingham.'

'And the night of the fire?' Corbett asked.

'Scoudas came to my chamber. I thought he'd come to make his peace. Joscelyn was with him. They sat and baited me, threatening to disgrace me. I couldn't bear their taunts any longer. I walked out of the room, slamming the door behind me, their laughter ringing in my ears. The manor was quiet. I'd left my wine in my chamber so I took a jug from the buttery and went into the grounds. I deliberately hid myself because I didn't want to meet or talk to anyone. I went around the maze and across into the trees. The night was warm. I fell asleep. I was tired and exhausted. I'd drunk a little too much. When I woke, it was dark, though I could see the sun was about to rise. I got up stiff and sore. I was about to go back to the manor when I heard the cries and saw the flames. Even from where I stood, the smoke hung heavy in the air.' He paused and scratched his chin.

'And you fled?' Branquier asked.

Baddlesmere paused as the door opened and Symmes and Legrave slipped in.

'The royal guards are feeding their faces,' Symmes barked. 'And, when they've finished at the trough, I will show them their sties.'

Corbett ignored the insult. 'Why did you flee?' he asked.

'I suppose I panicked,' Baddlesmere replied. 'It was obvious someone had died in the room. I would be blamed. Whatever I did, I'd be damned. My secret sin would be revealed. Worse, I might be accused of starting the fire and held responsible for the other deaths. It was quite easy: I had my saddlebag with me so I simply climbed the wall. For a while I stayed in the open countryside around York, but I needed a horse and a change of clothing.' He flailed his hands. 'The rest you know.'

'You guessed someone was in your chamber?'

'I went as close as I could to the manor house, I could tell from the shouts and cries. I started to think: was the assassin after my life? Even if I could prove my innocence, they'd still say I killed Scoudas.' He put his face in his hands and sobbed quietly.

'Joscelyn died too,' Corbett remarked.

'But why?' Baddlesmere asked. 'Both men were young and vigorous. They could have escaped.'

'You left a jug of wine?' Corbett insisted.

Baddlesmere blinked slowly.

'The wine?' Corbett repeated. 'How much did you leave?'

'A jug, five or six cups.' Baddlesmere's jaw sagged. 'You

are saying it was tainted? They were poisoned or drugged?'

'That is the only explanation.'

'But I wouldn't hurt him!' Baddlesmere wailed. 'I would never hurt Scoudas!'

'When did you put the wine in your room?'

'Early in the afternoon: the best Rhenish. I placed it in a bowl of cold water to chill.'

'And did you drink it?'

'Yes, yes, I did, half a cup: then Scoudas and Joscelyn arrived. I became so angry at their taunting, I threw the cup on the floor and left.'

'Sir Bartholomew,' Corbett continued, 'all your possessions were destroyed in the fire but, amongst Scoudas's, we found a map of York and the assassins' warning, both in your hand, as well as a receipt signed by Murston for monies received.'

Baddlesmere's eyes took on a secretive, cunning look: the change of mood was so quick that Corbett wondered whether the man was fully in his wits, or even if he might truly be the assassin, Sagittarius.

'The papers,' Corbett insisted, 'please. Why should Scoudas be holding these papers?'

Baddlesmere coughed and licked his lips. 'I'd like some wine, Sir Hugh.'

Branquier filled a cup from the side-table and thrust it in his hands.

'Answer my question,' Corbett insisted.

'You have no authority here,' Branquier broke in.

'Yes he has,' de Molay snapped. 'Sir Bartholomew, answer the question!'

'Yes, I'll answer your question.' Baddlesmere sat up. 'Though I don't like snooping clerks. Whatever my sins, I'm still a Templar. I resent you, Corbett. I resent you being here. The Order has its own rituals and rule.'

'The papers?' Corbett demanded harshly.

'I was making my own inquiries,' Baddlesmere snapped

back. 'I drew that map and the warning to help myself. I gave
a copy to Scoudas and asked him to keep his eyes and ears
open. If my chamber hadn't burst into flames, you'd have
found other copies there as well.' He shrugged. 'I know nothing
about a receipt for Murston.'

'Why did your room burn?' Corbett asked.

'I don't know.'

'There was nothing in it which could start such an inferno?'

'Nothing. Clothing, parchment, some books but nothing
else!'

'An oil-lamp?' Corbett asked.

'I said nothing.' Baddlesmere's eyes slid away. Corbett
knew this disgraced Templar had his own suspicions.

'What will happen to me?' Baddlesmere whispered. His
eyes pleaded with de Molay.

'You will be confined to a chamber on bread and water,' the
grand master replied. 'And, when these matters are finished
and the king's clerk has left us alone, you will stand trial before
your peers. The Crown, if it so wishes, may also punish you for
defiance of its writ.'

Baddlesmere nodded. 'I'll be broken, won't I?' he murmured
as if to himself. 'I'll have my spurs hacked off, my knighthood
removed. Sir Bartholomew Baddlesmere, Commander of the
Order of the Temple, reduced to a kitchen scullion in some
lonely castle.' He clenched a hand, glaring at Corbett so
furiously that the clerk's hand dropped to the hilt of his dagger.
Behind him he could feel the hate of Sir Bartholomew's
companions: disgraced though Baddlesmere was, like any
enclosed community, the Templars deeply resented the intrusion
of outsiders. Corbett got to his feet.

'Grand Master, I am finished. I must insist that Sir
Bartholomew is kept secure.' He walked to the door.

'Corbett!' Baddlesmere was staring oddly at him. 'Truth
stands on the bank.'

'What do you mean?'

205

Baddlesmere began to laugh, shaking his head, gesturing at him to go. Corbett bowed at de Molay and left for his own chamber. Ranulf and Maltote immediately began to question him.

'I don't know,' Corbett replied. 'I don't know if Baddlesmere is telling the truth, has lost his wits, or whether he is actually the assassin. Maltote, where are those books?'

The messenger pulled them out from beneath the bed.

'We'll all sleep in this chamber,' Corbett declared. 'But for tonight – ' he eased himself on the bed and opened one of the books – 'I'll see what secrets these hold.'

Corbett spent the night reading and rereading different pages whilst his companions snored, sleeping as peacefully as babes. Sometimes Corbett's eyes would grow heavy. He dozed for a while and then shook himself awake, going across to splash water on his face or replenish the candles when they burnt too low. At last he could do no more. The last chapters of Bacon's work were a mystery but Corbett felt elated. He knew the source of that mysterious fire and, just before dawn, drifted into nightmares lit by the roaring flames of the Devil's fire.

Ranulf shook him awake. 'Master, it's ten o'clock.'

Corbett rose and groaned, shielding his eyes against the sunlight pouring in through the open shutters.

'Maltote and I have been up hours. We broke our fast in the refectory, gobbling away whilst the community just glared at us. Montibus has gone.'

Corbett groaned. 'Oh, no!' He swung his legs off the bed and rubbed his face, pushing the books away. 'I wanted him to stay. He might have afforded us some protection.'

Ranulf's face became serious. 'The Templars wouldn't attack us surely, not royal envoys?'

'Oh, not attack, but you or I, my dear Ranulf, could suffer some dreadful accident.'

'Tell him what we found,' Maltote urged from where he sat perched on a stool busily sewing a stirrup leather.

206

'Oh yes.' Ranulf handed Corbett a rag tied in a knot at the neck.

'Undo it carefully, Master.'

Corbett did so and stared at the burnt leather fragments.

'What's this?' He touched one piece and it crumbled into flakes. One small part, however, still remained firm and smooth.

'It's leather,' Ranulf explained. 'Scraps of leather. We found them in the woods where those scorch-marks were: little pieces blown about by the breeze.'

Corbett placed the rag carefully on the bed. He took each scrap, scrutinising it closely before putting it back. He then got to his feet, stretched, and took off his jerkin and shirt. He went across to wash his face and hands, telling Maltote to get some hot water from the scullery as he also wished to shave.

'Well?' Ranulf asked anxiously. 'What do you think?'

'They are burnt scraps of leather,' Corbett replied, rubbing his hands with the small bar of soap he'd bought from a merchant in Beverley. 'They may be fragments of a sack used to carry what the Ancients called "Devil's fire".'

Ranulf immediately began to question him, but Corbett just shook his head and, when Maltote returned, concentrated on his shaving, asking Ranulf to hold the mirror steady in his hands.

'Once I am finished,' Corbett smiled at Ranulf, 'get me some food from the kitchen – but make sure you see who handles it. Whilst I eat, I'll tell you a story.'

As Corbett dried himself off, Ranulf hurried out and returned with a linen cloth bearing loaves and a stoup of ale.

'So,' Corbett rubbed his chin and sat down at the table. 'Now I have finished my ablutions, let me tell you what those books contained. First, the fire is not from hell, it's man-made.'

Corbett bit into one of the loaves, Ranulf shuffled his feet impatiently.

'At first,' Corbett continued, 'I thought the fire could have been started by some form of oil but that's not safe. Sometimes oil is difficult to burn, especially when it congeals. Now Brother Odo, God rest his soul, also realised this. He must have examined his chronicle and recalled the fire missiles the Turks threw into Acre. Now these were nothing extraordinary: a mixture of tar and pitch, poured over some rags, torched as they lay in a catapult, then cast in amongst the defenders. I've seen the same happen at sieges: straw or rags coated with sulphur and then lit.

'But this fire is different. Odo realised that. A student of warfare, he recalled two books. The first is an ancient tract called the "*Liber Ignium*" or "Book of Fires". The second is much more interesting: Friar Bacon's letter, "De Secretis Operibus Artis et Naturae". Now both these works describe a very dangerous substance, a mixture of elements which, if exposed to the naked flame, creates fire difficult to put out even with water.'

'And you think this caused these murders?' Ranulf asked.

'Perhaps. The "*Liber*" describes the mixture as sulphur, tartar and a substance called "*Sal Coctum*" or cooked salt. Bacon is more specific: he mentions a substance called saltpetre. Now Friar Bacon conceals his discovery behind riddles and anagrams but, if he is to be believed, this saltpetre mixed with sulphur and tartar will ignite immediately.'

'But you said,' Ranulf declared, 'that Bacon was regarded by many as witless.'

'I doubt it,' Corbett replied. 'Friar Bacon acquired his learning from the Arabs. According to them, this substance was known to the ancient Greeks as well as the armies of Byzantium which used it to destroy a Muslim fleet; hence its name: "Greek" or Sea fire".'

'And, of course,' Ranulf added, 'all the Templar commanders have served in Outremer. They might know of this secret.'

Corbett popped a piece of bread into his mouth. 'More importantly, the Templars have some of the finest libraries in the world, especially in London and in Paris,' he said. 'However, though de Molay and his companions might know the secret, they are too engrossed in what is happening to their Order: all they can see are these dreadful deaths and the consequent scandals.' Corbett sipped at the ale. 'Brother Odo was different: more detached, more serene, he was a born scholar. The assassination of Reverchien must have stirred memories. He was searching for what I've found.'

'But can you prove all this?' Ranulf asked.

'If necessary but—'

The door was abruptly thrown open and de Molay burst into the room. 'Sir Hugh, you must come immediately! It's Baddlesmere . . .'

The grand master strode out, leaving Corbett no choice but to follow, Ranulf and Maltote hurrying behind. De Molay strode ahead, not even bothering to look back. He went round the back of the manor into the servants' quarters, up a flight of stairs and along a narrow passageway. The guards outside the chamber opened the door, de Molay went in and Corbett followed.

'Oh, my God!'

The clerk immediately turned away. Baddlesmere, dressed in shirt and hose, swung from the end of a sheet which had been tied round one of the rafters. He looked grisly yet pathetic: his face had turned a dark purple, eyes popping, tongue clenched between half-opened lips. His corpse twirled like some grotesque doll in the breeze coming through the arrow-slit window. Corbett drew his dagger and, helped by Ranulf, got the corpse down and laid him on the trestle bed. De Molay stood just inside the door, his face marble-white, dark circles round his eyes. He opened his mouth to speak but instead just shook his head.

'Grand Master, what did you say?'

De Molay's lips moved but no sound came out. Instead he clutched his stomach, pushed Corbett aside and rushed out towards one of the latrines built into an alcove in the corridor.

They heard him being violently sick.

'Is it suicide?' Ranulf whispered.

Corbett studied the corpse, examining the nails carefully, the position of the knot behind the left ear. He lifted the shirt, examined the man's torso, then sawed through the knot with his dagger. He tried to arrange the corpse in as dignified a pose as possible and covered it with Baddlesmere's cloak.

'He committed suicide,' Corbett muttered. He pointed up at the rafters then at the bed. 'So simple, to walk from life into death. Baddlesmere stood on the bed, fashioned that noose, put it round his neck and kicked the bed away.'

'What's this?' Ranulf leaned across the bed and pointed to a carved scrawl on the wall.

Corbett studied this carefully and, looking amongst Baddlesmere's possessions, realised the dead man had carved this, using the buckle of his belt, now worn down on one corner.

'What does it say?' Ranulf asked.

Corbett studied the words. '"*Veritas*," he read, '"*Stat in ripa.*"' 'Truth stands on the bank,' he muttered. 'What on earth did Baddlesmere mean by that? The tag usually reads, "Veritas stat in media via"; "Truth stands in the Middle way".'

'I found him hanging!'

Corbett whirled round: de Molay stood in the doorway.

'He was here last night, with a jug of water and bread. Two guards stood outside.'

'And they heard nothing?'

De Molay shook his head. 'They heard him moving around early in the morning: he was singing the "*Dies Irae*". You know the sequence from the Mass of the Dead. How does it go, Corbett? "O Day of Wrath! O Day of Mourning! Heaven and Earth in Ashes Burning".'

'"See What Fear Man's Bosom Renders,"' Corbett continued, '"When from Heaven the Judge Descendeth on Whose Sentence All Dependeth!"'

De Molay knelt by the bed, crossing himself. When the others came, Branquier, Legrave and Symmes, Corbett walked back down the stairs and out into the fresh air. De Molay joined him there, Legrave beside him.

'Before you ask, Grand Master, Sir Bartholomew committed suicide.' Corbett shrugged. 'Overcome by remorse, fearful of what he had been implicated in, unable to accept the disgrace.'

'I came up,' de Molay remarked, 'just to greet him as a brother.' He glanced at Legrave. 'He can't be buried in hallowed ground.'

'But, Grand Master,' Legrave exclaimed, 'he was my brother as well! I knew Sir Bartholomew. We fought at Acre together.'

De Molay glanced expectantly at Corbett.

'Charity lies at the root of all laws,' Corbett declared. 'I do not think Christ will judge him as harshly as you do.'

'Strange,' de Molay murmured. 'All these deaths by fire. When I was a child, Corbett, playing in the fields outside Carcassone, I taunted a witch, an old woman, who lived in a shabby hut built against the wall overlooking the ditch. With all the foolishness and ignorance of youth, I shouted that she should burn. She approached me, eyes gleaming. *"No, de Molay,"* she screeched back. *"You will die in fire and smoke!"*' De Molay rubbed his eyes. 'I always wondered what she meant. Now I know: there are different forms of fire and there are different kinds of death.'

And, not waiting for an answer, the grand master spun on his heel and walked away. Legrave followed him. Corbett watched them go then beckoned Ranulf and Maltote over.

'Get your horses ready,' he ordered. 'I want you to go to York. Seek out Claverley.' He dug into his pouch and handed them a small scrap of parchment. 'Scour the city, buy these mixtures, but keep each separate. Claverley will assist you.'

'Where shall we look?'

'Among the charcoal-burners of the city. It may take some time, but remember what I said: keep each substance separate

211

and bring them back as soon as you can.'

Within the hour, Ranulf and Maltote had left the manor. Corbett decided to stay in his own chamber. He examined this carefully, locking the shutters on the window before going out to find a long ash pole to lie across the bottom of the door. As he did this, Corbett noticed the gap between the door and floor. For a while, he stood and stared at the long piece of leather hung on the back of the door to exclude draughts. Corbett smiled. 'I wonder,' he murmured.

He had a vague idea how each of the victims had died, but not of the motive or the identity of the assassin. He laid out his writing implements on the table and, for a while, studied what he had written, trying to recall conversations, incidents, gestures and expressions. His mind kept going back to Baddlesmere's death scene: the corpse swaying slightly and that enigmatic inscription carved on the wall.

'Truth doesn't stand on the bank,' Corbett murmured. 'It stands in the middle way. What did Baddlesmere mean by that nonsense?'

He slept for a while, then got up and went down to the kitchen to beg for some food; a surly, hard-eyed retainer almost flung it at him. Later in the afternoon there was a knock on the door, de Molay asking if all was well? Corbett shouted that it was and returned to his studies. He decided to concentrate on the first item of evidence: the assassins' warning. Once again Corbett noticed how there were two versions.

'Why, why, why?' Corbett muttered to himself. 'Why are they different?'

There was the message left in St Paul's with which the Baddlesmere version agreed, as did the words spoken in the library: these three differed slightly from Claverley's and the one pushed into his hand on Ouse bridge. Every story, Corbett thought, has a common source, be it a love poem or some message. It only changes when it's passed on. Baddlesmere learnt about the warning when the king met de Molay and the other Templar commanders at the Priory. But why was the warning delivered to him on Ouse bridge the same as that given by Claverley? Corbett's hand went to his face.

'Oh, sweet God!' he murmured. 'So much for your fine logic, Corbett!'

He returned to his scribblings, following a new direction, concentrating on when the warnings were given as well as the recent attack on him in York.

Corbett looked up. 'The Templars may have been in York when the warning was passed,' he whispered, 'but they were definitely gone when I was attacked.'

He snatched his pen up. Ergo, he wrote, the attack was planned by someone else. Corbett nibbled the tip of the quill. Once he had suspected Baddlesmere and Scoudas; in reality both men were innocent, more absorbed in their own sin than anything else. Corbett drew two circles on the parchment, then drew a line joining them. He got up, opened the shutter and stared out at the dusk. Some of the riddle was resolved, the how and the why, but who? Whom did Baddlesmere suspect? And what did that inscription mean? Was it a pointer to the truth? A warning to the assassin, or both? '*Veritas stat*' Corbett translated as 'Truth stands', but '*in ripa*'? He went back and began to play with the words, changing them round, but this proved nothing. He picked up the warning the little boy had given him on Ouse Bridge, then he looked down at his jottings: did I, Corbett wondered, tell anyone about that? And, if not, who amongst the Templars mentioned it? He racked his brains but his eyes were growing heavy. He made sure the door was secure, wrapped his cloak around him and lay down on the bed.

Chapter 13

Ranulf and Maltote returned later the next morning. Both were unshaven, rather bleary-eyed, but loudly protesting how they'd only found what Corbett had ordered after a thorough search. Night had fallen, the curfew had been proclaimed, the city gates shut, so they'd hired a room in a tavern just near Botham Bar Gate.

'Aye, and you tasted the local ale?' Corbett observed crossly.

Ranulf held his hands up, his eyes round with innocence.

'Master, a mere drop, a mere drop.'

'Let us see what you have brought,' Corbett snapped.

Ranulf undid the saddlebag and brought out three large pouches, each containing a powder. Corbett opened, sniffed and felt each of them carefully. The smell was acrid but not pungent.

'In the open air,' he observed, 'it would raise no alarm or suspicion.'

They slipped out of the guesthouse, around the manor and into the maze. Corbett took his hornspoon out of his pouch and, following Bacon's instructions, carefully mixed the powders together. He stirred them with his fingers until all three substances were mingled. He then piled it in a heap, took a lighted candle out of Ranulf's hand and placed it near the fire, urging Ranulf and Maltote to stand back. The candle flame gutted and went out. With some difficulty Corbett relit it. This time the flame was stronger, the candle melted, the flame moving back to where the dark powder lay in a small heap.

Corbett's heart sank in despair but then the flame caught the powder, there was a crackle and the flames leapt greedily into the air, scorching the earth beneath. Corbett studied the flames' blueish tint whilst Ranulf and Maltote stared in amazement.

'I've never seen oil burn so quickly or so fiercely,' Ranulf muttered.

'I've seen something like it,' Corbett declared. 'When farmers burn the dry stubble in autumn: sometimes the fire runs faster than a man.' He stamped on the flame, wary lest it raise the alarm.

They left the maze and walked into the ring of trees where Corbett picked up a dry stick. Once again he mixed the substance: he smeared the wood, leaving one end free which he lit with Ranulf's tinder. This time the effect was even greater. The flame, as soon as it reached the substance, burnt so fast and greedily that Corbett had to stamp it out with his boot.

'You should have used gloves,' Ranulf remarked, watching his master clean his hands on his jerkin. 'A thick, leather pair of gauntlets.'

Corbett looked down at his hands then back up at Ranulf.

'Gloves?' he whispered. 'Do you remember the leather fragments you found? Gauntlets!' he exclaimed. 'That's the only trace the assassin left.'

'What do you mean?' Ranulf asked.

'The fragments of leather,' Maltote volunteered, 'that we found near the scorch-marks: the assassin must have burnt the gauntlets he used.'

Corbett walked deeper into the trees. He now knew who the assassin was, but how could he prove it? What evidence could he offer? He told Ranulf to conceal the bags of powder and they returned to the guesthouse. Corbett asked his companions to find something to eat whilst he returned to studying Baddlesmere's map.

'It's not of the entire city,' Corbett murmured, 'but only the area around Trinity.'

He then studied the inscription Baddlesmere had written on the wall. Last night Corbett had thought the words formed an anagram, a complicated puzzle or riddle. He translated them back into English, rearranging the letters, but all his conclusions were nonsense. Finally he translated them into French and clapped his hands in surprise: Baddlesmere, too, knew the identity of the assassin. However, in those last moments before death, he could not bring himself to name his brother Templar, so he had purged his conscience by leaving this mysterious phrase.

Ranulf and Maltote returned, bringing food from the kitchen. By Corbett's face, Ranulf realised that 'Old Master Long Face' was closing his trap. 'Drawing up a bill of indictment,' he whispered to Maltote. 'Like any hanging judge.'

'You do know, don't you?' he called out.

Corbett put his pen down and turned. 'Yes, I know the assassin and I think I can prove it.'

'Logic,' Ranulf exclaimed, 'as always.'

Corbett shook his head. 'No, Ranulf, not logic. I applied that and made a dreadful mistake. You work on a premise and then believe that everything will fit into place.' He rose and stretched. 'Because of my arrogance and because of my logic, I made a terrible error. Poor Baddlesmere was closer to the truth than I.'

'What's a premise?' Maltote asked, his mouth full of bread and cheese.

'You start with a statement,' Corbett replied. 'Such as "All Men drink ale; Maltote is a man; therefore he drinks ale." But the premise is wrong. All men don't drink ale: it's not an undisputed fact. Therefore, every statement you make based on that must be wrong.' Corbett pulled his stool over to where his companions sat with their backs to the wall, sharing the bread and cheese piled on a pewter plate. 'I believed there was a coven in the Templar Order intent on wreaking vengeance against the Crown both here and in France. I therefore concluded that the murders here at Framlingham and elsewhere were merely the work of that coven. I was wrong.'

'So, what is the truth?' Ranulf asked.

Corbett shook his head. 'Eat your bread and cheese.' He paused as he heard a sound in the gallery outside. 'We have to leave here as quickly as possible,' he urged. 'Ranulf, pack our bags; Maltote, go down to the stables, saddle the horses. I want to be gone within the hour.'

Maltote grabbed a chunk of cheese and hurried out. Ranulf took one look at Corbett's drawn face and hurriedly packed their belongings. Corbett carefully put away his writing implements, checking the chamber, ensuring they had left nothing behind.

'Hide the books Maltote brought,' he hissed. 'And the three bags of powder?'

'They are kept separate,' Ranulf assured him.

They left the guesthouse and went down to the stableyard. Maltote had already led their horses out: he was busily trying to harness the small but evil-tempered sumpter pony. Corbett helped, checking harness and saddle girths. He was surprised at the silence of the manor, then he heard the clink of metal behind him and Ranulf's muttered curse. He swung round: the mouth of the stableyard was now cordoned off by Templar soldiers, helmeted and armed, each carrying an arbalest. On either flank stood their serjeants and officers.

'Mount,' Corbett ordered. 'If necessary, ride through them!'

Corbett edged his own horse forward. An order rang out: one of the crossbowmen raised his crossbow and a bolt whirred through the air over Corbett's head. Fighting to control his panic as well as his restless horse, Corbett rode on. Again the order was issued. This time the crossbow bolt whirred past his face; another smacked the cobbles in front of his horse, making it whinny and shy.

'That's as far as I'm going,' Maltote muttered.

Corbett reined in his horse: de Molay came out of the buildings and walked through the line of men. The grand master was dressed in half-armour, as were the other commanders, his hands resting on the pommel of his sword. He came up and grasped the bridle of Corbett's horse.

'You are not leaving us, Sir Hugh, without so much as a fond farewell?'

'You have no authority,' Corbett retorted. 'I intend to ride through and you must take the consequences!'

'Please.' De Molay's red-rimmed eyes had a pleading look. 'Corbett,' he whispered. 'You know the assassin, don't you? Your face betrays you.'

'These matters are for the king to decide upon,' Corbett replied.

'No, Sir Hugh, this is Templar land. I am the grand master. I must have some control, some say in what happens here. Templar justice is just as thorough and exacting as any king's.'

Corbett relaxed in the saddle. 'You know the murderer, don't you, Grand Master?'

'Yes, yes, I think I do: proving it is another matter.'

'And if I stay,' Corbett volunteered, 'I have your word that justice will be done and I will be allowed to go on my way?'

De Molay raised his hand. 'My oath on the Cross.'

Corbett dismounted. 'Then send four of your men to York. Don't worry, I will give them warrants and passes. They are to go to Monsieur Amaury de Craon, Philip IV's envoy at the archbishop's palace.' Corbett made sure he kept his voice low. 'Tell him what you like but invite him to come here as your guest. Say you wish to reveal secret matters affecting the Crown of France. Couch your letters in the friendliest terms.' Corbett glanced up at the pale-blue sky. 'It's about noon now. He's to be here by dusk.'

'I, too, studied Bartholomew's message scrawled on the wall,' de Molay retorted. 'It fits other pieces, fragments, mere morsels.'

'You should have told me,' Corbett replied.

'By nightfall we will all know,' de Molay whispered.

219

Corbett turned, telling Ranulf and Maltote to dismount: their horses were to go back to the stables, their baggage to the guesthouse. The Templars stood aside and Corbett returned to his own chamber. Guards soon followed, taking up position in the gallery.

'We should have rode on,' Ranulf declared, throwing the baggage to the floor, his face red with anger. 'They wouldn't have dared!'

'There was only one way of knowing that,' Corbett retorted. 'And I wasn't prepared to find out.'

He sat at the table and began to write out a short letter to the king as well as letters of permission allowing the Templar messengers into York. He sealed these hurriedly and Ranulf gave them to one of the guards outside. Corbett was then forced to kick his heels and wait, ignoring Ranulf's constant questioning, or Maltote's hushed observations about how many Templars were on guard.

In the afternoon they went for a walk and the guards followed. Ranulf counted at least a dozen. Corbett was tempted to seek an audience with de Molay but decided not to. He was still not fully sure, and concluded it was best that he wait until de Craon's arrival. He told Ranulf and Maltote to go back to their chamber and went into the Templar church. For a while he sat in the Lady Chapel, staring up at the dark mahogany, beautifully carved statue of the Virgin and Child. Above this was a small rose window with painted scenes from the life of Christ. For a while Corbett prayed: the statue and paintings reminded him of the small parish church near his father's farm.

I should go back there, Corbett thought: make sure my parents' tomb is well kept. He stared up at the window. Perhaps he could buy painted glass to light the dark transept where, under cold, dank slabs, his parents lay buried. He smiled; his mother would have liked that. She used to take him to church on afternoons like this, when his father and elder brothers were busy working on the land. She would describe the painted scenes on the walls or rood-screen: that's how Father Adelbert had come to know him and later agreed to school him.

'You are to work hard, Hugh,' his mother would say. 'Remember, great oak trees always start as little acorns.'

'I wish you were here!' Corbett whispered.

What would she have thought of him now, away from his second wife and child, preparing to confront a murderer and see justice done? That was his father's legacy: a former soldier who had fought in the civil war, his father had constantly preached about the need for a strong prince, good judges and sound laws. Corbett sighed. He got up from the small prie-dieu and walked back to the door of the church where his guards were waiting. He still wasn't sure what he would do: how he could trap the murderer? Evidence was one thing, proof was another. He turned and looked back at the rose window and the stories painted there: a vague idea formed in his mind.

'I want to see de Molay,' he told the guard. 'Now.'

The serjeant in charge shrugged his agreement and took Corbett around the manor house to the grand master's cell. De Molay had been busy: servants were packing chests and coffers, the bed was stripped, the desk had been cleared of all parchments and inkhorns.

'You are leaving, Grand Master?'

De Molay gestured at the retainers to go.

'You are my prisoner, Hugh,' he remarked drily. 'Whatever happens tonight, I will go back with you into York as your prisoner to meet the king.' He cocked his head to one side. 'You have not come about that, have you?'

'No,' Corbett replied. 'I have come to ask a favour. I wish you, Branquier, Symmes and Legrave to write out an account of all that has happened since your arrival in England.'

'Why?'

'Because I want it.'

'What will it prove?'

'Nothing – well, not really,' Corbett lied. 'But tell your commanders that, after my meeting with Monsieur de Craon, they may well wish to lodge their own complaint against me. Such an account might be useful.' Corbett went back towards the door. 'There are still a few hours left,' he called out. 'Plenty of time before dusk.'

Corbett returned to the guesthouse and dozed for a while. Food was brought in from the kitchen and, late in the afternoon, one of de Molay's retainers came to tell him that Monsieur de Craon had arrived and would Sir Hugh prepare himself? About an hour later Corbett, Ranulf and Maltote went into the refectory. The Templars were already assembled around the great table. De Craon rose as Corbett entered, his craggy face wreathed in smiles.

'Sir Hugh, the grand master says you are leaving, though there are matters we should discuss.'

Corbett limply shook de Craon's extended hand, fighting back the urge to smack that sharp, wily face. 'He's two people,' Corbett had once told Maeve. 'There's de Craon the envoy, but in his eyes you can see something else, dark and malevolent.'

Branquier, Symmes and Legrave were also there, as well as one of de Craon's black-garbed clerks: a young man, pale-faced with watchful eyes, his mousy hair cropped close to his head. He was there as de Craon's witness.

As soon as they took their seats, de Craon rose.

'Grand Master, I welcome Sir Hugh Corbett, but I was given to believe that you wished to consult me. Why is he present?'

De Craon's lawyer was already writing, busily recording his master's protests. De Molay smiled. His face became youthful, as if he thoroughly enjoyed baiting Philip's envoy. Corbett wondered what the real relationship between the grand master and the king of France was. De Craon, confused by de Molay's smiling silence, sat down.

'Sir Hugh is here,' de Molay rubbed his hands slowly together, 'because he is a hunter of souls and the searcher out of secrets.' He glanced down the table at Corbett. 'Time is passing,' he murmured. 'Darkness is drawing in.'

Corbett rose and walked to the end of the table so they could all see him and he watch them. Ranulf, as instructed, stood near the door, Maltote beside him; both had rested their loaded arbalests against the wall.

'Once,' Corbett began, 'there was a king of France, saintly but warlike; the holy Louis who wanted to plant the standard of the Cross on the towers of Jerusalem. He failed, died, and a martyr's crown was his reward.'

De Craon, his anger forgotten, was now looking curiously at him.

'At that time,' Corbett continued, 'this saintly king was helped by the Templars, a great fighting order of monks, founded on a rule drawn up by St Bernard himself. They were imbued with a vision, the capture and defence of the Holy Places in Outremer. The years passed, fortunes changed, and we now have a king of France, St Louis's descendant, Philip Le Bel, who would prefer to see his standards flying over the towers of London and Antwerp.'

'This is impossible!' De Craon sprang to his feet.

'Sit down!' de Molay snapped. 'And that's the last time you interrupt, sir!'

'But Philip's dreams crumbled,' Corbett continued, matter of factly. 'So he spun another dream. What he can't get by force, he'll acquire by stealth. His daughter is to marry our king's only son, so Philip knows that one day his grandson will sit on the English throne. Philip has to pay for this. He must collect a huge dowry, but his coffers, like those of Edward of England, are empty, so he looks around and sees the great Templar Order with its manors, farms, cattle and treasure. He watches closely because the Order has lost a great deal of its idealism. There are whispers of scandals; sodomy, drunkenness.'

223

Corbett glanced down the table and noticed Symmes's scarred face blush slightly. 'There are several rituals,' Corbett continued, 'gossip about covens and cabals; and a subtle plan forms in Philip's devious soul . . .'

De Craon made to rise but de Molay's hand went out and pressed him firmly down in his chair.

'The Templar Order itself,' Corbett continued, 'does leave a lot to be desired. There is a rottenness in it, but the Order is protected by the Holy Father in Avignon. Anyone who moves against the Templars moves against the Papacy, and Philip can't do that. He bides his time and selects his man: a Templar who will do for his Order what Judas did for Christ: betrayal with a kiss.'

The Templars stirred. Corbett fleetingly wondered how many of them had at least considered the path which the assassin had trod. Only de Molay remained impassive, hands before his mouth. He watched Corbett with the look of a hunting cat.

'A new grand master to the Order is elected.' Corbett leaned on the table. 'He holds a Grand Chapter in Paris. He wishes the Order to be revitalised and loudly proclaims his intention to make a progress through all its provinces. England will be first. He leaves Paris, lands in Dover and travels to London but, before he leaves France, the scandal breaks. A Templar serjeant, stupid and witless, is captured on suspicion of trying to kill Philip of France. A degenerate, probably dabbling in the occult, this Templar is handed over to the Inquisition. I suppose,' Corbett smiled thinly, 'if I was hung in the dungeons of the Louvre and left to the subtle cruelty of the Inquisition, I would swear black was white and white was black. God forgive me, I might even deny my faith, my family, even as I cursed myself as a coward. For that serjeant it was easier: bitter and resentful, he readily answered the Inquisitor, damning himself and the Order he once served.'

Branquier pushed himself forward. 'Are you saying that the serjeant was no assassin?'

'He was no assassin,' Corbett replied. 'A mere dupe. Philip was not attacked in the Bois de Boulogne or crossing the Grand Ponte: that was only to make us believe a sinister plot existed. There is no "Sagittarius",' Corbett continued. 'Or secret covens or cabals amongst the Templars: just a great deal of grumbling which a sinister Judas was willing to exploit.' He glanced at de Craon, who snatched the quill from his scribe's fingers.

'In England,' Corbett continued, 'the real plot began. King Edward had once fought in Outremer. The Assassins had tried to kill him. Such memories die hard and, naturally, when the Assassins' warning was pinned on the door of St Paul's, Edward paid heed. Such news chilled his blood. He came to York to hold a great council. He met our noble envoy de Craon to discuss the marriage terms. Our king, too, is bankrupt, so he also sought a loan from the Templar Order.'

'But the warning in London?' Branquier shouted.

'Oh, that was pinned to the door by one of you. A Judas who had become Philip of France's secret agent.'

'This is nonsense!' De Craon snapped. 'Stupid speculation . . .'

'Wait awhile,' Corbett replied. 'Now, when the traitor was in London, he not only nailed that message to the door of St Paul's, he also visited certain London merchants to purchase quantities of saltpetre, sulphur and other substances. This Templar had once served in Outremer where he had learnt of a mysterious fire which burns so fiercely that not even water can quench it: mingled with other substances and exposed to a naked flame, it seems the fires of Hell have erupted.'

'I have heard of that.' Symmes now put his pet weasel on the table: he stroked its ears and offered it a tidbit of dried meat. The Templar's good eye gleamed. 'We have all heard of it!' he exclaimed. 'The Byzantines used it to burn a great Muslim fleet.'

'No secret really,' de Molay interrupted. 'Certain books

225

discuss such a fire, and did not your Franciscan scholar, Bacon, analyse such mysteries?'

'The assassin certainly did,' Corbett answered. 'And it would not be difficult. Both the libraries in Paris and London are visited by scholars from all corners of God's earth. The fire itself is easy to make, once you know what to buy and how to use it.' Corbett now kept his eyes firmly on de Molay. 'Now this assassin,' Corbett continued, 'arrived in York. He mingles the substances and experiments with it here at Framlingham, in the woods, away from the inquisitive. Even so, the gossip begins. How the Devil's fire is seen. So, one night, he leaves the manor and goes along the lonely road towards Botham Bar. He hobbles his horse and, once again, experiments with the strange fire, perfecting its use. At the same time, being a consummate archer, he practises with an arbalest, loosing fire arrows into a tree: even in the dark his aim is true.

Now, all should have been well. However, on that night, a relic-seller, Wulfstan of Beverley, probably half-drunk, had left York to sell his tawdry goods in the villages beyond. Wulfstan, curious, ever eager for new stories, saw the fires, so he pushed his nag off the path and into the trees. The killer cannot allow this. Wulfstan will remember both his face and horse. He draws his great two-handed sword and strikes with such a great and powerful blow that he severs poor Wulfstan in two.'

'That death?' Branquier barked.

'Yes, that death,' Corbett echoed. 'As Wulfstan's horse bolts into the darkness, the assassin realises he has human flesh to play with. The fire will also destroy the identity of the victim. The remains are set alight but the assassin hears the cries of two good sisters and their guide, so he goes deeper into the trees and waits until they pass. He then leaves, removes the arrows from the trees: the burnt patches, the scratches on the bark and Wulfstan's mangled, burning remains are the only traces left.'

'Who?' de Craon shouted. 'Who is this assassin?'

226

'In a while,' Corbett taunted back. 'This assassin, Monsieur de Craon, is now ready to spread his web. Murston was a Templar serjeant, someone very much like the one who is lured into Paris. On the night before Edward of England enters York, Murston is told to go to a tavern near Trinity where the king will pass. He is ordered to hire a chamber and wait there.'

'Murston was a killer,' de Molay interrupted. 'An assassin.'

'He was no assassin,' Corbett replied. 'Just a stupid man, carrying out the orders of a superior officer. He stays the night like a good soldier would: the king enters York and so do you, Grand Master, with your commanders. However, one of them slips back along the streets to the tavern where Murston is waiting. He goes upstairs, slits Murston's throat and takes the crossbow Murston brought into the city. When the king processes up Trinity, the assassin fires two bolts, narrowly missing His Grace.'

Corbett turned and pointed to a chair standing in the corner, gesturing at Maltote to bring it across. Corbett sat down, easing the cramp in the small of his back.

'Murston was dead before those bolts were ever shot,' he continued. 'Greek fire has already been sprinkled over his corpse. Once the second bolt has been loosed, the assassin ignites the powder and flees down the stairs. He protects his face and body in a ragged cloak he'd bought from some beggar. I was the first to reach that garret but the assassin was already gone, leaving me to wonder how a man like Murston could shoot two crossbow bolts and then be half-consumed by those yellow-blue flames.'

'Did the assassin intend to kill the king?' de Molay asked.

'No, that was just the start. What the assassin really wanted – what Philip of France wanted – was to create a great scandal in the Templar Order.'

'Why?' Branquier shouted.

'So that the English crown would launch an attack upon the Order, seizing its properties, filling the exchequer with its treasure. And what Edward started in England, Philip of France would soon finish. And if the Holy Father complained?' Corbett shrugged. 'Philip would simply point to Edward of England, saying he was only imitating what his brother king had already done. Philip would destroy the Order, seize its lands and treasure, fill his own coffers as well as remove a movement which constantly reminded him about how his saintly grandfather had gone on Crusade. However, the Pope would hold Edward as the main culprit. Now the assassin knew that I would be sent to investigate. Hence the warning, followed by the attempt to kill me near the Shambles.'

'But we were all gone from York by then,' de Molay intervened. 'No Templar was in York when you were attacked.' The grand master spread his hands. 'True, one of us could have sent that warning to you but . . .'

'You never sent the warning,' Corbett declared. 'Nor was the mysterious archer a Templar. Was he, Monsieur de Craon?'

The Frenchman's eyes never flickered.

'Only you,' Corbett continued, jabbing his finger at de Craon, 'knew when I left for the archbishop's palace. You had me followed. You or one of your creatures also arranged that attack and, in doing so, deepened the mystery.'

'And Reverchien?' Legrave said hoarsely, not moving his head. 'None of us was at the manor when Reverchien died.'

'No, no,' Corbett replied softly. 'But you were there the day before he died: that was when the assassin entered the maze, carrying the Greek fire. He went to the centre. On the stone plinth, before the cross, are three candles on their metal stand. The assassin sprinkled the Greek fire over the candles, coating them, the stone plinth and the steps where Reverchien always knelt.'

'Of course,' Branquier breathed. 'And the old Crusader lit those candles, saying his prayers, his mind on God.'

'Yes,' Corbett replied.

He turned and gestured at Ranulf in the corner. The

manservant came over, carrying a small bowl. Corbett placed it on the table. He smiled apologetically at de Molay.

'I borrowed it from the scullery.'

He rose and brought back one of the many candles which burnt in their holders along the windowsill.

'In the bowl,' Corbett explained, 'is a very small portion of the powder which causes Greek fire.' He glanced up as the Templars pushed back their chairs. 'No, there's no danger.' Corbett took a long piece of dried vellum from his pouch, placed it in the bowl and lit one end. The flame licked it greedily, running down into the bowl. Even Ranulf jumped in alarm at the small, angry flame which shot up into the air. 'Reverchien did that,' Corbett said, pulling the bowl towards him and peering warily at the black scorch-mark inside.

'Reverchien lit those three candles, saying his prayers, unaware in the poor light before dawn of the death-bearing powder around him. The candles are lit. The substance is caught. The flames run down the candle stem, catching the powder on the step. It turned Reverchien into a living blaze. How subtle a way to kill your victim when you are far from the place of his death. And the flame burns fiercely,' Corbett explained, pushing the metal bowl along the table. 'Not only is it difficult to douse with water but the fire roars, leaving no trace of what caused it or how it began.'

Corbett retook his seat. 'The other deaths were similar. Peterkin the kitchen boy puts on an apron and oven cloths, not knowing they have been coated with that same powder. As he rakes the burning ash, Peterkin has a faint suspicion of what was happening before he died. Remember, his companions in the kitchen were discussing Reverchien's death and the other strange happenings. Peterkin made a joke about the air being tinged with sulphur. It was, on the very cloths he was wearing. The rest you know,' Corbett continued, staring at the murderer. 'A piece of hot ash or burning charcoal caught the cloths around his hand. The man tried to beat them out against his apron. Of course, the fire spread and Peterkin dies.'

'But why?' Symmes asked. 'Why a poor cook?'

'Because the assassin wanted to create terror. Spread the rumour, deepen the darkness, how the Templars were cursed, not only harbouring a possible regicide and killing each other, but allowing the flames of hell to burn freely and fiercely even amongst the innocents in their midst.' Corbett played with the Chancery ring on his finger. 'On a more practical level, Peterkin's death led to the flight of all the servants from Framlingham. Servants are curious, they look for the unexpected. Peterkin's death ended that and so protected the assassin.'

'And who, sir, is that?' Legrave snarled.

'Why sir, you sir,' Corbett remarked quietly.

Chapter 14

De Molay took some time to calm the subsequent uproar. Legrave rose and lunged at Corbett but Symmes, sitting between them, pushed back his chair. De Craon sprang to his feet, snapping his fingers at his black-garbed clerk as if they were on the point of departure. Corbett knew his old enemy and recognised the mummery for what it was: de Craon would only leave when it was to his advantage. Corbett was pleased the other Templars did not spring to Legrave's defence. There were shouts of disapproval, looks of concern, but the grand master's stern face and Branquier's troubled gaze reassured Corbett.

They know something, he thought; what I have said has touched secrets they harbour.

At last Legrave, red with fury, was forced back in his chair.

'You have no proof!' he spluttered.

'I will come to that in due course,' Corbett replied, 'when I have described the other deaths. Poor Brother Odo. You caught him as he went out to fish, didn't you? Waiting for him amongst the trees near the entrance to the jetty. I saw no blood there so you must have struck him a blow on the head, probably cracking his skull. Then you lowered him into the boat, fastening him upright in the seat, whilst in the stern and prow you sprinkled the Greek fire. The oars were tied to the old man's hands and fastened to their ratchet rings; the fishing line was slipped between the dead man's fingers and *The Ghost of the Tower* pushed out into the centre of the lake. A common sight here at Framlingham: old Odo dressed in his usual cloak and cowl, bending over a fishing rod, his boat bobbing on the lake. You hid amongst the trees, shot a fire arrow into the boat, and so the terror spreads. If a man like Odo, a hero of his Order, is devoured by the flames of hell, who can be safe? What is wrong at Framlingham? What is wrong with the Templars? And so the pool of poison spreads.'

'Why Odo?' de Molay asked. 'Why a gentle old man?'

'Because he was a scholar,' Corbett replied.

'And Baddlesmere?'

'Because he was a source of scandal,' Corbett continued. 'Legrave knew about Baddlesmere's little secrets, his passion for young men and the chilled white wine standing in his chamber. A sleeping potion was sprinkled into the jug; the fire powder spread on the floor beneath the rushes as well as along the leather sheet which hung against the door to keep out the draughts. Only Baddlesmere is not present: there's been a lovers' quarrel. Scoudas and Joscelyn drink the wine. Night falls whilst Baddlesmere sulks amongst the trees.' Corbett looked at Legrave's ashen face. 'And back you go, possibly carrying a small bowl containing a piece of burning charcoal. You slip that under the door. The rushes are dry, the powder is caught, the fire rages whilst those two drugged young men slip into death.'

'Grand Master.' Legrave pushed himself away from the table but, as he did so, Symmes placed his pet weasel on the floor; the creature scampered off into the darkness as its master caught Legrave's arm.

'I think you'd best stay, Brother,' Symmes remarked quietly. 'What Corbett says makes sense.'

'Of course,' Corbett continued. 'There was a connection between Baddlesmere and Brother Odo's death. The librarian was becoming curious. He was beginning to remember stories about the mysterious fire from the east. Legrave, however, was watching him. Perhaps Odo talked to him, told him what he was doing: that's why you came back into the library when I was there. If that door had not opened,' Corbett snapped, 'you'd have killed me as well!'

Legrave stared back, glassy-eyed, jaw tense. He kept gulping and glanced quickly at de Craon who refused to meet his gaze.

Corbett sighed: that glance alone confirmed his suspicions.

'For all his faults,' he continued, 'Baddlesmere was also edging towards the truth: he wondered who could have been behind Murston's death. On the morning the king was attacked, Baddlesmere knew where he was and where the grand master had gone. He also reached the conclusion, as I did, that two of his companions, Symmes and Branquier, had been at the other end of York near Botham Bar well away from Trinity when the attack was carried out.'

'That's true,' Branquier interrupted. 'Baddlesmere kept questioning all of us: where we had gone, which streets we'd walked down.'

'Even which taverns we'd drunk in,' Symmes added drily.

'But I was with the grand master,' Legrave shouted. He glanced down the table but de Molay just stared at him.

'The grand master was with the goldsmiths for at least two hours,' Corbett replied. 'You were supposed to stay outside.'

'And I did.'

'But if you look at Baddlesmere's map of York, you can travel from Stonegate to the tavern in Trinity where Murston was in a matter of minutes.'

De Molay took his hands away from his mouth. 'Sir Hugh speaks the truth,' he declared. 'We visited two goldsmiths on that street. On one occasion I came out and did not find you there.'

'I was amongst the stalls,' Legrave cried.

'Oh, yes, so you were,' Corbett declared. 'Buying what?'

Legrave licked his lips.

'Gloves,' Branquier replied, 'or gauntlets: that's what you told us.'

'Where are these?' Corbett asked. 'You bought more than one pair. Different stall-owners will attest to that. Why should any man want more than one or two pairs of gauntlets? You are a soldier-monk, Legrave, not some foppish courtier.'

'Where are the gauntlets?' de Molay demanded.

'Oh, you'll find them gone,' Corbett interjected. 'You see the powder Legrave used can be very dangerous. It leaves a stain: the grains become embedded in the cloth. Once used, they must be destroyed. Legrave did this. He burnt them in isolated spots in the manor. My companions found the remains.'

'You are lying! You are lying!' Legrave beat the table with his fists.

'We can search your chamber,' Corbett offered. 'We could ask you to produce these gauntlets. Who knows what we might find there. Some traces of the substances you used? It would leave its mark on boots and clothes. Perhaps traces of blood on a knife or sword?'

'Ralph.' Branquier leaned forward, looking down the table. 'You have the opportunity to answer these charges.'

Legrave refused to look up.

'Baddlesmere, too, studied the Assassins' warning,' Corbett continued. 'You see, the warning nailed to the doors of St Paul's Cathedral read as follows:

KNOWEST THOU, THAT WE GO FORTH AND RETURN AS BEFORE AND BY NO MEANS CAN YOU HINDER US.

Corbett closed his eyes.

'KNOWEST THOU, THAT WHAT THOU POSSESSES SHALL ESCAPE THEE IN THE END AND RETURN TO US.
KNOWEST THOU, THAT WE HOLD YOU AND WILL KEEP THEE UNTIL THE ACCOUNT BE CLOSED.

'That is the warning I read out at the priory when I was present with the king. However, the warning given to me on Ouse Bridge read a little differently:

KNOWEST THOU, THAT WHAT THOU POSSESSES SHALL ESCAPE THEE IN THE END AND RETURN TO US.
KNOWEST THOU, THAT WE GO FORTH AND RETURN AS BEFORE AND BY NO MEANS CAN YOU HINDER US.
KNOWEST THOU, THAT WE HOLD YOU AND WILL KEEP THEE UNTIL THE ACCOUNT BE CLOSED.

'And the same is true of the warning which Master Claverley took from Murston's gibbet.' Corbett shrugged. 'It was that which made me wonder. Were there two parties to this macabre game? Legrave in England and de Craon in France? Legrave posted the warning at St Paul's when the Templars passed through London. De Craon passed me the second rendering of the message as I travelled through York. He also had one of his clerks display one on Murston's gibbet just to deepen the mystery.' Corbett smiled bleakly at the Frenchman. 'You'll have to tell your master in France that you made a terrible mistake: you copied out a message wrongly.'

The French envoy did not stir but sat, head back, staring up at the ceiling, running his hands through his sparse red beard.

'But what's this connection?' Symmes asked. 'How did you know Legrave and de Craon were fellow conspirators?'

Corbett turned to him. 'Because on my arrival here – and you may not recall this – I told you that I had received a similar death threat but I did not tell you where. Later on, in discussion with all of you, Legrave casually remarked on how I was threatened as I crossed Ouse Bridge. How did he know that unless he and de Craon were fellow conspirators?' Corbett pointed to Symmes. 'You have written out your account, as the grand master ordered, of this whole sorry tale?'

The Templar nodded.

'And you, Branquier?'

'Of course.'

'And Legrave?'

'I was too busy,' he retorted.

'Whatever,' Symmes barked. 'I never knew about the warning being given on Ouse bridge.' He pointed at Legrave. 'Yet I do remember you saying it and Branquier kept a record of that meeting.'

'But this manor has been secured,' de Molay explained. 'None of us could enter York, nor has Monsieur de Craon been here.'

Corbett asked. 'If you wanted to correspond with someone just beyond the walls of this manor, would it be difficult? Baddlesmere found it very easy to slip away. I am sure Monsieur de Craon has envoys and clerks to run his errands – and so each kept the other informed about what was happening.' Corbett paused and stared at the window. The storm had passed but the rain was still splattering against the windows. 'In the end,' Corbett murmured, 'I must confess, I made a terrible mistake.' He glanced round the table. 'I thought this Order was rotten but, as in any community, there are bad and there are good. Grand Master, for my suspicions against you and the rest of your brothers, I apologise.' Corbett rubbed his face. 'But I am tired and my heart is elsewhere. "*Veritas in ripa*",' he murmured. 'Truth stands on the bank.' He stared at Legrave. 'That's what Baddlesmere scrawled on the wall of his cell before he hanged himself. He, too, had guessed the identity of the assassin. Perhaps he had seen something. Perhaps he had reflected on how close Legrave had been to Trinity when the king had been attacked. Perhaps he remembered what an excellent archer Legrave had been. A born warrior, he was not left-handed or right-handed but ambidextrous, who could shift a lance so easily from one hand to another. When I recalled the assassin in the library and asked my servant to play the part, I became confused until I remembered how the assassin kept moving the crossbow from hand to hand.' Corbett looked at the grand master. 'You know what the inscription meant?'

'Yes, yes, I do,' de Molay replied. '"*Ripa*" in Latin means bank, but in French bank is "*la grève*".'

Corbett pushed back his chair. 'Baddlesmere knew that,' he said. 'But he could not betray an old friend, a brother of his Order. Moreover, he lacked any evidence so, in leaving that cryptic message, he purged his conscience.' Corbett rose to his feet. 'I have finished. Grand Master,' he declared, 'there is no secret coven or conspiracy amongst the Templars but instead, as I have described, there has been an attempt to bring the Order into discredit, to provoke Edward of England into seizing it and thus pave the way for Philip of France to act. Legrave was their tool but the conspiracy had its roots – ' Corbett glanced at de Craon – 'with those dark souls who advise the French king.'

'I, too, am finished.' De Craon sprang to his feet, his chair crashing back to the floor. 'Grand Master, I refuse to stay here and listen to this nonsense: these insults offered to myself and my master. A formal protest will be lodged both with Edward of England and the Temple in Paris.'

'You can go when you want,' de Molay uttered drily. 'As you say, you are an accredited envoy. I have no power over you.'

De Craon opened his mouth to reply but thought better of it and, with his black-garbed clerk following, strode out of the room. Only when he passed Corbett did his eyes shift; the clerk flinched at the malevolent hatred in the man's eyes. Corbett waited until the door slammed behind him and listened to de Craon's fading shouts for his horses and the rest of his servants to join him.

'He will return to York,' Corbett declared, 'then protest

most effusively to His Grace and, by this time tomorrow, he will be travelling to the nearest port for a ship back to France. Now I, too, must go.'

He glanced at Legrave who sat, hands clasped together, staring into the darkness, his lips moving wordlessly. Corbett still hoped to spare this man the ultimate degradation.

'You cannot go,' de Molay declared.

'But you gave your word.'

'When these matters are finished!' de Molay snapped. 'And they are not finished yet!' He turned. 'Sir Ralph Legrave, Commander of this Order, what answer do you make to these accusations?'

Symmes, sitting next to the accused, grasped him by the arm and shook him. Legrave pulled his arm away as if he could see something in the shadows on the other side of the hall.

'What answer do you make?' de Molay demanded harshly.

'I am a Templar,' Legrave replied.

'You are accused of terrible crimes,' Branquier retorted. 'Your chamber and possessions will be searched!'

Legrave shook himself from his reverie. 'There's no need for that.' He ran a finger round his lips. 'Search my room and you'll find the evidence.' He chewed the corner of his lip and glanced fleetingly at Corbett. 'They might not find it but you will. De Craon warned me about you. I should have killed you immediately. We all deserved to die.' His voice rose. 'We are the Templars, men devoted to war against the Infidel. Now look at us: bankers, merchants, farmers. Men like Brother Odo living on past glories. Reverchien and his stupid pilgrimage every morning; Baddlesmere with his boys; Symmes and his drinking; Branquier and his accounts. What hope is there for any of us? I came into this Order because of a vision just as noble, just as holy as the search for any Grail.' He jabbed a finger towards de Molay. 'Philip of France is right. Our Order is finished. Why should we hug our riches to us? The Order should be dissolved, united with others, given a fresh purpose.'

238

'And you?' Corbett asked, curious at what Philip had offered this Judas.

'To be a knight banneret at the French court,' Legrave answered. 'Yes, to have manors and estates, a release from my vows. The opportunity to make up the time lost; to marry, to beget an heir. At least there's purpose in that. Sooner or later the storm will come, and the house of the Templars, built upon sand, will shatter and fall; and great will that fall be.'

Corbett went and stood over him. 'You're a liar,' he accused. 'You were a coward: you betrayed your Order years ago at Acre.'

Legrave's head snapped back at the hiss of anger from his companions.

'What, what are you saying?' he stuttered.

'I met a knight, a Templar in the Lazar hospital in York. A man kept prisoner for years by the Assassins: he did not give me his name. He called himself the "Unknown" but he talked of an English Templar who ran from his post in Acre and doomed his companions.'

'I have heard of such rumours,' Branquier interrupted.

'You ran, didn't you?' Corbett asked. 'And the French found out. They not only offered you wealth but threatened to reveal your cowardice.'

Legrave just nodded and, putting his face in his hands, sobbed quietly.

'You admit the charges?' Branquier whispered.

'He must stand trial,' Symmes barked.

'He has stood trial,' de Molay replied, rising to his feet. 'And has been found guilty.'

The grand master drew his great sword from its scabbard hanging on the corner of his chair. He walked down the other side of the table then stopped, glaring down at Legrave. He held the sword up just beneath the hilt like a priest holds a cross.

'I, Jacques de Molay, Grand Master in the Order of the Templars, do find you, Sir Ralph Legrave, knight of that same order, guilty by your hand of the terrible crimes of murder and treason. What have you to say?'

Legrave raised his head.

'Sentence is passed,' de Molay intoned. 'Execution will be carried out at first light tomorrow.'

'You cannot do that!' Corbett exclaimed.

'Go back to your Chancery!' de Molay retorted. 'Look amongst the deeds and muniments, your royal charters and licences. I have the power of the axe, the scaffold and the tumbrel, Brother.' De Molay looked back at Legrave. 'I ask you for the final time: do you have anything to say?'

'Nothing,' Legrave replied. 'Except, Grand Master . . .' He stared round the hall, seeing it for the last time. 'All this will pass,' Legrave whispered, 'for our cause is finished. Our days are numbered. Our house will surely fall.'

De Molay went towards the door and came back, leading a group of serjeants. Symmes pulled Legrave to his feet. De Molay removed Legrave's swordbelt, the sign of a knight.

'Give him a priest,' de Molay rasped. 'Let his sins be shriven.'

The prisoner turned and, without a backward glance, was led out of the hall.

Corbett went towards the grand master, hands extended. 'Sir, I bid you adieu.'

De Molay grasped his wrist; Corbett grew alarmed as the Templar seized it, holding it with all his strength. Ranulf cursed and stepped forward.

'You are our guest,' de Molay declared. 'It is too late for you to return. You are the king's commissioners. You must be his witnesses to our justice.'

Corbett's heart skipped a beat. De Molay was right. Legrave's execution would have to be witnessed. The king would demand that.

'You object?' de Molay asked curiously, still gripping Corbett's hand.

'I do not like to see any man die,' Corbett replied. 'Least of all at the block.'

De Molay released his hand. 'It will be swift,' he murmured. 'So, sir, tell your servant to withdraw. Branquier and I have something to tell you.'

'Master,' Ranulf protested. 'It is not—'

'Sir Hugh is safe,' de Molay reiterated. 'No harm will come to him. You have my oath.'

Corbett nodded; Ranulf and Maltote reluctantly went to the door.

'Wait for him in the guesthouse,' the grand master called out. 'He may be some time. You have nothing to fear.'

Once the door closed behind them, de Molay gestured Corbett to sit, he and Branquier on either side of him.

'You suspected,' Corbett began.

'I understood Baddlesmere's riddle,' de Molay replied. 'Though I could not see how it could be true.'

'And Philip of France's meddling?'

'The thought crossed my mind,' de Molay replied. 'At the Chapter in Paris, Legrave was often missing. I wondered if he was meeting some of Philip's coven. The French king has always found us an irritation. We constantly remind him about how his sainted grandfather went to the aid of the Holy Places in Outremer. But something else; about eighteen months ago Philip, now a widower, actually applied to be admitted into our Order.'

'Why?' Corbett exclaimed.

'For the glory. Perhaps our treasure. Or to learn our Great Mystery.'

'What Great Mystery?' Corbett asked.

De Molay looked across the table at Branquier.

'He deserves to know,' he remarked quietly.

Branquier breathed out noisily.

'I have decided,' de Molay repeated. He loosened the collar of his shirt, took out a gold reliquary, covered at the front by a piece of thick glass, and placed it on the table. He pulled the candle closer.

'What is it?' Corbett asked.

'A piece of the true cross,' de Molay explained. 'Taken before we lost it at the Battle of Hattin. Put your hand over it.'

Corbett obeyed.

'Now swear,' the grand master insisted, 'that what you see tonight, you will not describe, or hint at in any way, to another living soul.'

'I swear!' Corbett replied. He knew the Templars were about to reveal the Great Mystery of their Order: the source of all their secret rituals, hidden chambers, and ceremonies held at the dead of night.

'I swear,' he repeated, 'by the Saviour's Cross!'

De Molay slipped the reliquary back round his neck and, without another word, he and Branquier led Corbett out of the hall. They went up the stairs on to the gallery towards the secret chamber, still closely guarded by a company of soldiers. De Molay unlocked the room but he did not take Corbett aside. Instead, he came out carrying the tapestry Corbett had noticed hanging there on his first visit. The Templar soldiers stood like statues, heads lowered as Corbett was led up another flight of stairs and into a secret chapel. The tapestry was hung on a small hook thrust into the rim of the altar standing on the dais. Sconce torches were lit, as were the candles and the dark chamber flared into light. Three cushions were placed on the floor. Branquier gestured at Corbett to kneel, the Templar beside him. De Molay then played with the wooden rim round the tapestry. He took this and the tapestry away, revealing a pale linen sheet. Corbett could see the cloth was very old, yellowing with age, with a faint outline on it. De Molay then put two candles on either side of the sheet, etching more sharply the image it held. He came and knelt beside Corbett.

'Look, Sir Hugh,' de Molay whispered. 'Look and adore.'

Corbett stared. As he did so, he lost all awareness of his two companions or the chamber. His eyes adjusted to the contrast of light and dark, his heart skipped a beat, and he felt the sweat break out on his body: the image, as if painted in a rusty coloured substance, depicted a head crowned with thorns. The eyes were closed, the hair matted and bloody on either side of a long face, the nose sharply etched in death; the lips full, slightly parted, high cheekbones still bearing marks, cuts and bruises. De Molay and Branquier leaned forward, faces to the ground, chanting the prayer: 'We adore you O Christ and we praise Thee; because, by your holy Cross, you have redeemed the whole world.'

Corbett could only gaze. The image was so life-like; if he could stretch out and touch it, the head would surely move, the face would live, the eyes would open.

'Is it . . . ?' he whispered, and then recalled the stories and legends about a sacred cloth which once covered the face of the crucified Jesus. Some said it was at Lucca in Italy. Others in Rome, Cologne or Jerusalem. De Molay straightened up. He let Corbett stare for a while before going forward; he extinguished the candles and covered that haunting face behind the tapestry. He then sat down on the dais opposite Corbett.

'It is what you think,' he murmured. 'The sacred Mandylion. The cloth which Joseph of Arimathea and Nicodemus used to cover Christ's face in the tomb. Somehow the cloth took on the imprint of his face. For centuries it was hidden but when invading armies sacked Constantinople in 1204, it came into our Order.' He gestured with his hands. 'This is what we venerate in the dead of night. This is the source of the garbled stories about Templars worshipping severed heads or indulging in secret rituals. This is our Great Mystery, and it is this which Philip of France would like to seize.'

Corbett leaned back on his heels and nodded. Any king would give a fortune for what he'd seen. If Philip owned it, he would use the cloth to underline the sacredness of his rule and, if circumstances demanded, sell it on the open market for a fabulous sum. All of Christendom would bid to own it.

De Molay came over and helped Corbett to his feet.

'Only the chosen few in the Order are ever allowed to see what you have seen,' he explained. 'Now go, Sir Hugh, but *never* utter a word about what you have witnessed.'

Corbett rose and left the small, mysterious chapel. He returned to his own chamber in the guesthouse. Maltote was already asleep, but Ranulf was eager to congratulate his master and ply him with questions about what had happened. Corbett just shook his head. He took off his boots and climbed on to the bed, wrapping his cloak around him.

'Surely, Master,' Ranulf wailed, 'you can tell me.'

Corbett half rose, resting on one elbow. 'I'll say one thing, Ranulf, and you must not question me again. I am a singular man: in one night I have looked into the heart of evil and the source of light. I have glimpsed both heaven and hell!'

And, with Ranulf's muttered curses ringing in his ears, Corbett lay back down on the bed, praying daylight would soon come and this business would be finished.

The next morning Corbett, with Ranulf and Maltote in attendance, stood outside the front door of the manor house. The sun had not yet broken through the cloying mist which hung heavy amongst the trees, shifting under a sharp cold breeze which gave the manor gardens a ghostly appearance. De Molay had insisted that every Templar be present, formed in a square around a crude wooden platform on which a block had been set with a large, two-headed axe lying on one side. On the other stood a small basket filled with straw and coated with sawdust. The grand master stood on the platform intoning the '*De Profundis*', the psalm for the dead. He moved aside as a Templar soldier, dressed in black from head to toe, a red mask covering his face, stepped on to the makeshift scaffold. A single drum began to beat as Legrave, dressed in boots, hose and a white linen shirt, was led out through the main door of the manor. He looked pale but, apart from that, showed no sign of fear. He went on up on to the scaffold and knelt before the block. De Molay approached and whispered into his ear. Legrave smiled slightly but shook his head, refusing to listen. De Molay stepped back. The executioner lashed Legrave's hands behind his back and thrust his head forward over the block. For a few seconds the prisoner remained motionless, neck extended, eyes closed. He then abruptly lifted his head. The executioner was about to thrust him down again but de Molay shook his head. Legrave looked up at the sky and then round at the host of witnesses to his death.

'It will be a fine day,' he declared in a clear voice. 'The sun will rise, the mist will burn off. Brothers . . .' His voice shook a little. 'Brothers, remember me.' He laid his head on the block, the executioner pulled back his shirt a little then moved back. The drum beat began. The great axe went up. There was a shimmer of light as it swooped, cutting the air, piercing Legrave's neck, veins and sinews. Corbett closed his eyes, murmured a prayer and moved away, back through the crowd.

In the solar of the Archbishop of York's palace, Edward, King of England and John de Warrenne, Earl of Surrey, sat in the cushioned windowseat staring down at the scene in the courtyard below. Corbett, Ranulf and Maltote were preparing horses and two sumpter ponies, loaned from the royal stables, for their journey south. Corbett was on his horse, staring out through the yard gate, lost in thought, as if calculating how long it would take to travel from York to his manor at Leighton. The king stifled his annoyance and, opening his hand, stared down at the Secret Seal.

'Your Grace, I am going,' Corbett had declared. 'I wish to be on the road by midday. I kept my word and now you must keep yours.'

The king had fumed, sulked, shouted and pleaded, but Corbett was obdurate.

'Your king needs you!' Edward yelled in exasperation.

'So does my wife and family,' Corbett retorted and, taking the ring from his finger and the Seal from his purse, he'd walked over and thrust them into the king's hands.

'My Lord King,' the clerk had whispered, 'even a good dog gets his bone as a reward.'

'But why now?' Edward grasped Corbett by the front of his tunic.

'I . . .' Corbett had glanced away. 'I am tired,' he whispered hoarsely. 'I am tired of the blood, the violence. I resign my office. I wish to sit in my manor and count my sheep. Go to bed with my wife and stop sleeping with a dagger beneath my pillow whilst Ranulf and Maltote guard the door.'

Corbett had closed the king's fingers around the Seal and ring, then strode out of the royal chamber, shouting at Ranulf and Maltote that they were leaving. De Warrenne followed Edward's stare.

'I could stop him,' the earl offered. 'Give me ten good archers. I'll seize him at the city gates and bring him back.'

'Oh, for the love of God, don't be stupid!' Edward groaned. He leaned over and tweaked his earl marshal's cheek. 'You are a good man, John. If I told you to mount a destrier and charge the moon you probably would.' Edward tossed Corbett's ring and Seal into the rushes, though he made careful note where they fell. 'I made Corbett what he is,' he muttered hoarsely. 'What I fashioned once, I can fashion again.'

Even as the words were out of his mouth, Edward knew he was lying. He would miss Corbett: dark, secretive, with his wry sense of humour, his love of law. Corbett, his shadow-master or 'guardian angel', as the king had once referred to him.

'He did well,' de Warrenne grudgingly conceded. 'Do you believe Master Hubert Seagrave?'

Edward grinned. 'No, I don't. Truth comes in many guises, but a rich vintner coming to confess his sins, his chests full of ancient gold, craving the royal pardon for a momentary lapse . . .' Edward shrugged: he jabbed a finger at the courtyard below. 'Corbett's brain may be of steel, but he has a heart of wax. I suspect he had a hand in it. However, my coffers are full, my Exchequer clerks are dancing with delight at the profits, not to mention the low price Seagrave will charge for every tun of wine delivered to the royal household.'

'And de Craon?' the earl asked.

'Huffing and puffing,' Edward replied. 'Shocked, outraged. The lying bastard protests too much. He'll go back to my sweet brother of France and I'll have letters! Oh, by the moon's tits, I'll have letters! Angry protestations, fierce denunciations, then Philip will scuttle back to his spiderweb and plot again. He's set his heart on the Templars and the Templars he will have; but not while I sit on the throne at Westminster . . .'

Edward rose and went across to the table. 'Legrave is dead,' he continued. 'De Molay will return to France to accept Philip's protestations of innocence. He will even offer the French king a loan.' Edward sat down and began to leaf through the books Corbett had borrowed from the Archbishop's library. 'But this fire . . .'

'You had heard about it before, your Grace?'

'Oh yes,' Edward lied, snapping his fingers at de Warrenne to join him. The king leaned his elbows on the table, cupping his face in his hands. 'In the summer,' he mused, 'I intend to cross the Scottish march. I will teach Wallace and his rebels a lesson they'll never forget.' He tapped the pages of the book. 'I want my Clerks of Stores to read this. What Corbett discovered, so can they. That rogue Claverley, whom I'm going to reward, can help. Let us, my good Earl, take this fire north. I'll set the very heather ablaze!'

Edward heard a sound from the courtyard below. He pushed back his stool and went to look out of the window. His heart skipped a beat: Corbett was gone.

Author's Note

The events of this novel are based on historical fact. The city of York is as I described it, though sometimes I have used other spellings of well-known landmarks, e.g. Botham Bar for Bootham Bar.

The introduction of gunpowder into English warfare is well described by Henry W. Hine in his book *Gunpowder and Ammunition, Their Origin and Progress*, published by Longmans (1904). He gives a scholarly analysis of gunpowder, talks of the '*Liber Ignium*' as well as the secrets of Friar Bacon's work mentioned in the text. Even today scholars are puzzled by the complex anagrams and cryptic language in which Bacon conceals his formula. Perhaps the good friar realised the latent dangers of his discovery! Greek fire was used by the Byzantines and, for a while, was their jealously guarded secret. Edward I's remarks at the end of the novel are probably based on fact: the events of *Satan's Fire* are set in 1303: according to Hine's book (page 50), Edward did sweep north in 1304 and used this fire, for the first time, in the siege of Stirling Castle. By 1319 the Scots had learnt their lesson and also had the secret from a Flemish engineer.

The fall of Acre and the consequent effect on the Templar Order is also well documented. Philip of France did attempt to join the Order and was repulsed. There is evidence that he tried to stir up Edward's agitation against the Templars, but was prevented from carrying his designs through. In 1307, however, after Edward I had died, Philip launched his notorious attack on the Templars, accusing them of witchcraft, sodomy and of worshipping a severed head. The English Crown was one of the few institutions to raise a voice in defence of the Order and, for a while, Edward II tried to resist his father-in-law's demand for the destruction of the Templar Order in England. Philip, however, had his way: the Templars were destroyed and, in 1313, Jacques de Molay was burnt alive before Notre-Dame Cathedral in Paris. Before he died, the Templar grand master protested his innocence. He summoned Philip of France to meet him 'before the tribunal of God within a year'. He also cursed the French monarchy 'until its thirteenth generation'. De Molay's curse was prophetic: Philip IV was dead within the year. His three sons died childless; his grandson Edward III of England claimed the throne of France and plunged Western Europe into the Hundred Years War. Louis XVI, 'the thirteenth generation', died on the guillotine, his family's last prison being the Temple in Paris.

The Templars undoubtedly held the Mandylion, the cloth which covered Christ's face. This not only gave source to the legends about worshipping a severed head but figures prominently in Templar art, as recent excavations at Templecombe in Dorset prove.

© Paul C. Doherty
14 September 1994

X

Wilmette Public Library
Wilmette, Illinois
Telephone: 256-5025

GAYLORD M

everything in its place

jeremy p. tarcher/putnam
a member of penguin putnam inc.
new york

everything in its place

my trials
and
triumphs
with
obsessive
compulsive
disorder

marc summers

with eric hollander, m.d.

Most Tarcher/Putnam books are available at special quantity discounts for bulk purchases for sales promotions, premiums, fund-raising, and educational needs. Special books or book excerpts also can be created to fit specific needs. For details, write Putnam Special Markets, 375 Hudson Street, New York, NY 10014.

Jeremy P. Tarcher/Putnam
a member of
Penguin Putnam Inc.
375 Hudson Street
New York, NY 10014
www.penguinputnam.com

Library of Congress Cataloging-in-Publication Data
Summers, Marc.
Everything in its place : my trials and triumphs with
obsessive compulsive disorder / Marc Summers with
Eric Hollander.
p. cm.
ISBN 0-87477-990-1
1. Obsessive-compulsive disorder. Popular works.
I. Hollander, Eric, date. II. Title.
RC533.S86   1999   99-27534 CIP
616.85'227—dc21

Printed in the United States of America
1   3   5   7   9   10   8   6   4   2

This book is printed on acid-free paper. ∞

Book design by Amanda Dewey

acknowledgments

There have been many people along the way who have participated in this project. First of all, Kenneth Wapner and Jennifer
Wolfson, two of the most amazing people I have ever met. Their
intelligence and sensitivity are responsible for taking this project
from zero to sixty in record time.

Dr. Eric Hollander and Mariette Hartley who, by some stroke
of luck or fate or maybe the booking genius of Larry Ferber,
showed me the light and the path to getting rid of the silliness.

To the Kahn family, especially Darcie, Beatrice, and Marty,

and also Jake McDowell and his mom, Debbie, some of my first OCD friends. People like this definitely make the world a better place.

The people at Ketchum. They performed miracles in my life and, in turn, in the lives of others. A gigantic thank-you and a big hug to Colleen Brady and Hal Walker.

My new family at Porter Novelli, including Natalie Adler, Jeff Macdonald, Reisha Kelsey, and most especially to my travel buddy, Megan Pace. Megan and I do not necessarily agree on politics or sports, but her professionalism, dedication, and ability to go far beyond the call of duty at all times are to be applauded. Someday, she will definitely be that CEO in the corner office. See, I said it!

Mary Guardino, the most energetic woman I have ever met. Your sense of humor and your guidance mean more to me than you know. Tom Styron, the new man in charge, whose vision is inspirational. Trent Owen, for letting me share some time.

Fred Rothenberg at NBC News, who said all along it was the right thing to do. You were correct, and it helped many more with the visits to Matt Lauer and Oprah Winfrey. And to Sara James, the first person allowed to really mess up the place. You did good and thanks. To John Hannah at *People* magazine who jump-started all the media.

Mr. Steve Jennings, the hardest-working man in the business and one of the nicest. I value our friendship and will miss working with you. Good luck on the new gig. David Dodd for his wisdom and leadership. And to a very special lady, Janice McClure. Everyone should have a friend like you.

Wendy Hubbert, who understood the mission immediately and is a major supporter in so many ways. You always bring me good news. To Lori Fuller, you helped get it over the top.

Mark Reiter, a friend since the '80s who always stuck by me, pushed me, believed in my talent, and never gave up. It took over ten years, but we finally got a book! And thanks for almost always returning my phone calls! This would never have happened without you.

Richard Lawrence. If you look up "friend" in the dictionary, it is your picture that is the model. Thanks for absolutely everything.

My parents Martin and Lois and my sister Lori, who have a sense of humor about it and continue to try and understand this thing that has been handed down. Thanks for the support. To my brother Mike, the voice of reason, who dealt with this from the other side. And Clara Essak, Bobba, thanks for teaching me the wax paper trick, for letting me watch you sweep the street, and for providing me with all the summers of fun.

Burt, Lynn, Ali, and Liza Durbrow, for listening, understanding, and sharing the laughs. Mark Smith, a man who has been there from the beginning and shared the good times and the not so good. My other "sister," Merrie Dudley, who for the past eight years has somehow been involved in my professional life, even if it was just to take one of those phone calls at 2 A.M.!

A big thanks to Diane Considine, Vernal Cripe, Harold Hartman, and Chet Kubit for laying the foundation.

To Alice, Matthew, and Meredith, who know it has not always been easy to live with the guy who followed them and everyone else around the house, touched walls, and often made no sense. I love you all very much and appreciate your patience.

And for everyone else I forgot to mention, Thanks . . . especially Harvey for letting me vent. And last but certainly not least, Windex and Reggie. Who knew animals could be so much fun?

To Alice, Matthew,
and Meredith

*Because of your
love, patience,
and understanding,
I was able
to move forward.*

contents

foreword by eric hollander   *xiii*

introduction   *1*

one the public face and the private torment   *7*

two sunday, day of rest   *29*

three nurture and nature   *47*

four | adolescent ambition, adolescent angst *71*

five | waiting at the altar *89*

six | earthquake *111*

seven | the moment of truth *129*

eight | rock bottom *147*

nine | taking charge *167*

ten | waging war and winning *191*

resource guide *211*

foreword by eric hollander

I first met Marc Summers on his television talk show, *Biggers and Summers*. As a leading expert on obsessive compulsive disorder, I had become involved with the Obsessive Compulsive Foundation in a public campaign to increase awareness of OCD. I had been booked on radio and television programs as part of this public education campaign, and before I was due to go on Marc's show, he took me aside. "I've been up all night," he said in a shaky voice. "I was pacing back and forth, wondering whether I should talk to you. I think I have OCD."

I asked him a series of simple screening questions: do you

need things to be even, symmetrical, or "just so"; do you have to check over and over if the door is locked, if the oven is still on, or whether you've run someone over with your car; do you experience disturbing, repetitive thoughts that you can't resist, such as fear that people close to you will be harmed; do you worry about dirt, germs, or contamination; do you wash or shower excessively; do you have trouble throwing things away, such as newspapers or lists; do you have counting rituals, or touching or tapping habits?

When Marc answered affirmatively to many of these questions, I told him that he might, indeed, have obsessive compulsive disorder. We had to break to prepare for the show, so I gave him my card and told him if he wanted to talk further, I was available. Then we were hustled on stage. A microphone was clipped to my jacket's lapel, and the stage hand counted down ten, nine, eight . . . and then were on the air. The excitement of live television was a real change of pace for me, since I spend most of my time in hospital outpatient clinics, in research laboratories, or hunkered down in university libraries.

In the back of my mind, though, I was thinking that the obvious reluctance Marc felt to tell me, a doctor, in private, of his suspicion that he had OCD indicated that he was nowhere near ready to admit to the world that he might have the disorder. So imagine my surprise when Marc admitted to having obsessive compulsive symptoms right at the beginning of the show.

It was an incredibly brave thing to do, and I felt a surge of gratitude to Marc. He was doing for obsessive compulsive disorder what Magic Johnson did for HIV, Mary Tyler Moore did for diabetes, and Naomi Judd did for hepatitis. Whenever a celebrity comes forth and talks on television about his or her struggle with an illness, there usually is a huge response from people who have been suffering in silence, suspecting something was wrong with them but most of the time not knowing what it was or how to find out more about it. In a survey of 701 members of the Obsessive Compulsive Foundation, I found that approximately 25 percent of obsessive compulsive sufferers first seek treatment after seeing a report in the media about OCD. The first step in increasing recognition of OCD, which leads to effective treatment, is to get the word out. And the most effective way to do that is to have someone like Marc—who has a great sense of humor, who's bright, who people can identify with—humanize the disorder.

With the cameras rolling, Marc leaned over, a sheen of guilt and apprehension on his face. His voice came in a low revealing rush as he told his television audience about his neatness compulsions. I saw in him a truly outstanding spokesperson for the disorder—someone who could play an important role in educating the public and encouraging people to come forward and seek help.

OCD is a disorder that has desperately needed a spokesperson. It has long had a stigma attached to it. The Catholic Church in the Middle Ages attributed its symptoms to the devil. Shakespeare used Lady Macbeth and her compulsive handwashing ("Out, damn spot! out, I say!") to signify obsessional madness. In Victorian times, people with OCD provided the classic definition of insanity. And even recently, OCD has been significantly misunderstood. Freud wrote a landmark study of an obsessive compulsive patient he dubbed the Rat Man, a young man who was plagued by intrusive and repetitive thoughts that rats were going to eat him and his father. Freud, typically, attributed Rat Man's symptoms to problems with toilet training, and for most of this century that diagnosis held: the disorder was commonly believed to be a psychologically based problem, caused by early childhood conflicts, and treated with psychoanalysis.

Since psychoanalysis has proved to be ineffective in treating the disorder, the consensus in the medical community through the early 1980s was that OCD was not responsive to treatment. And the prevalence of the illness was grossly underestimated. It's only in the past 15 years or so that we have realized that OCD is a medical disorder, having to do with an imbalance of neurotransmitters in the brain, which we now estimate affects roughly six million Americans—none of whom are crazy or possessed by the devil. Happily, in the last 15 years, doctors and scientists have made important discoveries about OCD and its treatment. We can now effectively treat the disorder with medication and behavior therapy, and we have a startlingly high success rate. Seventy percent of OCD sufferers who undergo treatment report a substantial improvement in their symptoms and their quality of life.

But even with all these advances, there are still millions of OCD sufferers who don't know that they have a disorder or are afraid to seek treatment because of the stigma attached to OCD. One of the things I always wished I had to give these people is a story like Marc's. It's the story of a guy who was able to face OCD head-on and overcome it. Marc is living proof that there's no reason a stigma should be attached to the disorder.

I first became interested in studying OCD when I was a resident in psychiatry at Mt. Sinai Hospital in New York City, doing research on schizophrenia and Alzheimer's disease. While the science was fascinating, because these are disorders that didn't usually respond to treatment, working with these patient populations was tough. When I started reading the emerging literature on OCD, I realized that this was another common brain-based disorder, but one that might respond to treatment better than Alzheimer's or schizophrenia. A particular neurotransmitter, a chemical used to send messages between brain cells, had been implicated in OCD, and this neurotransmitter, serotonin, was known to be affected by drug therapy.

In 1986, I began to research the neurobiology and psychopharmacology of OCD. Nineteen eighty-six turned out to be a watershed year. Studies were initiated at 20 sites across the country to test Anafranil (clomipramine), a medication that in the past had been used to treat depression, on people with OCD. The studies were sponsored by the pharmaceutical industry to determine for the Food and Drug Administration whether this medication was a safe and effective treatment for OCD.

I was involved in a number of medication trials that took place at the Columbia University's New State Psychiatric Institute. We advertised on radio, television, and in *The New York Times* and *Daily News*, to find subjects to test new medications for OCD. The ads ran: "Do you have disturbing thoughts that you can't get out of your head? Do you wash your hands over and over? Do you need everything to be perfect?" We were overwhelmed by the response, and found ourselves inundated by people wanting to participate in the study. It was a strong signal that the number of people who had the disorder had been grossly underestimated.

The second thing that completely changed the minds of the Columbia researchers was the dramatic improvement we saw in the symptoms of 70 percent of the OCD sufferers that we treated with Anafranil. This result exploded the theory that OCD was psychologically rather than physically based, and completely changed the way the medical community viewed and treated OCD.

Successive trials showed that other drugs, called selective serotonin reuptake inhibitors (SSRIs), such as Luvox (fluvoxamine), Prozac (fluoxetine), Paxil (paroxetine), and Zoloft (sertraline) were just as effective as Anafranil in treating OCD but were better tolerated by patients.

This was an incredibly exciting time for me. I had found my life's work. I continued to do research on the neurobiology of OCD, and I started evaluating and treating people with the disorder. As I listened to their stories, I realized that many of these patients were suffering from other disorders along with OCD. This led to my discovery of the "OCD spectrum," a group of disorders which I believe to be closely related to OCD.

This OCD spectrum includes: body dysmorphic disorder (people obsessed with imagined bodily imperfections); eating disorders, such as anorexia nervosa; hypochondriasis (people obsessed with imagined physical illness); Sydenham's chorea (a rare disorder that follows a strep throat infection characterized by involuntary movements); autism; and Tourette's syndrome (characterized by elaborate motor and vocal tics: eye blinking, humming, and shouting profanity, for instance). We found that 50 to 90 percent of people with Tourette's, for example, also have

OCD symptoms, and 10 percent of people with OCD also have Tourette's.

I also began to study a whole series of impulsive disorders that involve repetitive behaviors and are driven by pleasure seeking and arousal gratification, such as pathological gambling, trichotillomania (pulling out one's own hair over and over), compulsive shopping, and compulsive sexual disorders. I found that the same medications that worked on people with OCD also worked on people with OCD spectrum disorders.

In 1993, my colleagues (Drs. Concetta DeCaria, Dan Stein, Daphne Simeon, Bonnie Aronowitz, and Lisa Cohen) and I moved back to Mt. Sinai and initiated the Compulsive, Impulsive, and Anxiety Disorders Program, which I currently direct. Our research focuses on the study of neurotransmitter and neuropeptide function, neuropsychiatric function, brain imaging by Positron Emission Tomography (PET) scans, assessing the impact of OCD on quality of life, and developing new treatments for unresponsive patients.

Unfortunately, there is still much that is not known about the causes of OCD and why some patients don't respond to treatment. To address these unanswered questions, I have organized the International OCD Conferences, which meet on an annual basis in Europe and North America. These conferences bring together the world's experts on OCD in small closed workshops to reach a consensus about the direction of future OCD research. I have also helped organize the International OCD Consortium, a cooperative of research groups around the world that work together to address the needs of OCD patients.

Doctors report that some OCD patients, up to 30 percent, don't respond well to medication. Many of these patients have subtle neurological "soft signs": problems with fine motor coordination, frequent facial grimacing, difficulty drawing a three-dimensional cube, and difficulties reading a map. These soft signs are a reflection of altered brain circuitry in OCD patients. The more severe the soft signs, the more severe the obsessions. Soft signs may be a way of predicting lack of response to serotonin-based OCD medications. Non-responders seem to differ in terms of their serotonin function and the activity level of certain brain regions, as measured by PET scans. Fortunately, a portion of these patients may respond to medications other than SSRIs.

I find my patients to be engaging, intelligent people who have good insight into their condition and a real will to get better. In helping them, I focus on finding what would motivate them to get better, something in their life that they really want to do but that OCD is preventing them from doing. One of my patients underwent a major breakthrough when she realized she wanted to be more involved with her kids. I've seen other patients who were motivated to get better when they saw how the disorder was interfering with an important relationship. This was the case with Jack Nicholson's character in the movie *As Good As It Gets*: he wanted the girl, and she made it clear that in order to get her, he would have to get better, or become "a better man," as he says in the film. As you'll read in the following pages, Marc Summers was moved to begin therapy when he hit rock bottom and realized the disorder was hurting his relationship with his wife and kids.

Some of my patients with OCD are high functioning like Marc, while others are more disabled. But the good news is that most respond well to treatment, and it's been very gratifying for me to help them get better. It takes tremendous courage for my patients to admit they have a problem and to seek out help. It also takes courage for them to overcome anxieties and face their fears, and to find the motivation to follow through with their treatment.

Marc has written a book for everyone with OCD, their families and their friends and loved ones. It's the book we've all been waiting for, a book that will entertain, inspire, and enlighten. As a doctor working in the field, I know that the biggest barriers to treating OCD are denial and silence. My deepest hope is that Marc's positive story will galvanize people suffering in silence to finally seek and receive appropriate and effective help.

introduction

From the time I was six years old, everything in my world had to be perfect. My clothes had to be folded a certain way. The shirts hanging in my closet had to be a quarter-inch apart, no more, no less, with all the hangers facing the same direction. My books were organized alphabetically and lined up so that they were exactly the same distance from the lip of the shelf. I shined my shoes each day until they glowed and I could see my face in them. If I erased something on a homework paper and left the slightest smudge or, God forbid, a hole, I'd redo the assignment on a fresh sheet of paper because I thought my failure to do so would result in something bad happening to me or to my parents. One of us would have a freak accident or contract a deadly disease. I thought I was the only kid in the world who felt this way. I thought I was crazy, so I kept the secret of my bizarre behaviors locked deep inside.

I was an odd kid, and not only because of my fanatical neatness and strange, fearful thoughts. I was odd because hosting television shows was all I ever dreamt about. I would come home from Miss Helms' kindergarten class and tune in to *Art Linkletter's House Party.* On each episode, Art talked to four kids about life. Unlike all my friends, I wanted to be Art, not the kids being interviewed! I can tell you who produced and announced programs that went off the air 40 years ago because as soon as I could read I was studying the credits on every TV show.

I had no idea I had obsessive compulsive disorder (OCD) when I was a child. In fact, I only learned about OCD a few short years ago. As a child and until my diagnosis in 1996, I didn't relate my fanatical neatness to my drive to be a TV personality. But looking back, those two parts of my personality were tightly entwined. At age six, I was driven, focused: I was determined that my room be spotless and my closet organized like a drill sergeant's; and I was just as determined to be on TV.

Either by luck or determination, my dreams came true. Those of you who discovered me as the host of a messy television program called *Double Dare* probably had no idea I was suffering from OCD. At that point, neither did I! All I knew was that I hated the part of my job that involved getting dumped in vats of goo or smeared with slime. On the air, I always laughed good-naturedly when I was slimed, but inside I was squirming.

Double Dare was *Jeopardy!* meets *Beat the Clock*. The kids who came on the show had to answer a question on history, geography, or pop culture. If they failed to answer the question correctly, they had to take on a physical challenge that usually involved being splattered with green liquid or some other disgusting concoction. The show's producers were ingenious in devising new ways for the contestants—and me—to become filthy. The kids loved seeing their adult host covered in gunk, and so we were doused, dunked, splattered, smeared, and slimed with oatmeal, applesauce, raw eggs, vanilla pudding, and chocolate syrup. Kids belly-flopped into a four-thousand-gallon tub filled with cold baked beans. It was truly repulsive. The most disgusting stunt the producers invented involved dog food. Competing teams of ten-year-olds with catapults on either end of the side stage heaved huge gobs of moist Alpo at each other. The sight of flying dog food and the smell that pervaded the studio that day sent me careening off stage, gagging.

As soon as the camera stopped on *Double Dare,* the instant we were off the air, I'd rip off my jacket, shirt, and tie, standing naked from the waist up in front of 300 eight- to eleven-year-olds. The producers hated this, but I couldn't help myself. I couldn't stand still with all that messy stuff on me. I took long hot showers, first in the studio and then at home.

After these showers I was generally fine until I'd scratch my ear and pull out a piece of green slime, or until the whipped cream that had been shoved in my face and had gone up my nostrils began to ferment, filling my head with the smell of sour milk. I'd have to practically snort cologne to mask that odor.

I'll never forget the smell of the Philadelphia television studio in which we first shot *Double Dare,* WHYY, a PBS station across from Independence Mall. The cleaning crew did a noble job of swabbing the place down after each show. But the food wormed its way into all the sets, into every crack in the walls, floor, and ceiling. The place smelled like a refrigerator where the food had been left to rot—a cruddy, putrid smell. One day the studio cleanup crew all broke out in skin rashes—that's how gross it was. Though I didn't know it at the time, it was exponentially grosser for me because it dovetailed with my obsessive need for cleanliness.

I left *Double Dare* in 1994 to do adult television, moving to New York City, where I co-hosted *Biggers and Summers,* a talk show on the Lifetime cable network. It was there, finally, at the age of 43 that I realized I had obsessive compulsive disorder. It happened by a fluke: we were doing a show to raise the public's awareness of OCD, and while scanning my prep material the night before, I realized I had the disorder. I actually "outed" myself on the air.

From the moment I went public with my OCD, my life changed. It was over a year before I sought treatment and began to get better, but I immediately understood that the bizarre behaviors that had made me different from other kids were caused by a chemical imbalance in my brain. I thought and acted the way I did because my brain had hiccups, as my doctor liked to say. The disorder was something I was born with, like the color of my eyes.

Now I work closely with the OC Foundation, going across the country, talking about OCD. Although it can be a grave and difficult condition, I like to inject a little levity into a disorder that was thought to have been spawned by the devil in the Middle Ages and that defined madness in Victorian times.

OCD affects roughly six million Americans. This book will give you a good understanding of the causes and treatments of OCD, but it's not meant to be a detailed clinical examination of the disorder's pathology, neurochemistry, or treatment process. Instead, it charts my sometimes harrowing, often humorous, and ultimately inspiring personal journey from compulsive room cleaner to family man, TV personality, and national spokesperson for the disorder. I want to clear up myths and misinformation and wipe out the bad vibes that have long surrounded OCD.

For those of you who suspect you have the disorder, I hope you will gain confidence from my story and learn to see the positive side of living with OCD. Frankly, I think almost everyone has a touch of the disorder, and we can learn to channel it in productive ways. It could be that the fast-track CEO in the corner office you know, the one who's always on time, who's on top of every detail and can find every piece of paper in her neat desk, is an example of someone who's learned to live successfully with OCD. If you suspect you have the disorder or know someone who does, I hope this book will help you realize the difference between superstition, caution, and true obsessive compulsive behavior, and help you understand a little more clearly what's going on inside the head of someone with OCD.

Enjoy my story, and, by the way, try not to bend the pages while you're reading. I'M JUST KIDDING!!!

Be well.
Marc Summers

the public face and the private torment

On October 18, 1994, I was finally going on *The Tonight Show,* where one appearance can make or break a career. Appearing on *The Tonight Show* would fulfill one of my lifelong dreams. Johnny Carson had been my idol as a child. Other kids had posters of Mickey Mantle or the Beatles on the wall, but not me. I had Johnny Carson. But by the time I made it to the show, Johnny was gone. Jay Leno ruled the big desk.

I knew Jay from way back. When I started doing bits at the Comedy Store on Sunset Boulevard in Los Angeles there were three guys you could tell were going to be stars: Robin Williams,

David Letterman, and Jay Leno. Jay was a journeyman comic—
he'd go out on the road, work anywhere. Big clubs, little clubs.
He was always working, and he is still one of the hardest-working
men in show business. Johnny took thirteen weeks off each year;
Jay takes two. He also has the reputation for treating guests like
human beings even if they're not as successful as he is, which is
more than you can say for most people in L.A.

After 25 years on television, I had finally cracked into that
dubious elite where—gulp—people will pick up the phone and
get back to you. My agents had been trying to book me on *The
Tonight Show* for years. Then, suddenly, Leno's talent coordinator, Mike Alexander, called to schedule me for an appearance to
talk about *Double Dare* and promote my new shows, *What Would
You Do?* and *Our Home.*

I was booked, bounced, and rebooked nine times. Late-night
talk show talent coordinators have a difficult job. Agents and
publicists call them constantly, trying to get their clients an appearance. A show will always lead with the biggest star and book
smaller fry that it thinks will get along with him or her. So, for
whatever reason—the producers didn't like the mix of guests a
particular week, or whatever—they'd book me, I'd get all excited
that "next week it was going to happen!" and then they'd call a
week, or even a day, before my scheduled appearance and cancel me. Sometimes they'd call and say, "We rescheduled your
appearance but we don't know for when." This went on for almost a year. I'd heard horror stories of people who were booked
for as long as three years and never ended up doing the show
at all.

It was nerve-wracking, especially for someone like me with

obsessive compulsive disorder. I didn't know the root cause, but I did know that being bounced time and again off *The Tonight Show* was making me nuts. Lack of punctuality and order awakened in me then—and sometimes still does now—strong emotional responses, from intense anxiety to anger. I was also aware that I had secret rituals, magic incantations and spells that I used to ensure that disaster didn't strike. I needed, for example, to read the back of the cereal box at breakfast over and over with complete fluidity or, I was convinced, the flight that I had booked for later that week would crash. I kid you not, I believed (as do millions of other Americans with OCD) that my well-being hinged on such absurdities.

Alexander and Leno wanted Marc Summers the magician, which was the way I had begun my career in show business, back in Indianapolis, where, as a teenager, I made rabbits pop out of hats at birthday parties.

"Do some magic with Jay," Mike said. "That will work well for your segment."

My segment was six minutes of the show wedged between commercials. It could catapult me to a new level of "visibility," as they say in the industry.

I had worked long and hard to get away from being billed as a magician. I was a television host, a teen icon, a comic. To focus my appearance on doing tricks made me shudder. What was I, a dancing poodle?

Finally, Mike Alexander gave me an ultimatum: if you want to do the show, you do a trick.

In this business you learn to kiss ass, or you die trying.

I'd do a trick.

If I was going to do a trick, I wanted it to be a card trick. No dice, they said. Jay wouldn't be sufficiently involved if I did a card trick. I called my friend Stan, a master magician. "Cut and restore Jay's tie," he suggested.

Jay's guys loved it.

What had I gotten myself into? I was going to do a trick I'd never performed before on the single most important television appearance of my life. I practiced and practiced my trick. Then I was bumped, and bumped again.

The tenth booking was the charm, or so it seemed. The show sent a limo to pick me up, but it arrived late. That was particularly unsettling since I was ready—as I always am—an hour early. I had laid out my suit, tie, shirt, and socks the night before. My magic props were in their little black cloth bag. I'd polished and brushed my shoes.

I paced the house. I lived with my family in a gated community, so I had to wait for security to telephone the limo's arrival. God, I thought, as I waited and waited, this is how they're going to tell me they bumped me again. They're just not going to pick me up. I would learn later that stress brought out my OCD symptoms, one of which was repetitive thoughts. At the time, I thought it was perfectly natural that my mind was on a loop, endlessly repeating the cut-and-restore tie trick.

Finally, the phone rang. The limo had arrived. It turned out that the driver had gotten lost.

I was in a state of acute anxiety as we whizzed down the Ventura Freeway—it was only a 20- or 30-minute drive to the studio from my house. I tried to make conversation with the driver—anything was better than being inside my head, replaying *ad nauseam* the tie routine. Suddenly, I felt a sickeningly familiar thud-thud thud-thud.

I leaned forward. "Is everything OK?"

"Sir, it seems we have a flat tire."

Had the show done it intentionally? Was this a premeditated break-down designed to strand undesired guests on the freeway? I couldn't believe it. God, I thought, is not pleased with me today. What else could go wrong?

The driver called the automobile club. I climbed from the car and started pacing along the shoulder of the Ventura Freeway. Auto clubs are the same the world over: sometimes technicians can arrive in 10 minutes; sometimes they take two hours. I kept checking my watch; it was a quarter to four, and the show started taping at 5:30. We were 15 minutes from the studio, near White Oak Avenue, and I was tempted to grab my suit and stick my thumb in the air.

AAA arrived. I stood in the swirling exhaust, cars whipping past, staring at the two guys who scrambled to change the flat on the big black limo.

When we finally arrived in Burbank, I arranged my belongings, as I always do before shows, in my small dressing room. I must have been nervous, because my OC symptoms were strong. I took my suit from its plastic dry-cleaning bag (I always put a plastic bag around a suit before putting it in an overnight bag) and hung it in the wardrobe closet, maniacally smoothing its nonexistent wrinkles and picking microscopic specks of lint from its crisp shoulders and lapels. I folded and refolded the plastic bag, placing it on the dressing-room couch in the middle of the right-side cushion, moving the bag around for several minutes until it was precisely centered. I could have been hanging a painting in the Louvre. I put my magic props on the vanity table, arranging and rearranging them until they sat at perfect angles to each other.

Jay came in, startling me. "Sorry you got bumped so many times," he said.

"I'm glad I'm finally here!" I replied.

We reminisced briefly about our Comedy Store days, and then I went to makeup. It was a thrill to be sitting in the same makeup room that Johnny Carson had used. *The Tonight Show* is one of the original, anchor shows of TV. It's living history. And I was a part of it.

I went back to my dressing room and put on my Joseph Abboud suit. This suit was my pride and joy, ridiculously expensive, with a subtle check design. I only wore it for special show biz occasions—like my first appearance on *The Tonight Show.*

Jay's audio man came in and clipped a microphone onto my lapel. Someone went over the questions Jay would ask and the responses I would give. (They pre-interview guests long before the actual show, but they go over the information again before taping to prevent guests from freezing up.) My mouth was parched. I was drinking gallons of water, but all it seemed to do was make me run to the bathroom every twenty seconds. My agent, Richard Lawrence, and my publicist, Coleen Gunderson, came in to lend support. But I was too nervous to carry on a conversation.

While waiting for my segment, we watched the show on the dressing-room monitor. The night before, Jay had made a nasty comment about Burt Reynolds' less-than-pretty divorce from Loni Anderson. Tonight, Burt was guesting on the show, and he was mad. We've all seen *Deliverance*, so we know Burt is capable of some odd behavior. But the night of this particular show, he was in an especially weird, vindictive mood. He said, in reference to Jay's nasty comment, "That was a cutting remark, so I'm going to even the score," and he brought out a pair of scissors and cut Jay's tie in half.

Out in the hall I heard a flurry of running feet. "Burt cut Jay's tie!" several people said. Leno's staff was in an uproar.

I sat there with my mouth hanging open. *Oh shit,* I thought. *Now what do I do? Jay doesn't have a tie! What am I going to do my trick with?* I had an overwhelming urge to hail a cab (with well-inflated tires) and go home.

But it had been a long road to *The Tonight Show*. I had rechecked my props ten thousand times in preparation. I was staying. I was relieved to see Jay return from the commercial break with a new tie.

A pissed-off, weirded-out Burt Reynolds makes good television, so Jay and his producers stuck with him. Instead of doing the usual star segment through two commercial breaks, Burt did three. The tone of the show was combative, confrontational. Burt was sullen, swaggering, sarcastic, and aggressive. It was a testosterone pissing match. Jay kept pummeling Burt, making references to the size of Loni's divorce settlement, making fun of Burt's being on a book tour for his autobiography, a book he hadn't actually written. Soon, Burt was on his knees. Jay wouldn't give in, which is not Jay's reputation—he's known as a nice guy. But Burt, in the kind of nasty supercilious mood he was in, brings out the worst in people.

Right before the third commercial break, after which I was

due to go on, Jay closed in for the *coup de grace*. He opened the book to a 1972 *Cosmopolitan* magazine photo of Burt naked. Burt recalled his embarrassment as the photo editors had peered over the print of the photograph with magnifying glasses, inspecting his body.

"They needed magnifying glasses?" Jay said, referring to the size of Burt's manhood.

The audience erupted. Burt had been set up, he knew it, and he was livid as the show went to commercial.

Jay had time for only one more guest, but there were two of us scheduled.

Chaos erupted in the hall. "Summers or Carrot Top? Summers or Carrot Top?" Leno's staff shouted. This was every performer's nightmare: me versus the then-biggest comedian on college campuses. To my horror, the consensus among the show staff was that Carrot Top had bigger mojo than Summers.

My publicist and agent came into my dressing room and said, "You may not get on tonight."

"Let's go with Carrot Top," said a Leno executive.

My publicist stepped into the hall. "This is enough already," she said. "You've canceled us nine times. You can run Carrot Top tomorrow. Put Marc on tonight."

It was incredible: Leno's staff saw things our way.

From there, everything was a blur. The stage manager told me to stand by the stage entrance and watch the monitor. When *The Tonight Show* insignia came on, the band would stop playing and I'd hear my name.

"Dear God, please let me get through this and not embarrass myself!" I prayed.

". . . Marc Summers!" was the next thing I heard. It was one of the most frightening moments of my life. I walked onstage, the audience from the corner of my eye appearing in what we call in film a slow-motion swish-pan blur. They were clapping, but I could feel their rhythm, skittish and on edge, as they were waiting, with a quickened sense of anticipation and embarrassment, to see what new humiliations would ensue. As a performer, you can't really see an audience, so you learn to have an aural sense of them. I angled toward Jay, propelled across the stage by instinct, shaking his hand and sitting down in the chair next to the big desk in one fluid motion.

I knew I was walking into the lion's den. Two titans of show business were going head to head. And I knew both of them were thinking as I sat down, who the hell is Marc Summers? I had six minutes to prove myself; I needed to score. It's a one-shot deal out there. There are no retakes, no second chances. I wasn't nervous; I was petrified. I began to banter with Jay, as all guests do. I felt Jay relax a little: he had been sparring with one of the all-time champs. I sensed he had no idea why I was on the show. And neither had I. I was sitting up there purely because of the superb work of my publicist.

Now, let's get one thing straight. I have no illusions about my status in the Hollywood food chain. I'm still best known for my long stint on *Double Dare.* My weekly adventures of being submerged in a vat of applesauce, or dragged through oatmeal or green goo, make good conversation fodder. Jay, with a nervous eye on Burt, jumped on my role in *Double Dare.*

"Now, do you like doing the messy stuff especially?" he asked.

This wasn't a question we'd rehearsed, but Jay's allowed to ask whatever he wants.

Do I give the pat Nickelodeon-type response? *It's great! At least once a week, I know I'll get dessert before dinner.*

No, I thought. Don't be pat. You made it to the couch. Give a thoughtful, genuine answer.

"No, it's very strange," I said. "I'm Felix Unger: I'm a neatness fanatic, so it's weird that for the last nine years I've been doing that kind of TV."

A neatness fanatic, I thought. That's interesting. First time I had ever mentioned that. Why was I saying it now in front of a national TV audience?

In fact, this was the first time I had acknowledged—in my own mind—that spending hours and hours and more hours putting everything exactly the way it should be wasn't normal. I'd spent almost four decades obsessed with cleanliness, neatness, order, spaces, angles, borders, and straight lines. Everything I touched had to be spaced with exact precision. To me, that was being a "neat freak."

I had said it. I wasn't ashamed of it. In a world full of Oscar Madisons, you need a few Felix Ungers to balance things, right? Call me Felix.

I continued, "We've done some weird things on the show. We once built a container with 4,000 pounds of baked beans and made kids dive into it, which was really great."

"Gee," interjected Burt, "I wish I'd seen that." The audience laughed. Jay laughed. I laughed. Burt was deadpan.

Jay tried to pull us back on track. "You force kids' heads under baked beans?"

More laughter. I explained, smiling, "We have an obstacle course, and . . ."

Burt jumped in, cutting me off mid-sentence: "Who told you you were a neatness freak?"

Alarm clock. Needle scratch. Wrong answer buzzer.

"I just say that," Burt said with annoyance, "because your back is to me and I was just talking to a back."

I guess he thought it was the Burt Reynolds Show. Why should they bring anyone else out? At the time, Jay was still pretty green as *The Tonight Show* host. He'd been at it only about a year. On the other hand, Burt had been on *The Tonight Show* fifty times with Johnny Carson, and a few more with Jay. Burt Reynolds was the most veteran man on the stage that night, a fact he seemed eager to exploit.

I wanted to keep the peace. "No, no, I can talk to you, too, Burt."

"Watch out," Jay cautioned, "he's got scissors."

Burt hammered away, the scorn in his voice palpable. "I was just wondering, who told you you were neat?"

This was one angry son-of-a-bitch. *Burt hates me,* I thought. *It's obvious.* I'm looking at this guy with a toupee and jeans that had been worn at least a hundred times and boots with a three-inch lift. Every morning he wakes up and has to transform himself into Burt Reynolds. I suddenly felt a wave of pity for the guy. In my mind I looked younger, dressed better, and was funnier. I tried to give him a quick non-answer grin, and go on with my segment. No dice.

"Who told you that you were a neatness fanatic?!" Burt repeated.

"My wife tells me that often," I said. "And," I patted his shoulder, "by the way, *I'm still married.*"

The audience went crazy. I glanced at Jay triumphantly. Jay jumped to his feet, eyes wide, and reached out to grab my arm. But it was too late. Burt dumped a mug of water into my crotch. I grabbed Jay's mug and tried to toss it on Burt, but Burt straight-armed me, bashing the mug into my mouth.

This is great, I thought. I'm finally on *The Tonight Show* and I'm engaging in fisticuffs with Burt Reynolds. It was, without a doubt, the most bizarre moment of my life. I was drenched, but I didn't even notice. At any other time, my normal obsession with my appearance would have made me acutely uncomfortable. I can't stand to have a hair out of place, the slightest spot or defect in my clothing. And here I was, sopping wet, my best suit blotched and spotted, my carefully coiffed hair hanging lankly over my forehead. But I was beyond concern for my appearance or comfort. I was trying to stay alive.

The audience roared. "You're not a neatness freak anymore," Burt scoffed.

I thought I'd lost a tooth; I was sure there was blood running down my face. I looked at Jay. He nodded comfortingly, which I took to mean—you're okay, you're blood-free.

"This is what's known as losing control of the program, ladies and gentlemen," Jay said. I think he felt a little protective of me. Yet he knew how good it was for the show.

I turned to the audience. "Burt Reynolds just dumped water on me. Did you notice that, folks?"

"And you'll treasure it later," Burt said, patting my hand.

"Don't touch me," I spat.

More laughter. Maybe I could still make this work. Maybe we could get along. I turned to Burt. "I used to be on your show all the time, *Win, Lose or Draw.* I loved that show."

"Funny," he shrugged, "I don't remember you."

"Oooooooh," said the audience.

So much for peace, love, and understanding. I turned back to Jay. "So, anyway, we were talking about being a neatness fanatic."

"Yeah," said Jay. "You started out as a magician, if I'm not mistaken."

Burt cackled like a hyena, laughing because the staff had tossed me a towel. He was sprawled on his chair, like he was soaking up rays at the beach. I couldn't resist. I blind-sided him with a mug of water, dousing him. The audience screamed in delight. Out of the corner of my eye, I could see folks in the balcony leap from their chairs to give me a standing ovation.

I learned later that my agent Richard was trying to stop the show. "My client looks like an idiot," he had said to the producers. "Stop taping!"

But my dignity, or career for that matter, was way down on the producers' list of priorities. They were looking for notoriety, ratings, hits in the press, and they knew they were going to get them.

Jay turned to his crew, appealing for a diplomatic solution. Before the show, Jay's producers had wanted to do a pie fight, but Jay had said no. Now, however, he mouthed to his crew, "Let's do the PIE."

Burt and I were drying ourselves off.

"It's all right," Burt said, "I deserved that."

"You deserved it?" I asked, quizzically.

"I deserved it. As I was saying to your wife the other night . . ."

Another wave of laughter. This would never end.

"Burt's been on a very rough book tour," Jay said, apologetically.

"I know!" I turned to Burt. "I once saw you on a PBS special. You were a nice guy then!"

"It's easy to be nice to nice people," he snarled.

"It is," I growled back.

"It's nice to see you two hit it off so well," Jay said.

Burt had his towel wrapped around his neck, his lips curled into a snarl.

"He's doing his Milton Berle impression, take a look at that," I said.

Jay cracked up, but the room was quiet. Whoops, I'd missed.

"Too obscure for the room," I said nervously, "anyway . . ."

"I'll bet that plays great on Nickelodeon," sneered Burt.

"At least *I* have a full-time job," I shot back.

"That's true . . ." Burt stopped mid-sentence. The two of us stared in disbelief. Jay walked toward us with what I could smell were pies made from shaving cream (an old show-biz trick) in his hands!

"What's this?" I protested, as Jay handed a pie to me and a pie to Burt.

"Shall we go back to back?" Burt said.

Before I knew what was happening, Burt and I were standing back to back with pies in our hands.

The band started a drum roll. Jay counted: "One, two . . ." We both spun before he got to three and smashed each other with pies. Mayhem erupted. There was shaving cream everywhere— on the wood floor, on the carpet, on the chairs, on me and Burt, everywhere except on Jay.

Burt hugged me, and then tried to hug Jay.

"Get away from me!" Jay said, running off stage into the band pit. It made me angry that Jay was clean. Johnny would have taken a pie; Johnny wasn't afraid to "pay off the joke." Jay was still too new to realize that getting dirty was part of the job. I was handed another pie. I said to the audience, "If I look like this and Burt looks like this . . . ."

"Jay! Jay! Jay!" they chanted. They knew he should take one, too.

Jay appeared back onstage and managed to say into the camera, "Oh, ladies and gentlemen, we are out of time. We'll be right back *right* after these messages." He dashed away as Burt pitched shaving cream at his back.

We came back on the air for the show's wrapup. Staffers wiped me and Burt clean. Burt hugged me and whispered, "I only did that because I really like you."

What a liar, I thought.

Jay suggested Burt sign a copy of his book for me.

"What's your broad's name?" Burt asked me.

"What?"

"Your broad. Your wife."

Broad. Now that was a term I hadn't heard in several decades.

"To Marc and Alice," he wrote. "All my love, Burt." I kept the book, as a memento of the night. I've never read it.

Burt walked offstage, got into his limo, and left. He was out even before the cameras had stopped rolling. That's unheard of: everybody hangs out onstage and chats with Jay until taping's done.

Jay and I were out there alone. He leaned over, "What was that about?"

"I don't know."

"I don't know either," he said. "But I do know that whatever else it was, it was sure great television."

The cameras stopped rolling and I staggered offstage. What had just happened? I felt as though I'd just gone 10 rounds with Muhammad Ali, but I had no idea how I'd come off.

"That's either the best thing that's happened for my career or the worst" were the first words I said to my agent.

Jay's staff was nice enough to say that the show would replace my suit (I never took them up on it) and kept telling me that I'd be "on the anniversary reel."

Jay came into the dressing room to make sure I was okay. So did a couple of NBC executives. I suspected they were attorneys who were afraid I was going to sue. They left when they were satisfied that I hadn't been injured.

The taping finished at 6:30 P.M., but the show didn't broadcast until 11:30 that night. By the time I arrived home at 8:00, NBC was already running promos with me and Burt getting ready to kill each other with pies. I was so overwhelmed by the whole experience, I didn't even get into the shower. They had started running the promos on the East Coast, where the show airs three hours earlier, as soon as we stepped off the stage. This was hot stuff, and they knew it.

I sat with my family later that night and watched the show. Alice was speechless. Finally, my son Matthew said, "Dad, you should have let him hit you. Then you could have sued him and you'd never have to work again."

It wasn't until the next morning that everybody realized the magnitude of the stir the show had caused. Phone calls poured in. People assumed the routine had been set up: "stunting," as it's known in the industry.

"I'm not that good an actor," I protested. "If I were a trained performer, maybe I could have pulled it off. But I'm not! It was real!"

Within a week, the incident had been covered by every tabloid and all the news-magazine shows like *Hard Copy* and *Inside Edition*. "Burt Goes Berserk on *The Tonight Show!*" screamed a headline in the *New York Post*. I heard from my friend producer-director Steve Binder that Burt felt like he deserved more respect as a major movie star and that he had referred to me as a "bottom-feeder in show business." My mother called. "My God," she said. "What's this going to do for your career?"

"Good things!" I assured her.

Four years later I still get stopped in the street and asked about *The Tonight Show* with Burt Reynolds.

I'm sure Burt thought he deserved more respect, but the audience was cheering for me that night, not him.

And how was Jay through all this? After he mopped himself off, he didn't mind at all. It was the first time he had tied David

Letterman in the Nielsen ratings. And my Joseph Abboud suit? I had it dry-cleaned three times, until the smell of the shaving cream was finally gone. I haven't worn it since. It's still hanging, immaculate, in my closet. I keep it in there as a memorial to the event, a reminder of the bittersweet culmination of my childhood dream. I have no desire to wear it again, and no heart to throw it out.

My admission that I was a "neatness fanatic" set off the fight with Burt, but it was barely noticed by the audience and completely ignored in the media coverage of our brawl. I later realized Burt had touched a nerve when he seized on that point and started needling me with it.

I didn't have a name for it at the time. I didn't know there was something called obsessive compulsive disorder. I didn't know that my fanatical neatness and propensity for lining things up at right angles were classic symptoms of OCD, a disorder I share with six million other Americans.

I was to learn that being a "neatness fanatic" was, in fact, only one of the many obsessions and compulsions that characterize my specific form of the disorder. I knew I was obsessed with neatness, but I had no idea that my obsession was clinical. I thought my obsessions were the normal type of day-to-day hang-ups the vast portion of humanity shares. But I was wrong. "Obsessions" for people with OCD are repetitive, intrusive, distressing, and anxiety-inducing thoughts. And "compulsions" are repetitive, ritualistic behaviors that we feel driven to perform in order to decrease our anxiety-provoking obsessive thoughts. The anxiety caused by obsessive thoughts is so strong that we repeatedly perform compulsive behaviors despite the fact that we don't enjoy performing them, and even though we're aware that our behavior makes no sense.

My obsessive need for order, symmetry, and exactness triggers my compulsion to align objects until everything is in its place. This is what I had been doing in *The Tonight Show* dressing room, arranging my bag on the couch and my magic props on the vanity table.

Obsessive compulsive disorder can be truly crippling, truly debilitating. People with OCD can become obsessed with contamination: the fear of dirt, germs, cancer, AIDS, bodily wastes, asbestos, poison, chemicals, radiation, and sticky substances or residues. Howard Hughes, a millionaire who once wined and dined with movie stars, was in later life so overwhelmed by his OCD- induced terror of germs that he sealed himself in one room. Servants, their hands covered with tissues, brought him his food. Hughes had curtains on all the windows to prevent sunlight from entering because he was afraid the sun might carry germs. He stored everything he was afraid might be "contaminated." He even saved his urine and feces in glass jars. My contamination obsessions are relatively benign. You'll read about my involved method of taking showers in hotel rooms so that my bare feet don't touch the floor. But that, fortunately, was about the extent of my contamination fears.

OCD sufferers can also be "hoarders": people who have trouble throwing things away because they feel they may need them later. Hoarders may save years of newspapers, and have no retrieval or filing system, but be unable to throw them out because they fear that someday they may need them. Some hoarders inspect household trash to make sure nothing "valuable" is being thrown out. I am fanatical about saving some things (I saved every paper from school since fourth grade, and have them stored in boxes), but I'm not the classic type of OCD hoarder, whose house or apartment is overflowing with junk.

Some people with OCD are besieged by thoughts of harming others. They fear that they will put poison in food, spread illness, smother a child, stab their spouse, push a stranger in front of a car, or run over a pedestrian. These people can become afraid to get into their cars for fear of hurting someone. I've never experienced these obsessive compulsive fears; but I have been convinced, as you'll see, that if I didn't practice certain rituals bad things would happen to me or to others (my plane would crash or my daughter wouldn't get a part in the school play, for example).

Another symptom I've experienced that is also common among OCD sufferers is an irrational urge to check things. For a brief period I was consumed by the thought that my car door was unlocked. I'd check it over and over. Others repeatedly check to make sure the stove isn't on or that they've turned off all the light switches before they leave the house. Anyone who's seen Jack Nicholson's Academy Award–winning portrayal of an obsessive compulsive sufferer in *As Good As It Gets* will remember his classic OCD checking antics: flipping the light switch on and off a certain number of times and locking and unlocking his door repeatedly.

Obsessions and compulsions that I've been lucky enough never to have experienced include: a fixation on lucky or unlucky numbers; religious obsessions and excessive moral concerns that lead to distressing "blasphemous" thoughts; repeatedly asking for reassurance; incessantly scrubbing one's hands; and, in more extreme cases, washing one's mouth out with Lysol because of contamination fears; counting things (signs along the highway or cracks in the sidewalk) or touching, rubbing, or tapping things (door frames, wall moldings). Radio and television personality Howard Stern admits that his OCD was once so severe that he was compelled to bang his head against the studio wall a certain number of times before each of his radio shows.

While almost everyone obsesses about something at one point or another in his or her life, people with OCD usually have multiple obsessions and compulsions. People are only considered to have OCD if their obsessions and compulsions are severe enough to cause them distress, consume an inordinate amount of their time, and interfere with their functioning in daily life. Like most OCD sufferers, I have found that performing compulsions does, briefly, alleviate anxiety; but the relief is temporary, and the anxiety-provoking obsessions quickly return, unabated.

In future chapters, we'll get into some of the science that concerns how and why the brains of people with OCD are different, and what happens in our brains when our symptoms occur. We'll see how tremendous advances in our understanding of OCD have helped to develop drug and behavior therapies that are extremely effective in treating our disorder.

On *The Tonight Show* with Burt Reynolds I had no idea that a chemical imbalance in my brain was what was causing me to be a neatness fanatic. But I did know that Burt had somehow cracked my public face, and underneath this carefully constructed public face lurked a very private torment. I had been tormented since I was a child with the constant anxiety of living in an inherently chaotic, imperfect world where I needed everything in its place. Most of the time that anxiety was at a low pitch. At other times it shrieked inside me like a siren. It was always there, lurking in the background.

I knew, intuitively, that this part of myself that needed everything in its place had a positive side. The same perfectionism that drove me to arrange my closet and dresser drawers like a drill sergeant's also spurred me on to succeed, to refuse to accept failure, to create for myself a public persona as a television performer in the brutally competitive world of show business. This public face was successful and self-assured. But this biggest night of my life in show business had opened a secret inner world that I had carried around inside me for nearly my whole life, since I was a very young child.

| *two* |

sunday, day of rest

Step on crack, break your Momma's back.
—*Anonymous children's rhyme*

On March 3, 1997, I appeared on *The Oprah Winfrey Show* with four other obsessive compulsive sufferers. Oprah, in a sleek black dress, made a dramatic entrance. The crowd, mostly female, leapt to its feet, hooting and whistling adoringly.

The crowd quieted, and Oprah read a page from the diary of Doron, one of my fellow guests on the show: "Today I went to the grocery store, and I was choosing a watermelon," Doron had written. "I felt gripped by fear. Someone had put poison in these watermelons and my fingerprints were all over them. I knew the police would accuse me of poisoning people who died after they ate these watermelons."

Knowing how difficult it was on a day-to-day basis for me to cope with the disorder, I wondered sadly how it was possible for someone as paranoid as Doron to function in the world. Doron was a perfectly normal-looking guy in his thirties, well-groomed with dark hair, wearing a black sweatshirt. I wondered how he felt about having his personal diary read aloud to 30 million Americans.

The first guest to appear on the show was Lorrie, who was so desperately afraid of contamination that she bathed in Lysol. Lorrie is a pretty woman in her mid-thirties with a sensitive face. Oprah showed a photo of her taken seven months earlier on her wedding day. She was radiant. But during those seven months the disorder had exploded, and the woman now facing Oprah was haggard and exhausted. She sat next to her husband Matt, weeping as Oprah ran film footage of what Lorrie went through each time she ate. Lorrie made Matt drive at least five miles from their house to buy her food. He had to inspect each item to make sure it was properly sealed. While Matt prepared her food, Lorrie locked herself in the bathroom, scrubbing her hands raw, "de-contaminating" herself. Matt would lead her to the table, where she sat shaking and crying. Eyes scrunched shut, she forced each bite into her mouth. Eating was pure torture for her.

"I depend on my husband and my mom," Lorrie told Oprah. "I have no life. My rituals are my life. I spend all day decontaminating everything."

I hugged her, put my hand on her arm. Her white gloves were pulled up past the sleeves of her red dress that helped, along with a "force field" she imagined around her body, to protect her from germs. Oprah asked Lorrie if my hand was bothering her. She said no, but that if her skin had been exposed it would have.

"I recently came to a realization," Lorrie said. "My thoughts are what is contaminating me, not the things I think are contaminating me. I have to learn to live my life all over again."

Next on was Don, a "hoarder" who hadn't thrown anything away in 40 years. A clip ran of Don's apartment, so cluttered with his art collection, hats, bags and boxes of clothes, Christmas trees he'd never put together, every receipt he'd ever gotten, a Yogi Bear punching bag he'd had since he was 10 . . . endless stuff. Don, á balding man with glasses, told Oprah that he could manage the disorder on his own. But I suspected, as did everyone else watching, that his compulsion to hoard was out of control.

We broke for a commercial and I realized that this show wasn't like any other television program I'd ever appeared on or hosted. There was an ease and naturalness about it. I leaned toward Oprah. "I understand why you're such a hit. We're just *talking*."

"That's right, honey," she smiled. "We're just talking."

It was Oprah's birthday that day, and Julio Iglesias was going to come out and sing to her. But she opted to go with one more guest with OCD.

Much as I felt for Doron, Lorrie, and Don, it was Oprah's next guest who broke my heart. Eleven-year-old Darcie had her dark hair bound in a ponytail on top of her head. She reminded me of my daughter Meredith. But Meredith didn't wander through the house, checking all the electrical outlets and light switches, terrified of fire. Meredith wasn't desperately frightened of germs.

Meredith didn't constantly check herself in the mirror, sometimes for hours on end, so worried about her appearance that she was often late for school.

"I get stuck in the mirror and have a hard time getting out," Darcie said, fighting back tears. "I know I look okay but I don't feel right. I don't feel comfortable if I leave. To people who hear this it might sound strange. When you have OCD you know how it feels."

I hugged Darcie before we went to commercial break. Oprah told her how brave she was to be there. "You're my hero for the day," she said.

She was my hero, too. My anxieties and compulsions as a child were not as crippling as Darcie's. But I knew what it was like to be consumed by doubts and fears. My childhood hadn't been particularly traumatic. But my OCD made it peculiar, perhaps even bizarre.

I grew up in a one-story limestone house in the northern part of the city of Indianapolis. My family had a one-acre lot, so our side yard was big enough for a good game of baseball or football. There were always a million kids around. One neighbor, David Rust, had a basketball court, so every day after dinner we'd go over to his house and play. Or, if David didn't want to play, there was another court behind the field in back of our house, near the farmers' pump house.

Every Sunday, after Sunday school, my brother, sister, and I came home and changed into our play clothes. Except I didn't play. Instead, I'd kick my older brother Mike out of the room we shared and start to clean. As my brother eagerly ran to watch TV or outside to play football, I'd turn on the radio or my little portable TV and shut the bedroom door. From the time I was eight years old until I was sixteen, every single Sunday of my life I cleaned everything in exactly the same way in exactly the same order.

This was no ordinary cleaning. First I'd strip my bunk bed, and dust the woodwork behind the bed and the bed itself. I'd walk around and around the bed as I made it, back and forth, until the bedding was perfectly smooth and symmetrical. The bedspread couldn't touch the floor. It had to be perfectly even along the bottom. I put the bed back into its indentations in our dark green carpet so I wouldn't make new ones. If, by chance, the bed had left any slight indentations in its temporary position, I would get down on my hands and knees and rub them out.

I then turned my attention to our bookshelf. I dusted each book with a rag—the cover, binding, spine, bottom, top, every surface. I dusted and Pledged the shelves, put each book back in its place, taking care that the edges were exactly flush with the lip of the bookshelf. The bookshelf alone could take an hour to clean.

On top of my brother's dresser was the stereo our dad had given him; he hated for me to touch it. "Keep your hands off my stuff," he'd say. But when it came to cleanliness, the room was my territory. I *needed* to dust underneath that stereo. I *had to* angle its hinged speakers in a particular direction.

To the right of the dresser was a bulletin board. It wasn't like other kids' bulletin boards with everything overlapping and helter skelter. My bulletin board was perfectly symmetrical, with all the items radiating in equidistant perfection from the big photo of Johnny Carson at the center. Below the bulletin board

was the desk I shared with my brother. I would dust the desk
drawers and then turn my attention to the dresser.

At age 11, I came to the earth-shattering realization that
"balling" my socks would stretch out their elastic, so I began
folding them. This made it possible to stack them. Browns with
browns, blues with blues, blacks with blacks. My ties, belts, play
pants, and T-shirts were all organized and folded according to a
system that I still use today. My good clothes were hung exactly
an inch and a half apart in my closet, organized by function and
color. They all faced (and face) the same direction. I hung my
pants perfectly, always folding them carefully to avoid the
dreaded double-crease.

Once a month, I'd binge, moving everything away from the
walls and dusting behind the furniture. My mother called those
Sundays "spring cleaning." Sometimes, a rag would come up with
so much dust that I'd run to show it off to Mom. "Oh, look at that!"
she'd exclaim. My mother never once had to say, "You'd better go
to your room and clean." She realized how important cleaning was
to me and accepted me as a quirky, clean little boy. There was
nothing in my room that wasn't Pledged to death, wiped,
Windexed, vacuumed. Nothing. Everything was shiny and perfect.
I loved the way a clean room smelled. Cleaning gave me an incredible feeling of satisfaction. It fulfilled a very deep inner need.

Occasionally, my mother or father would stick their head in to
see how I was doing. I barely glanced up. I was completely focused. Even at that young age, I needed absolute order. I needed
to do things in a way that felt right. I needed to have everything
in its place.

Cleaning was a recreational activity for me and my mother. I'd help her buff our floors until they shined, and she loved the way I vacuumed the house. As a kid I didn't think, "Let me do this so I can get rid of this horrible knot in my stomach," which is what I thought later in life. I enjoyed my cleaning rituals more as a child than later as an adult, when I derived no pleasure from carrying out my compulsions; when they became just a source of pain. I fondly remember cleaning with my mother as a child. Mom and I had a special bond that I don't think she shared with my brother Mike or my sister Lori.

A couple times a year I'd clean all the windows in the house, inside and out. I'd be up on a ladder and Mom would stand inside and point out dirt as I cleaned. My mother's special attention was particularly important to me because I was intensely competitive with my older brother Mike. His IQ was off the charts, and he had a photographic memory.

It wasn't Mike's intelligence I envied, however. He had played the drums from a very early age, and was a child prodigy. At 15, he was on the road with Henry Mancini and Johnny Mathis, and playing The Embers, the biggest nightclub in Indianapolis, when he was still underage. I envied him because he was closer to show business than I was. He hung out with celebrities. I eagerly drank up his stories of the people he'd met. While I dreamt show business, he lived it.

My father worked seven days a week at Berkys Supermarket, which my grandfather built and owned. The store closed at 8 P.M.

and Dad would usually be home by 9:00. If he wasn't, my mother would begin to pace and wring her hands.

"Oh my god! Where is your father?" she'd moan.

By 9:20, she'd panic. Passing headlights sent her running to the dining room window.

"Is that your father? Is it? Oh, no. Maybe he's had an accident! Let's call the hospital. Let's call the police."

My brother would roll his eyes and shoot her a "get a life" look. My sister was oblivious. But my mother's hysterics turned me into a wreck. I agonized about my father. Was he okay? Had something happened? As my mother paced, I paced right behind her. I prayed Dad wasn't dead.

Then, inevitably, headlights would swoop into our driveway, the garage door would swing open, and in would walk Dad.

"Where were you?" Mom would ask.

"Lois," he'd say, "I was working. Traffic was heavy."

"I thought something happened to you! I was so worried."

He'd sigh. "It's been a long day. Where's my dinner?"

Without further ado, he'd sit down at the table and eat the dinner she had prepared.

In some ways, I think my mom's behavior may have triggered my OCD. Although she's never been officially diagnosed, I believe she was (and is) afflicted by the disorder. She was a constant worrier, and, like many OCD sufferers, when she was under stress her symptoms flared. When Mom slipped into her obsessive compulsive behavior it seemed to bring out the same feelings in me.

Although I had specific types of anxieties, they didn't gener-

alize to make me a fearful person. My mother picked up on my
outgoing, uninhibited personality early on and encouraged it.
She gave me my start in show business. Even as a toddler I loved
to perform. I was always animated—like a cartoon character. I
had no fear.

I was infatuated with television. One day when I was four or
five my mother whisked me off to the NBC affiliate in Indianapolis to audition for *Romper Room,* one of the first educational
shows on TV. I hit it off with the show's host, Miss Sue, and immediately appeared for a week on the program. I did so well that
I became a fill-in for absent kids.

The coolest thing on the show was the magic mirror. Miss Sue
would look into the mirror and say, "Romper Stomper Bomper
Boo!" As she said it, film rolled in weird, psychedelic patterns.
Then she held the mirror, now only a frame. You could see clear
through to the other side. In the studio, I watched the stage manager run over and switch Miss Sue's mirrors. The studio had a
particular smell, a sweet smell with a hint of electricity behind it.
There was a tremendous soothing heat from the intense lights. To
me, the studio smelled like burning Graham Crackers.

I subbed on *Romper Room* for a couple of years and became
completely hooked on entertaining and performing, on the power
and prestige of being on television. Even at the time, television
was the only place I felt totally comfortable. At school, on the
playground, at home, I always felt slightly on edge, as though I
was on the verge of disaster: a drink spilled on my pants, my father coming late, dust behind my bureau.

My doctor and I think my feeling of comfort on TV is linked to my OCD. When I'm on television I'm in charge, in control. On camera, I never perform obsessive compulsive rituals. I can be a "normal" person. Television is like dream time or fantasy time for me, a hyper-reality. When the cameras start to roll I walk out of this world onto another planet. I am like the stutterer who stops stuttering when he starts to sing. Internally, I know I'm still fighting the demon of the disorder. But I don't have to fight it when I'm on television. I have felt that way since my Romper Room days. Performance has always been therapeutic for me. I'm completely in the moment, in the zone, all my attention focused on how I'm doing.

This kind of shifting of attention away from obsessive compulsive rituals and thought patterns is the thrust of behavior therapy, a powerful OCD treatment I'll discuss later in this book. When you shift focus, and become totally concentrated on something outside normal day-to-day activities, it's impossible to be run by obsessions and compulsions.

The first time I realized the full force of the freedom I felt from the disorder was when I was onstage. I was six years old. My parents took me to an ice show in Chicago. After the show, the M.C. encouraged kids to come up and tell jokes onstage.

"Tell a joke," he said, "and you can put your hand in our penny jar and keep whatever you can grab."

Without asking my parents, I slid from my seat. In a split second, I was standing next to a tall man in a tuxedo. Without a trace of nervousness, I told my joke: "If two planes crash in mid-air, where do they bury the survivors?"

"I don't know," the M.C. said. "Where?"

"They don't bury the survivors, only the dead people!"

I heard a tremendous roar of laughter.

At that moment I knew that this was what I wanted to do with the rest of my life. I wanted to be onstage, telling jokes or performing.

I stuck my hand in the big fishbowl filled to the brim with pennies. For good measure, I stuck my other hand in, too. With my two little fists filled with pennies, I ran back to my seat. My parents were rolling with laughter.

That was my first paid gig. I relived it in my mind, over and over. I experienced the same rush each time I pictured it. I dreamt about getting back onstage and getting that feeling again.

The Delaware Trail Elementary School was a block and a half from our house. My trip was five minutes shorter if I cut through the grass, but if I did that I'd get dew on my shiny leather shoes and my nicely creased pants. If my shoes got wet on the way to school, I went straight to the bathroom, pulled paper towels from the dispenser, and wiped them until they were bone-dry. After recess on the gravel playground, I ran into the bathroom and cleaned the dirt and dust off my shoes until I could see my face in them. If I got ink on my hands, I washed it off immediately. Lots of kids wrote on their hands—a repugnant thought! Dirt under my nails? Horrors! But not as terrible as ink on my clothes. I'd keep staring and staring at the stain. It was all I thought about for the rest of the day. I couldn't wait to get home and give the clothes to Mom to wash.

Despite these childhood "quirks," I was a popular kid. In Indianapolis in the early '60s, being a jock was the key to being well-liked. I loved sports, and I was good at them. I played in Little League and made the All-Star team several years in a row. I enjoyed and excelled at track and field. I never had trouble making friends.

I was in the Cub Scouts, and once a month my pack had inspection. We stood at attention and the pack leader would walk the line, scrutinizing us. Were our neckerchiefs properly rolled? Did our shoes shine? At home, there was a shoe-shine kit in the laundry room. Black wax, a polish brush, a buffer. I'd brush my uniform shoes until they glowed. Then I'd have shoe polish under my nails. I'd scrub them for 15 minutes until the polish was completely gone.

The scout who won inspection always got a gold medal. Well, it was more like a key chain. But to me, it was a gold medal. I had a ton of them. My whole two years in Cub Scouts I never lost an inspection. Not once. I'm very competitive: To this day my kids hate to play Monopoly or Scrabble with me. I'm a *pain*. I tell them I'm going to crush them. I rag them to death. I do whatever it takes to win.

Whether playing Monopoly or climbing the show business ladder, I have to be the best. This obsession with winning is part of the constellation of symptoms of OCD. It's part of my drive to be perfect. The drive to win, to be perfect, to be the best can be a positive. It can motivate people to pay attention, to struggle and not give up in pursuit of their goals. This is why I think that most CEOs in corner offices probably have a touch of OCD.

But there is a downside to this perfectionism. It can be crippling. Many people with OCD become so stressed-out and overwhelmed with their need to be perfect that they don't take on new things. An obsessive compulsive sufferer who gets straight-A grades in college may decide not to go to graduate school because he's afraid of not performing up to his undergraduate standard. This kind of thinking can prevent some perfectionist OCD sufferers from taking on new challenges.

Perfectionism can be a terrible burden, but it spurs me on. I'm driven to achieve, and I'm also a risk-seeker. I'm not terrified of losing; just intent on winning. Although I'm driven to be perfect, I survive when I suffer setbacks or fail. My life hasn't been a smooth upward progression, but I've shrugged it off when things haven't worked out for me. To my fellow obsessive compulsive sufferers I say: You too can learn to deal with adversity. You may have an extraordinary need to be perfect, but take that as a challenge, not a burden. Fight hard, and if you don't succeed, don't get caught up in a sense of failure. Go on to the next challenge, and put everything you have into meeting it. Then move on.

Typical of perfectionist OCD sufferers, even as a child I made lists all the time. There was always a pad of paper or an index card near my glasses on the night table. I'd often get out of bed after I'd turned off the light to write things on my list. When I woke up, I looked at my list: "Study for history test. Baseball practice 3 to 4. Call Mr. Kubit about props at 5."

If I didn't write it down, I was sure I'd forget it. Never mind that I kept a running list in my head that I recited like a litany, over and over again during the day. I doubt there was any chance that I would forget anything, list or no. I checked things off as I accomplished them. Looking back, that was pure OCD.

What I take to be my "manageable" obsessive compulsive

childhood traits—neatness, list-making, punctuality, infatuation with performing—had a darker side. On *Oprah* that day in 1997, as I listened to Darcie talk about her fears, I was taken back to feelings in my own childhood. Like Darcie, I was consumed by anxieties that were deeply disturbing. They began when I empathized with my mother's fear that when my father was late, it meant he'd been in an accident.

But my anxieties began to escalate. I thought my parents would die if I didn't do everything in exactly the right way. When I took my glasses off at night I'd have to place them on the dresser at a particular angle. Sometimes I'd turn on the light and get out of bed seven times until I felt comfortable with the angle. If the angle wasn't right, I felt that my parents would die. The feeling ate up my insides.

If I didn't grab the molding on the wall just the right way as I entered or exited my room; if I didn't hang a shirt in the closet perfectly; if I didn't read a paragraph a certain way; if my hands and nails weren't perfectly clean, I thought my incorrect behavior would kill my parents.

I didn't know why I was thinking these awful things. Where did these thoughts come from? Why was I saying all this to myself? "They're going to die. They're going to die," kept running through my head. "I've killed them. It's my fault!"

I started to wonder if other people had these feelings and intrusive thoughts. I knew that if I asked others, though, and it turned out they didn't share my feelings, they'd think I was crazy. So I kept these thoughts secret. Years later I learned that children with OCD commonly involve their families in their rituals (they demand, for example, that dishes be washed repeatedly).

But not me. Not only did I not want anyone else to physically take part in my rituals, I didn't want even my closest family members to know about them.

I was scared to death. I thought I was nuts. I knew the stuff I was doing was weird, and I was afraid that if I mentioned my strange thoughts to my parents they'd send me to a psychiatrist. And back then, in 1964, if you went to a psychiatrist, you were insane. Looking back, even if I had asked my parents for help, there was not a chance my mother would ever have sent me to that kind of doctor. And, come to think of it, if I had said to my parents, "I have these feelings that if I don't clean up perfectly something bad will happen," they would have said, "Yeah, so? What's the problem?" I believe now that both my parents had the disorder, so there was no way they would have seen my obsessive compulsive behavior as evidence that I needed help.

The rare occasions when I failed to perform a ritual or complete a task were sheer hell. I would wake up in the middle of the night and lie there, consumed by fear. I'd sneak out of bed, careful not to wake my brother, and tiptoe down the hall. I'd stand in the doorway of my parents' room, listening for their breathing. It was cold and dark in the house. It was the dead hours of the night. No cars passed on the street. I could hear the faint humming of the refrigerator. I was terrified. I was convinced I had killed my parents because I hadn't cleaned my room thoroughly.

I wouldn't leave their doorway until I heard them both breathing. Often I would fall asleep standing up, leaning against the door frame, and my father would catch me and say, "What are you up to? Go to bed!" He always thought I was sleepwalking, but I was making sure that Mom and Dad were both still alive. When

I saw that they were, and that my "failure" didn't have terrible consequences, for a brief time—perhaps a week or two, sometimes longer—the fears would decrease.

After we finished the *Oprah* show I offered to go visit Darcie Kahn at her elementary school in Lawrence, Massachusetts. She told me the kids in her fifth-grade class had been bothering her. She had seen a doctor who recommended that she try to alleviate her classmates' teasing by talking to them about OCD. But that had only made matters worse. Boys had been tormenting her, making cruel remarks about her OCD. She thought my presence in her classroom might help dispel some of the cruelty directed toward her, and I was glad to help.

The thought of Darcie having to cope with the ridicule of classmates on top of everything else she was going through made me shudder. As a kid I'd managed to hide my behaviors from my parents, siblings, teachers, and schoolmates. Darcie's openness impressed me.

I flew to Boston and then drove to Lawrence. I met first with the principal of the school, who asked if the kids would know who I was.

"I think so," I said.

Word had gotten out among the students that I was in the building. As I accompanied the principal to Darcie's classroom the halls were buzzing, kids sticking their heads out of doors, whispering and pointing. The school began to go wild. (Apparently they knew who I was!)

In Darcie's classroom we talked about how everyone was different, and how we need to appreciate each other's differences because that's what makes humanity rich. Darcie said later that my visit made a big difference in the way she was treated by her peers. Meeting a successful television personality with OCD helped the kids realize that suffering from the disorder doesn't mean you're weird or bad.

Darcie's family, however, continues to struggle. Her younger sister Teal has just been diagnosed with OCD. Beatrice, her mother, said that on a recent family vacation to Florida, Teal came down with strep throat. She ran a high fever, wasn't eating, and, within a few days, had full-blown OCD. (Later on, we'll discuss how strep triggers the disorder.)

Suddenly, Teal refused to wear her shoes and socks. She couldn't stand to have her clothing touch her waist. At night, she now has an overwhelming fear of fire. She won't go to sleep. Either Beatrice or her husband Marty has to stay up with Teal until she's utterly exhausted and passes out in their arms. During the day, Teal walks around the house with a Windex bottle in her hand, cleaning everything in sight.

"It's hard," says Beatrice. "But we'll get through it."

Beatrice and Marty are fantastic examples of how parents of children with OCD can respond to the disorder. "I'm not ashamed of my children," says Beatrice. "I would fight for them tooth and nail. I want them to feel proud of themselves. They're great kids!"

The Kahns are trying to find the right medication at the right dosage for Teal. When they do, they're confident her symptoms will decrease. Darcie says that while medication has helped her, it hasn't cured her. She's in behavior therapy, which she says can be pure torture, but which has been beneficial. In the past, she picked her arms until they were covered with scabs. This "picking" is actually a symptom of another disorder that is closely related to and often accompanies OCD. The behavior therapy got Darcie to wait to pick—first 10, then 20, then 30 minutes—until the urge diminished.

Darcie has told me that her therapy has made her confront her fears. "It's been hard work," she says, "and nerve-wracking. But each time I do it I become a little stronger."

Darcie and her family have been an inspiration to me and, I'm sure, to many others. Even if I had known in fifth grade that I had OCD, I would never have had the courage to stand before my class, describe my symptoms, and ask for help in my struggle to overcome them.

Can you imagine anything braver than that?

| *three* |

nurture and nature

DOCTOR: Look, how she rubs her hands.

GENTLEWOMAN: It is an accustomed action . . . I have
known her to continue in this a quarter of an hour.

LADY MACBETH: Yet here's a spot. . . . Out, damned spot!
out, I say! . . .What, will these hands never be clean?

—Shakespeare, *Macbeth* (Act 5, Scene I)

Dr. Hollander tells me scientists believe that OCD can run in
families, passed down from generation to generation. My family
history certainly bears out this theory.

My mother's parents came from Russia and Romania to
Toledo, Ohio, where they owned a laundry. I was five when my
mother's father died. Every summer after my grandmother was
widowed, I took a six-hour bus ride to Toledo to stay with her for
two or three weeks. My cousins lived down the block, and we
would ride our bikes to the zoo together, beneath the shade trees,

down the wide sidewalks. Grandma would send me to the grocery store, and she always let me keep the change.

My grandmother liked her windows spotless. As she got older, she had trouble stepping up on the ladder, so she would wait for me to come visit, and we'd clean them together. It was exactly the same routine that I did with my Mom. My grandmother would stand inside, pointing out dirt, as I cleaned outside. I loved it.

Grandma had a chrome breakfast-room table and chairs, and she had somehow figured out that rubbing the chrome with wax paper made it shine. She'd give me sheets of wax paper, and I'd get down on my hands and knees and rub the chairs and the base of that table until they sparkled in the sunlight.

As soon as you walked in the front door of her house you were overpowered by the smell of mothballs coming from a closet where winter coats were stored. People with OCD believe in overkill: if five mothballs are enough, fifteen are even better. So it was with Grandma.

On hot summer nights, my grandmother and I would sit out on the front porch. Grandma would sweep the sidewalk and street with her old-fashioned straw broom before coming onto the porch and settling into her glider. She'd start from the bottom of the porch stairs and, with short vigorous strokes, sweep every inch of pavement in front of the house. When she was done, not one leaf or speck of dirt remained. Relatives would stop by and chat. We would wait for the street lights to come on, and then go inside to watch TV, or walk to the drug store to get ice cream.

My other grandparents were also neatness fanatics. Their house in Indianapolis was perfect. They kept slippery plastic seat covers on their '56 Pontiac: heaven forbid the upholstery should get dirty. We never sat in their living room. The only time I remember being in that room was when my grandmother died. I distinctly recall a bowl of living-room candy, red peppermints with white stripes, that nobody ever touched. Both my grandparents' homes had a museum feel. Looking back on what I know about them and what my parents have told me, I feel quite certain that both my grandmothers and my father's father had OCD.

My parents, too, may be afflicted with the disorder. You've already heard about my mother's cleaning compulsions and OCD anxieties, and my father is also not a stranger to OCD symptoms. His closet is perfect, impeccable, like a fancy men's clothing store. It's amazing, a work of art. Every suit, every tie, every shirt is in perfect order. It looks like my own closet! When I was child, we had a cleaning woman come once a week. "Tell Laura not to touch my closet," my dad would say. If she moved a pair of his shoes a millimeter, he knew. Everything had its place and belonged in a certain order.

Our entire house was pretty much like that. I used to joke in my comedy routines that when I got up at night and went to the bathroom, I'd come back to find my bed had been made. I'd also joke that my mother put paper under the cuckoo clock. OCD has rich material for a comic! Growing up in a house like that didn't really bother me or my brother or sister—I just felt that other people's homes were a little different.

It has taken my parents several years since I outed myself on *Biggers and Summers* to recognize the OC part of their personalities. Initially, they resented my "airing my dirty laundry" and, by extension, *their* dirty laundry in public. They said there was absolutely no way they were afflicted with the disorder. I think deep down they blamed themselves for my condition and felt a tremendous amount of guilt. But as I have continued to campaign with the OC Foundation, my parents have come around. My mother brags to anyone and everyone about how many people I've helped. And the last time I was in Indianapolis, both my parents admitted that they "might have a touch" of the disorder.

So it seems that I got OCD genes from both sides of my family—a double whammy. What does it mean that "I got OCD genes from both sides of the family?" How does genetic inheritance work? I'm not an expert in the genetics or neurochemistry of OCD, but I've had extensive conversations with Dr. Hollander, who is, and I've tried to boil down what I've learned from him into layman's language.

When a sperm fertilizes an egg and creates a fetus, the cells of that fetus have their own set of genes, half from Mom and half from Dad. In identical twins, the original cell splits in half, and each grows into a separate person with identical gene sets. When two separate sperm fertilize two different eggs, fraternal (nonidentical) twins result, who are no more genetically related than any two siblings.

In a disease that is 100 percent genetically inherited, if one identical twin has the disease, the other twin will have it, because they have the exact same set of genes. But this doesn't seem to be the case with OCD. According to Dr. Hollander, OCD does have a genetic component, but researchers agree it is less than 100 percent. No "OCD gene" has been identified, and researchers generally agree that it is likely that more than one gene is involved in developing the disorder.

Studies are currently under way that may untangle the genetic causes of OCD. These studies involve hundreds of families with more than one OCD sufferer. Blood is taken from all family members and analyzed in a "gene scanner" to determine the entire content of each person's gene set. Comparing this information to whether or not each individual has OCD will enable researchers to determine which genes play roles in the development of the disorder.

Because several genes probably act together to produce OCD, isolating OCD genes is tough. To further complicate matters, the different varieties of OCD may each be brought about by different sets of genes. Dr. Hollander speculates that my subgroup of OCD, characterized by need for order and symmetry, is inherited through different genes than the OCD of people with, for instance, contamination fears. Pinpointing all the involved genes will probably take at least five more years. But the results will be worth waiting for: the disorder may be able to be treated, perhaps even cured, with new medications or with gene therapy.

Some subgroups of OCD—like my everything has-to-be-in-its-place-type—seem to have a larger genetic component than other subgroups. My type of OCD generally begins in childhood, and it mostly occurs in boys. People with my type of OCD want things to be perfect; symmetry is crucial to us. Repetitive touching, counting, tapping, eye blinking, shrugging, humming, and throat clearing are also common to my OCD type, although I never experienced these symptoms. People with adult-onset OCD are more likely to be women concerned with harm avoidance. These people are more worried that something bad will happen to someone close to them, and they are more likely to develop compulsions to ward off future ills. I have no idea why this is so, and neither do the most informed researchers. No one yet understands the gender breakdown, although it is generally accepted that OCD affects males and females in equal numbers.

Researchers have learned that having the OCD gene or genes does not necessarily mean you'll develop the disorder; environmental factors also contribute to whether a person develops or does not develop OCD. It seems likely I was genetically prone to OCD, but what was it about my environment that encouraged me to develop the disorder? According to Dr. Hollander, some researchers think certain types of personalities are prone to OCD. Eagerness to please and a tendency to feel responsible for others—both traits I had as a child (and still have)—may have predisposed me to the disorder. Being shy also may make a person more likely to develop OCD. I haven't been shy a day in my life, which goes to show you that these are all possible tendencies, not hard-and-fast rules.

Parents who are worriers, who are always afraid something terrible may happen (my mom, for example), may contribute to their children getting OCD. Growing up in an exceptionally rigid household, which I did not, with parents who demand their children stick to routines and do things until they're done perfectly, may also encourage a child to develop OCD. A stressful event, such as the death of a loved one, can trigger the onset of the disorder. Children, especially, may be sensitive to death or separation; in some cases it seems to sensitize them to the idea that bad things can happen. Sometimes children are haunted by this knowledge and may try to develop some sort of "protection" against the fundamental uncertainties of life, which can lead to the performance of magical rituals to ward off harm, and full-blown OCD.

OCD is found in people worldwide, often at the same rate as in the United States: 2 to 3 percent of the population. The symptoms suffered by a peasant living in a remote village in India and a businessman in downtown Tokyo are often similar: the peasant may fear he's contaminating his food with dirty fingers; the businessman with dirty chopsticks. Religious and cultural beliefs influence OCD: devout Catholics may compulsively confess, Protestants may suffer blasphemous urges at prayer time, orthodox Jews may be consumed with keeping the strict laws of Kosher, Moslems may pray excessively to Mecca.

OCD has plagued people for centuries. As far back as the Middle Ages, church writings vividly described monks, priests, and laypeople suffering from blasphemous thoughts, demoralizing indecision, compulsive scripture reading, and pathological doubting. It is now believed that many of these people were suffering from OCD. At the time, it was believed that these people were possessed by the devil, who besieged them with blasphemous or aggressive images. People were sometimes burned at the stake for these supposed demonic possessions.

Perhaps when Shakespeare created the character of Lady Macbeth he was responding to the medieval idea that OCD and the devil are intimately entwined. This character, Shakespeare's immortal depiction of evil incarnate, may have suffered from OCD. Dr. Hollander believes she was a compulsive hand washer. She had no insight into her condition, and while this is unusual for people with the disorder, it is not unheard of: about 5 percent of OCD sufferers are delusional.

In 1909, Sigmund Freud wrote a famous OCD case history: "Notes Upon a Case of Obsessional Neurosis," as the disorder was then known. He described the case of "Rat Man," a young, well-educated patient who suffered from blasphemous and sexual obsessions and vivid, recurring images of rats devouring him and his father. Freud attributed these symptoms to failures in toilet training and a regression back to infantile Oedipal urges, an explanation that held for much of this century.

Fortunately, in the last 15 years, psychiatrists and neuroscientists have made tremendous advances in understanding OCD. 15 years! That's nothing. Imagine: if I'd gone to a psychiatrist in 1970, even in the unlikely event I was diagnosed with OCD, it would have done me no good. I would have been treated with traditional psychoanalysis. The theory then was that if the underlying psychological problem could be understood and treated, the obsessive compulsive symptoms would vanish. It's ironic that traditional psychoanalysis, far from improving my symptoms, might actually have made them worse. Delving into the "meaning" of my obsessive thoughts might have encouraged me to attribute significance to them, exacerbating the anxiety they provoked in me and causing me to increase my ritualistic behaviors. The doctor might have convinced me that I had obsessive fears of my plane crashing because I secretly wanted to die, instead of helping me understand that these intrusive thoughts were a meaningless reflection of the imbalance in my brain chemistry.

The Freudian explanation for OCD has now been thoroughly debunked by science. Although many questions remain, it's now been proven that OCD is caused by a biological imbalance in the brain.

As is true with many medical problems, doctors are better at treating OCD than they are at understanding what's happened to create the condition or how the drugs work that help people get better. The first clue to what's actually going on in the brains of OCD sufferers was discovered because researchers noticed that OCD symptoms responded well to a medication whose effects on a different ailment were already known. In 1986, an exploration was made into the effect of a drug called Anafranil on OCD sufferers. Seventy-percent of OCD patients responded to treatment with Anafranil, which affects the serotonin system in the brain. This was a tremendous discovery. For the first time, doctors realized OCD was a treatable illness. At the same time it was discovered that this disorder was twice as common as the better-known psychiatric disorders of schizophrenia, bipolar disorder, and panic disorder, each of which is present in only 1 percent of our population. Two to 3 percent of Americans have OCD.

Since manipulating the body's serotonin levels worked to alleviate OCD symptoms, scientists assumed the cause of OCD must have something to do with this chemical substance. Serotonin is found in the billions of nerve cells, or neurons, in our brains. A neuron consists of a cell body and lots of tentacles, the longest of which is the axon. The tiny gap between the end of one axon and the next neuron is a synapse. An impulse begins in a neuron's cell body and travels to the tip of its axon. The impulse is then transferred into chemical messengers, called neurotransmitters, which are released into the synapse. These neurotransmitters cross the synapse and stimulate, or tickle, receptors on the receiving neuron. After they've done their duty, the neurotransmitters are usually taken back up by the neuron that released them. If enough receptors are stimulated on a receiving neuron, it will fire, and the impulse will continue along its way.

All this happens very quickly—impulses travel along some neural pathways at speeds over 200 miles per hour. Along with telling neurons to fire, a critical job of our brain is telling them *not* to fire. Many neurotransmitters are "inhibitory": they carry a message that discourages the receiving neuron from firing. If there weren't inhibitors and even a small fraction of our neurons were allowed to fire simultaneously, we would be completely unable to function.

Serotonin is one of the many different neurotransmitters that help our nerve cells "talk" to each other. It plays a role in regulating anxiety, appetite, sex drive, and mood. It also plays a role in assessing danger in the environment, and, by affecting the rate at which neurons fire, it modulates the activity of different brain regions. In the brains of people with OCD, something seems to have gone awry with the serotonin system. Only no one's really sure what. It's not as simple as having too much or too little serotonin. It seems likely that the receptors serotonin stimulates after crossing synapses are overly sensitive, so the brain has an exaggerated response to serotonin, which may help account for the constant sense of danger OCD sufferers feel. A small percentage of OCD patients don't seem to have anything wrong with their serotonin systems, further complicating matters. It seems likely that other neurotransmitters, such as dopamine, are also involved in OCD.

Not only is the serotonin system awry in most OCD sufferers, but different parts of the brain seem to have gone into overdrive. In the 1990s, studies have been done with technologies that allow researchers to actually see inside the brain. CAT scans (computerized axial tomography) and MRIs (magnetic resonance imaging) provide X-ray-like pictures that reveal the brain's structure, while PET scans (positron emission tomography), EEGs, and computer-assisted EEGs (electroencephalograms) allow researchers to observe brain activity.

Using this technology, researchers have learned that in people with OCD, three regions of the brain seem to be hyperactive. The first is the orbital-frontal cortex, the outer layer of our brain just above our eyes. This region is involved in assessing danger in the environment and planning behavior to respond to it. The orbital-frontal cortex is part of the most highly evolved region of our brain, which separates us from all other creatures. The second hyperactive region is the head of the caudate nucleus, part of the basal ganglia, a small cluster of cells buried deep within the brain. The basal ganglia is involved in coordinating movement. This is what enables us to learn to do something automatically after repeated practice. And, finally, the thalamus and anterior cingulate, located directly above the spinal cord, are overactive in OCD sufferers. These structures are part of the limbic system, the deepest and most primitive part of our brain. They are involved in driving the primitive impulses of emotion, sex, aggression, and anxiety.

Not only do these three brain regions seem to be overactive in OCD patients, but they seem to act in concert—not the normal state of affairs. Normally, these different regions fulfill their separate tasks independently. Using PET scans, researchers were able to monitor brain activity when OCD patients were presented with stimuli designed to provoke their anxiety (a towel dipped in a toilet bowl, for example). All three regions flared up, the neurons firing like crazy. Serotonin seems to play an important role in the regulation of this pathway and in "locking" these brain regions together. After an OCD patient has been successfully treated and balance has been restored to his serotonin system, PET scans have demonstrated that these regions return to normal: they decrease in activity and are no longer locked together in action.

Every time people with OCD respond to an obsessive thought by performing a ritual, they strengthen the brain circuit connecting the frontal cortex, the basal ganglia, and the thalamus—in effect worsening their symptoms. An OCD patient develops a "habit memory," akin to what happens when you learn to ride a bike or learn a new dance step. When you first try a new dance step, you have to think about it, about where each foot goes and in what order. The longer you practice, the less you have to think. In a practiced dancer, the steps become automatic, become a habit memory, "etched" into the brain.

The basal ganglia is instrumental in developing these habit memories. This part of the brain seems to be at the root of the trouble in OCD—when damage is done to it directly, through disease or injury, people who previously had no trace of OCD sometimes develop the disorder. This is what can happen when a child gets strep throat. Occasionally, the antibodies produced to kill off the strep infection actually start to attack the child's body. Sometimes the antibodies attack the basal ganglia. It's just been discovered that this attack, which leaves the basal ganglia bulging and inflamed, can kick in the hyperactive loop between the three regions of the brain involved in OCD.

Remember Darcie, my 11-year-old hero from the *Oprah* show? That is likely what happened to her five-year-old sister, who developed severe OCD immediately after becoming ill with strep throat. In fact, strep throat may be the precipitating factor in some of kids who develop OCD. To Darcie's family, and to me, the most exciting aspect of this discovery is that these special cases of OCD may be treatable and even preventable with antibiotics.

I think it's occurred to some of us with OCD to ask why we all have such similar obsessions and compulsions. Many, many people with OCD feel a compulsion to check to see if the stove is on. Why not have a compulsion to continuously dance? Or to continually write? Or climb trees? Why not get obsessed with money? Or with love? Why are we so consumed with fear? Why don't we feel overwhelmed by the compulsion to tell everyone how much we love them? Why do so many of us wash our hands until they're raw? Why do we feel compelled to order only our own belongings, but not other people's? Why are we consumed with order and not chaos? And why are OCD symptoms so similar regardless of cultural environment?

The typical concerns of OCD, which at first seem like such a hodgepodge of symptoms, can actually be grouped together in a few categories—hygiene, territorial order, sex, and aggression. These concerns are the same basic impulses or instincts found in many lower species (birds, dogs, and lizards, for example) and they seem to be hard-wired into our limbic system.

All animals engage in primitive fixed action patterns, which include grooming, nest building, reproducing, and defending territory. These primitive fixed actions are instinctual. They help species survive. Sometimes, something goes wrong with these instinctual behaviors. Acral lick syndrome in dogs is an example of this: the dog cleans itself with its tongue until it has no fur left. Parrots sometimes get a disorder in which they pluck all their feathers out. Animals suffering these disorders engage in pathological grooming—they're performing their primitive fixed actions excessively, causing themselves harm. Researchers have found that the same medications that relieve OCD symptoms by affecting the serotonin system help these animals stop their pathological grooming.

Humans, too, engage in fixed action patterns, but we have a thinking "free will" part of our brain that interferes with the instinctual impulses, usually giving us considerable control over our primitive behavior patterns. But OCD rituals—scanning for danger, fear of contamination—can be seen as fixed action patterns run amok. My obsession with everything being "just so" may be a pathological concern with territorial order. From an evolutionary standpoint, it makes sense to scan the environment for potential danger, germs, and contamination, especially when protecting offspring. This may be why pregnancy can trigger or exacerbate OCD symptoms, causing women to become obsessed with contamination, intruders, or the possibility of harm coming to their babies.

A reptile's brain is basically just a limbic system that serves to mediate primitive drives. In higher animals, however, with the passing of millions and millions of years, the neocortex developed and enlarged. In humans, this newer part of the brain system is involved in regulating or "putting the brakes on" the primitive drives coming from the limbic system. In people with OCD, it may be that the neocortex is overreacting to these primitive drives of hygiene, territorial order, sex, and aggression, sending out so many inhibitory impulses that the OCD sufferer feels as though he or she is in constant danger and must take action, repeatedly, against that danger.

Looking at it this way, OCD is just an exaggerated version of perfectly normal human behavior. Some researchers think that people develop OCD because, for whatever reason, they become far too upset when they have a completely normal obsessive thought. "This is a horrible thought," they think, "I can't have these thoughts. I'm a terrible person because I have them. I have to do something in order to neutralize them."

Almost everyone—people who never have and never will suffer a day of OCD in their lives—has had to run back home to make sure they really turned off the stove. Almost everybody doodles. Many people throw salt over their shoulder to ward off bad luck. I've heard from "non OCDers" that they sometimes feel a sudden urge to veer the car off the road or that they tell themselves, "If I make this sequence of green lights, everything I'm worried about will be fine." People have lucky numbers. Non-OCD friends tell me that they sometimes trace letters on their hands with their index fingers, or flex their fingers as they imagine typing words into a computer keyboard—classic OCD "tracing" compulsions. It has been comforting for me to discover that my OCD oddities are really just exaggerations of "normal" behavior.

What separates normal obsessive thoughts and compulsive

rituals from full-blown OCD? The answer is: severity. You'll re-member that in order to be considered OCD, obsessions and compulsions must cause a person distress, must be time-consuming, and must interfere with his or her functioning. This is what began to happen to me in my adolescence, which we'll ex-plore in the next chapter.

To give you an idea of the types of obsessions and compul-sions suffered by people with OCD, I've included a list of some of the most common OCD symptoms. Following that is the scale most commonly used by psychiatrists to evaluate the severity of obsessions and compulsions. It can serve as a gauge to get a sense of whether you have OCD and give you a clear idea of what's meant by "distress" and "interference with functioning." This test, Dr. Hollander cautions, does not replace a qualified doctor's diagnosis.

Yale-Brown
Obsessive Compulsive Checklist

OBSESSIONS

Aggressive Obsessions
- fear of harming self
- fear of harming others
- violent or horrific images
- fear of blurting out obscenities or insults

- fear of doing something else embarrassing
- fear of acting on unwanted impulses (e.g., stabbing a friend)
- fear of stealing something
- fear of harming others through carelessness (e.g., hit and run)
- fear of being responsible for something terrible (e.g., death of relative, fire)

Contamination Obsessions

- excessive concern or disgust with body wastes or secretions
- excessive concern with dirt or germs
- excessive concern with environmental contaminants (e.g., asbestos, radiation, toxic waste)
- excessive concern with household items (e.g., cleansers, solvents)
- excessive concern with animals (e.g., insects)
- excessive disgust with sticky substances or residues

Sexual Obsessions

- forbidden or perverse sexual thoughts, images, or impulses

Hoarding or Saving Obsessions

- excessive need to hoard or save "useless" items (as distinguished from wanting to save items as a "hobby," or because items have monetary or sentimental value)

Religious Obsessions

- excessive concern with sacrilege and blasphemy
- excessive concern with right and wrong or morality

Obsession with Symmetry, Exactness, or Order
- accompanied by magical thinking (e.g., concern that mother will have an accident unless things are in the right place)
- not accompanied by magical thinking

Somatic Obsessions
- excessive concern with illness or disease
- excessive concern with body part or aspect of appearance (e.g., nose too large)

Miscellaneous Obsessions
- fear of saying certain things
- fear of not saying just the right thing
- fear of losing things
- intrusive non-violent images
- intrusive nonsense sounds, words, or music
- belief in lucky or unlucky numbers
- belief in colors with special significance

COMPULSIONS

Cleaning and Washing Compulsions
- excessive or ritualized hand washing
- excessive or ritualized showering, bathing, tooth brushing, grooming, or toilet routine
- excessive cleaning of household items or other inanimate objects

Checking Compulsions

- checking locks, stove, appliances, etc.
- checking that one has not harmed or will not harm others
- checking that one has not harmed or will not harm self
- checking that nothing terrible has happened or will happen
- checking that one has not made a mistake

Repeating Rituals

- excessive rereading or rewriting
- repeating routine activities (e.g., repeatedly going in and out of house, repeatedly standing up and sitting down, etc.)
- stepping on cracks in sidewalk, or avoiding cracks in sidewalk

Counting Compulsions

- having to count over and over to a certain number

Ordering/Arranging Compulsions

- repeatedly packing and unpacking a suitcase, rearranging drawers
- repeatedly cleaning room
- excessively arranging items (e.g., food items alphabetically, closet by color or function)

Hoarding/Collecting Compulsions

- excessively saving old newspapers, mail, "useless" items (as distinguished from saving items as a "hobby," or because items have monetary or sentimental value)

Miscellaneous Compulsions
- excessive list making
- need to tell, ask, or confess
- need to touch, tap, or rub (e.g., touching moldings, tapping door frames)
- rituals involving blinking or staring
- ritualized eating behaviors
- self-damaging or self-mutilating behaviors

Yale-Brown
Obsessive Compulsive Scale

OBSESSIONS

1. How much of your time is occupied by obsessive thoughts? How frequently do the obsessive thoughts occur?

    0 = None.

    1 = Less than 1 hour per day, or occasional intrusions (occur not more than 8 times a day).

    2 = 1 to 3 hours per day, or frequent intrusions (occur more than 8 times a day, but most hours of the day are free of obsessions).

    3 = More than 3 and up to 8 hours per day, or very frequent intrusions.

    4 = More than 8 hours per day, or near-constant intrusions.

2. How much do your obsessive thoughts interfere with your work, school, social, or other important role functioning? Is there anything you don't do because of them?

    0 = None.

    1 = Slight interference with social or other activities, but overall performance not impaired.

    2 = Definite interference with social or occupational performance, but still manageable.

    3 = Causes substantial impairment in social or occupational performance.

    4 = Incapacitating.

3. How much distress do your obsessions cause you?

    0 = None.

    1 = Mild, infrequent, and not too disturbing distress.

    2 = Moderate, frequent, and disturbing distress, but still manageable.

    3 = Severe, very frequent, and very disturbing distress.

    4 = Extreme, near-constant, and disabling distress.

4. How much of an effort do you make to resist the obsessive thoughts? How often do you try to turn your attention away from these thoughts as they enter your mind?

    0 = Try to resist all the time (or the symptoms are so minimal that there is no need to actively resist them).

    1 = Try to resist most of the time.

    2 = Make some effort to resist.

3 = Yield to all obsessions without attempting to control them, but I do so with some reluctance.

4 = Completely and willingly give in to all obsessions.

5. How much control do you have over your obsessive thoughts? How successful are you in stopping or diverting your obsessive thinking? (Note: Do not include here obsessions stopped by doing compulsions.)

0 = Complete control

1 = Usually able to stop or divert obsessions with some effort and concentration.

2 = Sometimes able to stop or divert obsessions.

3 = Rarely successful in stopping obsessions, can only divert attention with difficulty.

4 = Obsessions are completely involuntary, rarely able even momentarily to alter obsessive thinking.

COMPULSIONS

6. How much time do you spend performing compulsive behaviors? How much longer than most people does it take to complete routine activities because of your rituals? How frequently do you perform rituals?

0 = None.

1 = Less than 1 hour per day, or occasional performance of compulsive behaviors (occur not more than 8 times a day).

2 = 1 to 3 hours per day, or frequent performance of compulsive behaviors (more than 8 times a day, but most hours of the day are free of compulsions).

3 = More than 3 and up to 8 hours per day, or very frequent performance of compulsive behaviors.

4 = More than 8 hours per day, or near-constant performance of compulsive behaviors.

7. How much do your compulsive behaviors interfere with your work, school, social, or other important role functioning? Is there anything you don't do because of them?

0 = None.

1 = Slight interference with social or other activities, but overall performance not impaired.

2 = Definite interference with social or occupational performance, but still manageable.

3 = Causes substantial impairment in social or occupational performance.

4 = Incapacitating.

8. How would you feel if prevented from performing your compulsion(s)? How anxious would you become?

0 = Not at all anxious.

1 = Only slightly anxious if compulsions prevented.

2 = Anxiety would mount but remain manageable if compulsions prevented.

3 = Prominent and very disturbing increase in anxiety if compulsions interrupted.

4 = Incapacitating anxiety from any intervention aimed at reducing compulsions.

9. How much of an effort do you make to resist the compulsions?

0 = Try to resist all the time (or the symptoms are so minimal that there is no need to actively resist them).

1 = Try to resist most of the time.

2 = Make some effort to resist.

3 = Yield to almost all compulsions without attempting to control them, but I do so with some reluctance.

4 = Completely and willingly give in to all compulsions.

10. How strong is the drive to perform the compulsive behavior? How much control do you have over the compulsions?

0 = Complete control.

1 = Feel pressure to perform the compulsive behavior, but usually able to exercise voluntary control over it.

2 = Feel strong pressure to perform the compulsive behavior, can control it only with difficulty.

3 = Feel very strong drive to perform compulsive behavior, must be carried to completion, can only delay with difficulty.

4 = Drive to perform compulsive behavior experienced as completely involuntary and overpowering; rarely able even momentarily to delay activity.

Add up your scores on questions 1 through 10. A score above 8 can indicate mild OCD. Most people receiving treatment for OCD score between 20 and 30.

four

adolescent ambition, adolescent angst

Aside from playing the trombone in our school band, in my teens, performing magic was the closest I could get to show business. I was desperate to perform, but I had no apparent talent. I wasn't funny, my singing sucked, and I couldn't dance. I had heard that television and film honchos like Johnny Carson and Orson Wells got their start as magicians, so I decided to give it a whirl.

But part of my obsessive compulsive condition is that for me nothing is ever casual: it's all or nothing. Once I commit that's it. I was determined to be the best kid magician in Indianapolis.

There was something about magic that hooked me: the ritualistic aspect of it, practicing the same trick over and over until it worked seamlessly, smoothly. Nothing in my hand and nothing up my sleeve. There was a cleanness, neatness, and precision about being a magician that gave me the same satisfaction I derived from my Sunday cleaning stints.

But the primary reason I liked magic was that it gave me a chance to perform. To stand up in front of people. To enthrall, entertain, and be the center of attention. I had a friend down the street, David Lawton, an accomplished magician, who helped build my show. I'd trot over to Dave's every night after dinner and pressure him into teaching me new tricks. By the time I was 12, I had my own act. Johnny called himself the great Carsoni, but I could never think of a moniker that rang right. I billed myself as Marc the Magician. It was the best I could come up with.

For $25 to $100 a pop I would perform at birthday parties. I practiced constantly, spending hours with a deck of cards or rolling coins over my fingers.

While I was doing so well at magic, however, something odd was happening to me academically. I had always been a good student, but I began to find studying increasingly difficult. My grades dropped. I lost the ability to concentrate on the written page. I found myself rereading the same paragraph twenty or thirty times, making sure I hadn't missed any words. I couldn't stop myself. I had no idea why. My lack of concentration made me frustrated and angry. I would stop trying to read and would roam around the house, trying to distract myself. I'd watch TV, get something to eat, talk to whoever was around. I *never* told my family or friends how I was feeling, what was happening to me. I thought maybe something was really wrong. "Why do I have to keep doing this?" I'd think to myself. "I must really be crazy." That's what happens to people who don't realize they have OCD—we figure we must be insane. It's terrifying. Although I later learned that my behaviors were typical of my OCD subgroup, at the time it was a nightmare. We have to do whatever it is that we do over and over until it's perfect, whether it's reading and rereading a passage or tying and retying our shoelaces until the loops are precisely the same size.

Professional pianists apparently have high rates of OCD. What distinguishes the professional pianist from the amateur is practice: the willingness, drive, or compulsion to play the same piece of music over and over. As Dr. Hollander has explained to me, in OCD sufferers these habitual routines form habit memory circuits in the basal ganglia of the brain. These circuits, while developed specifically for a piece of music or a series of ritualized actions to perform a magic trick, can generalize to other areas in the brain, broadening their application beyond their original purpose. Habitual actions loop in the brains of OCD sufferers like me. When the irrational fears that consume us don't actualize, we are convinced that we staved off whatever we were afraid of with our rituals, which reinforces our compulsion to do the habitual action. A vicious circle.

Grades were extremely important to me, as they are to many obsessive compulsive sufferers. We need things to be perfect, and we feel overwhelming anxiety if we don't live up to the strict guidelines we set for ourselves, whether it be checking a light switch 17 times or getting straight As. But, unlike your average perfectionist, I felt compelled to get good grades in order to allay feelings of unease and dread—in the same way I felt compelled to complete any one of my countless rituals to allay those same fears.

So I was deeply disturbed when my grades started to slide. By my sophomore year in high school, I had dropped to C-student level. My parents were completely unconcerned. Grades just weren't important to them. Unlike many of my friends, I was never praised or admonished for a report card. I had the only Jewish parents I knew who didn't push their kids to get into an Ivy League school. All the pressure I felt to be perfect I put on myself. Or, rather, OCD put the pressure on me.

One of my problems was that I couldn't turn in homework that had even a slight flaw—a smudge or eraser mark compelled me to redo the entire assignment. Standardized tests were hell. There was the stern warning, "Be sure you understand the directions before attempting to answer any questions." Great. I had to read the directions perfectly—my biggest nightmare. I'd get bogged down reading and rereading certain sentences and paragraphs of instructions. Then there was the announcement: "If you change an answer, be sure that all previous marks are erased completely. Incomplete erasures may be read as intended answers." It was a recipe for disaster. Heaven forbid I had to change an answer: I'd put a hole in the paper trying to erase it. Then I'd go nuts because you couldn't ask for another answer sheet. I'd have to live with that hole for the rest of the test.

I was disturbed by my inability to study and my academic performance, but the anxiety I felt about my grades was soon buried under my "obsession" with show business.

People use the term "obsession" all the time to refer to everything from their love of chocolate to their desire to rush home and watch *Dateline,* so let me explain what I mean. Technically, to qualify as an obsession in the OCD sense, a thought must be repetitive, intrusive, and unpleasant, and must interfere with one's life. My "obsession" with show business, therefore, was not a true obsession, but I've often felt there was something unnatural about it. Looking back, my instinct tells me that the intensity of my desire to perform, to enter the industry, was somehow related to my OCD.

I recently asked Dr. Hollander if he thought the two were related. Traditionally, OCD literature has firmly differentiated OCD, whose compulsions are never inherently pleasurable, from "pleasure seeking" compulsive disorders—compulsive gambling, compulsive shopping, binge eating disorders, and compulsive sexual addictions, which are all about pleasure gratification. Dr. Hollander, however, believes all these disorders are linked. They all have a common theme: it's hard for the sufferer to put brakes on the repetitive behaviors; we all have an excruciatingly hard time inhibiting or delaying acting on our impulses.

Dr. Hollander is currently investigating neurochemical links between OCD and the "pleasure gratification" disorders—it appears that they are all related to malfunctions in the same parts of the brain. So, according to Dr. Hollander, my tendency to fixate on pleasurable things—the elaborate fantasies I had as a kid about my future successes, my "obsession" with show business, my becoming determined to marry my future wife after laying eyes on her just once, my single-minded pursuit of my career— are all somehow related to my OCD. Which is not to say that everyone who ever fixates on a woman has OCD, but rather that, as an obsessive compulsive sufferer, my fixations and "obsessions" have an OCD-like quality—the same malfunctions in my brain that bring on my OCD also contribute to the intensity of my fixations.

Despite my academic woes, I felt hopeful about the future as long as I could watch Johnny Carson, Ed Sullivan, Steve Allen, Hollywood Palace, anything with *variety*. Variety is a television format you just don't see anymore. Variety shows came out of the great American traditions of vaudeville and burlesque, where anything could happen and anyone could perform: jugglers, clowns, dancing dogs, corny musical acts, slapstick comedy, the shtick meisters, the most ridiculous, outlandish talent was all paraded out onstage. You never knew when someone would crack you up, fall flat on his face, or capture your heart. So variety shows made for nervy, spontaneous TV. Talk shows have taken over this role today—the edginess, the unpredictability, the risk. But talk, with the exception of *The Jerry Springer Show*, doesn't quite have the zaniness of variety.

Age 13 was a big year for me. Dad lost Berkys Supermarket when Indiana University bought up the neighborhood. He was a nervous wreck. He picked himself up, though—went back to college, studied insurance, and became enormously successful: the vice president of the largest independent insurance agency in the state. But in the dawning of my manhood, that moment when the rug was pulled out from under my father's feet provided me with an acute sense of the fragility of life. Later on, when my career was hanging by a thread, when I felt my life was in shambles, I remembered my father's perseverance. His tenacity and grit were an inspiration to me.

I was bar mitzvahed on November 7, 1964. I had studied long and hard for the moment when I was called before the Torah. My rabbi, Maurice Davis, brought me close to religion. He didn't lecture to our Sunday school class; he talked to us as peers. When I studied for my bar mitzvah, Rabbi Davis was in his early fifties, a balding, gray-haired, distinguished man who always wore bow ties. His eyes were dark, deep, and full of humor. To me, they looked like he spoke to God daily.

My grandfather had studied to be a rabbi and had high expectations for my bar mitzvah, so I worked extra-hard to get the prayers right. Our synagogue was the ultra-reform Indianapolis Hebrew Congregation, located in an upper-middle-class neighborhood. In my comedy routines, I joked that there was a cross over the pulpit. It was the most modern temple in town. The rabbi pressed a button and the doors of the ark swung open to reveal the Torah. We had a huge choir. The place felt like magic—like showbiz.

I was particularly taken with the way Rabbi Davis orchestrated the proceedings on the day of my bar mitzvah. He seemed to have so much power, so much assurance. He was completely in control of the event. And yet there was no aggression about it. It was as if he had effortlessly picked up the congregation and was piloting us through sacred realms. And then he handed the controls to me. I was nervous and excited, filled with wonder and a deep sense of awe.

After that, I wanted to become a rabbi. What is a rabbi if not a performer? I wanted to be able to create the feeling in the room that Rabbi Davis engendered. That safe, enclosed space of ritual and magic. I know it sounds silly, but I think there are parallels between being a television show host and being a rabbi. Both professionals speak to, affirm, even define a community. Both have their prescribed sets of actions that have been determined beforehand, rituals reenacted at set times. Both the temple and the television studio are spaces separated from our everyday world.

After my bar mitzvah, I obsessed on my performance. The temple had recorded an audiotape of my speech and prayers, and I played it over and over, listening to each nuance in my intonation, imagining myself standing up in front of my friends and family, relishing how I looked in my black suit and tie, rekindling the attention and admiration that had flowed toward me from the audience.

My brief moment of glory in the synagogue redoubled my ambition to be a performer. I fantasized endlessly about playing *The Tonight Show*, the *crème de la crème* of television. Johnny Carson blew me away. He was hip and clever. Anyone who was anyone made an appearance on his show: Sinatra, Streisand, Woody Allen. Carson was topical. He spoke to what was going on in the nation. He brought the country together and made us feel like we were all privy to an enormous inside joke, and that we all participated in an endlessly weird, eternally fascinating, patently ridiculous yet somehow moving comedy of this country. He hooked me.

When I was 14, Rabbi Davis took our Sunday school class on a trek to New York City. In those days, *The Tonight Show* was taped at NBC Studios at 30 Rockefeller Plaza in Manhattan.

Some people say the show changed when it moved to L.A. I think that the L.A. shows were first-rate television, but in New York, Carson had that vaudeville feel. Ethel Merman, for instance, would come in and sing a song from her Broadway show.

When we went to New York, I was determined to break into national television in a big way. I would appear with Johnny on *The Tonight Show*, I thought. Having read *The Tonight Show* credits hundreds of times, I knew that the talent coordinator—and my contact to Carson—was Mike Zanella. I'd simply call Mr. Zanella and convince him that it would be supremely cool to have a 14-year-old magician from the Midwest on the show. If he balked, I'd remind him that his boss had started out as a magician from Nebraska (Johnny got his start in television doing *Carson Cellar*, a show for a CBS L.A. affiliate called KNXT, and as a writer for Red Skelton. Johnny got his big break in the late 1950s, when Red injured himself falling through a trap door. Johnny filled in for Red, and the rest is history.)

Typical of star-struck teens and OCD sufferers alike, I ran elaborate, repetitive fantasies in my mind. Johnny would dust off old tricks, and we would have a battle of the Midwest magicians. He would jump at the chance.

A month before our class trip, I began calling Mr. Zanella. I called him early in the morning, during my lunch break, and late in the day when I came home from school. He was always in meetings, prepping with Johnny for a show, out to lunch. He would get back to me, his secretary said. (At the time, I didn't realize that this was a perfect foreshadowing of things to come in L.A.)

My parents didn't know how focused I was on Zanella. I

called him on my private phone line. How, you might ask, was a 14-year-old able to afford a private line? I think my OCD was at least partially responsible. I had asked for my own phone.

"Fine!" my parents said. "You want a phone? You pay for it."

And I did. My savings account was flush from performing my magic shows, my paper route, lawn cutting, and other odd jobs. I had a sterling reputation. I was absolutely dependable. People knew I always showed up. I was always on time. I never made a mess.

At 6:30 one evening I made my obligatory call to Zanella. The voice on the line wasn't his secretary's.

"Marc Summers for Mr. Zanella," I said.

"This is Mike."

Zanella had actually picked up his phone! This was my chance. I made my pitch. Me. Johnny. Magic. The Midwest. I told him when I would be in New York and gave him the hotel's phone number. He was cordial. He'd discuss the idea with Johnny and get back to me.

When I arrived in New York, there was no message from Zanella. I checked the front desk every ten seconds. I saw my first Broadway play, *Fiddler on the Roof,* which I loved; went to the Statue of Liberty; searched for my Jewish roots in Williamsburg, Brooklyn. On my next-to-last day in the city, I frantically phoned Zanella to remind him that I was in town for another 24 hours. I would have to do the program that evening. Period.

He didn't return my call.

I was crestfallen, but I had the one trait essential to show business: never, ever give up. Take your licks and keep on coming. Looking back, my OCD-related traits—my uncompromising pursuit of perfection and my insistence on following through on everything I started—helped me achieve my goals. I had my eyes fixed on the prize. No disappointments, even at the hands of the likes of Mike Zanella, could shake me loose.

At 15 and 16 years old, I was torn between the rabbinate and the life of a TV broadcaster. Coincidentally, there was an assistant rabbi at our synagogue, Mr. Weitzman, who had majored in radio and television back in his pre-rabbi days.

When I was 16, I went to him for advice. He was a short man and wore glasses with thick black frames. His impish grin made him seem playful and approachable.

"What should I do with my life?" I asked him.

"What do you want to do?"

"Part of me wants to be a rabbi, and part of me wants to go into show business."

He closed his eyes and stroked his chin with his thumb and forefinger. "Why do you want to be a rabbi?" he asked.

"Because I want to help people."

"Well, as a rabbi you help a few people a lot. In show business, you help a lot of people a little."

I pondered his words, and opted for show business. But to this day I often wonder what my life would have been like had I decided to immerse myself in the Torah. Through my work with the Obsessive Compulsive Foundation I've had a chance to reach out and help people in a direct way, to make a difference in their lives. This is what I had hoped for as a teenager when I dreamed of being a rabbi. I hope I can, in this book, be something like a rabbi, someone people in distress can go to for guidance and help in making their way in the world.

In ninth grade, the intrusive thoughts of harm coming to my parents diminished. I no longer had that awful step-on-a-crack-break-my-mother's-back feeling (the person who thought up *that* ditty definitely had OCD). I no longer thought that if I didn't nail a test or do everything perfectly my parents would die.

But other intrusive thoughts didn't stop: they continued to plague me. It seems that many kids outgrow obsessive thoughts of causing their parents harm, but they develop other obsessions in their teenage years. My obsessions were multiple and omnipresent. I was obsessed with symmetry, order, neatness, and cleanliness. I was obsessed with the state of my room, the state of my clothes, the state of my homework, and with the countless rituals that filled my days. (Not all OCs are like this. Some people with OCD are focused on only one thing—keeping their personal appearance immaculate, for example. Most people with single-obsession OCD are probably undiagnosed and untreated because their symptoms are usually not as debilitating as multiply obsessed OCs.)

In adolescence, my obsessive anxieties with my parents' mortality branched out into a vast arena of placating and propitiating ritual. If I didn't put on my baseball uniform in a certain way (stirrup socks, then white socks, both pant legs pulled down evenly), I'd be tagged out at third base. If I didn't repeat a line just right, I'd forget it onstage. If I didn't check my magic props

15 times, I'd flub my gig. I turned everything into a ritual to appease some god of ill fortune who scrutinized my every move.

Checking magic props is something all good magicians do. There's no room for sloppiness in magic. For master magician Lance Burton, repetitive prop checking is probably just superstition. But my compulsion to check props was OCD related, as was my flirtation with the religious life. There's an interesting relationship between ritual, magic, superstition, and religion.

The ultimate goal of religion is to deal with fear of the unknown, fear of uncertainty, the doubt that comes from being born into a vast, largely incomprehensible universe. Religion uses ritual to lessen those fears in just the way an OCD sufferer uses magical and superstitious thinking to alleviate anxieties. My devotion to magic through my high school years was, I think, partially because magic was largely about practicing ritual. And being a magician allowed me to enter a realm where I was in control of what the world perceived as unseen forces, even if I knew it was all in the props. It's ironic that as an OCD sufferer I believed in magic even though as a magician I knew it was all smoke and mirrors.

In 1970, I graduated from high school. I was embarrassed about my mediocre class ranking since many of my friends were hotshot students, but my parents weren't concerned. Dad wanted a partner in the insurance business. "You'll be great with sales," he said. But I loathed the thought of working 9 to 5, stuck in an office all day. Show business was the life for me.

I thought I could make a career appearing on radio and TV that was aimed at and run for the armed services. Since the military's neatness and regimentation appealed to me, I enlisted in the navy. I was thrown out during basic training for bad knees, however, and I arrived home, deflated and beaten. My friends were away in college, and I had no idea what I was going to do next.

I haunted Indianapolis' radio and TV stations, futilely searching for work. No one would hire me, but broadcasting was the only thing I was truly interested in. I lay around the house all day watching TV, until my father set me up with a job in the commercial loan department of a local bank.

Stressed out about not being able to break into broadcasting, I would have chest pains every afternoon at the bank. My blood pressure was off the charts. "What's the matter with you?" said the doctor the bank brought in to check out its employees. "You'll be dead before you're 30 if you don't do something about this!"

I was 18.

Mom clipped an add from *Seventeen* magazine: "Come to Boston—learn radio and television at Grahm Junior College."

"Why don't you check it out?" she said.

I still have that little scrap of paper.

I interviewed at the college, staying with Rhonda, a high school friend who lived in an all-girls' dorm. The thrill of it! I was still a virgin, and when I woke up in the dorm room, Rhonda's roommate was stark naked, combing her long, dark hair. Boston was the place for me!

That school was just what I needed. I was a DJ at the college radio station and a host on the college television station. I learned that illustrious alumni had preceded me. The future creators of the *Alf, Sally Jessy Raphael,* and *Jerry Springer* shows had gone to Grahm. So had comedian Andy Kaufman. Everybody at Grahm wanted to work in the industry. We saw the school as a fast track to work. Grahm had real television studios and a real radio station. "Learn by Doing" was the school's motto. That was fine by me.

My compulsion for neatness didn't wane once I began living in a dorm. One night, a classmate came into my room and threw a wad of paper in the wastebasket. He talked to me for a few minutes, then left.

I didn't use wastebaskets. Ever. I couldn't stand the thought of garbage piling up in my room, even in a contained basket.

In school, if I had to throw something out, I'd march into the hall and deposit it into the communal garbage can. The guys in the dorm knew this, and they hid in the hall to see how long it would take me to empty my trash. Immediately after my classmate left, I walked out with the basket. All the guys laughed at me. I didn't like the laughter but I knew I couldn't control the compulsion.

As they snickered and guffawed, it was driven home to me that I was different. My dorm-mates were all inveterate slobs, their beds full of ancient pizza slices, their floors covered with filthy socks and underwear. I had to ask myself: why wasn't I a slob like a normal 18-year-old boy?

"Okay, you guys," I said. "I got it. You caught me." I was lucky that I had enough self-esteem not to be thrown by their teasing. But other teenagers aren't as fortunate. Many young people with OCD think they're crazy. They feel disturbed, even disgusted, by their obsessive thoughts and are too humiliated to seek help. They're lost in teenage hell.

I've traveled around the country hosting community discussions on OCD, and I've met countless teens with the disorder, and their parents. After talking with them I realize the most important thing is that parents recognize the pressures on their teenagers. It's tough out there! Teens need to forge relationships in a highly competitive social world. They face enormous peer pressure and they feel the need to conform. And to have OCD on top of that? Ouch! The parents who do best both for their children and for themselves make an effort to educate themselves through reading about OCD. They remember that OCD is not a character flaw but a treatable medical condition.

I doubt my college roommate Mike viewed my cleaning compulsion as a character flaw. He certainly benefited from it. Each Thursday the school issued clean sheets and towels. Thursday evenings I'd throw Mike out and clean the room, top to bottom. I *needed* to do it. It would have been torture for me, so intense would have been the physical discomfort, if I had not been able to clean the room from 7:30 P.M. until 11:00. Mike considered himself a lucky guy: he had a roommate with a bizarre eagerness to clean. What can I say, Mike? I was a classic case.

I sojourned in Beantown the summer before my sophomore year, living in a Brighton apartment with the two biggest pigs in the world. They couldn't stand me, and I couldn't stand them. The place was in total disarray all the time; the kitchen was a filthy, disgusting mess. There was so much grease in our oven that it would catch fire twice a week. I never ate a meal there; I *always* ate out. My high school sweetheart, Ann, once came to stay with me for a week. Before she arrived I cleaned madly, moving couches, dusting, Pledging, vacuuming. There was enough hair on the bathroom floor to fashion a full body suit for a gorilla. For a brief moment that apartment smelled the way my room at home smelled every Sunday evening.

Before the school year started again, I marched into Grahm's Director of Housing's office and demanded my own room. It was against college policy, the director informed me. I threw a fit: "I've tried living in doubles! I need to live alone! I need a single!"

He must have sensed I was absolutely determined, because he gave me what I wanted. I loved my single. It was the cleanest dorm room in Boston.

| *five* |

waiting at the altar

What happens when someone with OCD is left waiting at the altar? I'll tell you, he goes berserk.

Alice, my wife-to-be, was nearly an hour late for the wedding photos that were supposed to be taken before our marriage ceremony. I had arrived early, of course, at the temple in Westchester, an L.A. suburb, where we were to be married. My mother, father, sister, and brother were there. The photographer was there. The rabbi was there. The wedding party was there. The 250 guests had begun to gather. But Alice was nowhere to be found. And neither was her family.

The day was Sunday, June 16, 1974, and I was losing it, pacing and fuming.

"Where is she? Where is she?" I kept muttering. "I can't believe she's doing this!"

Think of a "normal" person's anxiety in such a situation, and then multiply it by a million. That was me. People with OCD are adversely affected by stress. Our symptoms tend to become more pronounced. And for my subgroup of obsessive compulsives—in addition to my need for neatness, I'm also a punctuality freak— lateness on one's wedding day was a capital crime. No punishment was too severe.

I couldn't stop looking at the clock. "I cannot believe this!" I was wound tight as watch. I kept storming outside, looking up and down the street.

Finally, finally they came.

I dashed toward Alice. "Jesus! Where have you been?" I grabbed her and hustled her inside. "What the hell happened?"

Instead of being a supportive, understanding future husband, I was a screaming maniac.

Alice was furious. "What's wrong with you? We're a little late. That's all."

We were screaming at each other right there in temple, in public. I remember my mother telling me to calm down, but I couldn't.

"Mom! You talk to her!"

"She's your wife," my mother retorted.

In the wedding pictures, you can tell Alice was pissed.

I felt no guilt. In my mind, my anger was completely justified. "How *dare* she arrive late?" I later learned that she and her parents had been trying to clean off nail polish that had spilled on her mother's dress. I was unmoved. "Well," I thought, "what a ridiculous thing to have done. They shouldn't have spilled that polish. They should have been more careful. They should have planned ahead." There was no excuse, ever, for lateness.

Nevertheless, I must have eventually apologized, because the wedding was terrific.

I still fume to myself when people are late. It's a horrible corrosive monologue that repeats and repeats in my head. I associate that kind of explosive anger with OCD. It makes no sense to me that people wouldn't show up on time. Why wouldn't they? I assume everyone lives his life the way I live mine. And my life runs with such precision that I'm never late. For me, there's no excuse for being late, short of being dead.

Funny that I should work in Hollywood, where big-shots keep you waiting intentionally. They play mind games with time. It pisses me off: you look like an idiot, sitting there, hanging out with the receptionist while the boss chats on the phone, files his nails, and does whatever other meaningless tasks he's doing. I won't wait more than 30 minutes for a meeting. It's partly OCD-induced irritation, partly business sense. You start to lose credibility if you've been sitting around for an hour and the guy you're waiting on finally calls in on his cellular to let his receptionist know he's just leaving his lunch date. If you think I'm pig-headed, I have friends in the industry who won't wait more than 15 minutes.

Alice and I had wanted to leave on our honeymoon that night, but I had a run-through the next day for a show. I had recently met Marty Pasetta, then the hottest television producer-director in Hollywood. He wanted to get into game shows and brought me in as part of the talent team for a pilot we were pitching to the networks titled *Discover America*. We were due for a final run-through the day after the wedding in front of network executives to see if they wanted the show. Alice understood this was a big chance for me. If the show had gone (it didn't) it would have been a big boost to my career. The chance to work with the hottest guy in town was what I'd been pushing toward since I graduated from college the previous May.

After graduation, I'd had two choices: L.A. or New York. I was a die-hard television person, and for die-hard television people, there are just two cities in the whole world. At the time, my brother was living in L.A., playing drums for Helen Reddy ("I am woman, hear me roar . . ."). He said I could stay with him. My decision was made: I left Boston and headed for L.A.

The previous winter break I had been out visiting my brother and had fallen into conversation with his next-door neighbor. The guy said he could get me into the Director's Guild Apprentice Program. The Director's Guild is the hardest Hollywood union to get into. You almost have to be born into it. Thousands of people apply to the apprentice program each year: you have to take a long test, and then a lucky 25 are accepted. Just 25 each year! Being accepted into the DGAP is basically a license to work the rest of your life, assuming you don't do anything incredibly stupid. The Director's Guild opens doors to the industry, introducing you to key contacts, which is what the L.A. world is all about. Schmoozing and ingratiating yourself. Kissing ass. Knowing the right people. Slowly, tenaciously clawing your way up the food chain.

Being in the Director's Guild Apprentice Program gets you assistantships on movies. Now, I wanted to work in television, and knew nothing about film. But I'd directed college TV, and I figured directing film and television were the same thing. (I've since learned they have nothing to do with each other.)

I was thrilled. It was all I talked about in my last semester of college—how I had this connection in L.A. who was going to get me into the DGAP.

Now, finally in L.A., I knocked on my brother's neighbor's door.

"Hi, remember me, Marc? I was visiting my brother? Last winter? You mentioned you could help get me into the DGAP?"

He didn't know what I was talking about. Denied ever having said anything about helping me. "Here's their address," he told me. "Go call them. And good luck."

To think I'd taken his promise to heart! Still in my Midwest mindset, back then I believed what anybody told me. "Indoctrination by hellfire" is what I think when I look back at the abuse I took in my early years in L.A.

I did go to the DGAP offices, though, down on Beverly Boulevard. They were filled with white leather couches and palm trees. I managed to convince a secretary to get me into a lower-level executive's office, but the guy had no time for me and told me to get lost.

I had one more lead: Michael Zinberg, the associate producer of the original *Mary Tyler Moore Show* and *The Bob Newhart Show*. These were major hits, which made him a hotshot.

I called. "Hi, you don't know me but your brother just married my best friend's sister and I'm looking for a job."

He chuckled. "If you've got the guts to make this phone call, I've got to see you."

He told me he might have something for me. It turned out to be the important sounding job of "production assistant," aka gopher. A chance to be at some egomaniac's beck and call. To run around like a lunatic slave. In other words, this job was what every 20-year-old fresh out of Grahm Junior College dreamed of.

Zinberg invited me to come in and talk to him. I was on my way.

His office was in Studio City, a five-minute drive from North Hollywood where I was living at the time with my brother. Zinberg was in his late twenties, tall, tan, and blond, with a thick, reddish-blond mustache. He looked like he'd just stepped off the tennis court. A typical Hollywood hey-babe-let's-do-lunch kinda guy. He told me I was overqualified for the job, and I told him, thanks for the kind words but my being overqualified wasn't his decision to make, it was mine. "You're too smart," he said. "You're going to get bored, you're going to find something else to do, and you're going to leave us. I need someone who'll stick around for a while." I was pissed but powerless.

He did have a friend, though, Bobby Roads, who was in charge of the pages at CBS. Pages bring honchos coffee, seat people in the studio, and give tours. They are the grunts of the industry, the first step into the business.

Eight years later, after I'd been around and climbed a few ladders, I asked Zinberg why he hadn't hired me for the job.

"Because you came across as the most arrogant, self-centered jerk I'd ever met in my life," he told me. Which, looking back, was kind of the way I was. I had always been taught that walking into a meeting with confidence impressed people. But I guess I took it too far.

Far from believing I had anything messed up in my head, I thought I was the "rightest" person in the world. Always on time, always correct, always neat—I wasn't odd, the rest of the world was sloppy, slow, and negligent.

I left Zinberg's office and made a beeline for CBS, which was 15 minutes away on Beverly Boulevard. CBS was a huge television factory with four enormous studio buildings. At that time, the network had a string of hits, including *The Price Is Right, Sonny and Cher,* and *All in the Family.*

Roads, a bottom-rung executive at CBS, was a scrawny, mousy fellow. His hair was always combed the wrong way. His face looked dried-out and pale, and his eyes were always darting around. He had a habit of constantly looking over your shoulder to see if there was somebody more important he should be talking to. He organized the weekly schedule for fifty or sixty pages every Monday morning. This was no small task, as many of the pages were still in school or working part-time. When I met him, he'd been at his position a year.

He gave me the same story Zinberg had—different job, but I was still overqualified. "I need pages who are going to be here for at least eighteen months," he said. "You're going to be here today, gone tomorrow." Well, of course, I thought. That's why people get jobs as pages—to move up. What I said was, "It's kind of you to say I'm overqualified, but I don't feel I am. I wouldn't be in this office if I didn't feel this job was the one for me."

No dice. Like Zinberg, in place of a job he gave me a lead. He'd heard that a new cable company (that was 1973, nobody knew what cable was back then) needed a production manager. I should give them a call.

I drove out to the cable company in Simi Valley. This was on the other side of the world from where I lived. I got lost, I had no idea where I was going. It took me nearly two hours to find the cinder block building that housed the company. The office was barren, no pictures on the walls. It exemplified the true meaning of the term "start-up." (Who knew at that time that cable was the future of the business? Everybody thought cable was a joke. The networks were God. Now, after being in the business for 25 years, I find it fascinating to watch the networks lose power as cable becomes king.)

I met with my contact and was hired right on the spot, as a production manager! It was a job beyond my wildest dreams, miles and miles above working as a production assistant. To think that I'd actually been eager to work that job! I was amazed, ecstatic. I was going to help run the production side of the company, and I'd be on the air part-time doing local news for Simi Valley. Experience on both sides of the camera, and good money to boot. It was a dream job. I drove the 30 miles back to CBS studios to thank Bobby Roads in person. I told him what a terrific job it was, and how grateful I was for the lead.

"Way to go," he congratulated me. "You nailed it!"

I was a kid from the Midwest; that was the right thing to do.

Two hours later, back at my brother's apartment, the phone rang. It was the person who hired me. "I'm sorry," he said. "I've had second thoughts. I can't use you."

I was flabbergasted. "What's changed in the two hours?"

It turned out that as soon as I'd left Roads' office, he'd picked up the phone and called the cable station.

"Mr. Roads is more qualified than you are," said my guy. "I had no choice but to hire him over you."

Bobby Roads had stolen my job! But he'd given me the lead! I jumped in the car and flew straight back to Roads' office. "How could you have done this?" I demanded.

Roads did feel guilty. Not guilty enough to say no to the job, but sufficiently guilty to offer me a post with CBS as a page. I was outraged, I wanted to kill him. But not so outraged that I didn't accept the page job.

The world of television was different in 1973. Without cable, there were only NBC, CBS, ABC, independent stations, and the syndication business. (These had independent producers and sold to local stations. Anybody could buy those shows, then as now.) There wasn't nearly as much work back then, and everybody wanted to work for a network. So, after my inauspicious beginning, I'd finally landed a job at CBS: the coolest of the cool, the Tiffany of all networks.

I began working as a page, the job for which I had been warned I was overqualified. I gave studio tours, ran messages to producers, took entrance tickets. If Carol Burnett said to me, "Excuse me, would you get me some coffee?" my job was to say, "Of course, Miss Burnett, would you like cream and sugar?" People were killing to get my job. I made $2.73 an hour, and I would have worked for free.

Bob Barker, the host of *Truth or Consequences* and *The Price Is Right*, was my role model. He was smooth, funny, and the nicest guy in the world. One day I dashed up to him as he was passing through the studio.

"I watched you every day when I came home from nursery school," I gushed.

His smile turned to a frown. This blunder was my first inkling of hyper age-consciousness in Hollywood and the pressure most celebrities feel after they reach a certain age. Back then, Barker would have called 39 "the dark year," but today I'd say the cut-off is more like 28, assuming you have spiked hair and an MTV look. If not, you're probably done for at 25.

Despite this dubious introduction, Barker and I went on to become friends. I modeled my career after his. We both idolized Jack Benny, whose stardom, we agreed, was due to his great generosity. Barker's theory, which became mine, was that if you make contestants look good, you, in turn, look good. Let your contestants and your guests get the laughs.

My best friend at CBS was a fellow page, Steve Weinberg. I was 21 and he was a little older, a wise man of 23 or 24. Steve was a hound: he used his post to pick up women. A smorgasbord of women were always lined up, waiting to get into the studio. He tried to get himself scheduled to work on *The Price Is Right*, since the women lined up for *The Price Is Right* were known throughout the page world as the cream of the crop. They were big-busted and came dressed to the nines, hoping to be chosen as contestants. So Steve would work the line, trying his luck: "Here's my card. I work for CBS." "Here's my card. I'll get you into the show." "Here's my card. I'll ask Bob to put you on . . ."

Television: for Steve, it was a great way into women's pants. For me, it was my introduction to my bride-to-be.

A month into my new job, Steve and I were standing on the set of *The Mary Tyler Moore Show*. I glanced up at the line of people waiting to enter the studio for the taping of the day's episode, "Angels in the Snow." And then I saw her. At least on my end, the chemistry was instantaneous. She was about 5-foot-2, with long dark hair, dressed in an ankle-length skirt, knee-high boots, a thin silk top and dark jacket.

I leaned over to Steve: "That's the woman I'm going to marry."

"That's nice." He was skeptical. "But I think she's already engaged to a friend of mine."

Oh.

I watched my newfound mate (Alice was her name, Steve told me) file into her seat with her boyfriend. She looked like she was having the worst time of her life. Suddenly, she stood up and walked toward us. Unlike my buddy Steve, I was shy with girls. My pulse was racing, but I had to talk to her. Was it fate? She was right in front of me.

"Excuse me," she said. "Could you tell me where the bathroom is?"

Her words were poetry to my ears. "What's it worth to you?" I grinned.

She laughed, and I walked her to the bathroom. It was beautiful.

After the show, Alice and her guy hung around to chat. He was a fake-producer type. Turn over any stone in Hollywood and you'll find one with his own "production company." They whip out fancy business cards, but they've never worked in the industry. That was as true in 1973 as it is now. I could tell how miserable Alice was, but I'm not sure how I knew. Maybe it was the way she carried herself, the look on her face, the way she glanced up and around the room when her boyfriend was speaking.

When they left, I said to Steve, "Let me know when they break up." Steve shook his head and sighed. "Don't hold your breath."

A month later, Steve called to tell me Alice and her boyfriend had broken up. He agreed to call Alice, who remembered meeting me, albeit vaguely. Then I called Alice and asked her out. She said she'd be more comfortable if we double-dated with Steve.

So it was that we went out on a double date that night.

I knew just the place. An old Victorian castle in the Hollywood Hills called the Magic Castle Night Club. Celebrities walked around the club with drinks in their hands watching magic acts. People called it Disneyland for adults. Back then, nothing was bigger than the Magic Castle. You couldn't get in unless you knew somebody. Cary Grant was on the board of directors. To buy a club membership cost $1,000. They had 17 valet parkers running around outside to get you your car.

The Magic Castle Night Club is still around. The bloom is off the rose, however. Bill Larson, an executive at CBS who started the place and ran it in its heyday, died a few years ago. But a booking at the Magic Castle is still a huge event for a magician. And I had just landed a part-time job performing there, which made me a performing member. Which meant I could get us in. As a page, you saved up for dates; Steve and I had been saving for weeks for a night like this. Since I was out with the girl of my dreams, money was no object.

I remember the night like it was yesterday. The four of us strode up to the Castle. I was giddy. Alice held my arm. I gave the receptionist my name and she checked her list. My heart was pounding. She flipped pages for what seemed like an eternity. Finally, she nodded her head. We were in! Except, as we glided through the door, another host reached his arm out and barred Alice's way.

"ID, ma'am?" She looked 21 to me, but it turned out she was only 20. The host was sorry, but he couldn't let her in. They could lose their liquor license. I don't know who was more embarrassed, Alice or me. She'd been carded, but my vaunted clout hadn't pulled us through.

We ended up at a small restaurant in Beverly Hills for wine and as much free cheese as we could eat. Steve's date was Susan Bierfisher, a mature woman of 27 and a secretary in CBS's executive offices. The four of us wandered the streets of Westwood after our wine and cheese. We passed through a little arcade where people sold jewelry on the street. That's when I first kissed Alice. You have to understand, although I was outgoing, a ham, and lived to be on TV, I was desperately shy around girls. For me to ask a girl out was a major move. And to KISS a girl! Incredible. But everything was different with Alice. There was something special about her, a warm glow. Everything felt right. I was loose and able to open up and express my feelings.

Steve drove us back to the rendezvous point where I'd left my car. Alice lived with her folks, and I delivered her home at 1 A.M.

We kissed goodnight at her door. I was on cloud nine. I walked back to my green '68 Oldsmobile and cranked the key but it wouldn't start. It was completely dead. I swallowed my pride and knocked on her door.

She came out, laughed, and we drove around in her car at 2 A.M. looking for a gas station to get someone to come jump the car.

"We're going to look back at this and laugh," I told her.

"What are you talking about?"

"I'll tell you later," I smiled to myself. I was determined to marry her.

The next day I sent her a dozen long-stemmed red roses.

We dated five nights a week. I was very skinny then, and full of piss and vinegar. I couldn't afford food: my page's salary was less than $350 a month, and I paid $125 in rent. After putting gas in the car, I could afford little else. I'd show up at *The Joker's Wild,* a daytime game show, an hour before call time, slip into the room where lunch was laid out for the contestants, and stuff my pockets with sandwiches. If a page got lucky, he or she would be assigned to a show over at the Studio Center in Studio City in the Valley, where they actually *fed* you lunch.

Five weeks after our first date I asked Alice to marry me. "You're crazy," she told me. "You don't even know me."

Two weeks later, in October, I asked her again. This time she said yes.

Until this point, Alice hadn't encountered my OCD symptoms, which didn't exhibit themselves on dates. She knew, of course, how focused I was on my work, and how fanatically punctual I was. I was a nut for being on time. Sometimes I'd arrive at

6:00 for a 7:00 date. I'd drive around the block for 15 minutes, and then say, ah, forget it, and go ring Alice's bell. She wouldn't be ready, and it frustrated her. But she accepted it. Better than having a perpetually late boyfriend, I suppose. And I guess she thought I was just incredibly eager to see her. Which I was.

But, of course, it was more than that. When Alice came to my apartment she saw it was neat, but in those days I was living in a tiny one-bedroom with a queen-size bed and a bookshelf that I'd made from plywood and bricks. There wasn't much to obsess over. So she was completely unprepared when I screamed at her on our wedding day for being late for the photo session.

After the wedding, which, despite my hysteria, was wonderful, as I've said—lots of dancing and toasting and the feeling of happiness, joy thick in the air, new beginnings, and our families embracing us in a circle of love and sending us out into the world, we went back to my little apartment, which was now our little apartment. Our wedding night was bliss. Alice seemed to have completely forgotten my outburst. I did my run-through the next day. When I came home, we started packing, getting ready to leave for our Hawaiian honeymoon.

Alice's red Amelia Earhart suitcase was sitting in a corner. She opened it, banging its top against the spanking white wall. I had the same response that I had had at our wedding. I started yelling, screaming, upbraiding her, telling her to be more careful, stomping around the room, throwing up my hands. She was completely baffled. She had no idea what had caused my explosion.

I didn't know if there was a scratch in the wall. If there was, it was certainly nothing a normal person would have noticed. The point was that Alice had banged the wall, and I hated that. Know-

ing that she had done it, I then had to go over and touch the spot
the suitcase had dinged. I had no idea why at the time, it was
something I'd been doing all my life. If I saw a mark on the wall,
I had to go touch it. It didn't make sense. It still doesn't. Today,
when I see a wall nicked or marred, I still have to keep putting
my hand on the damaged spot. I can't explain what goes on in my
head. It's not like I think I'm Oral Roberts and can heal the wall
with my hand. There's no logic to it. All I know is that for most of
my life the compulsion was so strong I never even considered trying to override it.

I was sarcastic, self-righteous, fuming. "Try to be a little more
careful, okay?" I remember saying. "Try not to bang the wall."

Finally, she realized what had set me off. It was her turn to ex-
plode. "The suitcase hit the wall! So what? What is the matter
with you?"

And somewhere I must have sensed how crazy I was because
I apologized. Alice had hurt feelings, but eventually we kissed,
made up, and had a terrific week in Hawaii.

Back at home we settled into domestic life. Alice's parents
bought us a new couch. Wedding money bought bookshelves. I
didn't have much of a wardrobe, but Alice, being a dental assistant, had actual outfits. We shared closet space. She had her side,
I had my side. There was a little partition down the middle.
Whatever she did on her side was fine, as long as it didn't touch
my side. Now don't get me wrong, Alice was (and still is) an incredibly neat and clean human being. But nobody, short of my father, could keep a closet the way I kept mine.

When I was promoted to head page, I got a small raise. My
salary was now $87 a week, and Alice took home about $100,

maybe $105 a week. (I recently found our first combined tax return out in the garage. I save everything. That first year, Alice made $9,000 and I made $4,000.) I worked as much overtime as was available, and on a good week I made $135. I also worked part-time doing warm-ups on *The Joker's Wild*. Shows with studio audiences often have someone warm the crowd up before filming begins, to get them so geared up, giddy, and giggly that they'll laugh at just about anything. I continued to work part-time at Magic Castle, which paid a measly $125 for seven straight nights, four shows a night. Even back then, that was highway robbery.

Alice didn't like The Magic Castle. Too many creepy people hanging around. Too many characters.

I worked sunup to sundown, going from job to job. I was driven to do any work at all in the industry. I ate, slept, and drank television. For me, L.A. was the best place to be in the world.

Alice and I were happy together. Show business wasn't important to her, but her attitude was "If he's happy, I'm happy." She let me go out and do my thing.

I was a hustler, trying to hustle up work. I still am, and I still try.

A year or two into our marriage I got a job for Hertz Rent A Car. They billed me as "The Great MIRAHCFU (May-I-Rent-A-Hertz-Car-For-You), the Magician." I stood in their booth at conventions dressed in a yellow brocade tuxedo and did magic tricks. The object was to draw people into the booth. And would you believe it? It worked! When Hertz had me come to San Francisco to do a travel show, I invited Alice along. The morning after we arrived, I woke up and started to dress. "Where are you going?" asked a groggy Alice. I'd somehow neglected to tell her that I had to perform every day from 10 to 5. She thought we were on vacation. She was not happy. She spent the days at museums, being a tourist. Marc Summers on vacation? Forget it.

On Sundays, we made breakfast together, and then our mission was to clean. We had a stereo, books, the living room, bathroom, kitchen, and bedroom. And we cleaned them all. I dusted all the windowsills. We had venetian blinds, filthy with L.A. smog. There were five windows in the living room and three in the bedroom, all fitted with venetian blinds. Actually, every window in the house had venetian blinds. I'd painstakingly run a rag along each slat, wiping the grime from both sides.

Alice lived up to my standards for bathroom cleaning. She'd scrub and scrub the floor, toilet bowl, bathtub. Lemon pledge wafted through our house. We did the vacuuming. We did the wash. That's the way it was on Sunday. We cleaned all day in our one-bedroom apartment. I didn't like it, but I had to do it. In order to function properly during the week, everything in my brain and in my life had to be in order by Sunday night. I don't know what would have happened if I'd woken up Monday morning and something had been out of place; it never happened.

A few years ago, I asked Alice, "Why did you do it?"

"I thought it was normal, just part of married life," she said.

At the beginning of a relationship you jump through hoops to please your partner. But after a while, you want go to the beach on Sundays, to Fisherman's Village, to walk around and see the shops, to look at the boats.

I wish there had been the knowledge about OCD then that we have today. Alice and I had no idea what was going on; why I exploded, why I was compelled to clean. Today, however, the disorder is identified and out in the open, and there are proven approaches to helping someone you care about who is an obsessive compulsive.

OCD can put a huge strain on relationships. After Alice and I had been married for six years, we felt we were finally ready to start a family. In 1980 Matthew was born, and three years later, Meredith. We were thrilled, but gradually my OCD became torturous for Alice. She felt that my rigid cleanliness and need for order prevented me from living up to my full potential as a loving, embracing father. I was too uptight to have small kids in the house, she said. It took a toll on our marriage. I was frequently consumed with my compulsions when I should have been spending time with my family. I still hadn't heard of OCD then, and unrecognized, untreated OCD is far more devastating for relationships and family life than is managed, acknowledged OCD.

If your date or mate is exhibiting OCD symptoms, the first thing I recommend is not to overreact. Contact a doctor or OCD hotline. Get as much information as possible. Don't say to your partner, "You're crazy." Say, "Can I have a conversation with you? I think there may be something we should look into. Do you think it's normal that you have to flip the light 11 times, check the door 19 times, wash your hands 30 times?" It was at Alice's bidding that I finally sought treatment. And that was the best possible thing for me, for her, and for our kids.

I've met many couples at Foundation meetings, and have seen a wide variety of responses to OCD. I've talked to some couples in which the partner without OCD says, "I will do everything I can to help my mate," and couples in which the non-OCD partner says, "I don't know if I can handle this." I think back to Lorrie and Matt, the lovely couple who appeared with me on the *Oprah* show. Matt was an incredibly supportive husband, but a lack of professional guidance and his love and concern for his wife led him unwittingly to become an "enabler." Along with Lorrie's mother, Matt helped Lorrie enact her rituals. By helping Lorrie carry out her compulsions (buying her food five miles away, bringing her cigarettes in her prescribed manner, assisting her in her tortured eating rituals) the two people closest to Lorrie were probably exacerbating her symptoms.

When you are the partner or close loved one of somebody with OCD, it's important to seek professional help, because strangely enough, acting on instincts is not always in the best interest of your loved one. Giving in, reassuring, or debating are generally not constructive in helping to decrease the symptoms of OCD. It is an incredibly difficult thing, to refuse to alleviate the fears of your most dearest, even if you know it's in their best interest. Lorrie's mother said that when she tried not engaging in Lorrie's mealtime rituals, Lorrie wouldn't eat. There are numerous support groups and family therapy groups which the OC Foundation or any other of the groups listed at the back of this book can put you in touch with. You don't have to go it alone.

Once I was diagnosed and began receiving treatment, Alice and my kids were a great help to me. They still are. My kids say, "Dad, you're doing that again. You just did that. Do you really need to neaten your desk again?" I find it very helpful when they point out my repetitive actions with love and patience. What I had to do, as the OCD person in the family, was, first, admit that

I had a disorder. The next step was deciding I wanted to get better and stop performing my rituals.

I'm aware of the strain my obsessive compulsive behavior has put on my family, and I'm as understanding as possible. When Alice or someone I really trust tells me, "Hey, you're doing it again," I laugh and say, "You're right!" That helps me say to myself, "Stop it. You don't need to do it."

earthquake

Howard Hughes is the most famous example in our century of someone with OCD. Hughes, who had inherited millions from his father, was a playboy, aviator, inventor, and movie producer. At one time, he was the richest man in America. But throughout his life, Hughes suffered from OCD. He had severe contamination fears. No one could touch his private refrigerator. Like me, he couldn't bear to wear clothing that had the least little spot on it.

Hughes was immensely successful. His OCD probably fostered in him the same kind of drive and perfectionism that has ruled my life. Sadly, his compulsions were doomed to destroy him.

After a near-fatal plane crash, Hughes' OCD intensified. Afraid to go out, to see anyone, or to come in contact with a world he was convinced was full of deadly germs, Hughes lived in self-enforced solitary confinement, holed up in the baronial splendor of his top-floor suite in Acapulco's Princess Hotel. It's hard to visualize how this powerful man went from *bon vivant* to a guy so consumed by his OCD anxieties that he couldn't leave his room.

What's truly striking about Hughes' story is that piloting his airplane, he was totally focused on the task at hand, which was a matter of life and death. I feel that kind of focus every time I'm in front of a camera: my OCD recedes. But there was one short period in my life where I experienced a *complete* remission of my OCD symptoms. It occurred when, like Hughes in his plane, I was completely preoccupied with survival.

It was the winter of 1994. I had finally attained many of the goals I had strived for since I was a kid ogling the credits scrolling at the end of my favorite TV shows. I was in the midst of a long, successful run in my career. In 1986, I had been signed to do *Double Dare.* The show took off: it put Nickelodeon on the map, made me a household name, and had a phenomenally long life, as cable programs go.

Cable television is a unique animal. Sixty-five episodes is the typical limit of almost all cable shows. After that, the show is yanked off the air and sent into reruns. That's how it works. But with *Double Dare* we did 525 episodes between 1986 and 1994, probably more episodes of one show than any cable network has ever done.

In all those years working as the star of what was at that time Nickelodeon's biggest hit, I never knew what was going to happen next season. The Nickelodeon powers that be were always vague. "Do I have a job next year?" I would ask them in so many words. "We don't know," they'd say. That's show business: no matter how high you climb, you're always at someone's beck and call.

By 1994, *Double Dare* had played itself out: Nickelodeon had enough episodes on tape to do reruns forever, so I wasn't surprised when they decided to stop shooting new shows. I then signed a contract with the network to produce and host live performances of *Double Dare*. We took the show on the road, performing on weekends in arenas across the country, often in front of ten or fifteen thousand people.

I'm asked whether I would go back to *Double Dare* if it was resurrected. There are murmurs at Nickelodeon from time to time of doing just that. To slime or not to slime, that is the question. It would be a tough call for me. I want to do adult television; I don't want to be pigeonholed as a kiddy host. But I wouldn't mind going back to *Double Dare* as a producer.

In 1994, I was also working for ABC's *Home Show* as a roving correspondent, which provided me with the opportunity to do serious news. I covered tornadoes in Kansas, the unveiling of the astronaut memorial at Cape Canaveral, and the return of troops from the Gulf War.

The *Home Show* broadcast live at 8:00 A.M. West Coast time, 11:00 A.M. on the East Coast, Monday through Friday. My correspondent job required that I be in the studio only two or three mornings each week. The show shot at ABC studios at Prospect and Talmedge Streets, a seedy part of Hollywood. I had to be there at 5:30 or 6:00 A.M. I'd wake up at four, shower, hop in the car, and get on the Ventura Freeway as dawn washed the sky with beautiful pastel colors in the omnipresent smog. Traffic was light at this time in the morning. But in L.A., people are always on the road, always moving.

The Prospect Street studios had once been used for film, and even though they were old and decaying they had a certain charm. Most television studios in L.A. are enormous cinder block buildings, enclosed universes that look like they could survive a nuclear attack. But at ABC you could wander the lot, from sound stage to sound stage. There was a neat old commissary where, during my warm-up days when *Welcome Back, Kotter* was shot at the studio, I'd see John Travolta lunching with the other sweathogs.

It was a schlep to the studio from our house in West Hills, which is north of Malibu and west of the San Fernando Valley. To make an 8:00 breakfast meeting in Beverly Hills, I'd have to leave the house by 6:00. But the schools were good, and it was an all-around better place to raise a family than anything we could have afforded closer to town.

We had moved to West Hills in 1984, buying a four-bedroom house with a nice backyard. Our neighborhood was exactly like the one in "E.T." Wide, gently winding blacktop sloped up into a middle-class subdivision that had settled into the mountain landscape. The lawns and plantings around each home were irrigated, a lush oasis set in the midst of stark arid hills. The wholesome Main Street, USA innocence of West Hills reminded me of my Midwestern childhood.

One of the perks of broadcasting at 8:00 A.M. was that I was out of the studio by 9:00 or 9:30, and back home by midmorning. I'd hang out with friends, go out to lunch, spend time with Alice. One of the biggest reasons I relished this period was because of the time I was able to spend with my kids.

In the past, I'd had tremendous guilt feelings about leaving my family for work. When Meredith was three and four years old, I was away for months at a time, shooting *Double Dare* in New York and Philadelphia. When I was on the air, she'd search behind the bookcase on which the television sat, saying, "Dada! Dada!" During one period, she was so angry I was away that she refused to speak to me when I called home.

I was there for her third birthday party, though. We had just moved into the house, and my OCD symptoms were strong. The thought of 20 three-year-olds marauding through our pristine space made me anxious enough to try to convince Alice to have the party at a bowling alley, ice cream parlor, McDonald's, anywhere but in our house.

Alice put her foot down: "We bought this house and we're going to use it!" she said.

What to do? The day approached, and I became more and more distraught. Finally, I couldn't bear it: I measured how tall Meredith was, and then I ran out and bought yard upon yard of butcher paper and taped it along the base of the wall to well above the height of your average three-year-old. I taped it to the wooden posts in the corners of the room so the tape wouldn't scuff the paint on the sheetrock.

The neighbors heard about this and came by to see my handiwork, chuckling and shaking their heads.

Our kids grew up in that house. I put up a professional NBA backboard on a pole sunk into the edge of the driveway (if I had put it up over the garage the ball would have made marks on the house), and when I was home Matthew and I played basketball most evenings after dinner. We'd always bonded around sports. We went to batting cages together, and I coached his Little League team. He was fast, a great base-stealer. I loved watching him take off, streaking around the diamond, sliding into second base. He was ballsy, a risk taker, completely unafraid.

Going one-on-one with Matthew on the blacktop in front of the garage, I was my usual competitive self. I never let him win. And not only that, when he was a young kid, I taunted him as I trounced him. The hardest day of my life was the first day he beat me. I had known it was inevitable: he was 12, thin, wiry, already my height, fast as a greyhound and agile. The fateful day came when he was half a step ahead of me, and he beat me by four points. In my mind it might as well have been a thousand.

"A new world champion!" he crowed as the final shot went in, taunting me in the same way I had taunted him. I had to laugh, but I was burning inside. It was payback time, the changing of the guard.

I rarely beat him after that. We'd play as the sun set and the air turned cool: the minty smell of pine and freshly mowed lawns and dry desert night coming down around us. I had mounted lights on the garage, and we'd play into the darkness. The neighborhood kids would be out, rollerblading and riding their bikes and skateboards. They'd often ask to play, and we soon had a game going. When he was young, Matthew and I played against all comers. But after a certain age he wanted to lead his own team to beat me, and I was always ready for the challenge.

On Labor Day, 1993, my life was complete. After much thought, we decided to move into a new house in Mountain View Estates in the city of Calabasas, a five-minute drive from West Hills. The house was 6,000 square feet, a mansion as my friends said, although I didn't think of it that way. Mountain View was a gated community, which I felt we needed at that point in our lives. The popularity of *Double Dare* was such that kids were always showing up at our front door in West Hills. Whenever anyone in the neighborhood had relatives in town, they'd bring them over to meet Marc Summers. Privacy started to become something all of us craved. But then something happened that spurred me to move sooner rather than later. I was working at home in my upstairs office when I suddenly noticed a towheaded kid with pale blue eyes standing on the landing. I was startled. He had come out of nowhere, like an apparition.

"Who are you?" I asked.

"Harold," he said, which struck me as an odd name for one so young.

"What are you doing here?"

"I heard this was where you lived, and I wanted to meet you."

I signed a press photo for him: to Harry from Marc Summers. But he shifted on his feet and looked down at the carpet.

"What's wrong?" I asked.

"Could you make it out to Harold, please?"

I let out a little embarrassed puff of laughter, and he glared at me. I quickly took another press photo from the shelf, inscribed it to his specifications, and then led him downstairs and out the door. I had begun to feel visible and exposed, but this was the capper. Though he was just a kid, having an intruder in my home frightened me. I was traveling a lot, and I wanted the extra protection for Alice, Meredith, and Matthew that a gated community would supply.

The new house was beyond anything I'd ever imagined being able to afford living in. On the wide terrace that connected Meredith's room (French doors, walk-in closet, private bath with Jacuzzi) to the master bedroom, I could look out over the stunning vista from the Santa Monica Mountains to Malibu. I never took the house for granted. I had earned it; nobody gave it to me. But inside, I always felt my family was like the Beverly Hillbillies in this ritzy exclusive community.

That was the way it was the evening of January 13. I went to bed that night next to Alice, happily married, in the house of my dreams with my wonderful family, my career going great guns. As usual I couldn't get to sleep. I always say that if my neighbor sneezes, I wake up. Almost every night I toss and turn, thinking about work, the people I need to call back, the appointments I've scheduled, upcoming travel plans. I find it almost impossible to relax: some nights I don't sleep at all.

It must have been one or two in the morning when I finally drifted off into a dreamless sleep. The next thing I knew I was awake, in the pitch black, feeling intuitively before I could grasp what was going on that something was very wrong. Faintly, on the edge of my hearing, glasses tinkled and there was a tight rumbling. The air was thick and bristling, and then I was wide awake and so was Alice. The house began to shake.

Alice and I had a prearranged earthquake plan. I was responsible for Meredith; she for Matthew. We leapt out of bed. The floor heaved under my feet, the whole house cracking and groaning. I lurched to the door of Meredith's bedroom and then the quake's peak hit. The floor fell away, and I was thrown against the wall. It felt as though a giant had picked up the house and dropped it.

The quake's peak seemed to go on and on, although it probably only lasted a few short seconds. When I finally got to Meredith, she was sitting bolt upright in bed, white as a sheet, in a state of shock. She threw her arms around my neck, and she was trembling and rigid.

Matthew, typically, had slept through the whole thing. He was rubbing his eyes sleepily as we hustled downstairs in our nightclothes. I grabbed the battery-powered radio by our bed and a flashlight. We flung open the front door and ran into the driveway. Car and home alarms were going off, and the whole neighborhood was out on the street in front of their homes. The power was out, and we stood out under the stars, flashlights flickering in the dark.

Living in L.A., it's an accepted fact of life that you don't want to be inside when the big one hits and your house collapses on top of you. It's much better to be tossed around like a piece of popcorn in the open air.

There was an aftershock every couple of minutes, lasting from 5 to 20 seconds. Any one of them could have been bigger than the initial quake. We sat on the stairs by the front door and listened to radio call-ins from reporters and people on the street.

At first, I wasn't thinking about the state of our house. But as dawn broke over the hills, I began to mull over the damage that had been done. When the aftershocks finally quieted, we went back inside, and I toured the house. It had moved, and everything inside it had moved as well. The books, Alice's china cat collection, Meredith's doll collection, everything had all come tumbling off the shelves. There was broken glass everywhere. There were fissures in the walls of every room, and our marble entryway had shifted and cracked.

As I walked through the house, surveying the damage, it began to dawn on me that I didn't feel the need to clean or straighten. I was confronted with the biggest mess of my life, but I didn't care! My OCD seemed to have disappeared, magically vanished. All I was thinking about was my family.

The quake was 6.9 on the Richter scale, and the aftershocks, which came every couple of minutes, were big ones, too: 6.2, 5.9. There was no relief.

Two days after the quake, I did a *Home Show* segment in Northridge, the quake's epicenter. I drove the streets at dawn. It was a weird morning, quiet and still, different from the hum of traffic and movement that always pervades L.A. at any hour of the day or night.

There was destruction everywhere. The streets had buckled and cracked. Streetlights tilted at crazy angles. Trees had toppled onto cars, crushing them. Businesses had plywood covering broken windows. Security guards prowled the streets to keep away looters. It looked like a war zone.

I passed a hospital, where there was a line of people waiting outside for treatment. The night of the quake, fire had erupted in Northridge. A gas main had exploded, and the trees along the street were scorched and charred. I found the house where we were shooting the segment, and we set up to interview its owners, a married couple with kids. They gave me a tour with the camera and audio guys trailing behind us. The house was intact enough to walk through, but barely.

I couldn't believe 22 seconds of the earth's power had destroyed these people's lives. I felt frail, shaky from all that my own family had been through in the last 48 hours. While we were on the air, Gary Collins, who hosted the *Home Show*, asked me, "How are you doing?"

I almost broke down.

Later, I heard that a neighbor of ours had been watching the show while Matthew was visiting her son. The neighbor had snidely said to Matthew that she was surprised at how emotional I had become during the interview. This was Southern California: earthquakes were a part of life.

Her insensitivity infuriated me, but Matthew took her comment with a grain of salt. He's used to having me derided. His friends in school were huge fans of *Double Dare*—until they grew out of it. Then they started making fun of me to his face. I know Matthew: he was loyal. He knew the jabs were part of having a father in the public eye.

Alice's brother, sister-in-law, and mother were worried about structural problems in their apartment building in West L.A., and they moved in with us. Having company, the stress around the earthquake, and, most important, the deplorable state of my house would normally have sent me into an obsessive compulsive frenzy. The desire to order and straighten would have overwhelmed me.

But I was so focused on the welfare of my family that I didn't even notice the chaos that surrounded us. It was an intense relief to be free of the gnawing anxiety to have things perfect.

I've never heard of this kind of spontaneous remission in other OCD sufferers, but it's not uncommon for the reverse to happen: for people to have one bout with OCD in their life and then recover. Someone I'll call Bob, a successful lawyer in the entertainment industry, told me he had severe symptoms of OCD when he was in his stressful first year at Harvard Law School.

When you meet Bob, you'd never think that a man with such poise and confidence, so at ease with people and at home in the world, would have been, at one time, afraid to open the door and walk out of his Cambridge, Massachusetts, apartment. Like Howard Hughes, Bob was convinced he would be contaminated by germs. For several weeks, he cowered in his apartment, consumed by dread. His roommate brought him tins of food, which he ate straight from the can with his hands, which he would meticulously scrub, afraid to let the food touch pots, pans, plates, or even silverware. All of these, he thought, were crawling with deadly germs.

Bob feels that his bout with OCD was brought on by the pressure of final exams. He showed up at the exams with his hands encased in gloves, although the May weather was warm and sunny. After the tests were over (he scored in the top 10 percent of his class), his symptoms vanished, never to return, as mysteriously as they had appeared.

Bob's is not a typical case of OCD, which continues over a long period of time and impacts one's whole life. Many OCD sufferers think that they're going to somehow mysteriously get better. But studies have shown that if you have OCD, you've got it for life.

Howard Stern is an example of someone with OCD who thinks he has somehow mysteriously cured himself of the disorder. He's fooling himself. Howard and I battled it out on the radio one day when I came on his show as the spokesperson for obsessive compulsive disorder. Howard was obviously sympathetic to the OC Foundation cause. He admitted that at one time he had OCD, but he insisted that he had "cured himself."

"You're not cured, Howard," I told him.

He became huffy. "Yes, I am."

"No, you're not!"

He said he had cured himself of his OCD in the same way he had cured himself of back pain: he realized that it was psychosomatic and had no basis in physical reality. He told his listeners about his bizarre rituals: banging his head 16 times before going on the air to make sure the show went well; mentioning a certain number in every sentence to ward off disaster when he was on the air; believing that even numbers were good and odd numbers were bad (then, somehow, they switched); being a germphobic and an obsessive hand washer to the point where he had his own bathroom built in the radio studio.

"Howard," I said. "You acted that way because your brain chemistry is screwed up."

"No way!" he said. "Absolutely not!"

Robin Quivers, his longtime foil, started goading him.

"Howard," she said. "Aren't you a hypochondriac?"

At the time of my appearance on the show, Stern had lightly bruised his ankle. He had just recently been obsessing on the small injury, overwhelmed by intrusive thoughts, convinced that the bruise would lead to a debilitating condition that would fell him.

Robin kept badgering him. "It's ridiculous, Howard, admit it!" Finally he acquiesced.

"Okay, okay, okay!" he said. "But that's not OCD. I'm cured."

I laughed as he quickly went to take calls from listeners.

After the show, I told Howard that OCD is not like depression. With depression, you can suddenly become better without going through treatment. But he fixated on the idea that he no longer suffered from the disorder. After appearing with him, I thought about my own spontaneous cure, and how short-lived it was.

After the earthquake, I wanted to talk to my shrink about the sudden relief from my cleaning compulsions, intrusive thoughts, and ridiculous rituals. I didn't know I had OCD, but I did know I had been carrying around a deep dark secret, thinking I was crazy for as long as I could remember. Now that I was symptom-free, I was finally ready to confess to someone just how weird I had been.

I had started therapy in the early 1980s with a psychiatrist who I'll call William. I was frustrated with busting my butt but not getting anywhere in my career. I saw everyone else in my clique at the Comedy Store (David Letterman, Jay Leno, Robin Williams, and Garry Shandling) becoming famous. But I seemed stuck in the land of perpetual warm-ups. I was making good money, but I was bored. That changed after I scored on *Double Dare*, but I kept going to William, occasionally seeing him when I felt overwhelmed by life. I'd go to him for two or three sessions and then wouldn't call him again for six months.

I told him intimate parts of my life, but I had never touched on my OCD symptoms. I thought I was the only person in the world with my symptoms. I was profoundly afraid to talk about them, so afraid that not even Alice knew about my intrusive thoughts and secret rituals.

William's office had been trashed by the earthquake, so he had moved to the Agoura area. His new space was off the Ventura Freeway, in one of southern California's ubiquitous strip malls.

A tall man in his late forties with prematurely gray hair and a soft, soothing voice, William rose to greet me as I entered the office. You had to listen closely to catch his words. He was always calm and collected, and he was very successful. We had a little ritual at the beginning of each session.

"So, Marc," William began, "tell me about your dreams."

"I don't dream."

"Yes, you do."

That's how it went.

During this session, for the first time, I told William about my compulsions to clean and straighten: I had to vacuum in perfect rows, no one could touch the walls in our home, as a child I had secret rituals that I performed so my parents wouldn't die. And, in fact, I still had such rituals: if I didn't correctly read my script for the show, disaster would befall me or my loved ones.

He listened with his mouth hanging open. "Very interesting," he said, when I was finally finished.

"But Doc, now I don't feel compelled to do that stuff. I think I'm cured."

We spent the whole hour talking about my "odd behaviors," and how none of them meant anything anymore.

Had William recognized my odd behaviors as classic symptoms of OCD, he might have been able to resolve my problem. I still wonder what my life would have been like if he had caught the disorder years before it was eventually diagnosed by Dr. Hollander. As it turned out, William was clueless about OCD. But he was very excited about the earthquake session. We decided the quake had been a terrific thing for me.

"Do you mind if I mention your case in an article?" he asked. He wanted to write up how his patient had been cured by the great earthquake. I went to see him two or three weeks in a row, continuing to talk about the absence of my drives to straighten.

Years later, after my diagnosis, I called William. I told him that the whole time I was his patient I was suffering from OCD.

"You never suspected it?" I asked him, incredulous.

"Nope." He was not the least bit apologetic. "The thought never crossed my mind."

Whenever I talk about OCD, people suffering from the disorder tell me horror stories about misdiagnosis. I've heard countless times that someone spent years and thousands of dollars in therapy only to be told that his fanatical need to clean or wash his hands came from his potty training when he was two years old. A few years ago, I was at an American Psychiatric Association Convention, signing a book by Connie Foster about children with OCD for which I had written the foreword. A psychiatrist walked by and asked me what I was doing.

"We're trying to help out kids with OCD," I told him.

"Oh," he snorted, "I never see anyone like that!" I stared after him, incredulous. Two to three percent of the population has OCD, and many find their way to a psychiatrist's office, only to face a doctor with almost no knowledge of the disorder. Of course he had patients with OCD. He just hadn't diagnosed them correctly.

Unfortunately, my remission was too good to last. My obsessive compulsive behavior came roaring back, sparked by a particularly severe aftershock that occurred exactly one month after the big quake. That one month was the only time since I was about six or seven years old that I wasn't plagued by compulsions.

Alice and I were driving in West L.A. when the aftershock sent our car lurching across the road. I took Alice to her mom's and rushed home. The mirrors and paintings were askew. There were a few odds and ends lying on the floor, and I was surprised that I didn't rush to clean them up immediately. I felt remarkably calm given the circumstances.

Then I went into the family room. A big wooden bowl had fallen off the top of a shelf, gouging a big chink in our beautiful oak floor. I stood there looking at this hideous blight, feeling the anxiety well up inside me. It was a defamation, a desecration. I wanted to scream. I crashed straight from sanity into the sense that my life wasn't perfect—and that I *needed* it to be perfect or I'd go nuts. In our old house, I'd lived through the mess of having the floors stripped, sanded, and stained. Now we would have to live with that misery again because there was a chip in the floor. There was *absolutely no way* it could stay. As I stared at the chink in the floor, the infinite things pushed out of place in the house by the quake descended upon me like the plagues on Pharaoh.

The aftershocks went on for months, during which time I had

to live with the cracks in the walls and floor. It was useless to try to fix them before the earth settled. I tried to cope by spending lots of time out of the house. And when the aftershocks finally abated and the renovations began, I tried not to go into the rooms under repair. The upstairs was in better shape than the ground floor, so that's where I spent most of my time when I was home.

When I did have to go downstairs, I'd stand on the top floor landing, knowing that downstairs I would see the corners and joints in the living room where the walls had separated. I'd find myself returning to the same crack in the wall over and over again, staring transfixed in front of it as though it was a mesmer-izing work of art. Had it widened slightly? Or was it mysteriously coming back together?

Forcing myself to walk away, I'd be drawn irresistibly back against my will. It was a morbid fascination. It was grotesque, yet somehow it transfixed me. I stared and stared. I went away. And then I came back to stare some more.

| *seven* |

the moment of truth

I'd always wanted to host my own live talk show. *Marc Summers, Live from New York City!* I'd hosted game shows: *Double Dare, Family Double Dare, What Would You Do, Couch Potatoes,* and *Pick Your Brain.* I had also produced *Double Dare* and created, hosted, and produced *Pick Your Brain.* They had been "mine." But to do a live talk show? I loved the prospect of working live, of talking to a potpourri of guests: celebrities, authors, quirky people. For me, a live talk show was the best of television. From 1990 to 1994, I had been a contributing reporter on ABC's *Home Show.*

I was disappointed when *The Home Show* was canceled, but word was out that Lifetime Television was creating a new show and looking to me to handle it. I walked from one job to another.

The smooth transition was fortunate: I'd noticed when there was stress in my work life, I'd start cleaning fanatically. I couldn't bear to have the house messy. I couldn't even bear the thought that the house might *become* messy. I couldn't tolerate it when my son or daughter wanted to have friends over who might make a mess, scuff up the carpets, leave crumbs on the floors, or inadvertently move the furniture. I needed the whole house to have the feel of a museum: immaculate and untouched.

Under stress, I'd begin to have anxious thoughts. Not the kind of morbid thoughts that I'd had as a child, when I thought my parents would die if I didn't read a paragraph "perfectly." But anxious feelings that led to repetitious rituals: the compulsion to make lists and go over and over them in my mind, as I had as a child; a fanatical need to arrange knickknacks; hours spent on my hands and knees on our wooden floors, rubbing out the slightest scuff-marks.

I was offered the job hosting the Lifetime show *Our Home*, which was designed to scoop up the *Home Show* viewers. The show shot in New York City, to which I moved in 1994. I took a ridiculously expensive apartment on 56th Street and Second Avenue and commuted back and forth to L.A. to see my family, whom I missed terribly. But *Our Home* was not only a great career opportunity, it was extremely high-paying. At this point in my career, I was one of the highest-paid people on cable.

I was the only man on Lifetime Television, which billed itself as television for women. "Great job you've got," people used to tell me. "Being the only guy in a sea of women."

Our Home gave instruction in everything from faux marble painting to new cooking techniques from some of the world's best chefs, who came on the show direct from New York City's finest restaurants. Initially we shot the show at 57th Street and 10th Avenue, and eventually moved to a studio in Astoria, Queens. Several months into the program, I guested on *Queens*, a Lifetime talk show hosted by Sissy Biggers and shot in a basement studio in that same building in Astoria. Sissy and I hit it off immediately.

We were total opposites. I was a Jewish guy from a middle-class family in the Midwest. Sissy was a tony East Coast blue-blood, 5' 2", slender, stylish, with short blond hair. She knew all the hip fashions and loved to hang with an old-school moneyed crowd. She was extremely well connected because of the years she had spent as an executive at NBC, where she had handled *The David Letterman Show* and *Saturday Night Live*. It was an unusual transition, going from executive to working on-camera, but she'd always wanted to be a TV personality.

Sissy loved to go out in the evening, romping around the city with celebrities while I holed up in my apartment, read the script for the next day's show, talked to my family on the phone, and watched TV. I teased her about her social activities, and spun ridiculous tales of eating at fancy restaurants and hobnobbing with stars.

Upper management at Lifetime had me guest on Sissy's show a couple more times, to be sure the initial chemistry wasn't a fluke. They loved us together; we were incredibly compatible.

Sissy was very sensitive to how I was feeling, what was going on in my mind. Management was so impressed with our rapport that they decided to create a show specially for us. They found a new host for *Our Home*, and *Biggers and Summers* was born.

I had a show. A live talk show! Monday through Friday, 11 A.M. to noon. I was thrilled. It was exactly where I wanted to be. (Well, I would have preferred to be on a network, of course, and then in syndication. But I figured they'd try to syndicate the show: we had a clause in our contract explicitly stating the terms should the show be syndicated.)

We covered topics from celebrities and health to lifestyle and fashion. Our guests all had something to push, plug, or sell—we gave them a platform and they gave us something to talk about every morning. We were hip. We were fun. We were *Biggers and Summers*.

Shooting out in Astoria was a drag. I had come to New York to do a show in Manhattan, not to cross the 59th Street Bridge into the boroughs. But Astoria did have some perks. Don Imus, Sesame Street, and Bill Cosby had their shows there. It was where Bette Midler, Diane Keaton, and Goldie Hawn had shot *The First Wives Club*. To my daughter's great delight, I once rode the elevator with Leonardo DiCaprio. The studio was an exciting place to work: there was always a celebrity in the elevator or down the hall.

I found the one hour a day doing live television to be an enormous emotional relief. Whenever I was on the air, the stresses, strains, and loneliness of the life I had in New York, far from my wife and children, evaporated. When the cameras rolled, I was on another planet—planet TV—where I felt completely comfortable, totally in control. When I was off-camera I felt isolated and off balance, prey to constant low-grade obsessive compulsive anxieties that would flare up at odd moments.

I was living in a spacious rental apartment, which I kept neat as a pin. First thing every morning, I made the bed. The spread didn't have a wrinkle on it. It looked like a sheet of ice. Before going to sleep each night, I spent 10 minutes fluffing and arranging the pillows on the couch. Even with all these details taken care of, during the evenings I would always have a lot of trouble concentrating: when I went over the script for the following day's show, I'd read the same paragraph again and again without absorbing it.

In New York, the most disturbing symptom of my disorder occurred not in my apartment but on Madison Avenue. I'd walk up and down Madison when I returned to Manhattan after a day in the Queens studio. I would read the signs in the shop windows over and over again. If I didn't read the signs correctly, I was convinced Meredith wouldn't get a part in the school play or Matthew wouldn't make the sports team. I was afraid that if I didn't read the sign just right, the plane I took every Thursday to California would crash.

I obsessed endlessly about those Thursday flights, following strict rituals to ensure that disaster didn't strike. I was especially drawn to the window of one particular watch store. I vividly remember standing in front of the store's window one blustery fall evening. A sale was on for Breitling watches. There was a sign in the window that explained the watches' special features: dual time zones, perpetual calendar, day-and-date display. I read the sales pitch from top to bottom at least 25 times, a sickening feeling gripping my stomach and chest, utterly convinced that if I

didn't read the ad copy perfectly my plane would hurtle down-
ward in a ball of flame somewhere over Missouri.

Reading perfectly meant with complete fluidity, without hesi-
tation, from beginning to end. Even the slightest moment of distraction, the least little glitch in the smoothness of the way the
words scrolled in my mind, and I would be compelled to start
over from the beginning. I must have read that sign over and over
for nearly half an hour before I finally got it right.

My weekly commute to and from L.A. was hell. Matthew was
13 and Meredith 10. I'd get into L.A. at 5:00 or 6:00 P.M. on
Thursday, and leave for New York again on Sunday. Soon, I
started leaving later and later on Sundays, in order to spend precious extra hours with my family. Eventually, I was leaving L.A.
at 4:00 P.M. Sunday and getting back to New York at midnight. It
was difficult for all of us.

For two years this misery continued. Sometimes Matthew and
Meredith wanted to do things with their friends on weekends, but
they felt obligated to stay home and spend time with me, since I
was away all week. My kids didn't want to move East: they were
in the middle of their lives. Alice's mother wasn't well, and Alice
wanted to be with her on the West Coast. So I made the regular
3,000-mile weekend commute.

My phone bills were enormous. I talked to Alice seven times
a day; called the kids two or three times each night. Meredith and
I did her homework on the phone. On the upside (and I always
like to look on the upside), the kids spent summers with me.
They both liked to visit the East Coast, and I was off the air at
noon, so we'd have the whole afternoon to play.

We loved walking around the city. I remember riding the elevator in my apartment building with Meredith one summer when she was staying with me.

"Dad," she said, "I want hot dogs for dinner, and I want to cook at home."

I gulped. The lady across from us in the elevator watched intently. She was older, conservative, with a snooty, uppity upper East Side attitude. I thought hard for a long moment, trying to figure out how to phrase what I wanted to say. "Meredith, my goal is to never use that kitchen."

The lady in the elevator raised her eyebrows.

I wanted to keep the kitchen perfect. The apartment had been completely redone before I moved in, and I was not going to be the first person to despoil its pristine surfaces. I also knew that a hot dog dinner was going to cost me $100, because I had no pots or pans. I couldn't just go out and buy a $5 pot—that's not the way I do things. If I bought anything, it would have to be an entire set of matching pots and pans. But Meredith wanted hot dogs. And macaroni and cheese. So we walked to Macy's, bought pots and pans, and had our dinner. It was warm and close.

We cleaned up. But after Meredith was asleep, I went back into the kitchen and recleaned it, buffing the countertops and the stovetop with paper towels until they gleamed. When I was done in the wee hours of the morning, only the most discerning eye (mine) could tell that the kitchen had ever been used.

I was 43 years old. I had been driven by these compulsions for as long as I could remember. I thought I was just someone who liked a neat, clean house. A man who liked everything in its place. I had no idea there was something wrong with me. But that was about to change.

It was a warm summer evening. Meredith and I had just finished a meal of Chinese take-out. The lights in the buildings of midtown were coming on, glimmering in the dusk. Traffic flowed south down Second Avenue, a river of light and movement. The sounds of the city were faint through the thick glass of the living-room window and the soothing hiss of central air-conditioning. I felt good. The show that day had gone well, and I was about to prepare for the following day's show. Meredith was watching television.

Prepping for my role as talk show host was nothing like my tortured attempts to do homework in high school. The producers lined up our topics and guests and did the research necessary to keep Sissy and me from looking foolish, assuming we reviewed the material they prepared for us. I'd usually spend an hour going through the material, a little longer if the following day's guest was an author. I'd focus on two or three passages of his or her book, so I'd be able to engage in an informed discussion.

Tomorrow's guests were Dr. Eric Hollander, a New York psychiatrist and director of the "Compulsive, Impulsive, and Anxiety Disorders Program" at Mt. Sinai Hospital, and Mariette Hartley, a well-known actress and television host, who had written *Breaking the Silence*, a book about alcoholism in her family.

Mariette wasn't coming on the show to discuss her career or her alcoholic father, but to talk about her role as the National Spokesperson for the Obsessive Compulsive Foundation. My producers had provided information from the Foundation on OCD and its symptoms.

"Some symptoms," I read, "are neatness, checking, cleaning,

placing things symmetrically, compulsive rereading, retracing, intrusive thoughts."

I recognized myself instantly. I couldn't read anymore. I was choked up. My heart was racing. I threw the papers down, stood up, and paced around the room. What I had just read described my habits perfectly. It made me nuts; I was freaked out. I needed time to absorb the information, but my immediate concern was the show the following day. Should I let Sissy handle it? If I talked about OCD, would I be able to get through the segment without breaking down? Could I, should I, go on the air and pretend that I didn't think I had the illness?

True to form, I was more worried about my job performance than anything else. Meredith was in the next room, oblivious to my inner turmoil. I didn't want to alarm her. When she came in to say goodnight, I acted as if nothing was wrong.

Before that evening, I had never heard of obsessive compulsive disorder, even though I'd been working in the media for years. I was stunned: it was clear to me I'd been afflicted with the disorder since I had been a child, and, not once, even with all my blatant mannerisms and public rituals, had anyone suggested that I might have OCD.

That was five years ago. Today, far more people are aware of OCD. But there are still many people who have never heard of the disorder. Each time I discuss OCD in public I get letters that read, "Thank God this thing has a name. I really thought I was crazy. Thank you."

Relief is the typical reaction of people who suddenly find out that they're not crazy but are instead victims of treatable disease.

It's still a shock to realize that your brain chemistry differs from most of the rest of humanity's.

I didn't sleep at all that night. I kept thinking: do I avoid the fact that I have the disorder? Do I try and fake it? What was best for me as a performer? What was best for the program? I had never dissembled on the air. I had always tried to play the what-you-see-is-what-you-get type of host.

I reviewed my life. The Sunday cleaning binges. Pacing around the living room with my mother, waiting for my father to come home. Reading and rereading the signs on Madison Avenue. I realized that one of the reasons I had been keeping the apartment neat was that I was afraid if I didn't I would flub my performance on *Biggers and Summers*. The material I read said OCD could be genetically inherited, and I began to suspect that both my parents were afflicted with the disorder.

It was a lot to absorb, and I tossed and turned. But when I climbed out of bed the following morning, I wasn't tired in the least. I woke Meredith up, since she was coming to the studio with me that morning. We had a quick breakfast and then a car service picked us up to take us to the studio. It was one of those hideous New York August mornings. Although it was still early, the pavement was hot and steamy as we left the sanctum of the air-conditioned lobby of my apartment building and ducked into the backseat of the black Lincoln that sat idling at the curb.

I was nervous on the way to Astoria and barely said a word to Meredith. She looked out the window at the sparkling surface of the East River, the tram swinging on its high wire, making its way toward Roosevelt Island. The sun blazed through a heavy haze of humidity and exhaust. We glided along in the air-conditioned car, sunk in its plush upholstery. My palms were sweating, while my fingers were ice-cold.

At the studio, Meredith went to hang out in the makeup room while I met with Sissy and the show's producers in the Green Room. We sat in the same spot every morning—Sissy and I on the big black couch, the producers around the coffee table.

The meeting's first few minutes were light and breezy. We chatted about who had appeared the night before on *Politically Incorrect, The Tonight Show,* and *David Letterman,* until, in the midst of the typical chaos that goes on before live television (late guests, lost guests, technical problems), we focused for 45 minutes, talking down the show (an industry phrase that means going through the show segment by segment). The producer who put together each segment told us what the guests wanted to discuss, what they didn't want to discuss, what they were plugging, critical questions to ask, and what to get to if we had time.

I couldn't concentrate. I got emotional. Finally, I just got it over with. I told them all I thought I had OCD. "I don't know if I can go on," I said. "I might have to walk out during the taping."

I put my head in my hands. Tears squeezed from the corners of my eyes. Everyone was supportive, though. Sissy said, "You open it up, Marc. See how you feel. If you can't continue, just leave. We'll handle it."

As soon as Dr. Hollander arrived at the set, I approached him and introduced myself.

"I think I have OCD," I said.

Dr. Hollander is tall and donnish. He looks far too young to be as smart and knowledgeable as he is. "Why do you think so?" he asked.

I described my symptoms. I might, indeed, have obsessive compulsive disorder, he told me. But he cautioned me that lots of people have traces of OCD, and that I shouldn't jump to conclusions. He gave me his card and told me we could talk after the show.

Air time, 11:00, arrived as it always did. I felt raw. TV had never made me nervous, but that day I was queasy. Sissy and I chatted as usual on a predetermined topic: her life in Connecticut, her kids, her husband's road trip, my family, the fantastic things I'd done the evening before in Manhattan. (I always made my social life seem much grander than it actually was in order to have comic biplay with Sissy.) I was stiff. I was talking—my mouth was moving and sounds were coming out— but I was in a fog, the whole time thinking about the upcoming topic.

We went to commercial break and returned with Dr. Hollander and Mariette Hartley. Dr. Hollander began defining OCD. As he described intrusive thoughts, the compulsion for rituals, and fanatical neatness, the pressure built inside me. I couldn't meet his eyes. I felt numb. Suddenly, I leaned forward.

"Dr. Hollander, I think I have this," I said.

I confessed that I was the father of the only five-year-old in the world who could eat a chocolate ice cream cone without spilling a drop on himself. And I'd been proud of it! For years, I had been forcing my compulsions on my kids. I told a story about getting a call from Matthew's nursery school teacher. In all her years of teaching, our son was the first kid who refused to finger paint because he didn't want to get his hands dirty. Matthew's teacher had asked me to go buy finger paints and show Matthew that getting green gobs of goo under his fingernails was okay. I completed my assignment, despite my total aversion to having paint under my nails. The following Monday at school, Matthew proudly completed his first finger painting.

When we went to a commercial break, I took the deepest breath of my life. Dr. Hollander, who was very approachable, told me, in his soothing bedside manner, "You may find that you do better with treatment. Help is available when you want it."

Later, Dr. Hollander would tell me that I seemed anxious and agitated when I spoke to him before the show.

"You were pacing back and forth, Marc," he said. "You had a pained look on your face. I was surprised when you brought up your OCD on the show. I thought it was a brave, courageous thing you did."

Everyone in the studio wanted to make sure I was okay, and told me I'd done a terrific job. Exercise guru and flamboyant personality Richard Simmons, who'd been another guest that morning, hugged me. "That was a very brave, good thing you just did," he told me. "You helped a lot of people." I welcomed the support, considering the doubt coursing through me—had it been a bad move to "out" myself on the air? How would the viewers react? Would it hurt my career? What would my family think? What now?

I called my parents afterward to discuss the show. I knew they'd seen it. They watched every single one of my shows (you know Jewish parents). They were nervous.

"Do you think that was a smart thing you did?" my mother asked. "Don't you think it will hurt your career?"

My father said he felt the same way.

Later my parents would express their personal discomfort and fear at the public disclosure of my OCD.

After an article appeared in *People* magazine about me coping with the disorder, my dad said, "Just because you're in the public eye doesn't mean we have to be in it, too." My parents felt exposed in their tight-knit Indianapolis community. They thought having a son with OCD was a put-down in their friends' eyes. I tried to reassure them that my OCD had nothing to do with them. It was something I was born with: it wasn't their fault.

I phoned Alice to tell her about the show. She, too, was concerned that I had damaged my career, but on the whole, she was extremely supportive. She said I sounded happy and excited; she was glad I had finally found an answer, a name to put to the behaviors that had perplexed us since our explosive wedding day.

"Things fit together for me," Alice said in a television interview, remembering that call. "Marc's OCD had put a strain on our marriage. I wouldn't say it was a major strain. We tried to make a joke of it. Before Marc talked to Dr. Hollander he and I had chalked his odd behavior up to 'eccentricity.' It was perplexing. His inflexible neatness put a strain on our kids, and I was in the middle. That was difficult for me. I was happy when we got an answer. And I knew Marc. He's an extremely capable man. He *always* follows through. I knew whatever lay ahead, he would overcome it and we would come through it stronger."

It moved me that Alice had such faith in me. And, finally, for the first time in our relationship, I could admit to her (and to myself) how deeply my rituals and anxieties disturbed me. I could finally share that part of myself with her, which was an enormous relief and brought us even closer together.

Before Dr. Hollander left the Astoria studios, he gave me his card. I tucked it into my pocket. But I knew I wouldn't call him. "I can handle this on my own," I thought. "Now I know that what I've been doing all these years has a name, and so I'm fine."

The reaction I had turns out to be a common one among people who have OCD. On average, it takes us seven years from the onset of symptoms to the admission that obsessive compulsive thoughts and behaviors are caused by the disorder. And once we discover we have OCD, we don't seek help for another ten years. We fool ourselves into thinking we're in control.

While I insisted to myself that I was doing fine, secretly one of the reasons I knew I wouldn't call Hollander was because I was scared: I couldn't stand the idea of taking pills. On the show, Hollander had talked about medication as key to treating the disease. I hate to take even an aspirin, so it was horrifying to contemplate taking pills every day to get better. Aversion to pills is common among OCD sufferers and contributes to the delay between diagnosis and treatment.

But something else even more profound keeps many people with OCD from seeking treatment: the stigma surrounding mental illness. Countless obsessive compulsives say that fear of ridicule was what kept them from seeking help or even admitting to themselves that they had the disorder.

I'm encouraged by the recent attention the media has given OCD. Daytime talk shows have been instrumental in spreading the message that different doesn't equal bad, and illness or disability doesn't mean crazy or worthless. Jack Nicholson's Academy Award-winning portrayal of a severe OCD sufferer in *As Good As It Gets* did incalculable good. With every *Oprah*, *Date-*

line, *20/20*, or *Biggers and Summers* show on OCD, someone out there suffering from the disorder feels less alone. With each *People* magazine or *USA Today* article that gives us glimpses of the "normal," healthy, productive people who happen to have OCD, someone suffering in silence is encouraged to take that next step toward getting help.

Along with the media attention, organizations such as the OC Foundation and many other groups listed in the resource guide at the back of this book have turned around the lives of countless sufferers of the disorder.

The week I identified my disorder on the air, thousands of calls flooded the Obsessive Compulsive Foundation's 1-800 number. The PR firm handling the Foundation called me to say it had been a terrific segment; the public's reaction had been tremendous. They asked if I'd be interested in working alongside Mariette, or even in her place. No way, I said. Not a chance. I didn't want to be identified as the guy with OCD.

A couple weeks later the PR firm called and asked again. This time I told them to let me think about it. I called publicists and agents to ask their advice. How would I be viewed? Public service jobs are viewed differently in the industry than they are by the general public. People in the industry tend to think that if someone is crusading for a cause it means they've got nothing else going on work-wise. It is viewed as a move someone makes when his or her career is waning.

The agents I talked to reassured me. They said that so many famous people are confessed drug addicts and alcoholics, becoming known as "the guy with OCD" was a gift in comparison. I finally decided that working on behalf of OCD awareness was the right thing to do. I remembered my early dream to be a rabbi, and I thought: here is my chance to do good, to help people, to make a difference.

But I still didn't call Dr. Hollander. I didn't think of needing help myself, or of the way I tortured myself and occasionally those nearest and dearest to me. I thought, instead, of helping all the OCD sufferers sitting by their phones, staring at the Foundation's number or the number of their doctor. People who desperately needed help but were afraid to call. People who were practicing their inflexible rituals, who were consumed by anxiety but, for whatever reason, were in denial. I still separated myself from those tortured souls. I could not yet admit that I, too, was ill. I was one of them.

eight

rock bottom

"Oh! Blessed rage for order, pale Ramon . . ."
—Wallace Stevens,
The Idea of Order at Key West

In February of 1996, six months after Dr. Hollander appeared on *Biggers and Summers*, the show was canceled. Sissy and I stepped offstage after a Thursday filming and the programming people came over and said, "You just did your last show." That's how it is in TV. They don't want you to bad-mouth the station or the program on the air, so they give no warning when they cancel you. We were lucky. Generally, when a show is canceled they escort the staff directly from the building. The *Biggers and Summers* people were nice; they gave us a week to get out.

Lifetime paid out our contract, which ran for another five

months. "Why can't we stay, then?" I asked the head of programming. "It doesn't make sense to pay us and not use us."

My plea fell on deaf ears. We were done taping new shows as of that day and paid an arm and a leg not to work.

I was never given a clear answer about why we were canceled. Was it because Sissy and I pressed for more publicity for the show or complained about taping in Astoria rather than in Manhattan? The network might have thought we were too uppity. We were supposed to take whatever Lifetime dished out and be grateful. Were we canceled as punishment for bad behavior? For making waves?

Sissy and I were told our show "just wasn't working." Our ratings were middling, as were our ad revenues. We hadn't set the world on fire. But that's the way it is in daytime television on cable—every show gets about the same rating. I felt that management's expectations were unreasonable, especially given the fact that they had done nothing to promote the show.

Although there was some acrimony at the time, Lifetime and I didn't part on bad terms. The old saying "You'll never work in this town again until I need you!" held true for me. You don't want to burn your bridges in television, and so you want to make sure you're nice to everyone. Doug Herzog, the guy who held my cue cards on CNN's *Lee Leonard Show,* now heads Fox Television. It's the same pool of people holding different and better jobs. It just doesn't pay to make enemies.

Sissy took our cancellation harder than I did. She hadn't come to realize the sad truth of television: eventually you're going to get canceled or canned. It's only a matter of time. She eventually ended up on the TV Food Network hosting a game show called

Ready, Set, Cook, which is what she does today. Sissy and I are both driven to be on camera. That's essential for a television personality; you have to want to be there. If you don't, the audience will sense it.

Since I was back living full-time in our L.A. home, I had to break the lease on my New York City apartment with seven months left. At $3,200 a month, that wasn't a small chunk of change for an unemployed guy. But in a bizarre twist of fate, the kind that sometimes seems to come around just when you need it, my daughter's soccer coach's wife's brother was my landlord, who, courtesy of that great connection, was willing to negotiate: if I got out in 12 days he wouldn't hold me to my lease.

Alice flew to New York to help pack up the apartment. We kicked around the city between bouts of packing and labeling boxes. I had developed a love-hate relationship with New York. I loved the pace, the action, the ambition, the professionalism of the city. But I regularly got into or witnessed at least one fight a day living there, with dry cleaners, cab drivers, shopkeepers, anyone and everyone. I got into a fight with the dry cleaner because my shirts came back with black spots. The cleaners insisted the spots were on the shirts when I brought them in. One night my cab slammed into another cab. Both drivers jumped out. My guy was a wiry Asian who started yelling at the other driver, a heavy-set black guy. The other guy punched my guy in the face and knocked him out flat on his back in the middle of Sixth Avenue. Another time, I hailed a cab in the rain, and as I was getting into it, an older woman came up and started beating me on the shins with her umbrella. "That's my cab, Sonny," she said, and pushed me aside and jumped in.

At first it had been fun, but all the attitude and the constant confrontations had begun to wear on me. I was washed out, on edge. I just wanted to relax and be in a place where people were friendly and polite. I won't say L.A. is a bastion of civility (it's not nearly as calm as Indianapolis, for example), but it's more laid-back than New York, sunnier in both weather and temperament.

After Alice returned to L.A., I spent a few days in the city on my own. I wandered the streets, thinking about the ups and downs of the volatile life I had chosen for myself. It was a cold, bleak time. The city seemed strange. I didn't feel part of its life and vitality anymore. I was a ghost wandering through the dark streets and freezing pavement, coming home to an empty apartment that felt like a waiting room for transit to God-knows-where. On Madison Avenue I practiced my sign-reading rituals, only instead of Matthew's success in basketball tryouts, I fixated on what I saw as my future job possibilities. I hadn't the slightest idea of what awaited me in L.A.

Finally, the day came to leave the city. I closed the door on my apartment for the last time and heard the familiar faint sound of wind, a subdued whoosh from the heating vents in the hall. I stood in the elevator with its banks of glowing numerals, my luggage at my feet. It was cold on the street, with stark February early-morning light. I waited under the long canopy of the awning outside while the doorman flagged me a cab. He put my bags in the trunk and I bid him farewell and tipped him. I slid into the cab's backseat, leaning back as we accelerated off the curb into the jockeying traffic, bouncing over manhole covers, idling at cross-street lights, and then taking the hard turn onto the FDR Drive, the first leg of the short journey to Kennedy Airport.

On the plane, I looked out the portal into a vista of cloudless blue sky. I thought about my dreams to host a television show in New York City, and how that dream had come briefly to life and then faded, as dreams always do, in the harsh light of day.

Alice picked me up at LAX. We drove north along the freeways, through the dazzling midday sun, up the coast to our new home north of Malibu in the plush bedroom community of Calabasas. We'd bought a new house during the period when I was commuting between New York and L.A., and I didn't feel entirely at home in it yet. If Alice was cooking and asked me to pass her a ladle, I didn't know where to start looking for it—extremely disconcerting for a guy who has to have everything just so. ,

I had been making a small fortune for the past couple of years, but our cash flow would soon dwindle to nothing if I didn't get more work. Alice and I had been poor when we were young. But it's different to face hard financial times in middle age. There was the kids' college tuition to think about, and our future retirement. Plus, we had grown accustomed to a high standard of living that would be hard to relinquish.

I keenly felt my responsibility as a father and husband. I looked back at my career path, and I wondered how I had come to this point in my life. I was feeling my age in a town and a business that can make you feel over the hill at 40. I looked back at my life and tallied my accomplishments. It seemed that everything I had worked for had come to nothing. I was faced with the prospect of living off dribs and drabs of ever-shrinking residuals and royalties.

I obsessed, going over and over my career path, trying to identify the misstep that had led to my present sorry state. I obsessed over money. When I first started doing warm-ups for sitcoms and game shows in 1974, I was paid $160 a night. By 1982, warm-ups were still my primary source of income, but I was making $1,200 a night.

After 1982 I moved from doing warm-ups to hosting rehearsals for game shows. The rehearsals were dry runs of the shows that were done before a live audience but weren't taped. Rehearsals paid better than the warm-ups, but they still were nowhere near as well paid as hosting the shows themselves. The game shows in those days were an old boys' club. The hosts were older men with gray hair. They jealously guarded the gates of a closed world, partially because the money was so good: they made $10,000 and up per week, and they didn't want to share the spoils with any young upstarts.

There was an irony in this because the game shows had a tainted feel. They were looked at as the bargain basement of daytime television, which was looked at as the bargain basement of television by the show business world. Daytime personalities are perceived in New York and L.A. as people who can't make it at night. But that's not true. Look at Rosie or Oprah. They work brilliantly on daytime, but I don't think they'd work nearly as well at night.

Back in L.A. I keenly felt the stigma attached to game shows. I had experienced the higher reaches of daytime television with *Biggers and Summers* and in my work as a roving correspondent for the *Home Show*. The *Home Show* was network. If you work on a major network, you've arrived. Both the *Home Show* and *Biggers and Summers* were informational live television, with that sense of excitement of working without the safety net of editing.

The prospect of going back to being dipped in goo or taking part in the shenanigans of game shows felt like a huge step backward.

Not that I was being offered a game show. This was the first time I'd been unemployed since 1978, and I'd been working seven days a week since 1986. There was a time when I had four shows on the air simultaneously, hosting all of them and producing some. My work provided income, which was, of course, extremely important, but it was also a way for me to channel an aspect of my disease: my need to win, to be perfect, to be the best; to accumulate as many credits as possible and reach the pinnacle of my career. People would tell me, "I can't turn on the TV without seeing you." "Good!" I'd say.

Now my career had come to a screeching halt. After a few days at home, I started to go nuts. I'd read the paper in the morning, and then couldn't figure out what to do next. I was going through a mid-life crisis, doubting myself and everything I had done. I'd been on a long run. I had kept driving relentlessly forward. Suddenly, it all felt shallow and meaningless.

"What should I do?" I asked Alice. "I've done game shows and kids' shows, and I don't want to do them anymore. I've done talk—I was *good* at talk, and they canceled me."

"Be patient," she said. "You have time. Look around. Get your bearings. You've always landed on your feet. And you will this time, too."

I couldn't hear her. OCD had begun to run my mind. I obsessed on the cancellation of *Biggers and Summers*. The show *had* been great: the marvelous TV and film director Carl Reiner had watched us in action and been blown away. He couldn't believe Sissy and I had just started hosting together. He said it seemed like we'd been together for years. Tom Selleck, Tony Randall, Michael Bolton—they all came on the show as guests, and loved doing it. I had been good at my job. And I had been canned.

I think almost anyone in my situation would have had these thoughts spinning around in his head. But I obsessed on the praise I'd received from Tom Selleck and Carl Reiner. I ran their words over and over in my mind. I couldn't stop. I felt that if I replayed the shows in my mind again and again, somehow I'd fix what was wrong. I'd magically bring back to life what had been taken from me. For hours on end, I'd sit in my favorite chair and visualize the scrolling credits of all the shows I'd hosted. In my mind, I would greet the guests, chat them up, make them feel comfortable, feel the warmth from the audience as they laughed and applauded.

My self-confidence was in meltdown. Was I damaged goods? Could I work again? Maybe I had had my shot. Perhaps the life of show business was simply too volatile, too uncertain.

As it turned out, a big part of my problem was timing. I had come back to L.A. in March of 1996, but January and September are the times in television when shows are traditionally cast. I held my finger up and gauged the wind. Once I realized nothing was going to happen until autumn, I settled down to wait out a long dry summer in the Santa Monica Mountains.

I set about doing what you do in television if you're someone like me who is back in town without work and has missed those hiring windows. You have to constantly remind people who you are and what you do. You take them out for lunch, for drinks, you call them just to say hello—you wine and dine and you have to constantly keep up a cheerful face. Of course, it's exponentially easier to get work in this business if you already have work. If you have work, you have confidence. And people have a sixth sense for someone whose confidence is at an ebb. They smell the fear coming off you. There's nothing you can do to hide it.

In my current state I knew it was risky taking people out to business lunches because I was so emotionally shaky. But I had to send out feelers and let people know I was back in town. So I'd try to kill as many birds with one stone as I could, planning business lunches in places where I knew I was likely to run into show business movers and shakers.

Conversation in L.A. runs like this: "Hi! How are you? What are you up to?" Everyone lives to work here, and work is the first thing on everyone's mind. So chance encounters, running into people at restaurants, can be productive. Everyone knows everyone. It's important that people see you, know you're around.

I wined and dined television executives at Citrus, an upscale restaurant in the bowels of Hollywood. I hosted producers at Hugo's, a Hollywood coffee shop and industry hangout. I took programming people to Nate 'n' Al's, a deli in Beverly Hills. I sprung for the check at The Palm, a steak and lobster joint between Beverly Hills and CBS Television City.

The conversation at these lunches was entirely predictable.

"Gee, what happened at Lifetime?" said the exec.

I told him, trying to sound as upbeat as possible. "Well, they loved the show, but, you know, their programming was moving in another direction. They wanted to cut back on costs."

That's L.A. for you. That's show biz. Even if you get run over by a truck you'd better look on the bright side. You'd better come up smiling.

Inevitably, the conversation rolled around to the question: "What do you want to do now?"

What the hell did he think I wanted to do? Play lead violin in a symphony orchestra?

"I want to do what I do," I said, smiling my best rendition of a Marc Summers A-list smile. "I want to host television shows."

I asked if he was developing anything, and he talked up all the earth-shattering programming he was busy getting off the ground. Isn't that exciting! Isn't that wonderful! I said. What brilliance! Was there a place for me in anything he had in the works? I was sucking up, selling myself like a piece of meat. It's wasn't fun and it wasn't pretty, but it is a big part of this business.

After these lunches, I would drive back on the endless L.A. freeways, cars belching exhaust, the interminable strip malls, the glare of the harsh sun beating down on the concrete that stretched unbroken for mile after mile, the relentless commerce and the unbridled ambition of the world of show business. I thought about the tree-lined street where I'd grown up in genteel Indianapolis, and the boy I had been who made rabbits pop out of hats and dreamt of a life in television—a life that would one day eat him up and spit him out. I came back from those lunches defeated, bloated, the false smile I had plastered on my face making my jaw ache. In hindsight, it's clear that I was overreacting, but at the time, I thought I'd never work again.

My close friends said the cancellation of *Biggers and Summers* was a sign: I needed to make big changes in my life, shake things up, bring in new energy. They urged me to leave my agent and close friend, Richard Lawrence, at Abrahms, Rubaloff, and Lawrence, a successful boutique agency that had handled me for 15 years. So I defected, going over to Ken Lindner and Babette Perry at Ken Lindner and Associates with offices in Century City. Lindner and Associates was another agency that specialized in handling television hosts. The move to my new agents buoyed me momentarily (I've since moved back to the agents who launched me; Richard welcomed me back with a graciousness and lack of resentment that warmed me to my core.)

When I wasn't futilely wining and dining industry executives, I was hanging out at home all day. At first, I was waiting for my belongings to arrive from New York. Then I was unpacking. Then I was neatening.

The stress from being unemployed sent me into an OCD tailspin. I became obsessed with keeping the house straight, and constantly arranged and rearranged paintings, vases, furniture, pillows, curtains, glasses, window blinds, photographs, rug fringes. If it could be moved, adjusted, or rearranged, I was powerless to resist. Every couple of hours I'd have to go through the house, straightening everything, although nothing had been touched since my last round. I'd feel anxiety start to well up. It was like a maddening itch that I couldn't quite scratch. The straightening and restraightening made the itch better for a little while, calmed it, but then it would catch fire again, crawling under my skin, and I'd have to go back and do the whole bloody thing again, moving the cushions by only millimeters, making sure the vase with flowers was placed in the exact center of the table in the foyer.

I didn't clean, dust, or vacuum, as I had when I was a kid. The house was too clean for that, since I had a cleaning woman come in on Mondays and Fridays. If I saw dust on a table I would wipe it off, but the house was basically kept dust-free. So I focused on the symmetry of vases, glasses in the kitchen cabinets, pillows on the couch, food in the refrigerator, the space between the chairs at the dining room table. Everything had to be at just the right angle.

The Monday cleaning lady changed sheets and towels and did the wash and vacuuming. The Friday woman did the hard-core, physical cleaning. She moved everything, picked up pieces of furniture—couches, tables, chairs, beds—and dusted behind them. She left around 3:30 in the afternoon. As soon as she was out the door, I'd go to it. I'd fix everything. The plant on the kitchen table went directly under the middle ceiling lamp, salt and pepper shakers had to be in perfect alignment, the throw rug precisely centered in front of the fridge, the pattern on one couch cushion had to mesh perfectly with the next, the photographs on the mantle had to be just so, the paintings had to be perfectly level. Two hours later everything would be back in its place.

Friday afternoons the kids were away at after-school activities—soccer or theater practice. Alice asked me, "Do you want to come with me to pick up the kids, or do you want to stay here and do your thing around the house?"

You can guess my choice. I knew that I should have gone with her to pick up the kids, but my compulsions came first. As I worked my way through the house, I thought to myself over and over, "I should be spending time with my wife and family." But then I'd think, Oh God, the curtains aren't hanging right. If I just fix it quickly, maybe I can take the kids out for ice cream when they come home.

But, of course, one thing would lead to another. I'd fix the curtain, then notice the photographs on the mantle were out of alignment. I'd fix the photos, then straighten all the paintings on the dining room wall. Then I'd have to straighten all the paintings in the entire house. So when the kids came home, needless to say, there was never time to take them out for ice cream. God forbid they should interrupt me in the midst of my Friday afternoon rounds. When my compulsion was in charge, everything that got in the way of serving it was an interruption—even the needs of my kids and wife.

It was horrible knowing I should be investing energy in the relationships most dear to me. But I was helpless. My helplessness began to make me furious at myself. This kind of self-directed anger is common among OCD sufferers. Our self-knowledge can be devastating—we see that our behavior is ridiculous and self-destructive, yet we can't control it. But it's also one of the blessings of the disorder that we have the sense that our behavior is out of bounds. Unlike people suffering from schizophrenia (another disorder caused by chemical imbalances in the brain), who truly believe their distorted vision of the world, people with OCD do not assume that our obsessions or compulsions make sense or have any bearing on reality. On the *Oprah* show, both Lorrie, who had such acute fears of contamination, and Don, the hoarder, were quick to admit that what they were doing was "out of hand" and "a little bit crazy" but that they had no control over their actions.

I felt the same when Meredith would have friends over, and I would stick my head in her room, "Can I straighten in here a sec?"

Her friends would look at her as if to say, "Is your dad crazy, or what?" Even though I knew teenagers need nothing as much as they need privacy, I couldn't stop.

The embarrassment I caused myself was far outweighed by the embarrassment I caused my daughter, and I knew it. But I couldn't help myself. The most restraint I could muster was to gloss over Meredith's room when she had a friend visiting, instead of giving it the usual detailed straightening.

I became obsessed with the green curtains in the dining room. They had to hit the floor in perfect, even waves, with none of their white lining showing. I'd arrange them, and then, though they hadn't been disturbed, I'd arrange them again. And then a third time. Each time I walked by a carpet I'd straighten it. I spent hours in the kitchen. I wiped and wiped the countertops and straightened the chairs. Our drinking glasses had to be arranged in perfect rows on the cupboard shelves. I should have been trying to write up ideas for shows, to pitch programming. But I was at a creative low. I was usually buzzing with ideas, jotting them down on legal pads. But now I was flat. Empty. My work life was a mess, but if I could make the house perfect, at least something would be right.

I was at a low point in my life. Nothing was developing in my career. When this happens, you always hope that people will find out you've been canceled and call with job offers. Not this time. I felt rejection like a knife.

I started to stay in bed as long as I could each morning. I

didn't want to get up: I didn't have anything to do. A major depression settled over me.

What I had is called "comorbid" depression, meaning a depression that co-existed with my OCD. Two-thirds of obsessive compulsives develop clinical depression at some point in their lives. We suffer classic symptoms of depression: loss of interest and energy, poor concentration, difficulty with sleep, and, in extreme cases, suicidal thoughts. Thankfully, my depression never reached that point. It did, I think, exacerbate my OCD symptoms, which in turn made me even more depressed. A vicious cycle developed, as happens frequently in the lives of depressed people with OCD. It's not always clear if the depression is secondary to the OCD—that is, brought on by the stresses of living with OCD—or a separate illness, labeled "primary" depression. In any event, at the time, the distinction was pointless.

Normally, I'm awake by 5:30 or 6:00 A.M. I spend an hour on the treadmill, watching the early morning news. But now I languished in bed all morning, finally getting up at 11:00 A.M. After staggering to the shower and getting dressed, I would or would not shave, depending on whether I had a depressing business lunch scheduled that day with a producer or agent or lackey whom I thought might help me get work.

I'd hang around the house and finally skulk into my home office. It was set up with a TV and VCR, all the tapes of my appearances on various shows meticulously organized, a big overstuffed chair in one corner, pictures of me with various celebrities hanging on the wall, a private business phone on a spotless desk. Two French doors opened out into a big backyard and the Santa Monica Mountains. The room was quiet, hushed, at the very back of the house. No one went in there except me.

It should have been my haven but now it was my hell. Sitting at the computer was torture. I had no idea what I was going to write. I had vague ideas for show concepts, ideas to pitch. But I told myself that I couldn't begin work until the room was clean. So I killed hours fluffing pillows, straightening furniture, re-arranging videotapes on the shelves.

I should have been taking time off after working like a slave for all those years without a break. I should have been regrouping, looking at my options, planning my next move. But I was incapable of slowing down. A pit of emptiness was opening inside me—a gnawing anxiety I couldn't control. When I unpacked my stuff from New York I found all the material the *Biggers and Summers* producers had given us to prepare for the show we did on OCD. You'd think I would have noticed my behavior and connected it to what I'd learned about OCD from Dr. Hollander on the show that day. I'd admitted to the whole world that I had the disorder—why couldn't I admit it to myself now?

I played the kids a videotape the producers had included of a woman afflicted with OCD straightening her apartment. "I can't believe somebody else does what you do," Meredith said.

Alice and the kids used to look at my compulsions as "eccentricities" and "quirks." They had always felt that cleaning made me happy, so they gave me license to indulge that kind of behavior. They had no idea that I was afflicted by a clinical illness that played havoc with my brain chemistry.

It wasn't until I appeared on *Oprah* that the kids felt self-conscious about having a dad with OCD. After the show, kids in their school would approach them and ask them about their "weird" father. Reporters wanted to interview them on what it was like to have an obsessive compulsive dad. Matthew and Meredith told me they didn't want to be constantly fielding questions about their father, and they asked me to shield them from media people.

"That's your life," Matthew, age 16 at the time, said. "I don't want to be sucked into it."

I respected that, especially because our family dynamic was close, and the kids had never reproached me for my eccentricities. But I do remember one night when I was rearranging the living room, Meredith kept running past me *en route* to Alice, who was helping her with her homework. On one trip she stopped, and said "Dad, please stop doing that. I hate it when you do that."

"Okay," I said as she vanished up the stairs.

I sat down for a minute, feeling lost and confused. I wanted to stop, but anxiety welled up inside me. It grew and grew until I couldn't help myself. I got up and went back to fluffing the couch pillows.

"Dad! Stop!" Meredith had been watching me through the banister rails.

I hung my head. I'd been caught.

At night I watched *David Letterman* and then whatever else happened to come on. I stayed up as late as I could, going to bed around 2:00 A.M. And then it would be 11:00 in the morning again, and Alice would be saying, "Come on; you have to get up; this isn't good for you."

I still didn't consciously realize how driven I was by the disease. I was in denial. I hadn't been officially diagnosed with

OCD, and, although I was pretty sure I had the traits of an obsessive compulsive, I didn't think I needed help. I resisted the thought of taking drugs or the idea that therapy might help me. I still thought I could handle everything myself.

Late one night I was up watching TV. I walked past the oriental rug in our dining room. I knew the fringe was straight, but, as usual, I couldn't help myself—I got down on my hands and knees and started running my fingers along each tassel, placing each on the floor in a perfectly straight line, parallel to all the others. I had to make them perfect. It was a soothing feeling. I knew that if I straightened all the fringe, I'd feel better.

"It's 1:30 in the morning!" Alice's voice, raw and edgy, pierced the stillness. "What the hell are you doing?"

I looked up at her through the darkness. "I have no idea."

There was a long pause.

"Do you have the card of that doctor from the show?" she said. "I think you need to call him."

"I think you're right."

I stood up, went into my office, pulled Dr. Hollander's card from my alphabetized business-card filing box, and placed it by the phone. I resolved to call him as soon as I got up the next morning.

From my work with the Foundation, I now know it's common for OCD sufferers to reach a nadir before seeking treatment. I suppose it's human nature to wait until things get desperate to make changes in our lives. But it doesn't have to be that way. I was terrified of the pills, but, as you'll see in the next chapter, they aren't so bad, and they can make an enormous difference. I think it's important to realize we can't handle the disease on our own. The help lines listed in the back of this book can help you find a doctor or support group in your area. You don't have to go the distance alone. I know that it's doubly hard to address your obsessive compulsive disorder when you're also battling depression. Depression often exists without OCD, but one of my compatriots in the campaign to publicize OCD, Connie Foster, a writer on the disorder, says that OCD is almost always accompanied by depression. Like me, Connie was spurred to seek treatment by her family when she found herself in the throes of a major depression.

"I was overwhelmed with fatigue," she told me. "I wasn't eating. I wanted to sleep all the time. With three children, two horses in the barn, and a business to run, I obviously needed to be on medication. I was so depressed I didn't realize I was depressed. It was my family, my husband and three sons, who sat me down and told me that I needed to get help."

Even though she bottomed out with OCD before seeking treatment, Connie feels that overall her OCD has contributed to the success she's achieved.

"OCD has been more of a help than a hindrance to me," she says. "I wouldn't have accomplished what I accomplished without it. When I sought treatment in 1989, only a few doctors had heard of the disorder. I had to go out of state to Massachusetts General Hospital in Boston for treatment. At that time, Anafranil wasn't approved for use in this country, so I got it from Canada. It helped immediately. First the depression lifted and then the OCD."

When Connie counsels OCD sufferers she likes to remind us and our families that OCD is a chronic illness. "You always have it," she says. "It waxes and wanes. Some days are harder than others. But as we age we tend to live with it more gracefully."

The morning after I resolved to seek help I rolled out of bed before dawn. It was three hours later on the East Coast, and I wanted to catch Dr. Hollander by telephone before his busy day began. I felt acute apprehension. I was worried that I would have to go on medication. If I hadn't promised Alice that I would call I probably wouldn't have followed through.

Alice and the kids were still asleep, and so I felt completely alone in our big dark house. First light was just creeping through the windows. I made my way to my office. I could see the brightness coming up over the jagged spine of the mountains; it was not enough to read by so I flicked on the desk lamp. A small circle of light pooled around Dr. Eric Hollander's card, lying on the desk where I had left it the night before. I felt an overwhelming urge to straighten up the room. Instead, I picked up the card, took a deep breath, and lifted the receiver.

| *nine* |

taking charge

The phone rang twice. "Good morning, Dr. Hollander's office," said the woman who answered.

"Can I speak to Dr. Hollander, please?"

"What is this regarding?"

"My name's Marc Summers." I was nervous. "Dr. Hollander told me to call if I ever needed help. I think I have OCD, and I need help."

After a few minutes, Dr. Hollander's warm voice greeted me. "Marc! What's going on?"

"Hi. Remember that conversation we had in the studio about

my disorder? You said help was available when I needed it. I think I need it."

"Why?"

I took a deep breath. "I straighten all the time," I said.

"What do you mean, all the time?"

I told him about losing *Biggers and Summers* and returning to L.A., about the days spent straightening my immaculate house and getting caught by Meredith, and, finally, about my confrontation with Alice late the night before when she had caught me fixing the fringe on the dining room rug.

"I need to get control of this," I said. "It's running my life. It's hurting my relationship with my wife and kids."

We talked for 30 minutes and then made another appointment to speak by phone in two days. I hung up with the feeling that a burden had at least partially been lifted from me. I didn't have to carry the weight of the disorder alone anymore.

When I spoke to Dr. Hollander again, we talked for an hour. He asked me in detail about my rituals and intrusive thoughts and about when I had first expressed my OCD symptoms. Then he let the bomb drop. "I think you need to go on medication," he said.

I wasn't surprised. We had talked about medication on the show. I knew it was ultimately part of the solution to my problem, but that didn't diminish the anxiety and resistance I felt at the suggestion.

"Why do you say that?" I asked.

Dr. Hollander told me that in his experience, which I knew was extensive, a combination of medication and behavior therapy usually provided the best results for people with OCD. Behavior therapy, he explained, provides lasting benefits by changing the way OCD patients respond to their obsessive thoughts, which eventually leads to a reduction in the thoughts themselves. At first, though, the therapy was likely to increase my feelings of anxiety. Medication, Dr. Hollander said, would take the "edge" off my OCD symptoms, lessening the severity of my anxiety and making the behavior therapy a little easier.

I was foggy on exactly what behavior therapy was, so he went over it on the phone in order to let me know what I was in for. He explained what's called "exposure and response prevention," a regimen familiar to the thousands and perhaps now hundreds of thousands of people who have used it to control their OCD. In exposure and response prevention, an OCD patient is encouraged to face his fears, to expose himself to the very things that induce his obsessive thoughts. A person with contamination fears might be asked to touch a T-shirt he considers germ-covered. That's the exposure part. In the response prevention part, the patient is asked to resist, for a certain length of time, doing the compulsive rituals he would normally do to ease his anxiety-provoking obsessive thoughts. The patient who has touched the "germ-covered" T-shirt and is terrified he's been contaminated must now resist his urge to run to the bathroom sink and scrub his hands. At first the OCD patient is asked to resist for only a short time, and then gradually to do so for longer and longer. As it becomes clear to the patient that he hasn't gotten sick and that nothing bad has happened because he hasn't washed his hands, the power that his obsessive fear of contamination has over him begins, bit by bit, to diminish.

Dr. Hollander suggested we begin behavior therapy by using

the ferocious compulsion I had to straighten after the cleaning woman left on Fridays. Our goal was to help me begin to recognize that if I didn't rearrange the house after she left, nothing would happen. No one would get hurt.

"Do you think you can wait five minutes after she leaves before you begin straightening?" he asked.

"Yes," I said.

"10 minutes?"

"Yes."

"15 minutes?"

"Don't push it."

We decided I'd wait five minutes that Friday after Nati left, and that as the weeks and months passed I would increase the time I resisted acting on my compulsions from five minutes to an hour. This process, Dr. Hollander explained, might actually begin to correct the biochemical processes in my brain. Psychiatric researchers have only recently discovered that behavior therapy seems to have much the same effect on the brain as OCD medications: through therapy, the different brain regions that are hyperactive and "locked" together in OCD patients (the orbital frontal cortex, the basal ganglia, and the thalamus) become less hyperactive and less "locked." Dr. Hollander told me, unable to conceal his excitement, that this is one of the most exciting discoveries ever made in psychiatry.

It is well known that therapy can change patients' moods, understandings, views of life, and behavior without the help of medication. For a long time psychiatrists have suspected it can change patients' brains as well, but they've never been able to prove it. Using imaging devices that provide pictures of brain activity, it has recently become possible to see how the hyperactive, locked regions of the brain become normal during treatment with behavior therapy. It's the first (and only) evidence of therapy resulting in a specific change in the brain.

Dr. Hollander asked if I was going to be in New York any time soon.

"I can be."

"Why don't you come in and we'll talk some more?"

When I told Alice that my first OCD treatment was to wait five minutes after the cleaning woman had left before I started straightening on Friday afternoon, she smiled.

"I'll believe it when I see it," she said.

I saw she was teasing me. "Oh, ye of little faith!" I said.

"I know you can do it, Marc. You can do anything when you put your mind to it."

That Friday at 3:30, after our front door clicked shut behind Nati, I stood in our kitchen, eyes closed, hands clenched. I felt the insidious anxiety gripping my belly and chest. I was short of breath. I checked and rechecked my watch, pacing through the house, trying to keep my eyes away from couch pillows that were slightly off-kilter, the dining room curtains that didn't hang quite right.

I made it through the five minutes—barely. As soon as my allotted time was up, I began frantically straightening and rearranging. The waiting had been torture, but I felt stronger afterward, as though whatever it was that had a stranglehold on my psyche had loosened its grip somewhat.

A week later, I flew to New York to see Dr. Hollander. I stayed at the RIHGA Royal, my hotel of choice at the time. It was a great place to run into people in the industry. There tend to be hot hotels for celebrities in New York that change every four or five years, and in my business, every chance encounter can lead to work. In television, you must constantly position yourself to run into people, to be seen—until you reach a certain level, that is. Stars, at that level, crave anonymity.

I didn't choose hotels only because there were celebrities in the lobby. I also factored in my need for cleanliness. The RIHGA was a new hotel, and the staff kept the place spotless. I have a terrible time in hotels. I never walk barefoot anywhere but in my own house. I carry a pair of flip-flops to use in the shower when I travel, and I have a highly evolved system for showering and getting dressed so that my bare feet never touch the floor. I take off all my clothes, except my socks, while sitting on the bed. One at a time, I slip my feet into my flip-flops. I lay clean socks on the bed—only on the sheets, of course; *never* on the bedspread. (Who knows *what's* been on the bedspread?) Then I get in the shower. I have a phobia about the shower curtain, which can't be completely closed when I'm behind it (I don't know if it's claustrophobia or the sense that the curtain is dirty). This means that water inevitably sprays on the floor, so I put down plenty of towels beforehand. I wash my feet one at a time, slipping first one and then the other out of its flip-flop. I can't let any part of my body touch the shower curtain or the bathroom wall, so I stand, balanced precariously, on one leg like a flamingo.

The night before my meeting with Dr. Hollander I felt my life was about to change. I was still struggling to accept that my need for help was not an admission of defeat or a sign of weakness, but actually an indication of strength, growth, maturity. We're conditioned in this culture, especially as men, to think we have carry our load alone. We think that if we can't handle it on our own there's something wrong with us, something lacking.

Not only am I an OCD sufferer and a man to boot, I also have a type A personality. I like being in charge. I prefer not only to host but also to be involved with writing and producing my shows whenever possible. My need for control was so intense that I needed to go into hypnotherapy in 1987 to cope with my fear of flying. When in an airplane I was terrified because my life was in the pilot's hands, which meant that I had no control. Sometimes when we hit turbulence I would even start to cry. In 1986, being the host of *Double Dare* meant that I was suddenly airborne several times a month, since we shot the show at a variety of locations. It was unbearable. I knew I needed help, and I finally confessed my fear of flying to my doctor. He said hypnosis would help.

"You can't hypnotize me," I said. I thought I was too much in control of myself.

"Oh yes, I can!"

He was right. I lay down on his examination table, and he turned down the lights. He started talking in a soft, soothing voice, and in no time at all I was deep in a trance.

Dr. Hollander has since told me that one of the reasons he thought I'd make a good candidate for behavior therapy was the success I'd had with hypnotherapy. It indicated that I could follow directions and was motivated to change. He said hypnosis had been tried on people with OCD, but it had been largely ineffectual: less than 15 percent of patients showed signs of improvement.

Hypnotherapy helped my fear of flying, but I must admit I'm still queasy on planes. It takes a long time for guys like me to realize that we don't have all the answers, that we need help, that we can't control life. That night in my hotel room I lay awake wondering if I was surrendering a core part of myself by ceding control of my psyche to someone else. I didn't suspect that by sharing my fears, instead of insisting that I had all the answers and was completely self-sufficient and independent, I was about to take charge of my life for the first time.

The next morning I walked from midtown Manhattan up Fifth Avenue. It was a breezy spring morning. White clouds raced low and fast over the glittering tops of buildings. Kids skipped down the steps to the Central Park Zoo. Nannies pushed baby carriages, and elderly women leaned on walkers, guided by nurses in starched uniforms. I passed the Metropolitan Museum of Art and the Guggenheim, finally coming to 98th Street and Mt. Sinai Hospital, where Dr. Hollander has his office.

I took a seat in a small waiting room and nervously flipped through a magazine. Dr. Hollander soon appeared. We shook hands, and he led me into his office, a large room with a view out over Central Park.

I smiled to myself at the clutter of the office, so unlike my own with its pristine surfaces. There were tons of books strewn all over the floor, shelves, and desks. I noted several that Dr. Hollander himself had written on OCD. It looked like a professor's office, not in the least pretentious. Dr. Hollander was dressed in one of what I came to recognize as his typical off-the-rack rumpled suits. His manner was warm, and I was again struck by his youth.

I reported my attempt to resist my compulsion to clean that previous Friday.

"You might be able to get better on behavior therapy alone," he told me, "but I recommend you try medication."

I hedged. "I don't want to rely on pills for the rest of my life."

"It's your decision."

There was a long pause. "As much as I hate pills, I hate more how I've been feeling," I finally said.

When I left Dr. Hollander that day I felt great; all the discomfort and anxiety had been drained from me. I marched, prescription in hand, to a pharmacy on Madison Avenue. I strolled around the Upper East Side while the prescription was being filled. The pills might make me better, but I still resisted the thought that I might have to rely on them.

After an hour wandering the streets, I reentered the pharmacy and emerged with my vial of Luvox.

Fluvoxamine (Luvox) is one of several medications approved by the Food and Drug Administration for treating OCD and was first approved to treat children and adolescents. Luvox is the drug that worked for me; other, equally effective drugs used to treat OCD include clomipramine (Anafranil), fluoxetine (Prozac), paroxetine (Paxil), and sertraline (Zoloft). There are also several other promising drugs awaiting FDA approval. In his office, Dr. Hollander had explained how the medications work. You'll remember that neurons release serotonin, among other neurotransmitters, which carry impulses across synapses. OCD drugs are known as serotonin reuptake inhibitors because they block, or inhibit, the "reuptake pumps" whose job it is to collect serotonin from the synapse and bring it back to the neuron that released it.

Blocking these reuptake pumps allows the serotonin levels in the brain of an OCD patient to rise, which, after a number of weeks, changes the sensitivity of serotonin receptors. This restores balance to the serotonin system and normalizes the hyperactive and locked regions of the brain that had me on a continual feel-anxious, must-straighten-fringe loop. Almost all of these drugs affect only serotonin and no other neurotransmitters, and they are therefore known as *selective* serotonin reuptake inhibitors. All five OCD drugs are also effective in treating depression, which Dr. Hollander pointed out was often useful, since so many OCD sufferers also suffer from depression. Some people respond better to some medications than others, and side effects vary from person to person. It can take three months before a medication shows its full effect, and it often takes trial and error to find the right medication. But I was lucky: Dr. Hollander's first choice was right for me.

I figured I'd go on meds for a few weeks, get cured, and get off them again. I flew back to L.A. and resumed my life: looking for work and straightening fringe. I checked in with Dr. Hollander once a week. I made progress with behavior therapy, which wasn't as difficult as I thought it would be. The Friday after my visit to New York I extended the time I waited to start straightening up after the cleaning woman left to 10 minutes. The week after, I waited 15 minutes. I was taking baby steps, but at least I saw progress. Other sufferers of OCD have a harder time of it. They find that behavior therapy initially increases their anxiety level, and so they stop the therapy before it has a chance to work. Behavior therapy is not instantaneous and it takes effort.

My resistance to behavior therapy came when Dr. Hollander asked me to wait 40 minutes before straightening. Half an hour had been manageable, but waiting any longer than that, for some mysterious reason, sent me into a panic. The sight of the mussed fringe of the dining room rug made me nervous. I tried to watch television to distract myself. But I couldn't sit still. Dr. Hollander suggested that if I began to cave in to my compulsions I should leave the house, get in the car, and drive away. But that would have been an admission of defeat. Just as I always have to win when I play Monopoly with my children, I was damned if I would "lose" to my OCD. My perfectionism extended to behavior therapy. I had to be the best patient possible. So I stayed and suffered. Hollander told me that he has treated other OCD patients who are hypervigilant, obsessed with how well they respond to treatment.

For most OCD sufferers, family participation is necessary for successful treatment. The OC Foundation believes optimal treatment includes medication, behavior therapy, family education, and the right kind of family support. On the one hand, it's common for families to get sucked into OCD rituals because they want to ease the anxiety of their loved one. Parents of kids with contamination OCD often do their children's laundry repeatedly, performing their children's rituals for them. On the other hand, there are families who become enraged at the obsessive compulsive sufferer's strange behavior. They scream at him or her: "Just stop it!" They blame the person with OCD for his or her behavior.

Neither approach is productive, and the pattern my family fell into wasn't, either. Although they didn't actively participate in my straightening and ordering compulsions, Alice and the kids did cater to my idiosyncrasies. Because I didn't like having people in the house, we had very few guests, and my OCD made my family neater than they otherwise would have been and even somewhat uncomfortable in their own home. My disorder curtailed all our freedom.

In the beginning of my treatment, the producers of *Dateline NBC* asked if they could come into my house and film my obsessive compulsive life. I was making progress with behavior therapy, but my medication hadn't kicked in yet, and I felt far too embarrassed about my compulsions to let cameras in the house to film me. After Nati left, although I was up to a full hour before straightening, I still, inevitably, ended up down on my hands and knees, running my fingers through that carpet fringe.

The *Dateline* appearance had been suggested by Ketchum Communications, a public relations firm hired as part of the OC Foundation's campaign to promote public awareness of the disorder. *Dateline* had already done a piece on a woman with OCD who was much more severely afflicted than I was. She had strong contamination fears. She didn't like dirt, and I remember that *Dateline* shot her walking barefoot through dirt. It made me wince.

Dateline wanted to revisit the disorder. The producers liked the fact that I was a celebrity and I had a tie-in with *Double Dare*. "Neatness freak slimed for a living" made a good lead for a story that would focus on what we hoped would be my successful treatment.

I was nervous about doing national publicity on OCD. When I agreed to work on behalf of the Foundation, I never thought I'd be doing national shows like *Dateline* or *Oprah*. I pictured myself doing radio spots for a local station in Des Moines, not opening my house to national TV. I told the *Dateline* producers to give me a few more months, and we scheduled filming for that fall. (After the *Dateline* piece, some people actually asked me if I did it for notoriety, to increase my visibility. People in this business are relentlessly cynical. The truth is that I never thought that way.)

Dr. Hollander suggested that I go to group therapy sessions at a behavior therapy clinic for OCD sufferers organized by the neuropsychiatric division of the UCLA Medical Center. He thought that being around people who were successfully treating their OCD through behavior therapy might inspire me. I thought I'd give the clinic a shot, even though I had the same resistance to group therapy that I'd had when I sought Dr. Hollander's help in the first place and went on medication: it was hard admitting to myself I still wasn't in full control, that OCD still had a grip on me.

This admission was especially tormenting with the *Dateline* piece fast approaching, because I couldn't imagine being less than completely cured on television. But I was committed to the treatment process. I was determined to do whatever it took to get better.

The group was run by Courtney Jacobs, a psychiatrist in her thirties with a professional New York manner. Her office was a couple of blocks from UCLA's Westwood campus. The members of my group of OCD patients would gather in the waiting room while Jacobs finished up with a private patient. We would sit there, with only our OCD in common, not saying a word. It was creepy. Four to seven people came to each weekly Thursday night session. The members of my group were a shy, eccentric bunch. Most had trouble talking about the disorder, but I had no trouble at all. Once I was finally diagnosed and began to receive treatment, I never hesitated to discuss the disorder or my symptoms. After all those years of internal suffering, I was through with keeping secrets.

A 17-year-old kid who reminded me of my son Matt drove from San Diego every week to attend the group session. He barely said a word. I thought of myself at 17, how much more outgoing I was than this poor kid who sat staring at the floor and didn't seem able to tell us about his symptoms.

A Hispanic man in the group had severe contamination fears, which was particularly unfortunate because he made his living as a phlebotomist. His job was to draw blood from people. Although he wore gloves, he was convinced that he was exposing himself to viruses. I told him he should look for another job. But he said he wanted to work in the medical field and someday hoped to become a doctor. It was heartbreaking.

One young woman in the group was a writer. She was very open, even flamboyant, about her disorder. She was a hoarder, and her apartment was filled to the brim with junk. She loved to talk about how many medications she was taking and how many different doctors were looking after her case. She went on and on about it. One session I asked her, "Are your doctors talking to each other? Do they know what medications the other ones are prescribing for you?" She said they did, but I didn't believe her.

The sessions involved going around the room, each of us

telling the group what kind of week we'd had and how our behavior therapy had gone. This was the first time that I'd seen, up
close and personal, the spectrum of people with the disorder. I
saw how broad it was, and how the severity of symptoms varied
from one person to another. I felt lucky that my own symptoms
were relatively mild and not as disabling as those of some of the
other people in the group.

Very soon, the sessions became painful for me. I would sit
there during the frequent tortured periods of silence and think,
"Why am I here?" Someone, usually the flamboyant girl, would
pierce the silence with a lament of how hard it was to have OCD,
and I would think, "Why are *any* of you here? You don't even
want to talk about ways to get better!" Maybe they just hadn't gotten to that stage yet, but I felt unforgiving; my mission was to go
in, get better, and get out.

By the third meeting, I was exasperated. I felt the others were
just coming to therapy to feel sorry for themselves.

"You guys don't want to get better," I told them. "You just
want to complain." There was a silence in the room. "You can
take control of this, but if you don't want to get better, you won't."

No one said a word. That was the last time I went to group
therapy. I talked to Dr. Hollander about the decision to stop going. He said he had hoped I'd find positive role models at UCLA:
people combating the illness successfully. But, given the situation of silence and stasis in the group, we agreed it was probably
a waste of time.

One positive experience did come from my visits to the clinic
at UCLA. The group leader, Courtney Jacobs, worked on an OCD
children's ward at the UCLA Medical Center. She told the par-

ents I was in her behavior therapy group, and the parents invited me to speak to their kids. I became friends with a boy named Trent who had been hospitalized for a month because his obsessive thoughts had him convinced that his family was contaminated. Of course, he knew they weren't, but his OCD was so overwhelming that he couldn't function at home. He wouldn't let his family near him. If they touched his jacket, he'd have to throw it out. If they touched his sneakers, he had to get new sneakers. He was a fabulous kid who was fighting his symptoms valiantly and who desperately wanted to get better.

I recently talked to Trent's parents, who told me that he is now in his own apartment, working and living with roommates. He's talking about getting ready to go to college. Life is going well.

During the time I was going to the clinic, Dr. Hollander had me on 50 milligrams of Luvox a day. I didn't notice any improvement, and I gained five pounds in the first month of treatment. Extremely concerned, I called Dr. Hollander. I photograph heavy on television anyway, and I was afraid additional weight would hurt my career. But I started to carefully watch what I ate, and the weight gain stopped. Medications for OCD are miracle workers, but, like all medications, they have side effects. This is why you'll frequently see people going on and off them. It's a balancing act—the dosage against the side effects, and how much you want to get better against how the medication makes you feel.

I was frustrated when I noticed nothing but extra pounds after my initial Luvox regimen. There was no change in my desire to straighten and control. So Dr. Hollander recommended I break a pill in half and try 75 milligrams daily. That's when I started to notice a difference. Suddenly, I didn't have the need to straighten as much. It was the strangest feeling. For my whole life I had felt the need to clean. But now, after Nati left, I didn't need to get down on my hands and knees to straighten fringe. I felt jubilant. But I also wondered if there was something wrong with me. I'd trained myself to think that compulsive straightening was a healthy, normal activity. It was the rest of the slobbish world that was demented.

In the early phases of treatment, before the medication had kicked in, *Dateline* had been to my house to film my Friday afternoon post-Nati cleaning binges. They filmed me moving through the house with manic energy, rearranging dishes in the dishwasher, tilting mirrors until they were perfectly level, and, of course, straightening the fringe on the dining room rug.

"The fringe drives me the most crazy," I told them.

I straightened for 57 minutes, with TV cameras following my every move.

"57 minutes," Alice scoffed later. "That's nothing, Marc. You used to go on for almost two hours."

Later *Dateline* filmed me and Sara James, the reporter covering the story, watching footage of my straightening binge that Friday afternoon. Watching myself I felt deeply ashamed. I saw just how sick I was. How driven. I looked away from the screen as I saw myself entering Meredith's room, an adolescent girl's haven, and asking her if I could tidy up.

When Sara James asked how I felt watching this footage, I nearly broke down.

"It upsets me," I choked out. "It doesn't make me happy."

Even now I wince to think of it.

Altogether the NBC crew must have filmed 8 or 9 hours of

Marc Summers battling OCD, most of it in my house. I would hate to have been the one to edit all that. The crew was sensitive to my family's needs, conscious of being in our space. They were nervous, too; careful never to let their cameras hit the walls. If they had, and a single black scuff mark had appeared, they knew I would have to haul out paint and brush and get rid of that spot.

I'm still amazed that I let people into my house to film such a private part of my life. It has helped people, though: colleges and high schools all over the country use the *Dateline* piece to teach about OCD. I'm not saying it was easy for me. In the middle of filming, I had second thoughts.

"I'm not sure this is a good idea." I said to the producer, Fred Rothenberg.

"This is very good thing," he countered. "You're helping a lot of people."

Of course, he had to say that to me: he couldn't afford to lose me mid-way into the filming. But his words were genuine. I wanted to follow through. The thought that I was helping people continued to motivate me.

Dateline wanted to shoot me in a session with Dr. Hollander, to give viewers some background on our relationship. We flew to New York so they could shoot an hour-long session of the two of us talking in his office, of which only moments appeared in the final cut. That's television for you.

Spring turned into summer, and I still hadn't found work. But things were looking up. One of my best friends, Mark Maxwell-Smith, had developed a new game show, *Majority Rules,* and sold it to Dreamworks SKG, the charismatic start-up company founded by Steven Spielberg, Jeffrey Katzenberg, and David Geffen.

The idea of the show was to poll 99 audience members on questions that ranged from who had the worst hair on television to whether Martin Luther King's birthday should be a public holiday. If you voted with the majority you got to enter the next round. The polling eliminated contestants until two came onstage for an opportunity to win $5,000.

Mark, a fellow magician, was one of the first people I had met in L.A. We'd worked together writing *Truth or Consequences* in 1974. He had since become a prolific producer of daytime television and had been extremely helpful to my career, always believing in my talent and helping me find work. Mark was involved with the *Majority Rules* hiring process, but it was Katzenberg and a tight circle of people around him who made the decisions.

Dreamworks had auditioned literally scores of people, looking for a host. At first they didn't think I was famous enough to audition for them, but Mark got them to take a look at me. After my long dry period without work, I was under a lot of pressure. I was a veteran. I'd been around the block; I was in my mid-forties, and I needed this show. Driving to the NBC studios in Burbank I wondered if I would be perceived as a has-been. When *Double Dare* became a hit, the show generated lots of attention. I was asked to host programs like *Couch Potatoes* without even an audition. The same was true when I hosted the twentieth anniversary show for *NOVA* on PBS. But now I was back in the position of proving myself all over again.

Mark had been feeding me information for months, keeping me abreast of the show's development. Dreamworks had gone down a list of literally 100 people, looking for the right host. Each time they rejected a prospect, Mark said to them, "Why don't you try Marc Summers? Let me bring him in." But they wanted a star, someone with big-name recognition. After months of rejects, they finally said, okay, let's take a look at Summers.

I wasn't nervous on the way to the audition because I didn't think I had a shot. This was a good thing because I kept telling myself that if I was nervous I was going to screw up. I knew there would be a live audience at the audition, which, in fact, would be a run-through of an actual show. I'm just going to keep doing what I do, I thought. I'm a touchy-feely kind of host. I throw my arm around contestants' shoulders; I ask about their families.

The audition went extremely well. I felt completely comfortable on the stage, totally in control. I got in a few good lines, and the rapport between me and the audience was strong. I knew I was right for the show.

Mark was upbeat. He said the inner circle was due to meet a couple of days after the audition to make a decision. He'd let me know what the outcome was.

But when the inner circle met they couldn't come to a consensus. Katzenberg said the show was called *Majority Rules,* so they should take a vote, and whoever won would be host.

I won the vote. I had a job, a plum job. Except that they wanted to hire me and start taping shows even as they continued to look for another more famous host who would then take over. But Mark refused to let them bring me on the show under those conditions.

"I told those guys that even if you had not been a friend, I would never have set you up in that way," Mark said to me, recounting his battles with Katzenberg and Co. "There was silence after I said this. Then the same guy who said we should keep looking for someone else while you hosted the show said 'Okay. The job is his to lose.'" Meaning that I had the job until I screwed up or proved I couldn't handle it.

It often strikes people outside the industry as odd that a company as classy as Dreamworks wanted to produce game shows. But there's a ton of money to be made in the games. If you hit it big with a *Wheel of Fortune* or a *Jeopardy*, it's like you're printing money. The shows don't cost anything to produce: one set, a host's salary, and that's it. The costs are fixed. If your ratings are good, you drown in money. That's why Dreamworks was involved.

I ended up co-hosting the show with Arthel Neville, zydeco musician Arthur Neville's daughter. The pay was great. I never saw Spielberg, but Katzenberg was involved in everything. He was a total perfectionist . . . something I could really relate to!

We ran the show in two test markets: New Orleans and Phoenix. It came in first in its ratings in New Orleans and third in Phoenix, but when we shopped it around for syndication, no one picked it up. Dreamworks promptly canceled the show, took a two million dollar bath, and I was out on the street again, looking for work.

I was shaken, but a different man from the one I'd been a year ago who'd had no confidence after losing a job and ended up compulsively straightening fringe at 1:30 in the morning. I felt relaxed. My whole demeanor was different. By the winter of 1998 when the show was canceled, I was so relaxed that I was worried my television persona would be affected. I thought viewers might see a Marc Summers with diminished energy. My producers had to keep reassuring me that I was the same man on camera I had always been. But internally I felt completely different.

The change hadn't come all at once. Through the late summer and fall, my compulsions to straighten, to read signs over and over, and to make endless lists in my head would still show themselves from time to time. And I felt a chronic recurrence of anxiety. When Dr. Hollander upped my dosage to 100 milligrams, the effect was incredible. The desire to arrange and rearrange disappeared. The desire to have everything in its place just vanished. The anxious hum that had buzzed in the back of my brain all my life was suddenly silent. That silence felt to me like a miracle.

It was at this point that *Dateline* met me with cameras rolling at the door of my home and filmed me as I walked inside. They had set up all their equipment in my living room, a room which was *never* used. That room, like all the living rooms in all the houses I had ever lived in, was a museum piece, perfect, immaculate. When we had company over, we sat in the den because the living room was out of bounds. But *Dateline* had rearranged all the furniture, set up cameras, monitors, lights, run cables and wires everywhere, and generally made a mess. They had turned my pristine environment into seething chaos.

This was the acid test. Sara James and her crew watched closely to see if I'd buckle. But I was actually able to sit down in my invaded sanctum as the cameras rolled. I won't say it didn't bother me, that I didn't have the urge to rip the place apart and put it back together to my liking, but the urge was distant, not pressing; a faint, inconsequential echo of its former self.

I felt good. It was a nice closure to my treatment process. I knew the crew so well that I ordered in sandwiches for everyone. We all sat around laughing about how afraid they'd been to eat in my home at the beginning, for fear of spilling anything; how they'd been afraid to sit down, practically afraid to breathe. Now as crumbs and chips littered the carpet, I barely noticed.

| *ten* |

waging war and winning

[Until OCD] no other disorder in the history of medicine
has ever experienced such explosive growth in scientific
understanding that has led to such a revolution in how it
has been viewed: from regarded as rare to recognized as
common; from presumed psychological to proven neuro-
biological; from written off as hopeless to accepted as one
of the most responsive of all mental disorders.

—Ian Osborn, M.D.,
Tormenting Thoughts and Secret Rituals

When *Majority Rules* went off the air, I found myself pounding
the pavement again, looking for work. That doesn't mean quite
the same thing in L.A. as it does in New York City. In L.A., no
one walks anywhere, least of all to work. So, for me, "pounding
the pavement" meant cruising around to meetings and lunches in
my SUV, a Toyota 4Runner, in air-conditioned comfort, cell
phone at my side.

I had my confidence back. I had been working at Dreamworks, which had cachet, an aura of power and class. When the
company's founders, Spielberg, Katzenberg, and Geffen, had first
started out, the industry thought they were invincible; that everything they touched would turn to gold. Hollywood is a strange
town: there was some glee and not-so-discreet snickering when
Dreamworks' syndicated television division, which had developed *Majority Rules,* went belly-up. Nonetheless, even early on,
when some of Dreamworks' projects were floundering, the magic
and charisma attached to its principals' names counted for a lot
in a town where image is everything.

During this period, I acted as a spokesperson for people with
obsessive compulsive disorder, making appearances across the
country. I was also working for the Game Show Network, spear-
heading the Network's Coast to Coast Search for a Host. It was a
marketing project designed to boost the Network's visibility. I'd
arrive with a Network PR person in a city like Cincinnati, Cleve-
land, or Minneapolis and work the press, giving prearranged in-
terviews for local radio and television stations, spreading the
word that Marc Summers had come to town looking for the next
Bob Barker or Pat Sajak.

The following day we would build a mini-set for a television
game show in a shopping center or a nightclub. The would-be
Barkers and Sajaks came to audition. Some had some broadcasting experience, but most had never been in front of a camera.
They were librarians, schoolteachers, accountants, truck drivers.
I was the master of ceremonies as we ran them through a mock
game show in front of a live audience. Sometimes the performances would be surprisingly good. But, more often, our would-

be hosts would sweat and stammer through the run-throughs. A group of people from the Game Show Network flew in and acted as judges along with local celebrities. The winners of the local auditions competed against each other for the prize of hosting a nationally televised game show for a week.

The job was fun: I felt like Ed McMahon, fronting a company. As always, going on radio and television fulfilled my craving to perform, to be on the air. And the money was good. But I wasn't doing a television show, which was where I really wanted to be. At other times in my life, the stress from not having a show of my own might have sent me into an OCD tailspin. But the medication and behavior therapy were working well, and for the first time in my life, I was free of rituals and anxious thoughts. The distress I felt about not having a show didn't have the same gnawing quality that it had had in the past. It didn't lead to repetitive circular thoughts, my mind going round and round like a rat in its cage running on a wheel for hours on end.

I was going to auditions, meeting people, working to develop ideas for shows. But it was touch and go. Nothing jelled. Then, in August, I auditioned to host *Hollywood Squares*. Sean Perry was heading the show. I didn't want to do another game show, but *Hollywood Squares* was a plum, a classic which, in its heyday in the late 1960s, had been about entertainment, not prizes. Those were the days when Charlie Weaver, Wally Cox, and Paul Lynde sat in the Squares. Lynde sat in the center, and he drew in viewers. He was quick, sharp, perpetually dissatisfied, nasal, almost sneering, and his outrageous sense of humor let him get away with some very politically incorrect answers. Once he was asked the question, "Paul, you walk into your house. The walls are brown, the ceiling is brown, the floors are brown. What happened?"

"The maid exploded," he answered.

Back then, game shows still had importance. Anyone who was big on television played *Hollywood Squares,* and the show also drew film stars like Henry Fonda and Glenn Ford.

Hollywood Squares, like the other classic game shows—*Family Feud, Wheel of Fortune*—is a perennial. It went off the air only to be recast and resurrected. When King World, the biggest, most powerful syndication company in the business, decided to bring *Squares* back, there was a lot of buzz around the show. It was an opportunity for a host to have a high degree of visibility. That's why my agent, Babette, was excited when she called me during our family's vacation in Hawaii.

"Perry wants you to audition for *Squares,*" she said. "Tomorrow."

I was feeling really good at this point. On family vacations in the past I would have been on the phone half the time, wheeling and dealing, taking care of business. My family understood that this was who I was, and that my efforts made it possible for us to have a comfortable life. But on this vacation, I checked my voice mail only once a day, and I only made a couple of calls a day, just to take care of urgent business. Given the new me, you can imagine how torn I felt when Babette called.

"Fly home," she said.

I thought about it for a moment. Even a year earlier, I would have jumped on the first plane back to L.A.

"If they want me bad enough, they can wait," I told Babette. "I'll be home in a couple of days."

"If that's what you want to do," she said. "But I can't guarantee anything. You may be cut out of the auditions."

"Screw it," I said. "I'll take the chance."

For once, I felt unwilling to part with my family and put work first.

As it turned out, I wasn't cut out of the audition, and I showed up at the appointed time, rested and tanned. It took place in a little office building on Cahuenga Boulevard, near the NBC studios in Burbank. It was the first of three auditions, all of which went well. I was dealing from a position of strength: I wasn't going to run when they whistled. My attitude was that if I got the show, I got it; if not, fine.

I was hired in October. I got a nice fat chunk of money on signing, and then additional funds for *not* working, since shows for syndication are cast a year ahead of the time they're due to air. Rehearsals for the show weren't due to start until the following summer. *Hollywood Squares* didn't want me taking another job in the interim, so they paid me not to work. I still did my OCD speaking engagements, but, basically, I was hanging out. And I felt relaxed! I wasn't running around every minute of every day, and I still felt calm. I spent time with my family. Saw friends. Enjoyed life. Looked forward to the summer when I'd start working again.

Then I was fired from *Squares* in March of 1998, even before they had taped any shows. A new management team had come in and cleaned house. Out with the old and in with the new. Welcome, once again, to show business! By this point I knew that I would never feel secure in the entertainment industry. Never.

The reality of show business is that even though you have a

contract, it doesn't mean anything. Contracts are never in favor of
the talent; they're always in favor of the network or the producers.
It's a scary business: yes doesn't necessarily mean yes, as I
learned my first week in L.A., when I was promised a job that was
snatched from me hours later by the very guy who had given me
the lead.

After I was released from *Squares* in March of 1998, my work
with Porter Novelli, a PR firm that coordinates my speaking appearances at OCD conferences with groups such as the OC Foundation, the National Mental Health Association, Freedom from
Fear, and others, became increasingly important to me. On the
day preceding a conference I would do radio and TV spots, explaining OCD and its common symptoms. "Come attend a free
seminar tonight. Talk to experts in the field," I'd say on the air. I
was always amazed at the turnout: we'd fill ballrooms.

I would speak for 30 minutes, capsulizing my life story. After
I was done, medical experts would discuss childhood OCD, the
serotonin system, why the disorder occurs, and some of the treatments available. Then we'd open the discussion to questions. I'd
go down into the audience with a microphone, keeping the show
rolling. It kept me sharp with my career skills: working any big
audience is a lot like hosting a television show. The OC Foundation organized events like these in six cities last year. This year
we'll do eight.

But it's hard to get up and tell my story over and over and over
again at Foundation meetings. It gets harder and harder. I feel
played-out sometimes, like I'm repeating myself; I want to move
on. It's difficult to talk about my symptoms, to keep the disorder

in the forefront of my life. I often just don't want to deal with it. I want it to go away. But keeping it in my face has been as important in my war against OCD as medication or behavior therapy. It renews my vow not to fall back into my old OCD behaviors. By leading conversations about the disorder every four to six weeks, I stay on track. I tell people about what I've been through, and in doing so I'm also reminding myself that you can get better, but you have to *want* to get better.

Very few people are ever fully "cured" of OCD. I expect a continuous battle to keep my symptoms at bay for the rest of my life. It's a day-to-day war, and most days I'm winning. I like to say that I'm 80 percent cured. When I'm feeling good and fully employed, OCD is number 17 on my list of things I have to worry about. But occasionally, when I don't have enough going on, when I'm not busy and occupied with my career and family, things get hairy.

Even after undergoing intensive therapy, relapses are common for OCD sufferers. A relapse happens when you're on the path to success; after taking three steps forward, you suddenly find you've been kicked two steps back. When I was speaking in New York recently, I met a woman suffering from OCD who worked in a hardware store in Fort Wayne, Indiana. One of her jobs was to mix paint. She had paint on her hands all the time. You can imagine how she felt: her job was pure torture for her. When she went on medication, her symptoms disappeared, but she wanted to get off medication quickly. As soon as she did, her symptoms came back in full force.

My own relapse came last summer, when, without warning,

my symptoms came rushing back. My mother-in-law had just died. Matthew left for his first year of college, and I knew that even when he came back for weekends and vacations, things wouldn't be the same. A part of my life seemed to have died with my mother-in-law (we had been very close), and another part of me died when Matthew left. I wasn't prepared to lose him, even if it was the normal separation that occurs when children become adults. To top it off we had just moved into a new house in Calabasas. The upkeep on the 6,000-square-foot palace had been enormous, and, with Matthew gone and Meredith never home, it seemed ridiculous to have so much space.

Several months before the move, I had taken myself off medication without consulting Dr. Hollander. One day I just went cold turkey. I felt I had the disorder licked, and I suppose I was like many other people when I decided to go off medication. I didn't like the thought of being dependent on a pill. I wanted to feel that my body was functioning naturally. Subconsciously, perhaps, I thought that as long as I was medicated I officially *had* OCD: by stopping the medication I would be cured.

Unfortunately, I soon learned the fallacy of this magical thinking. For a while everything was fine. I felt I had the disorder under control. I was not as stressed, rushed, or pressured as I had been in the past without medication. When I started to obsess on cleaning, organizing, and my various rituals, I was able to just walk away, to leave the dirty dishes in the sink, the fringe of the dining room rug messed up, the pillows asymmetrical on the couch. I was damned proud of myself.

I didn't know it at the time, but going off medication abruptly, as I did, is a dangerous maneuver. You're supposed to wean yourself off the medication under careful supervision. You need to pick the right time, when your life is stable. Going off medication suddenly can lead to what's called SSRI discontinuation syndrome. This syndrome can produce vivid dreams or nightmares, depression, an increase in anxiety, and flu-like symptoms. Fortunately, even though I stupidly went cold turkey, I didn't experience the syndrome, perhaps because I had been on a relatively low dose of medication.

But going off medication also sometimes leads to an immediate relapse of OCD symptoms, and this is what happened to me. It's hard to know how an OCD sufferer will react without meds: in general, the more gradually you taper off the medication, the more work you've put into behavior therapy, and the less stressful your life is at the time you quit, the better you'll do.

Even though I had worked hard on my behavior therapy, I was not immune to a relapse. During the move to our new house, our whole life was in boxes and in storage. There is something about living out of boxes that sets my teeth on edge. I was overwhelmed: it would be months before we had everything in its place. Everything was in disarray. I despaired; it had taken five years to get our last house "in shape."

In the midst of this, I started to obsess on the death of my mother-in-law, Matica. When I first started dating Alice, I was a skinny kid. Every time I'd go to the house to pick up Alice, Matica would have a big steak ready for me. She couldn't feed me enough. She doted on me, the exact opposite of Alice's father, Alberto, who once chased me around the house, shouting that I was not good enough for his only daughter.

After we were married, Matica made sure Alice and I had

enough money to live on. She gave us money to landscape the first house we bought—a loan which she never let us repay. Later in her life, after Alberto died, Alice and I looked after her.

I gave the eulogy, my first, at Matica's funeral. I talked about how she had survived the concentration camps of Dachau and Auschwitz. How she had sent me special care packages of Kudalakia, a biscuit-like cookie, when I was living in New York City. How she was the sweetest, most incredible person.

Months later, as painters, plumbers, and carpenters ripped our new house apart, I found myself repeating the eulogy I had delivered over and over again in my mind. It looped through my consciousness. It was clearly an intrusive, obsessive thought, but I didn't identify it as such. I thought I was mourning a wonderful woman whom I had loved.

It didn't occur to me that my OCD might be coming back until one night, nearly dead from moving-induced exhaustion, I decided to cease and desist carrying boxes from the car into the house. I felt slightly uneasy: I couldn't put the car in the garage, which was full of unpacked boxes. In the best of circumstances, I don't like to leave our cars in the driveway; at night, cars belong in the garage. A nice clean driveway makes me feel good. But on this particular night I realized my uneasiness was amplified, although I wasn't sure why. I activated the Toyota's car alarm and went into the house, intending to go straight upstairs to bed.

As soon as I entered the house, though, I felt the old familiar gnawing anxiety. I rushed back outside and checked that the car was actually locked, which, of course, it was. When I reentered the house, the same anxiety came back in full force. That night I went out and checked and rechecked the locks on the car five or six times.

Why am I doing this? I wondered. Calabasas is not the South Bronx. It's a gated community, tightly patrolled by a security force, and crime is nearly nonexistent. My car was in the driveway: even if I'd put out a giant neon sign with big arrows pointing at it that said "Come steal this stuff!" no one would have touched it.

At first, I tried to deny that this was the beginning of a relapse. It was like trying to convince yourself, when you have a sore throat and your body aches, that you're not getting sick. By not recognizing the symptoms for what they are, you think they will go away, but the next morning you have a fever of 102. That's what happened to me. Even as I slid into my relapse, I was up to my old tricks. I would surreptitiously straighten the mirrors, paintings, and glasses in the kitchen cabinet. But I kept it quiet, hidden from my wife and children. I found that I was angry all the time. Angry that the house was in a shambles and my mother-in-law had died and my son was off at college.

I began to lapse into my old state of mind, a state of simmering anxiety, impatience, and anger. I was back at square one, forgetting all the lessons I'd learned from a year and a half on medication and all the hard work I'd done in behavior therapy.

When I went off medication, I tried in vain to recapture the jubilation I had felt when I first went on Luvox and started therapy. Under medication, I had quickly come to feel that my constant anxieties and compulsions no longer controlled me. I'd seen another reality, another way to be. A friend of mine with OCD, a teenager I'll call Gina, describes this shift or transformation as "getting the gorilla of OCD" off her back.

Gina's symptoms were particularly bizarre. She felt overly protective of her younger sister, even felt that she actually controlled her sister's destiny. Whenever her younger sister coughed, sniffled, or sneezed, Gina had to make a specific sound, *baa!*, like a sheep, to ensure nothing bad would happen to the sister. Cough. *Baa!* Cough. *Baa!* The younger sister grew to detest that noise: it drove her into fits of rage. Yet Gina was convinced that if she didn't make the noise something terrible would befall her sister. This created ongoing battles and crazy tension in Gina's household. Imagine yourself as a parent trying to mediate this particular conflict. After Gina started on medication, she improved. The gorilla of her OCD began to loosen its grip.

Another friend of mine, whom I'll call Karen, described a similar feeling when she started treatment for her OCD. Karen is a highly successful conductor of orchestras and choruses. Like me, her OCD has probably helped her in her professional career, by giving her ambition and drive and the perfectionism necessary to be a first-rate musician.

Karen's gorilla had intense checking compulsions. It was convinced that every time she hit a bump in the road, she had run someone over. Whenever she hit a bump, she had to get out of the car and check and recheck that no one was dead on the pavement.

It was moving for me to learn that Karen had OCD, because we had been friends for years, and OCD had hurt our friendship. Before she told me she had the disorder, I hadn't known it. When Alice and I had had Karen and her husband over for dinner they'd often been late—40 minutes, an hour, even more. Well, you know how I react to lateness: I went ballistic. Finally, I asked

Alice to terminate the friendship, because I couldn't stand Karen's lack of punctuality. Then Karen saw me on *Oprah* and called immediately to tell me that she, too, suffered from OCD. That's why she had been late all those years: she couldn't drive the short distance from her house to our house without checking umpteen times whether she had killed someone. Karen has tried medication and behavior therapy for her disorder, but they haven't worked. The gorilla is still there, riding her. Now that I know she suffers from OCD, we're close again.

When I went off medication, I thought my gorilla was gone for good. And I still didn't acknowledge, in the early days of my relapse, that it had come sidling back and had taken its habitual perch, looking over my shoulder, whispering in my ear.

After my checking episode with the locks on the car doors, an incident occurred that made me recognize just how far gone I was. Meredith has a friend who I'll call Jill. She's a great kid: sweet, funny, with an open, trusting personality. Whenever she comes into the house she makes me smile.

I grew up in a house where my parents would always say, "Keep your hands off the walls!" I passed that rule down: my kids and their friends, Jill included, know about my obsession with clean walls, and they're generally careful and cooperative.

Jill came over one night soon after we moved into the house. She's a tall girl, and as she was leaving after visiting Meredith, about 10:00, she slung her daypack over her shoulder. The pack hit the wall, which was freshly painted, and left a thick black streak.

Jill left, oblivious to the horrendous black mark, and to the frustration rising inside me. As soon as she was out the door, I rushed to wash the streak out with a rag, soap, and warm water. "Out, out damn spot!" Nothing doing. There it was, plain as day. I knew what I had to do. Not a moment to lose. I went to the garage. Found the ladder. Found the paint. Found the paint brush. Stirred the paint and put two coats over the mark. Put the paint back on the shelf. Washed out the paintbrush. The whole procedure took over an hour. "Why hadn't I been able to wait at least until morning?" I thought, standing there over the sink in the laundry room, washing the last bit of white latex paint from the brush. I felt ashamed.

Fortunately, I snapped out of my relapse. Our house got back into shape, and life assumed a semblance of order. I felt much less stressed.

I've had other relapses since then, and now I can predict when they'll happen. I'll be overloaded, spread too thin, trying to satisfy everybody. That's what happens to other OCD sufferers I know: they become overwhelmed with their need to be perfect, to return every phone call, to always show up on time, to keep their homes clean. They become exhausted and strung out. I think it's important for all of us to consciously refuse to let ourselves be pulled in twenty directions at once.

New action on the work front also helped snap me out of my first relapse. An old friend, Michael Young, went out of town and asked me to fill in as host for him on *Great Day America,* an afternoon talk show on PAX TV, which is a cable network owned by Bud Paxson, the man who had created the idea of home shopping on television and made millions from it. I took to the show like a fish to water, and when Michael got back into town he asked me to take over as host. He wanted to spend time growing Alton Entertainment, the business he runs which developed *Great Day America* and a number of other shows. Michael also brought me on as Alton's vice president in charge of development.

Since we've been working together, Michael and I have had to realistically assess what's happening in the industry. It's totally different than when I got into the business in '73: the years of risk-taking are gone. It's impossible to put a show on the air just because you believe in it, and then give it time to grow. *Hill Street Blues* and *The Dick Van Dyke Show* were at the bottom of the Nielsen ratings when they were first broadcast. But the heads of the networks on which those shows were broadcast, Fred Silverman at CBS and Brandon Tartikoff at NBC, were both visionaries. When they had a gut feeling about a show they went with it. Now nobody has those kinds of gut feelings—or they're scared to act on them. The industry today is all about dollars and cents. You'd better hope you grab an audience by the throat right away or you're going to be out on the street looking for work. You're always dealing from a position of fear.

On top of this, television is now being aimed at a teen audience. When you're in your forties, like I am, and most shows are geared to fifteen-year-olds, you begin to say, "Wait a second, what am I doing?" I've done warm-ups, I've been the Great MIRAHCFU, I hosted *Double Dare* for years, I did serious news with *Our Home,* and Sissy and I did live talk from New York. You'd think that I'd be content with my success. But television is almost like a drug to me, and I'm not happy unless I'm on camera and performing. It's not something I have a choice about.

I've accepted my role as a daytime television personality. I wouldn't do a nighttime talk show. I'm just not made for it. I don't have the sarcasm, the acerbic wit, and I'm not exceptionally clever—things nighttime guys like Leno, Letterman, and Carson need. Hipper, cooler people are better at night. During the day people want me in their houses. They trust me.

Hosting *Great Day America,* I have the live, informational, news-you-can-use kind of show I do best. We lead off with a celebrity like Ed McMahon, Alan Thicke, or magician Lance Burton. Or we do informational stories on women's health or financial information women can use. I help produce the show and sometimes pick the talent.

But I still haven't attained my goal of hosting a network show that focuses on serious news. I recently came close, but, would you believe it, it was the stigma and ignorance that still surround OCD that kept me from being hired.

I can't mention the name of the show or the personalities in-volved, but, take it from me, it was a plum of a show, a network job, and I would have been perfect for it. I sent in my tapes, sev-eral of the producers loved them, and the show was ready to be-gin serious discussions about hiring me. Then a powerful executive nixed me because she knew I had OCD. She refused to work with me because she said I would have inflexible perfec-tionism. If the sound was bad, she said, I wouldn't let the seg-ment run. I'd make them do one shot over and over. It was reported to me that she said, "You can't work with those people," meaning people with OCD.

I suppose I could have sued, but that would have been the end of my career. And one thing I know about this business: people move on. When that executive is gone I'll go to the well again.

Who knows what will happen next time? "The harder you work, the luckier you get" has been my motto.

But, whatever happens, it's been a great ride. If it doesn't get any better than this, I'll die a happy man.

I've had to accept that relapses are a normal part of the disorder. Depending on what's happening in my life I become vulnerable. I've had to learn to say no to people, and to avoid scheduling so many meetings and conference calls one on top of the other. To not be constantly traveling. But even if I have to experience two or three relapses a year, I'd rather be off medication than be relapse-free. That's the life I've chosen for myself. It's an intuitive choice that feels right for me, but it may not be for you. There's nothing wrong with being on medication if that's what feels right. It's a personal decision. If it comes to the point where I feel I'm being overwhelmed by the disorder, I won't hesitate to go back on medication, and I couldn't have gotten where I am now without it. But I think I would need to experience a fairly steady parade of OCD symptoms to start taking the pills again.

I'm immensely grateful for all the medical research that has been done on OCD. Because of many doctors and scientists, I don't obsessively need to fluff the pillows on my couch. I can leave the house with the bed unmade. I can walk down Madison Avenue, see a sign, have an urge to start reading it, and say "Stop it!" to myself. At moments like these, I remember Dr. Hollander's words: "How important do you really think you are? What's your fear? Are you really afraid the plane is going to crash because you haven't read something perfectly?"

And my answer to the last question would always be: "No, I don't really think that."

I'm learning to deal with kids' backpacks banging into walls. Before I was treated for OCD, I would never worry about the child or the child's feelings, just about the wall. Now when a kid scuffs something in the house or stains a carpet I just let it happen. I figure I'll deal with it later, after the kid has gone. I'm conscious of the feelings of others. I don't want to embarrass my own children, and I don't want them or their friends to feel inhibited in my house.

People with OCD have a hard time compromising and putting the needs of others before their own needs. The disorder makes you selfish—your mission is to get rid of your intense feelings of anxiety, and you have to take immediate action. It's hard to worry about anyone who's in the way. Take my friend Karen, for example. She knew I was fuming waiting for her to arrive, but my feelings took a distant second place to her need to stop the car and make sure she hadn't run someone over. One of the greatest side benefits of waging war against OCD and winning is an awakened empathy for others. It's a wonderful feeling to be connected to the rest of humanity instead of being consumed by my own needs.

And it's been an enormous relief to understand that the success of those I love isn't bound up in my rituals. I no longer think the outcome of Meredith's audition for the school play hinges on the fluidity with which I read a sign. In fact, she just got the lead in her high school play, *Once Upon a Mattress,* without my doing one superstitious thing to help her. She doesn't need my help!

OCD has been a shadow lurking in the corners of my life. It wasn't something I enjoyed having, but in some ways it has helped me. It has had a positive side.

It's a great feeling to have faced and overcome OCD. People

who have fought back from a life-threatening illness often feel a special glory in being alive. People who conquer OCD often feel a special kind of freedom or liberation from the obsessions and compulsions that have driven them for years.

Too often we plod through our lives, figuring, "This is just the way I am, this is the way I'll always be." Well, waging war against OCD gives us a chance to step back, take stock of our lives, and make changes. If my story has encouraged one person to gather the courage to get help or feel more confident living with OCD, it will have been worth the telling.

My wife and kids have seen the change in me—that I'm better. But there are still things I'm working on. I want people to walk into our house and feel comfortable, but I'm still uptight, and it gnaws at me. I still get antsy when there are little children in the house; I think they're going to put their hands on the walls, or toddle around with a mouth full of cookies, dribbling crumbs on the floor. And I'm still waiting for the day when I'll be able to say to Meredith, "Why don't you invite fifty of your friends over for a party?" That's my goal: to feel comfortable with fifty teenagers partying hard late into the night in our house, leaning against the walls, dancing on the carpets, their jackets tossed hither and yon, bowls of chips knocked over on the living room floor, glasses spilled, glasses broken, chaos and mayhem, everything out of place.

resource guide

Anxiety Disorders Association of America
11900 Parklawn Drive, Suite 100
Rockville, MD 20852-2624
(301) 231-9350
www.adaa.org

Freedom from Fear
308 Seaview Avenue
Staten Island, NY 10305
(718) 351-1717
www.freedomfromfear.com

National Alliance for the Mentally Ill (NAMI)
200 North Glebe Road, Suite 1015
Arlington, VA 22203-3754
(800) 950-6264
www.nami.org

National Institute of Mental Health
c/o Information Resources and Inquiries
5600 Fishers Lane, Room 7C-02
Rockville, MD 20857
(301) 443-4513
(888) 826-9438 (publications)
www.nimh.gov

National Mental Health Association
1021 Prince Street
Alexandria, VA 22314-2971
(703) 684-7722
www.nmha.org

National OCD Resource Center*
(800) NEWS-4-OCD
(800) 639-7462
OCD Resource Center Website
http://www.ocdresource.com
*Presented by Solvay Pharmaceuticals, Inc., and Pharmacia &
Upjohn

Obsessive Compulsive Foundation
P.O. Box 70
Milford, CT 06460
(203) 878-5669
www.ocfoundation.org

about the author

Marc Summers is the former host of Nickelodeon's popular *Double Dare* game show, ABC's *Home Show*, Lifetime's *Our Home*, and PAX TV's *Great Day America*. As a national spokesperson for the Obsessive Compulsive Foundation, he has appeared on *Oprah*, *Today*, *Dateline*, and the *Howard Stern Show*, and has been profiled in *People* and *USA Today*. Summers lives in Los Angeles. **Eric Hollander, M.D.**, is professor of psychiatry, director of clinical psychopharmacology, director of the Compulsive, Impulsive, and Anxiety Disorders Program, and clinical director of the Seaver Autism Research Center at Mount Sinai School of Medicine. Marc's collaborators on this book are **Kenneth Wapner** and **Jennifer Wolfson**, who run Peekamoose Productions in Woodstock, New York, a company involved in developing, writing, and editing books.